Litter

John Doriot

Litter

Dedication

For my brother. I think he would have liked this story.

&

For all the Healthcare Heroes. I worked at two great hospitals in my career of 40 years – The University of Tennessee Medical Center in Knoxville, Tennessee and Doctors Hospital in Augusta, Georgia. I am very proud to have called so many of you a coworker.

Acknowledgements

Thank you to my wife who has an amazing deaf ear toward loud noises that sometimes emanate from the room in which I write, and who did a terrific job in helping me to edit the book. Thank you also to my son for doing the final edit of the book. Thanks to Particular for the book cover art and thank you, Jill, for proofreading the final edition.

Chapter 1

Private Road

"There can't be any more fires," Sean said as they drove down Davis Road toward the realtor's office.

"I know, Sean, I know," Maggie replied. "The doctor said it was just a way for him to rebel. About moving. She said it should never happen again."

"He's 16 years old, Maggie. We won't, at least I won't, keep him from going to jail the next time. He could have burned down the house. And the neighbor's house. And, oh my God. What if someone had been hurt? It's just impossible for me to think about."

"I know. Believe me. I have thought about the same thing more times than I can count. But I've talked to him a lot and he's assured me it wouldn't happen again."

"Yeah, I know he says that but I'm not sure I believe it. We've heard it before," Sean sighed as he looked over at his wife. "This is my dream job, Maggie. The one that I have been wanting for years. Finally, the COO at the largest type of hospital in our organization. I can't have a son that's an arsonist or screwed up on some drugs or on some bullshit journey to find himself. I can't believe that child psych idiot said that. 'He sets fires to things to find out who he is.' Fucking asinine."

"Well you didn't help things by asking her if she perhaps thought he was an Apache setting fires to the white man's land," Maggie answered sarcastically.

"Legitimate question based on what she was passing off as insight. I almost asked her if she had gotten her diploma from Auburn or some Caribbean school, but I held off. Out of respect."

"Funny," Maggie said as she punched her husband in the arm. "Let's see how much you have to say after Auburn plays Tennessee this year. Then we'll see if you still have questions as to whether Auburn is a real school or not."

"Hey, even after Auburn beats Tennessee, I'll still have questions about whether it's truly a university. Hell, the last time we were there, cows were grazing in the parking lot next to the stadium."

"Keep talking," Maggie said as she smiled at her husband. *At least we've stopped talking about Connor*, she thought. She knew her husband was right. They wouldn't be able to do much more for their son besides send him away if he did anything again. But he had promised her. And he hadn't broken a promise to her. Not to her. Not yet. *Now, I just need to keep Sean focused on the present.*

"Who is this realtor we're meeting?" she asked.

"Bob Williams, he's with Re-Max. The hospital set it up. Has lived in Augusta most of his life as I understand it. When I talked to him on the phone, he told me he had found the perfect place. He said he knew we would like it so much he only scheduled this one place to show us."

"Oh, my God," Maggie groaned. "It's apparent he knows nothing about you and how particular you are. I'll just be happy to see you get out of the car when we get to this house."

"Ha-ha, very funny. I guess we'll find out soon enough," he said as he pulled into the Re-Max parking lot. "You can just wait here and I'll go get him." Within a few minutes, Maggie saw Sean wave to her as he stood beside an older, stocky man with short blond curly hair and a bushy light brown caterpillar mustache. There were sprinkles of white within the mustache that indicated either age or a fondness for doughnuts. She couldn't tell which from her position in the car until she got out to meet him. *Age,* she decided, *though I still think he loves doughnuts* as she got closer and glanced at his stomach jutting out over his belt. Before Sean could make an introduction, the agent introduced himself.

"You must be Mrs. Brodie. I'm Bob. Real glad to meet you. Your husband has told me nothing but great things about you."

Maggie shook Bob's hand and smiled. "That's because there are only great things he can say about me."

Bob started laughing and then winced.

"Are you okay?" Maggie asked.

He paused for a moment and then nodded. "I just get these electrical bursts in my head every once in a while. Doctor said not to worry about them. They'll go away," Bob said as he started walking toward his car. "Mine's the red Cherokee over there. I would have had y'all meet me at the home I'm showing you, but I thought it would be a good idea for me to drive you around Augusta a bit so you get a good feel for the area and how to get from point A to point B. 'Cause I know you're going to want this place," he grinned as he pressed his key fob and opened the doors.

Maggie glanced at her husband and wondered if he was going to say anything before they got into a car where the driver had just announced that he got electrical bursts within his head, but Sean ignored her and opened the passenger door. Maggie rolled her eyes and got in the back seat of the Jeep as Bob drove out of the parking lot.

"You just take Davis Road here and you can follow it all the way to Washington Road. Washington Road is one of the main thoroughfares that takes you from Evans and Martinez to downtown. You can never get lost if you find your way back to Washington Road. From there, you can go just about anywhere. Traffic is pretty bad on Washington from 5 to 6 in the evenings through the week and can be a little bit of a problem in the morning, but it's never really that bad. Not like a big town. Nothing like Atlanta, even though people around here complain like it is. You two are coming from somewhere in Florida, aren't you?"

"Yes, Ocala," Sean replied. "It's a small town. About 60,000."

"And you're the new COO at Doctors Hospital, right?"

"Yes, that's right."

"I can remember when that hospital was built 40 years ago. Just a dirt road and woods before it was built," Bob explained. "Things sure have changed. We're going to turn on Bobby Jones now, which takes you to the airport and South Augusta, which is where we're going. If you stay on it long enough it will even take you into South Carolina and back to the Interstate."

"Just a minute ago, you mentioned Martinez and Evans. What are those towns?" Maggie asked.

"They're in Columbia County. It's where the growth is these days and normally that's where I would show you some homes. But when this house became available, I just had to show it to you. It's a beautiful custom-built home and I know you're going to love it. There's not another setting like it anywhere in Augusta."

Maggie wasn't so sure about what Bob was saying, but for now, she would go along with it. She knew her husband wanted to find a home as quickly as possible, but he was also very picky. And if she didn't like this place, she was certain Sean wouldn't either, and now she knew where she would have Bob take them next.

"Now, this is the Peach Orchard and Windsor Springs turnoff. We'll go down to the second stop sign and then turn right onto Peach Orchard and then go about ten miles. Your address would actually be in Hephzibah. I usually don't show houses out in this area but a developer friend of mine created this small subdivision out of an old pecan farm some years ago and it is something to behold. It's a gated community. Sits way back from the road. A lot of people drive right past it and don't even realize there is anything back there. Will only be about fifteen homes in here when it's fully built out. There's just about ten now, I think. YEEEOWWWW!" he cried as Maggie watched him clench his fists around the steering wheel and shake his head.

"Those damn firecrackers going off in my head again. That's something, isn't it?" Bob asked while he continued to drive as if nothing had happened.

"Are you sure it's safe to be driving with firecrackers going off in your head?" Maggie asked.

"Oh yeah. No big deal. I'm fine. Just feel a brief shock – it's like touching some live wires - and then I see some explosions of color for a few seconds, but it always goes away. Doctor said it's nothing to worry about."

"The doctor you're referring to," Maggie asked, "he does have a medical license, correct?"

Bob laughed as he looked at Sean. "She's a pistol, all right. Just like you said she would be."

Sean felt his wife lean over and grab his neck and act like she was being affectionate, while she twisted his right ear. "Ahh, honey, A pistol? How nice of you to refer to me that way," Maggie replied as she turned the ear a little more before letting go.

"Thanks, Maggie," Sean replied. "You're going to make Bob think we're still on our honeymoon with all that affection."

Bob just smiled and then turned onto a paved road leading into a forest of pine trees.

"This is it, folks. It's called Sycamore Springs. Just look at those pine trees. I bet some of them have been here for a hundred years. Look at some of those trunks - see that one over there! A grown man couldn't even put his arms around that big boy. There are a lot of trees like that in this neighborhood. Like I said, this is called the Hephzibah community. Not sure if you are familiar with the Bible or not, but the name means 'delights in her,' and I think you're going to be delighted with this place. All the lots are three to seven acres. The house I'm showing you sits on four acres of woods. White oaks, red oaks, pines, sweetgums, and several of the largest sycamore and pecan trees you have ever seen. Plenty of dogwoods, crape myrtles, and even some mimosas. Just real pretty landscape. And most of it was already there. Just had to clear away the brush," he boasted.

Bob parked the car in front of the gate. A small dark green stucco sign that read "Sycamore Springs" sat in front of a massive sycamore tree bisecting the entrance and exit to the subdivision. The limbs of the sycamore extended over the roads on both sides of it.

"Now let me see what this code is, I have it here somewhere. I can't remember it for the life of me," he said as he fumbled around in his billfold.

Sean looked back at Maggie and shook his head no. He knew she wanted to say that the electrical bursts in his head may have erased some of his memory but he was silently urging her to refrain from commenting. Maggie understood and just smiled at him.

"Here we go, it's 6-2-3-5-4," Bob said out loud as he entered the code. The gate opened and he drove just inside before stopping to put the piece of paper back in his billfold. "The lower limbs of that sycamore had to be cut down or trucks couldn't get in here. Ain't that something? Would you look at all these old pecan trees that line the road? My goodness. I'm telling you folks, this place is special.

"Look at that. Another old sycamore over there on your right. That one's over a hundred years old. And check out that waterfall. The guy who owns that house put it in a couple of years ago. Has koi in the pond. Just beautiful. He's a bit of an eccentric though. Was in the Vietnam war and I think he still deals with some issues on occasion."

"What are you talking about, Bob?" Maggie asked. "Is he going to re-live the TET offensive and lob a few grenades over into our yard or something?"

Bob chuckled. "Do you ever stop laughing around her?" he asked as he looked over at Sean.

"Only at my own peril."

"No, he won't lob any grenades at your house, Maggie, but he may take a few shots at you. I heard he was a sniper in the war," Bob chuckled as he replied.

Maggie opened her eyes wide as Sean managed a nervous grin. Before she could say anything, Bob began to laugh. "Couldn't help myself," he said. "There ain't nothing wrong with old Amos. I've even taken him fishing and hunting with me. Those issues I mentioned are self-inflicted wounds. He over-medicates himself in one way or another. I hear from my builder friend that it's been happening a lot more often these days since his wife died about a year ago. But the only thing that you may see from old Amos if he gets in one of those dark places, is him walking around the yard without any clothes on. I'd just stay away if you see that. Beautiful dark brown stucco home. Those bay windows. And that stone driveway is something, isn't it? Always has a real nice flower garden too. I'm sure you'll meet him soon enough, once you buy the house."

What the hell does that mean, stay away from him when you see him naked? Why the hell would I even think of going over there if he was naked?

Maggie wanted to ask but she again showed restraint. After all, he was a veteran and he had just lost his wife. She guessed she could live with that, especially considering that this property Bob was showing them was stunning. It looked like something out of a magazine. *Driving by that waterfall and seeing the flowers every day and, on occasion, a naked man, wouldn't be that bad. I think I could get used to that.*

"Now, this covered bridge here connects the two large ponds in the neighborhood and the house that I wanted to show you is over on your left up on a hill overlooking the water. The road is… YEEEEOWWW! Whew! That was a good one… made a little narrower than most, because the builder wanted the canopy of the trees to reach over the road. Isn't it beautiful?"

He went from one sentence to the other with an electrical burst erupting in his head as if nothing happened. But Maggie was not going to address that now. She was too enamored by the covered bridge and the ponds. The water lilies and swamp irises that bordered one area of the pond were like prisms that magnified their color onto the top of the still water.

"Look at that color and all those pitcher plants! I even see some Venus fly traps down there in the boggy side of the pond. That was smart. Natural insect control. Bob, can you park the car at the bottom of the driveway and let us walk up to the house?" Maggie asked.

They got out and walked up the winding driveway without saying a word. The house appeared to have been built into the side of the hill and the rocks that framed the house looked like they had been there forever. There were large boulders in the yard, surrounded by flowers and Japanese maples. With each step they took, another little garden seemed to emerge. The garage doors on the side of the house resembled old wooden barn doors. As they neared the front of the house, the large flagstone porch, accented by the dark oak door, came into view. Bob opened the front door and as soon as Sean caught a glimpse of the heart of pine wood floors, he knew Bob was right. They would not be looking at any other houses.

"I'll just wait for you two on the back porch," Bob said as he strolled through the den and out the French doors.

"Oh my God!" Maggie squealed as she threw her arms around her husband. "This house is amazing, Sean! I don't even care about naked Vietnam war vets. I want this house!" She kissed him and then went into the den. There was a large fireplace of burl mahogany sitting atop a marble base with brown swirls of color. At one end of the house were three bedrooms of different colors and complementing hardwood floors. Two of the bedrooms had bay windows and the other had three very large picture windows.

Next came the kitchen that was supported with strong wooden beams and a wooden ceiling. A Sub-Zero refrigerator with maple doors was designed to blend in with the cabinetry and granite countertops that accented the wood. From there, they entered the master bedroom which had a cozy sitting area and a large master bath with a spa tub. Maggie flicked on a switch labeled "HEAT" that was next to the lights. She took off her shoes and wiggled her toes when she felt the warmth emanate from the tile.

"Can we really afford this?" Maggie asked, standing barefoot on the heated bathroom floors.

"Let's go find out," Sean said as they walked onto the back porch.

"Oh my God!" Maggie repeated when she saw the backyard with its waterfall and the beautiful gardens built on the hillside, all leading to the large pool that resembled a mountain pond. The waterfall, bordered by various kinds of ferns and more Japanese maples, meandered twenty feet down from the top. The pond-like pool was encircled by elm and pine trees, large azaleas, and crape myrtles. Maggie had never seen anything like it and her desire to live there became hypnotic.

"How much do they want for the house?" Sean asked Bob when Maggie returned to the porch.

$600,000, and they won't budge on it," Bob replied. "This house out in Evans would cost you over $750,000."

"Why the difference?"

"South Augusta is still being developed and there aren't as many businesses or amenities out this way. In the past ten years, Martinez and Evans have grown by leaps and bounds and continue to do so. The houses with land are getting to be few and far between and will cost you over there. Columbia County is 'the' place to live right now and would be where I would say you should buy, except for this one subdivision. This house is a steal. In two years, it will be worth another hundred thousand easily. Shall I write up the contract?"

"Yes!" Maggie shouted before Sean could answer.

"How much?" Bob asked.

"$600,000, just like you said," Maggie replied.

"OK – I'll get right on it."

"By the way, what's the name of this street?" Maggie asked. "I never saw the sign. There is one, isn't there?"

"Yes. It's there as you turn off of Peach Orchard. It gets missed all the time. The county will only do so much sign-wise. You neighborhood folks may decide to do something different, but then again you may not. But regardless, the name is Lavender Lane. It's a private road."

"What does that mean?"

"Well for starters, it means that no one is supposed to be on this road that you don't want here. And it's your road," he explained.

"What do you mean it's 'my' road?"

"Privacy comes with a price. Road floods or tears up, you - the homeowners - fix it. But don't worry about anything. This road will still be here when we all keel over and die."

That's probably true, Maggie told herself as she thought about Bob's head explosions. Sean just shook his head as he looked into his wife's eyes because he knew what she was thinking. *She can't help herself. Maybe that's where Connor gets it,* he thought, as he looked over at Bob and his wife and smiled.

Chapter 2

Circle K

Their offer on the house was accepted immediately and they moved in within a month. Maggie took care of most of the moving activities since Sean was working twelve to sixteen-hour days in his new role at the hospital. Maggie didn't mind doing any or all of the moving coordination though; she actually preferred it that way. She loved the new house and enjoyed setting it up exactly the way she wanted. Each day as she drove across the covered bridge, she stopped and admired the flowers around the pond and marshy area. It made her happy to see that unframed picture and think about how lucky they were to be living here. She knew Connor wasn't afraid of snakes, but she still would make a point of telling him to be careful around that pond.

Connor and Maggie were on the back porch setting up the patio furniture when they heard the doorbell ring. Since moving in, they had not seen a naked Vietnam war vet or met any of their neighbors. As Maggie started toward the door, her son yelled out to her.

"If that's the old guy from across the street and he's naked, holler at me. I want to get an Instagram of you and him. I think it would be a great way of saying we moved to a new neighborhood. We may even want to make it our Christmas card photo for the year. A variation on the yule log and mistletoe."

"What a great idea," Maggie replied. "I can put that photo with a picture of your report card and make it a contest. Ask all of our friends which one they find more disturbing."

Connor chuckled. It was very seldom when he got the last word on his mom, but it never stopped him from trying.

Maggie looked through the peephole just because her son had put that image in her head, but she did not see a naked man standing there. She saw a young blonde-haired woman who was holding a casserole dish in her hands.

"Hello," Maggie said as she opened the door.

"Welcome to Sycamore Springs," the young woman said. "I baked this for you and your family. It's my world-famous macaroni and cheese. It has five different kinds of cheese in it, with bacon and mushrooms and green peppers. I've been meaning to get by here and welcome you guys but wanted to let you get settled in a bit before dropping by. My name is Elizabeth, but everybody calls me Beth. Beth Stevens. We live at the end of the cul-de-sac. Red brick and stone two-story."

"World-famous, huh?"

"Well, within the world of Stevens," Beth replied modestly.

Maggie laughed. *I think I'll like her.*

"Come on in, Beth. My name is Maggie Brodie."

"Oh, I know who you are," Beth said. "I'm the treasurer of the homeowners association. I'm the one who will be bugging you to pay your annual homeowner's fee."

"I wanted to talk to someone about those fees," Maggie said as she motioned for Beth to follow her. Maggie could see Beth checking out the house as they walked to the kitchen. *I don't blame her. It is a beautiful home,* she thought.

"Your kitchen is just gorgeous," Beth said as she handed the casserole dish to Maggie.

"Thank you. I'm in love with it too. Let me put the world-famous mac and cheese in the fridge and get us a drink. Would you like a bottled water or iced tea?"

"Yes, some iced tea would be great."

Maggie filled two glasses and led Beth onto the back porch where her son was sitting on the couch looking through his phone.

"That body over there with an inability to acknowledge human life is my son, Connor. Hello! Hey, Connor!!" Maggie yelled before he looked up. "That's right, humans here on earth. New human at our house. This is Beth Stevens, one of our neighbors. Beth, this is my rude son Connor who thinks deafness is a convenience."

Connor looked up at Beth and said hello as he nodded his head and then went back to his phone. Maggie looked at Beth and shrugged her shoulders. "Teenagers. What can you do?" she said in a light-hearted manner.

"Take away their phones for one thing," Beth answered matter of factly as she frowned at Connor and then back at Maggie.

"Yeah, I could do that, but then he wouldn't have a hand and arm," Maggie laughed as she thought Beth's response was said in jest. It wasn't.

"My husband and I don't allow our children to use their phones at home except after they do their homework and only for an hour each evening. They retrieve their phones from the phone basket each day when their homework is finished and cannot get them any earlier. They can decide to use their phones or the computer or watch tv between 7 and 9 each evening.

And only then. We don't make exceptions. We find it helps us bond more as a family. Children today are just bombarded with too much unhealthy material and we try and minimize that. And you should never joke about deafness," Beth concluded.

Connor glanced at his mom. Maggie knew that look. She could not stop him from saying something that would not go over well with their new neighbor.

"Hope your children don't get bitten by one of those cottonmouths out by the pond that I saw the other day before 7 p.m. Seeing how they wouldn't have a phone to let you know they had been bitten. It might be too late by the time they crawled to the house," Connor said as he walked back inside.

Beth's jaw appeared as if it had been broken and become unhinged. Her mouth was open and didn't seem like it could close.

Damn it, Connor. But as Maggie looked at Beth and thought about what Connor said, she knew it could have been worse. He was making a good point but she didn't remember him telling her that he saw a cottonmouth out by the pond. *I wonder if he was just saying that or if he really saw one.* The perturbed look on Beth's face made her realize she needed to say something to diffuse the tension that had been created by his comments.

"Sorry, Beth," Maggie said. "Connor speaks with an unfiltered tongue. I apologize. And I didn't mean anything by that deaf comment. I was just making a joke about my son who ignores me half the time."

Beth took a sip of her tea and stood up. Maggie realized that today would not be the day when she asked her about the homeowner's fees.

"It's all right. Do you have an email address that I can use to correspond with you about the homeowner's meetings and things regarding the neighborhood?"

"Of course, I'll email it to you," Maggie replied and as soon as she said it, she realized she didn't have Beth's email address. "Uh, it's MaggieMayBrodie1@comcast.net. The M's and the B are capital letters."

"Got it," Beth said as she stood up to leave. "Thank you for the iced tea. Just return the casserole dish whenever you are through with it."

Maggie escorted Beth to the door. "Thanks for stopping by," she said and Beth smiled and waved as she walked down the driveway. Maggie leaned up against the closed door and yelled out "Shit!" *I need to rethink that friendship idea with Beth. Not sure we would get along. Wound a bit tighter than I thought at first glance. Those rules and a phone basket? Damn. And she would never get along with Connor. No, not at all. I'll need to tell Sean about this and I don't think he'll be too happy.*

That evening Maggie filled Sean in on her visit from Beth and she was surprised by how well he accepted all the information. He agreed with Maggie: Beth would not be someone that would become a close friend. But he told Maggie he was okay with that.

"They live at the end of the street. It's not like we have to be good friends. We just have to be good neighbors." Hearing that, Maggie felt better about things. She asked Sean how his job was going and he talked about it for thirty minutes before saying he was tired and going to bed. Maggie agreed that was a good idea and she would be there after she checked in on Connor.

Maggie walked back toward the end of the hall and knocked on their son's door.

"Enter," she heard him say and she opened the door and saw him on his computer.

"What are you doing?"

"Looking at some stuff on the Nat Geo channel. Some things about the world's deadliest reptiles. They had a picture of a 26-foot anaconda. 26 feet? Unbelievable. That would swallow a few of those Stevens kids and no one would know about it, seeing how there was no one there to snap a picture with their phone."

"Connor…" Maggie started.

"Just kidding. But, Christ. Didn't know we had the Amish living down the road from us," Connor replied.

"Connor, give it a rest. I'm not sure what their religion is, but it doesn't matter. Amish, Catholics, Presbyterians, Wiccans. Whatever. Your father made a good point this evening. We don't have to be friends with them. We just need to be good neighbors. You can do that, can't you Connor?"

"Well, I don't mind handing them my phone when they get bitten by that cottonmouth I saw."

"Yeah, I meant to ask you about that," Maggie replied. "Did you really see a cottonmouth down there?"

"Yep. A big one. I stood there for a few minutes and tossed a stick toward him and watched him head for the water. As long as you aren't in their way, you're pretty safe around them. They get a bad reputation about being aggressive but they're only aggressive if you're keeping them from going where they want to go."

"Aggressive or not, I don't want you bringing any of them around here to prove a point," Maggie said. "You know I don't like snakes. And for God's sake, don't be throwing sticks at them. The only thing that can do is piss them off."

"Actually, it was toward, not at him, and the only thing it does is tell them to move on."

"I don't want to debate this. Not tonight, okay?"

"Yep," Connor said.

"Good night, son," Maggie said as she closed the door and went down the hall to their bedroom.

The next morning, Sean got up early to jog down the street. From the end of the cul-de-sac to the front gate was 1.5 miles so he could do a quick 5k with two up and backs. He loved running in the morning in his new neighborhood. He felt safe. The houses were beautiful and everyone kept the yards looking nice. His neighbor's yard was his favorite though and he told himself he needed to make a better effort to get to know him. His brother had been in the Vietnam War too and it would be nice to meet another vet even if all he did was just say thanks.

While he was running by the old man's house, he noticed some trash laying on the edge of his property. As he got closer to the pile, he could see that it was some coffee cups and a potato chip bag. *I'll get that on my way back* he thought and, on his return, he stopped and picked it up. Among the trash, he found a check stub for an Emiliano Martin from Forest Lawnscapes Company.

As he was walking back to his house, he kept looking at the paystub. The more he thought about it, the more he felt he should do something. He didn't allow his staff at the hospital to litter the grounds. The landscaping company shouldn't allow their employees to do so either and he was certain that the owner would appreciate the input. So, he made the phone call when he got back home and informed the owner of what he had found. The owner was very professional as he listened and thanked him for the call. Sean was impressed when Mr. Forest told him that he expected more from his staff and that he would take care of the issue. He felt good about how well his call was received and made a mental note to ask some of the neighbors about the company to see if he would be interested in having them care for his yard.

Doug Forest brought Emiliano into his office later that afternoon to discuss the call. He told Emiliano that he was tired of his screw-ups, explaining to him about the trash and how that type of stupid little thing could hurt his business. He was in the job of making landscapes look nice, not putting trash in them. He told him his company could not be associated with that type of behavior and when Emiliano heard that, he knew what was coming next, and he gritted his teeth as he listened for those words. The words he knew all too well.

"Sorry, Emiliano," Doug said as he told him he was fired.

Emiliano got up from his chair and glared at Doug for a moment before he walked out of the office. "Fuck this job," he muttered. He was getting paid minimum wage for working his ass off. He knew he only got the job because of his aunt's relationship with Doug, and he didn't really give a shit about losing it. *What do those people at Sycamore Springs even know about what it's like to work minimum wage jobs? What would they think if they knew half the people that were working in their yards had been working out in prison yards earlier in their life? Probably wouldn't like it too much* he thought as he drove to the Circle K and got a six-pack of Budweiser.

He opened a beer and drove to Peach Orchard Road right up to the Sycamore Springs front gate. He punched in the numbers: 6-2-3-5-4 and watched as the gate opened. He was certain that Doug would not tell any of the homeowners that he fired someone for leaving trash in their neighborhood because he wouldn't want them to feel bad, even though he doubted that any of them would give it a second thought. As such, they would have no reason to change the entry code and he had no doubt he would be able to come and go in this neighborhood anytime he pleased. He gulped his beer and laughed as he thought about how safe the homeowners thought they were behind this stupid gate.

Chapter 3

Cypress Mulch

Emiliano drove his old blue Chevy pick-up truck down the road as he looked at all of the nice homes he had seen numerous times. He slowed down at the spot where he had dumped the trash and wondered if it had been that old man who had complained. Doug didn't tell him who had called. He wouldn't even tell him which neighborhood it was, but when he heard about the check stub, he knew. He remembered the day clearly because he was pissed that last payday. He had caught his girlfriend with another guy and had gotten into a fight. He wasn't pissed off about his girlfriend cheating on him. He was mad because he had gotten into a fight over it. She wasn't worth it and he knew losing control like that could send him back to jail.

He opened another beer and thought about all of the locks on all of the doors on the nice homes he was looking at. He wondered if they knew that none of them were burglar-proof. Sure, some of them were harder than others to open, but he could always get in. If only those kids hadn't been home on that last job. He had just stood there looking at them and wondered what he should do before the police arrived. But he froze. They recognized him and he didn't do anything. He took another sip of beer and promised himself that he would not make that mistake again.

Beth spotted the truck parked at the end of the cul-de-sac. She recognized it as one of the landscape trucks, so she wasn't too worried, but she wondered why it was just sitting there. She watched it for ten minutes before deciding she needed to go out there and see what was going on. She picked up her youngest child and walked through her yard toward the truck. As she got nearer, she saw the driver lift the beer to his lips and that made her angry. *They can't come in here and drink while they're working!* She picked up her pace and even though she was barefoot, the little rocks and sticks on the ground did not deter her from marching toward Emiliano's truck.

Emiliano saw her approaching and got out of his truck. He waved at her but she was not acknowledging him. He yelled, "Stop!" and Beth awkwardly looked at him and stopped. She wondered if he was drunk as she stood there glaring at him.

"Don't move," Emiliano said quietly.

"What do you mean telling me not to move?" Beth asked. "This is my property and you can't be sitting out here in your truck drinking beer."

"Yes, it is your property, but if you take two more steps forward, you are going to step on something that doesn't give a rat's ass about it being your property."

Beth looked down but she didn't see anything. Emiliano inched toward them and bent to pick up a large stick. It wasn't until he was placing the stick on the base of the head of the copperhead that she saw it. Emiliano reached down and picked up the snake and took it over to the vacant lot on the other side of the cul-de-sac. He let the snake go and then walked back over to them.

Beth hadn't moved an inch and wasn't sure she could move now as she nervously looked at the ground.

"There aren't any more around you," he said.

"How did you see that from where you were?"

"When you work in the yard all the time down here in this part of the country, you develop good eyes. Or you get bit. It's that simple."

"Ummm, well, thank you…"

Emiliano knew she was trying to determine what his name was so he told her a name. As long as it wasn't his name it didn't matter.

"Jorge," Emiliano told her. "George."

"Well, thank you, Jorge."

"No problema," he replied. "You need to be careful though. I don't think I would be walking around barefoot. Maybe out by your nice pool, but not in the yard or around the mulch. The copperhead is very hard to detect. Never see them until they let you know they are there."

"Yeah, I know, I know," Beth replied. "I just wasn't thinking. Are you on a break or something? Where is the rest of the crew?"

"Just taking a lunch break. I like the quiet back here."

"Yes, it is very quiet," Beth agreed. As she stood there looking at the young man, she began thinking of how bad it might have been if she had been bitten and dropped her little girl. She knew she would have probably survived the copperhead bite, but she also knew that her daughter probably wouldn't have. The more she considered that, the more she realized that confronting him about the beer wasn't as important as she first thought. After working hard all morning, she doubted if one beer was that much of a problem. *He probably deserves it.*

"Well, again, thank you, Jorge. Hope the rest of the day goes well for you," Beth said as she turned away, making sure to walk over to her driveway to get back to her house.

Emiliano smiled as he watched Beth. He went back to his truck and opened another beer as he turned his key. *Who would have thought a little copperhead would bring him such good luck?* He knew that blonde-haired woman would talk to her neighbors about what he had done and though he doubted she would remember the name, she would remember the truck. The old blue Chevy truck would be a welcome sight in Sycamore Springs anytime he wanted to come back. And he was certain he would be coming back.

Connor was out by the pool thinking about what he would do today. His first option was to just sit there and veg all day, but he remembered that he wanted to go back and check to see if that cottonmouth was still there. He wondered if it was just passing through or if that pond was its home. He went into the house and put on some jeans and hiking boots and though he looked for his mom, he couldn't find her, so he just left.

Still no naked man running around the yard. He smiled at the thought as he looked up at Amos' house. After passing through the covered bridge, he turned toward his neighbor's yard and that side of the pond. That was where he had seen the snake the other day. He started slowly making his way toward the marshy reeds. He was always careful when he was stalking something like this. You could not be apprehensive. You had to be calm. Maintain a steady heartbeat. Remain focused. He was good at doing that.

"What the hell are you doing down there, boy?" Connor looked up and saw the old man on his front porch.

"Looking for snakes," he answered.

"Well, you're sure as shit in the right place," the old man replied. "None of them are too happy when you find them, you know."

Well, the man knows something about snakes. "Yeah, I know. I won't bother them. Just looking for them."

"Hell, boy. They don't know the fucking difference."

He's got me there, Connor thought. *Let's just go talk to the Mad Hatter.*

The old man said nothing else. He just watched Connor coming up his stone driveway.

Connor had learned more about their neighbor than the fact he was known to walk around in his yard naked. He knew that he was a veteran of the Vietnam war and that he had recently lost his wife. He didn't know what he looked like though and as he walked up toward the porch, he assessed his appearance. He was in pretty good shape for a seventy-some-year-old. They were about the same height he figured and looked about the same weight. He was bald but had long sideburns ending in a gray and black speckled beard. He had dark brown eyes that were staring at him as he got closer.

"Hey. My name is Connor Brodie, I live…" he began before the old man cut him off.

"I know where the hell you live. Hell, I saw you move in." He leaned down and pulled a Bud Light out of a cooler beside his chair. "You want one of these?" he asked and Connor shook his head no.

"Name's Amos," the old man said as he took a sip of beer. "Amos Hunt Morgan," he added and Connor wasn't sure why he was telling him that. *Maybe that's what old vets do. So used to telling everybody their entire name, they just do it.*

"How old are you, Connor?"

"Sixteen. Be seventeen later this year. I'm a junior in high school."

"Well, ain't that just special."

Connor laughed. *Oh shit, I have got to get him and my mother together.*

"What do you do with your time these days?" Amos asked.

"Not much. Look at Youtube, Facebook, tv, listen to music. Play video games."

"Ever thought about reading a damn book?" Amos growled as he took another drink of beer.

"A what? Book? What's that?" Connor answered as seriously as he could.

"You know what a god damn book is. But you're right, fifty years from now, maybe people your age won't. Everything will be on some shitass computer pad of some sort, I suppose."

"Does that matter? Who cares what the outside of the book looks like if the words inside of it are worth reading?"

Amos looked at the young man in front of him and leaned back. *Hell, this boy has some smarts about him. Looks a little like me body-wise. Good looking kid. Except for that damn hippie ass hair. Shaved off on the bottom with the hair hanging down over it. What the hell is that? And those eyes. He's got the eyes of a sniper, I can tell. Those eyes can handle death.*

"Ever read any books about the Revolutionary or Civil War?" Amos asked.

"Not any specific books," Connor replied. "But you know, studied them in history class."

"I doubt if what they teach you in history class tells you everything you need to know about the wars. About the people that fought them. Reading about the people, then you know about the war. What they were thinking, what it was like. Really like.

"My great, great, great uncle, was John Hunt Morgan. Was a general in the Confederacy. Fought at Shiloh. Died in Greenville, Tennessee in 1864 trying to escape from the damn Yankees. Distant relative of Daniel Morgan. He was a general in the Revolutionary War. Fought at Saratoga and at Cowpens. Some say Cowpens was the turning point of the war. And my relative was the person responsible for that. You said you were sixteen. Right?"

"Yeah."

"You say you play a lot of video games, huh?"

"Yeah, 'God of War' is my favorite."

"Well, based upon the average life expectancy of a male in the United States, which is 78 years old, you have about 543,120 hours in your life to do something meaningful. Do you really think playing 'God of War' is going to do that for you?" Amos asked. "And considering what I can tell about you, I suspect you have about 90,000 hours less than average."

"Sounds to me like I could get real good at playing 'God of War' in that amount of time," Connor retorted.

Amos suppressed his smile as he leaned over to get another beer out of the cooler.

"How old are you?" Connor asked.

"Seventy-three."

"So, you have about 43,000 hours left to do something meaningful. What are you doing?"

Hell, he calculated that pretty quick, Amos thought. *Yep, the boy's got some smarts about him.*

"I get up every morning and see the sunrise and I sit outside every evening and I watch the sunset. And I paint them. I paint the way the sun makes the trees look. The way the plants stand up tall to greet the sun. And say goodbye as it sets back down into the distance. Then I set fire to what I painted," Amos explained as he took another drink.

"Why do you set fire to them?"

"Because they're always a poor imitation of the real thing. Don't waste your time with poor imitations." His voice trailed off as he looked up into the sky.

Connor followed his gaze up at the sky. *Interesting philosophy*. When he turned back around and looked at Amos, he saw someone different staring at him.

"Are you from Kansas?" Amos asked.

"No," Connor replied.

"Good. Bunch of devil worshipers in Kansas. God damn bunch of devil worshipers."

"I thought they were mostly Republicans."

"Republicans – Democrats. Same god damn thing."

"Wasn't Bob Dole a Senator from Kansas? A war hero? And his wife, Elizabeth Dole. Wasn't she the CEO of the Red Cross?"

"Yes, the sneaky bastards. You know, where we are living, it's not really Sycamore Springs. It's Eden," Amos stated.

Holy shit. I'm getting ready to see the naked man running around the yard. "I believe that the inhabitants of Eden got thrown out of that place," Connor replied.

"Yes. Yes, that's right. I suggest you keep some bags packed."

"Does it actually matter if we have luggage considering that would probably be the end of the world?"

"Up to you. Can't ever have enough clean underwear. And socks. You need clean dry socks. And one more thing," Amos added. "Beware of the woman that welcomes the serpent."

"Uh, thanks," Connor said. "I'll take that into consideration."

He could see that Amos wasn't there anymore. He was still sitting in that chair but he wasn't there. Connor left and went back toward the marsh. He didn't find the cottonmouth but he did see a young black snake that was a little over four feet long. "Probably ran it off, didn't you?" Connor said as he leaned down and touched it. It sped off as soon as it felt what it considered to be a large predator and disappeared into the brush.

The next day, Beth saw the blue Chevy truck drive through the neighborhood as she was taking some mail out to the mailbox. She waved at George and he waved back. Several hours later, she heard a dog yelping and screams coming from her neighbor's house. She ran outside and saw them loading their large Labrador retriever into their car and speed off down Lavender Lane. She found out later that the dog had been bitten by a copperhead. The owners were planting flowers around the house and heard the dog and then saw it limping. Mr. Thompson, the owner, glimpsed something out of the corner of his eye as he rushed over to check on his dog. The mulch moved just the slightest bit. Had he not seen the cypress mulch move he would have never discovered the reason for the dog's injury. The intruder would have gotten away. Hiding in plain sight. It was the best camouflage. But if someone slams a hoe down onto your head, even the best camouflage doesn't work.

Chapter 4

Hot

Within several hours, Beth had sent out an email to the neighborhood association about the Thompson's Labrador getting bitten by the copperhead. The dog was going to be fine but that didn't stop most of the neighbor's from becoming increasingly anxious and maiming a lot of sticks that appeared to move over the next several weeks. Later that evening another email was sent out by Jasmine Bartholomew. Her husband Caleb had seen something coiled around the base of a shrub and shot it. They had a picture attached to the email showing what a 12-gauge shotgun could do to a six-foot gray water snake shot four times within a three-foot distance. The harmless snake looked more like snake jerky due to the buckshot but it didn't matter. It was dead and to most of the owners in the neighborhood, the only good snake was a dead one.

Maggie knew she was in for a long, hot summer when she found out they were moving to Augusta. She had checked the Farmer's almanac for the region and found that the average temperature from July through August was 92-95 degrees. But the temperature had already been over a hundred for three days since they had moved in and the humidity was stifling. If there had been more sand and palm trees around the neighborhood, she would have sworn they had moved to the Philippines. As soon as she stepped outside, her body started to sweat. Simply changing the light bulbs on the patio fans made her look like she was in the tenth mile of a marathon and she knew that if she planned to do any more work outside, it would have to be done in the early hours of the morning or late in the evening.

After replacing the last light bulb, she jumped into their pool to cool off. She wasn't sure if she was ever going to get out as she sat there on the flat surface of the rock ledge that had been made for just that purpose. She didn't care that the t-shirt she was wearing clung to her breasts. She was sure her son was still asleep and wouldn't be coming out anytime soon or that anyone else would just stop by with a casserole. She was pretty sure that neighborly gesture had been squashed because of her interaction with Beth. As she felt the cool water on her body, she just sat back and thought about how it would take some time to get adjusted to the new neighborhood, but this part she liked. *I may never leave the pool*, she thought. *At least not today.*

\--------------------------------------

Emiliano laid on his bed as he waited for his aunt to get home from the hospital. His Aunt Luna worked the night shift as a nurse and usually got home sometime around 8 in the morning. He knew an argument would ensue when he told her that he got fired from his job, but he didn't care. He was still mad about it. Doug had never liked him and was just looking for an excuse to fire him. The faces of the prison guards flashed before him as he thought about Doug and it angered him. When he imagined the conversation that he was going to have with his aunt, he knew it would be the match that ignited some of the coals. Coals that she wasn't even aware existed.

Prison had done nothing to rehabilitate him. The only thing it had accomplished was to change the structure of his intestinal tract. Though undetectable by x-ray, beside his small bowel and stomach was now a small bag of pre-soaked briquettes. Briquettes that were shaped by feelings of isolation, disrespect, and anger. Each day he spent inside that cell, another segment of those small black bricks, was formed. They aged with the disgust he felt for where he was and the hatred he felt for the people who tried to control every aspect of his life. Many of the prison guards were unaware of what was being manufactured within his body, but the older guards knew. They could always tell. They were aware that the person being released from jail that day carried something combustible inside of him. They knew that person would be coming back to see them because he was now an arsonist; those coals would grow into fires with each future crime he was certain to commit.

The conversation with his aunt went as expected. She yelled. He listened to her yell. She asked him what he was going to do now, and he told her he didn't know. She yelled some more and he felt the match strike against his gut and an ember start to smoke. She told him that he needed to find a job and he told her he would try but he was only saying that so that she would not kick him out on the street. Even when she held his head in her hands and kissed his forehead, it did not lessen the burn he felt inside. He told her that he was going out to look for a job and left. But he was not going to look for a job. No, today, he was going to the three places he went every day since he was fired: The Circle K, Sycamore Springs, and Strom Thurmond Lake.

A little after 9 a.m. Emiliano pulled up to the Circle K and picked up a twelve-pack of Budweiser. He popped one open and drove to Sycamore Springs before he headed toward the lake and to the park that he knew was vacant most of the time. He entered the code for the gate and passed by the waterfall and through the covered bridge. He looked at the beautiful homes and yards. He turned around in the cul-de-sac and drove back to park his truck inside the bridge so he could get out and look at the waterfall pond. The rainbow colors of the fish almost glowed as they swam around the shadow he cast onto the water. The koi knew those shadows often provided food and he bent down and provided them with something they had never tasted before. He wasn't sure they would enjoy it as he remembered the many times he had eaten something in prison that had made him sick.

He finished another beer before he arrived at the park he had found some time ago. He thought its name, Essie May Washington Branch Park, was a stupid name, probably honoring someone that he was certain didn't look like him. No, in his mind, this would always be Emiliano's Park and he treated it as such.

Entering the park, he found the booth empty where a person at one time asked for entry fees to use the area. He threw a penny into the box on the open door before proceeding. *Can't keep Emiliano's Park open without funding* he thought as he took several beers out of the twelve-pack after he parked the truck.

This area of the Strom Thurmond Reservoir system was a seldom-used inlet and had very few of the amenities that people generally wanted when they went to the lake. The beach could hardly be considered a beach. It was just a little bit of sand next to a marshy piece of land overlooking the lake. There was a rundown playground with a few rusted swings and a slide, alongside five cracked picnic benches and three dirty grills. It was obvious why few people utilized the area, and that is why he loved it. In his mind, it was his land. His own "lake view property," like many of the people who lived in the big homes with the big yards that he worked on owned.

He walked toward one of the benches and wondered if the carcass was still there. It was. When he first saw it he had thought it looked like some prehistoric fish. It was over six feet long and one part of its head was still somewhat intact; the flies and ants had destroyed everything else. All that remained was that small segment of a head with the gray milky eye and the bones that were scattered over the ground. He realized it was actually a catfish but it was one of the largest he had ever seen. He wondered what had killed it and what left it there. Perhaps it was just its time and it had floated to the surface and as the other fish pecked away at it, ended up on the ground where the flies and ants could finish the job. Sometimes you just never know why things die, he thought as looked out onto the glassy surface of the water.

Connor came outside in search of his mother. He found her lounging in the pool.

"Nice look, Mom. I would put it on Instagram, with the caption, 'neighborhood wet t-shirt competition' but then there would be this perverted mother-son vibe and I'm not sure that would help Dad at his new job."

"Yes Connor, I have breasts," Maggie replied. "It's hot as hell and the pool was here and so, there you go. What are you doing?"

"Don't know, but you are right."

"About what?"

"You do have breasts."

"Hilarious. I knew as soon as I asked the question, it was a mistake."

"I don't win many with you mom," Connor said. "Gotta give me props when I do."

"Run along child, or get in the pool. I'll even go put on a bathing suit."

"No thanks. I think I'll just go back down by the marsh. Saw a cool black snake there the other day."

"Yeah nice try, Mr. Brodie," Maggie retorted. "You are going back down there to see if that cottonmouth is there. Damnit, Connor. Be careful. Don't do something stupid."

"Don't worry Mom. I don't do anything stupid. Life's a lot like video games. Gotta be thinking several moves ahead or you're dead."

"Great philosophy. You should go far with that line of thinking," Maggie stated sarcastically.

"Yes, I probably will." Connor went back inside to put on his snake boots. He was going into the marsh a little deeper today and though he knew a lot about snakes, he understood he needed to anticipate the unexpected. *Like the video games*, he thought and grinned.

On his way to the marsh, he looked around the neighborhood and wondered what the people were like in those homes. They were now called neighbors, but what did that really mean? In their old neighborhood in Florida, neither he nor his parents were familiar with many of the neighbors. His mother and father knew their names but that was about it as far as he could tell. *Saying hello or waving to someone as they drove by in a car didn't constitute a relationship, did it? Well, maybe it does,* he told himself. *After all, you have learned something about them. You know they speak English and they can wave and still drive at the same time* and that made him laugh.

The trees are enormous in this neighborhood, he thought. The pine trees were some of the biggest he had ever seen. He remembered his father telling him that this was an old pecan farm at one time. *No shit,* he thought as he looked at the line of pecan trees that still grew along the road and in the yards. With all this heat and water around here, he understood that the shade from the trees and the coolness of the water was a perfect place for snakes to rest. He wondered if his neighbors were as aware of that as he was. His mother showed him the email about the copperhead and the water snake but he could tell by just looking around, there were other things here that could hurt someone if they weren't careful.

This morning, he walked to the marshy side of the pond on the other side of the covered bridge and looked around. He saw a few frogs and a brown water snake just laying in the weeds watching him.

"One of your relatives got blasted the other day," Connor said as he looked at the snake. "I would recommend staying away from the yards now. Nothing up there that would interest you anyway. Take my advice or not. It's up to you. But, if you do decide to go up near those nice-looking homes, I suggest you have all of your affairs in order. Have your bags packed as our friend Amos would tell you."

He was waist-deep in the water when he saw what he was looking for. The cottonmouth was headed toward him and he knew he just needed to remain calm. He kept his eyes on the snake as it slithered atop the water and he kept a steady movement toward the right of its path. *Just keep moving right and do nothing to alarm him* he told himself as he kept his eyes focused on the twisting motion of the snake. At times when Connor moved, the snake seemed to stare at him and change its direction for a moment as it if was coming toward him. If Connor moved again, the snake would realign itself, headed in another direction. This dance went on for only a minute but to most observers, that minute would have seemed like an hour. He watched as the snake ignored him while it went right past him, two feet away from where he stood. It didn't even bother to look back as it disappeared into the reeds, marsh grasses, and pitcher plants that were thriving within this perfect environment.

About five feet long, he thought. *Big snake.* He continued through the pond, just to see how deep it was. At one point he was required to swim, which wasn't that easy with his snake boots on. He was glad he didn't have to do that for very long before he felt the bottom of the pond again and walked out on to the other side.

He suddenly stopped as he was walking by Amos's waterfall pond on his way home. He knelt for a closer look at the fish and realized that they were not moving. At least not on their own. The only movement pushing them along came from the waterfall. They were all dead. He trudged up the driveway and knocked on Amos's door and told him that he needed to come take a look at his fish.

"Why the hell do I need to look at the fish? I know what they look like."

"I doubt you have seen them look like this before."

Amos grumbled but walked out the door with Connor. When they got to the pond, Amos saw the multicolored fish floating on top of the water; the color of their bodies beginning to dull as their internal organs had failed some time ago.

"How in the hell did this happen?" Amos barked as he glared at Connor.

"I don't know much about fish, but it looks like something you would see on the six o'clock news. Fish dead due to industrial spill. Story at eleven."

"God damnit! Are you trying to be a smartass?"

"Not trying to be," he replied sheepishly, "but I'm afraid it's part of my genetic makeup. I am really sorry about your fish, Amos. I mean that."

"You can say it all you want, but I'm not so fucking sure about anything you say at this point."

Amos began to examine the pond, trying to figure out what had happened to his fish, stopping to pick up a rock every so often as if he would be able to tell what killed his fish by something he found underneath them. "Shit," he heard Amos mutter under his breath as he lifted a rather large rock next to the main skimmer.

"What is it?" Connor asked. "Did you find something?"

"God damn right I found something. Salt. God damn fucking salt."

"Salt?" Connor repeated.

"Yeah, God damn salt. Somebody poisoned these fish." Amos looked suspiciously at Connor.

"It wasn't me, Amos," Connor replied. He had seen that type of look too many times before to not know what he was thinking. "I didn't kill your fish."

"That's exactly what the fish-killing son of a bitch would say."

"Look, Amos, if I killed your fish, would I come knock on your door and tell you that your fish were dead?"

"That's exactly what the fish-killing son of a bitch would do."

"I didn't kill them, Amos," Connor stated again. *What would he do if I told him I was from Kansas now?* Connor asked himself. *Devil worshiping Kansans have killed your fish, Amos. As you knew they would. That would be funny but I know better than to say anything like that. Just like in the video games, stay several steps ahead.* With regard to Amos, that meant to expect he had a loaded gun somewhere on his body.

"What's going on here?" Maggie said as she walked up. "I was outside and you two looked like you were up to something interesting." She looked down in the pond and saw the dead fish and shook her head.

"Oh my God! What happened to the fish?"

"Somebody poisoned them with salt," Amos replied. "And I'm looking at the number one suspect standing next to you."

"Amos, my mother. Mother, Amos," Connor said.

"Hello, Amos," Maggie replied as she thought how stupid it was for her son to make introductions now. "Connor didn't kill your fish. He isn't a suspect."

"Everybody's a suspect until I tell them they aren't a suspect."

Maggie pulled her son closer. "Tell Amos you didn't kill his fish, Connor," she said calmly. *Tell Amos you didn't kill his fish* she screamed inside her head.

"I did tell him, Mom, but he doesn't believe me," Connor said as he smiled at his mom.

When Amos saw Connor smile, something inside of his brain took him back to another time. The smile reminded him of the children he had seen at the edge of the village. Smiling at them. Knowing that death awaited them behind the straw walls. Hiding. Waiting for them to let their guard down or if they didn't leave, to ambush them. That smile made Amos pause and he knew he would have to keep his guard up around the two people that stood in front of him. They looked foreign and similar to him at the same time.

"I'm very sorry about your fish, Amos," Maggie said. "It's not a very good way to make an introduction and I hope we can get past this. My son and I didn't kill your fish. In fact, we would be happy to get you some new fish if you would let us."

" So, your guilt is weighing on you, is it?"

"No, no, that's not what I meant. I was just, uh, just…" But Maggie stopped when she felt her son's hand on her arm. Connor was nodding his head as if he was telling her it didn't matter what they said from this point forward. Looking into Amos's eyes, Maggie could tell that her son was right.

Amos had heard those types of denials before. They never ended well for anyone involved with them.

"You - and him," Amos said as he pointed toward Connor, "need to leave. I'll take care of the dead. Bury them and get their tags. I knew this mission would result in too many casualties. Watch your back as you head back. It's not safe around here. There's death lurking there in the marsh. I can sense it."

Maggie and Connor started walking back toward the covered bridge. She glanced over her shoulder and saw Amos picking the fish up out of the pond and laying them carefully onto the ground. Connor looked at his mother and told her it was sad that the fish had been killed.

"Yes, it is, son," Maggie said as she put her arm through his and thought that it was going to be a long, hot summer.

Chapter 5

Uncle Arthur

When they got back to the garage, Maggie turned to Connor.

"What the hell happened with those fish?" she asked angrily. "And don't try and bullshit me. Tell me the truth."

"The truth is that someone poisoned the fish. With salt. You heard what Amos said."

Maggie grabbed his hands, turning them over to inspect both sides, and then held them up to her nose. She could not see any salt but his hands smelled like the pond.

"Your hands smell like pond water. Why?"

"Uh, maybe because they were in the pond," Connor replied. "Hell, you saw Amos, didn't you? That look on his face. I'm not so sure he didn't kill them himself. Thinking he was on a mission of some sort."

Maggie didn't say anything as she stood there looking at her son.

Connor had seen that look before. In the past, that look from his mother would have intimidated him, but it didn't now. Nothing really scared him anymore. This interaction he was having with his mother was just that, another interaction. One he had grown accustomed to and one he knew he would always have with her. It was just another part of their relationship now.

Maggie thought about what her son said regarding Amos. He was right. She saw the change in his face, the faraway look in his eyes. The way he referred to the fish as casualties and the reverent manner in which he removed the dead fish from the pond. He was reliving some part of a war. Connor was right. He could have killed the fish and not even remembered doing it.

She looked at her son's face and eyes and now saw truth where she once saw guilt. He wasn't lying to her about the fish. And she always knew when he was lying. She told herself that, but somewhere in the back of her mind, she could see someone waving at her. Trying to get her attention. Telling her that she couldn't be sure of that anymore.

"Why are you so wet?" Maggie asked.

"I waded through the pond."

"And?"

"And what?"

"And didn't I tell you before you left home not to do something stupid?"

"You did indeed, Mother. And I followed your advice."

"You don't think wading into a pond with a water moccasin is foolish?"

"No, I don't. Not if you know what you're doing."

"So, what did you see?"

"There were some frogs, another water snake that Mr. Thompson can obliterate with his 12-gauge, and there was that cottonmouth that I saw earlier. I'm pretty sure it was the same snake. That pond is probably its home. Good-sized snake, about five feet long. It swam by me as I was wading through the pond."

"Swam by you?" Maggie asked as she shook her head. "Really, Connor? Really?"

"Yes really. He saw that I wasn't a threat, and he ignored me."

"Well shit, Connor. Why don't you just get it and bring it up to our pool? Let it live there. That way, the two of you could go swimming every day."

"That wouldn't be a good idea," Connor replied as he sat down on the steps and started to remove his snake boots. "First of all, you can't really go swimming with cottonmouths. You can be in the water with them, but if you started going toward them or started to swim, you would alarm them, and then there could be trouble. And second, if I brought him into our pool, it would be his pool then, not ours. We would just be his guests."

Maggie just shook her head as she watched her son stand up. "So, what are you going to do now?" she asked.

"I am going to go in and get changed and jump in the pool," he announced. "It's hot out here. But unlike you, I am actually going to be wearing a swimsuit."

"Very funny," she said as she followed him into the kitchen. She poured herself a glass of tea and got her iPad. She was scrolling through her email when she saw one from Beth and opened it. The message stated there would be a homeowners meeting at her house that evening at 7:30. She apologized for the late notice but hoped to see everyone there. It was signed with a smiley face emoji and "Beth."

I wonder if all the meetings are at a last minute's notice, Maggie said to herself. *That's something I am going to bring up. We need more warning.* She wasn't sure that Sean would even be home by that time so she sent him a text about the meeting, telling him to make sure he was home in time. He answered that he would try. When Maggie saw the word "try," she responded by telling him to BE THERE in bold letters and added that she didn't want to go to this first meeting by herself. Sean knew there was no sense in arguing with her. He just said he would be there even though he knew there was a chance he wouldn't be. He'd just have to deal with the cold shoulder and angry looks if he didn't make it. He had done it many times before and was certain he would again.

Maggie spent the rest of the day unpacking boxes in the kitchen and organizing the cabinets. There were a lot of empty boxes piled up against the garage door when she looked up at the clock on the kitchen wall and saw that it was 6:45. *Shit.* She turned on the oven and started taking the boxes out into the garage next to the trash can. She pulled a couple of frozen pizzas out of the freezer in the garage and took them into the kitchen. *Damn. Is Connor still out at the pool? I hope he used some sunscreen.* She realized he must have because she didn't see anything that resembled a strawberry with legs and arms when she saw him sitting on one of the pool chairs. He had his earbuds in and his eyes were closed as she walked over and touched him on the shoulder. He opened his eyes and smiled. "What's up?" he asked, pulling out his earbuds.

"We have to go to a homeowner's meeting tonight," Maggie replied.

"Who is 'we'?"

"The entire family. Apparently, they have an award for the best-dressed family at these meetings and I want to make sure we make a good first impression."

"So, are you wearing that wet t-shirt without the bra?" Connor asked.

Maggie tried to keep from laughing but she couldn't. "No, smartass. Just your dad and I are going. I am putting some frozen pizzas in the oven for you. I hope that your dad will get home in time to eat but if he doesn't, he doesn't. They should be ready in about 20 minutes."

"Cool."

Maggie turned around and started walking back toward the patio when she heard Connor yell out to her.

"Mom! Are they having a fish fry tonight at the meeting?"

"Connor! Don't even joke about something like that. What if someone heard you?" she scolded as she looked around.

"Looking for drones or someone lurking in the bushes?"

"Dammit, Connor. You know what I mean. Your Dad doesn't need that kind of shit. Not now with the new job."

"Look. If I hadn't brought it up, you would have probably said something like it at the meeting making things worse. I know you."

Maggie tried to glare at her son as if she was mad, but she couldn't. He was right. She probably would have said something like that, but she wasn't going to let him know it.

"I would not have said anything like that, whatsoever," Maggie replied. "No one in their right mind would fry carp."

"Uh, the key words there: 'in their right mind.' Some of our neighbors may not be in their right mind."

True, Maggie said to herself as she thought about what Connor was saying. "Pizza ready in about twenty minutes," she said robotically as she went into the house.

She thought about what Connor had just said while picking out what to wear. *Was that the reason for the short notice of the meeting? The dead fish? What if Amos is there? What if he accuses her or Connor of killing his fish? There's no telling what Amos would say. But that's okay,* she told herself as she changed into a nice floral dress. *They all know Amos. They know what he says is suspect.* She would just have to play along with whatever he says. She could convince them that he probably did it himself. She was certain she could do that.

Maggie checked her watch. Sean still wasn't home. She would wait a few more minutes before sending him a text about the fish. She preferred to tell him about it in person but she also didn't want him to be surprised should someone at the meeting mention it.

"Pizza's ready!" Maggie called out as Connor came in from the pool. She took the pizzas from the oven and placed them on top of the stove to cool as she looked at her watch again. It was now 7:15 and Sean was still not home. Connor cut off about half of one pizza, put it on a plate, and turned on the TV.

"I'll hold off on watching any of the new 'Electric Dreams' till you get back," Connor said.

Maggie smiled. As her son got older, they had begun to share a love for science fiction and horror movies. They had just started watching "Electric Dreams," a show that reminded her of the "Outer Limits" television series. Connor had searched for the "Outer Limits" on Amazon and they had ordered the whole set. They were still going through all of those shows.

Sean drove into the garage at 7:25 p.m. Maggie grabbed several slices of pizzas and put them on a paper plate. She picked up some napkins and a ginger ale and met her husband as he was getting out of the car.

"Just get back in there, Mister," Maggie directed. "Here's dinner. I don't want to be late for this first meeting. We're already on shaky ground with Mrs. Stevens and our neighbor across the street."

Sean could tell by his wife's demeanor, that there was nothing he could do except get back in the car and do as she said. He restarted the car as he took the pizza from Maggie and began to eat. Before he could ask what she meant about their neighbor, Maggie proceeded to tell him what happened to Amos's fish.

"Damn, Maggie," Sean said as he took several long drinks of the ginger ale. "Are you kidding me? Tell me that this isn't happening again. Tell me that, Maggie," Sean implored as he stared at his wife.

"Connor didn't do it," Maggie stated emphatically. "We talked. I am certain he had nothing to do with it. I told Amos that even though we were not responsible, we would be glad to buy him some new fish. And then that's when I saw what Connor saw."

"What are you talking about?"

"The look on Amos's face. The look that made us think that maybe he had done it himself and was not even aware that he had. He was back there in Vietnam. We were standing there in front of him, but we weren't there anymore. At least not as Maggie and Connor Brodie. I saw it in his eyes and heard it in the way he talked to us."

"You are sitting here, telling me that our neighbor killed his own fish," Sean said, shaking his head. "That he thought he was back in Vietnam and killed the fish for some reason. Is that what you are saying?"

Maggie nodded her head.

"Well, what are we supposed to do if he brings this up at the meeting? Hell, is this the reason for the meeting?"

"It could be," Maggie shrugged. "But I've already thought about that. Everyone knows how Amos can be. Just let me do the talking if it comes up. I will handle it. I can handle it, Sean. You don't need to worry about anything except making a good impression on our neighbors."

Sean looked at his wife and nodded his head. He had seen that determined look in her eyes before and knew what she was capable of doing when she had everything planned out in her mind.

"Where is this meeting?" Sean asked as he backed the car out of the driveway.

"At the Stevens' home – end of the cul-de-sac. The large two-story stone and brick home."

There were already several other cars there when they arrived. Sean recognized one of them, a yellow Corvette. It belonged to their neighbor, Phil Gillespie. He had met him while he was out running and he seemed like a nice guy.

The door opened before they could even knock and Beth was there with her husband greeting them.

"Glad you could make it," Beth said. "Darrin, this is Maggie and Sean Brodie. They just moved into the river rock house that's built into the side of the hill."

"Love that house," Darrin said as he shook Sean's hand. "Come on in. Everybody is out on the patio which is straight back that way. Beth and I need to get some more stuff out of the kitchen. Be right with you."

"Did you just hear who we were introduced to?" Maggie said as she tugged on her husband's shirt sleeve.

"What?" Sean said as he was looking out onto the patio.

"She said her husband's name was Darrin. Darrin Stevens? Don't you hear what I'm saying? Beth and Darrin Stevens. Like on 'Bewitched?' Beth is short for Elizabeth. Bet her maiden name was Montgomery. Want to bet?" Maggie asked as her eyes widened.

"Oh shit. Please don't go there and start asking her where Endora is. Remember? Shaky ground? Bad first impression? Maybe dead fish on the agenda? She probably doesn't even know the show you're referring to. And then when you explain it, she'll just think you are calling her a witch. Think about it, Maggie," he begged.

"Can't I just please ask her about Uncle Arthur?"

"Definitely not."

Chapter 6

Deer Feeder

As they made their way outside, Sean was concentrating on the people on the patio while Maggie checked out the house. The living room furniture was all white and though beautiful, Maggie wondered how Beth could keep it clean with three children. *Maybe they weren't allowed in here. Or if they were, probably only in thirty-minute increments under direct supervision. Or maybe she was a witch and just twitched her nose when company came over. Yep, that's it,* she thought and smiled.

She watched as Sean turned the knob and within an instant, went into corporate android mode. The smile filled up his face and he was ready to converse about anything and everything. He could make anyone feel comfortable within minutes. Both men and women loved being around him. He was a handsome man with his dark brown hair and brown eyes and he kept his body in good shape. He could be quite the charmer but Maggie never worried about other women.

They had been married for twenty years and she was certain he had never cheated on her. There would be no reason to. They connected on so many levels. She knew she was at least an 8 on the looks scale, and, sexually, she doubted if many women could do all the things she could. Well, maybe a seasoned prostitute but they came with a lot of baggage, some of it which could not be stored away in a closet.

Sean also knew that Maggie would cut his nuts off if she found out he had cheated on her. She had told him that several times and he believed her. He had been tempted before but he always remembered her talking to him about the lack of testicle transplant centers and it would make him laugh. Even so, he made certain his actions were never mistaken for anything of a provocative nature when interacting with a member of the opposite sex.

She watched him shake hands with the middle-aged man with black hair sitting in the recliner. *Damn,* she said to herself. *The patio furniture is even white wicker. And not a speck of dust or dirt on them. She really is a witch.* Watching Sean talk to the man, she could tell that he already knew him. Then she heard him make an introduction.

"Maggie. This is Phil Gillespie. He owns that beautiful yellow Corvette out in the driveway. Works out at the Savannah River Plant. Met him running the other day. This is his wife Barbara," Sean said as Maggie smiled and shook Phil's hand, and nodded toward his wife.

I wonder if those things are real, Maggie thought as she glanced at the 38 double d's that were semi-restrained by the blue cotton t-shirt Barbara was wearing. *I'm not sure I like her* she said to herself without any reason to think that way other than the fact that Barbara's bosom may not be real. *Why do I care about things like that?* She heard Phil and Sean talking about the Corvette. *I should be talking to Barbara,* she told herself, and then she realized Barbara's lips were moving. *Shit. What did she just say? Just nod your head and smile and compliment her clothes.*

"That's a pretty top you're wearing," Maggie said. "Seems nice and comfortable for this type of weather."

Yes, that was what she was talking about it. She asked me about the weather and the heat. Continue talking about the weather, Maggie.

"Yeah, I had read that Augusta could be hot in the summer but I didn't realize that we were moving into an actual jungle. I'm beginning to wonder if we should be worried about the mosquitos around the pond and Dengue fever and the Ebola virus," Maggie added with a smile.

Sean scowled at her. *What the hell are you doing* she could tell he was asking her with those brown eyes of his. But before she could respond, Phil and Barbara started laughing and Maggie saw the concern leave Sean's eyes almost as fast as it appeared.

"I know," Barbara said as she leaned forward and touched Maggie's arm. "When we first moved here from Virginia, I told Phil we wouldn't be staying here very long. But these types of summers only come every once in a while. You'll get used to it. It's not always this hot."

Correction. I do like Barbara, Maggie said to herself as she looked over at Sean and gave him her "I just beat you at Scattergories" look but before she could really rub it in, Beth and Darrin came out onto the patio with a tray full of cheese and crackers, stuffed mushrooms, and a bowl of shrimp with cocktail sauce.

"Dig in guys. There can be no leftovers," Darrin announced as he put the bowls and platters on the large table in the center of the patio. "There's beer and wine over there in the coolers and I believe, according to my wife, we are ready to get started with the meeting. So as soon as everyone gets settled, we'll get going with the agenda."

Everyone got up and helped themselves to the food and Maggie felt like she was watching some show on "Nat Geo" when all the animals headed down to the watering hole. Tentative. Aware of the danger that was there, but unable to see it. But unlike the others, Maggie could see it. It stood over there next to her husband Darrin. And it was looking for her casserole dish. *Dammit*, Maggie said to herself. *I forgot the casserole dish. I'll be the first antelope that gets pulled into the water with the crocodile's jaws around its neck, so I better be careful.*

As people started to settle, Beth began to talk. "Hello, everyone. Please feel free to continue to get food and drink but in the interest of everyone's time, I'll go ahead and get things started. First of all, I would like to tell everybody that Mrs. Cayman will not be with us this evening. She has pneumonia again and is in the University hospital downtown. If you get a chance, please send her a card, or give her a call. It would be best not to go by there with her having pneumonia. The less exposure to germs the better, you know."

No shit, Maggie thought as she looked around at all the clean white furniture on the patio. *I wonder if she cleans this furniture every day. I can't see any dirt. She has to. Either that or she is a witch for sure. I don't care what Sean says, I think I will ask her about Uncle Arthur.*

"Also," Beth continued, "Neither Frances nor Jennifer can be with us tonight. They're both in Washington lobbying for more diversity within the automotive industry. I'm not sure what that is all about, but I'm sure we'll learn a lot from both of them when they get back. Having said that, I believe the rest of the homeowners are represented here by at least one person so we can call the meeting to order."

Wait a minute Maggie said to herself. *How can she say that? Amos isn't here. He's a homeowner, isn't he? Of course, he is, and she knows that. But I get it. Amos doesn't attend these meetings. I wonder if he ever did.* Maggie looked over at Sean and smiled. She tried to tell him with her eyes that Amos wouldn't be attending but she could see that he didn't understand what she was trying to say. She picked up a napkin and wrote on it, "Amos won't be here - you need to work on your telepathy" and slipped it to him as she walked over to get a beer.

He was smiling as he read her message and stuck the napkin in his pocket. He looked at her and motioned toward the cooler. She brought him a beer and whispered, "See - I practice." She heard her husband chuckle and turned her attention back to Beth.

"Jim, since you are the president, do you want to officially call the meeting to order?" Beth asked the older gentleman sitting next to the patio railing.

"Meeting called to order," Jim said and Beth continued with the agenda.

I suspected as much, Maggie said to herself. *Beth runs the show. But I understand. It's a thankless job.*

"Thank you, Jim," Beth said. "Also, before we get further into the meeting tonight, I'd like to introduce the two newest members of our Sycamore Springs community. Sean and Maggie Brodie. Welcome. I hope you get a chance to stick around a little after the meeting to meet everyone."

Maggie smiled as everyone turned toward her and Sean. *Just keep smiling Maggie. Remember, she can turn you into a mongoose or something by just twitching her nose.* That thought made Maggie smile even more and now she didn't really care how long they stared at her.

"Ok, the main reason for this meeting has to do with Jim's dog. As you know, Sandy, his Labrador, was bitten by a copperhead. She's fine now but that's not the first snake that has been up in our yards recently. Caleb killed a large six-foot gray water snake, but it could have just as easily been a poisonous one. He only saw it because he noticed something curled up under the shrubbery and then it struck at his dog. And I almost stepped on a copperhead the other day. One of the landscapers, a young man named Jorge, happened to see it before I did, and he stopped me from stepping on it. I think about what may have happened if he hadn't been there. I was holding my little one, Summer, at the time and it just makes me shudder to think if I had been bitten and dropped my little girl."

Where is she going with this? Maggie asked herself. *We are in the woods. In the south. There are snakes around here.*

"And you can remember last year," Beth continued. "Phil killed a four-foot rattlesnake down close to the covered bridge. In this heat, the snakes are just attracted to water. I asked a naturalist about it the other day and he said that if you didn't want snakes around, you should eliminate the water sources."

Oh shit. Now I know what you're doing. You're getting back at my son and what he said about the cottonmouth, aren't you? I don't like snakes either but you aren't getting rid of the pond. I am not going to let you do that.

"So, what are you suggesting?" one of the men asked. He was a rugged-looking man. Sharp nose. Square jaw. Long black hair and eyes that looked almost black. Maggie thought that he could have been of Native American heritage.

"What I am suggesting, is that we drain the pond. We could put some nice rocks and flowers in the area and keep the covered bridge. Make it look like a dry water bed. It would cut down on the number of snakes we see in our neighborhood," Beth informed the group.

The man that asked the question shook his head no as he spoke. "That's a bad idea. Even poisonous snakes have a purpose. We will not eliminate the copperhead, or the occasional rattlesnake by getting rid of the pond. You cannot make a wooded area like the one we live in snake-free. It's impossible. You cannot subdue Nature."

Maggie wanted to speak up but she felt Sean tugging on her shirt sleeve. She looked up at him and he was shaking his head in a very subtle manner telling her not to say anything.

"Thank you, Red," Beth said. "I respect your opinion. Does anyone else have anything to say?"

No one said anything.

"Ok then, let's vote. I already spoke with Sarah Cayman and she told me that she was fine with draining it. I have also spoken with Jennifer and Frances and they are for it. Darrin and I are for it. Anyone else for it, please raise your hand. Ok, Jim and Renee Thompson for it. Caleb and Jasmine Bartholomew for it. Now, all opposed? Sable and Red Skye, Agathe and Ulf, Maggie and Sean, Phil and Barbara Gillespie. So, the vote carries. I'll start working on the…" but she could not finish her sentence as Maggie spoke up.

"Wait a minute. You failed to count one other person's vote."

Beth glared at her. She knew who she was referring to.

"I am not sure we can rely on his vote."

"Why not?" Maggie asked as she felt Sean pulling on the back of her shirt.

"Because he is not always 'there.'" Beth made air quotes around the last word.

"Well, he's here now," Maggie said.

"What are you talking about?" Beth asked. "He never comes to these meetings."

"Look out there at your deer feeder." Everyone turned toward the backyard.

"Now look there to the right in the woods. See the naked man with the green and black markings on his face? I believe that is Amos."

Amos was standing in the woods gazing at some deer. Maggie called out to him, causing the deer to run and Amos to start chasing them.

"Amos, do you want to drain the pond?" Maggie yelled.

"Hell no!" he yelled back as he disappeared into the woods.

Beth was seething, but managed to say, "So, that's nine for and nine against. This meeting is adjourned," as she turned and stormed inside.

"Uh, everyone, you're welcome to stay here and socialize," Darrin said, a bit uncomfortably. "I'll be back in a minute. I just need to check on something."

Barbara whispered to Maggie. "I wouldn't recommend staying. I've never seen her glare at anyone like that before. She won't be happy with you for quite some time," and then she started to laugh.

In the car, Maggie knew she needed to say something to distract Sean from what had just occurred.

"Sable and Red Skye seem nice, don't they?" Maggie said. "Red or Skye, you can call him either one apparently, retired from the lumber industry, and now they both make art. They invited us over to see it. I'd like to do that. And Agathe and Ulf. I would have never known how to spell those names by their pronunciation. Ah-get. Well, maybe Ulf. Yeah, I think I would have gotten that one. Strong accents. He's some type of engineer. He likes trains and she likes antique porcelain dolls and Renaissance Fairs. Yeesh, that's a little scary, isn't it? Don't you think he looks a little like Lurch from 'The Addams Family?'"

Sean was silent until he pulled into the garage and turned off the car.

" Beth and 'Bewitched.' Ulf and 'The Addams Family.' Don't you think the old TV show references are a bit much?" Sean asked.

"Oh, come on, Sean," Maggie laughed. "We never did find out if Beth's maiden name is Montgomery, did we? And I promise you, either Agathe or Ulf has someone in their family that looks like Cousin Itt."

"Maggie," Sean said as he shook his head. "Let's make sure Amos remains 'crazy neighbor number one,' ok?"

"What are you saying?"

" I know you. The TV show references are just a distraction. You confronted Beth and you won't stop there. You think I don't see that?"

"Sean," Maggie said. "What she was proposing was crazy. It wouldn't have gotten rid of the snakes."

"Not completely, no."

"Plus, it would have broken your son's heart," Maggie said. "He loves going down there. He likes snakes, you know. He told me about a black snake, and several water snakes he saw down there. And the pond is so beautiful with the covered bridge. It would look stupid without a pond."

She failed to tell Sean that one of those water snakes was a cottonmouth. She knew she would have to do so sooner or later but this was not the time.

"Yes, I agree that it wouldn't look as good, but I don't think a dry stream bed would be all that awful," Sean replied.

Sean had that look on his face that she hated. The "lecture look" she called it. And she knew one was coming.

"You have got to stop making snap judgments on everyone that you meet too. It's not wise and it does nothing to help frame a positive impression of you."

"Yeah, ok," she replied. "But how often am I wrong?"

"Oh, several hundred times a year, I'd guess."

"That's not true," Maggie said defiantly.

"Your first impression of Barbara tonight was negative, wasn't it?"

"Um…." Maggie said as she looked away from Sean.

"I know exactly what you were thinking. You thought she was some kind of Barbie doll with breast enhancements and not a brain. And then you found out she had a sense of humor and everything changed. Why do you even care if they were real or not?"

"Because I don't like fakes."

"What if she had breast cancer and they were reconstructive surgery? Is it okay then?" he asked.

"I don't know. Maybe."

"And Agathe and Ulf. Even though they voted with you, you have a negative impression of them because they have interests in something that you find unappealing."

"Unappealing?" Maggie said as she interrupted. "Trains, antique porcelain dolls, and Renaissance Fairs? Have you seen what those antique porcelain dolls look like? We might as well go over to their house and start digging around in their backyard. I promise you we will find a dead body."

"Maggie. Come on."

"I'm kidding, Sean. I'm kidding."

"Yes, this time you are, but I know you. In your mind, they are still crazy people. TV characters. Not real. And then here we are back to where we started. Beth. Sometimes you just become unhinged about things, for whatever reason, and that can't happen with our new neighbors. Even if you don't like them, we have to be good neighbors. Not with half of them. All of them. Tomorrow, you need to start the recovery phase with Beth, ok?"

Maggie thought about what Sean had said. He was right and she hated when he was right. She nodded her head and started to mumble, making sure that the mumble was loud enough for him to hear.

" You have to admit one thing," Maggie said.

"What's that?"

"I think I would be at least crazy number four in this group," she said "Amos, Agathe, Ulf, and then, maybe me."

Sean smiled and leaned over and kissed his wife. He knew that was her way of saying she was sorry and that she would try to make amends.

As Maggie walked into the house, she thought about Amos. *He showed up just in time. I wonder if anyone else saw that knife in his hand. Well, if he happens to catch one of those deer tonight, I hope he catches the one that has been eating my hosta plants around the house. I wouldn't mind if he killed that one.*

Chapter 7

Casserole Dish

Sean was gone before Maggie woke up the next morning. She didn't even hear him shower. *I must have really been out* she thought as she went over to the sink and splashed some water on her face. "Good morning, Maggie," she said as she looked at her reflection in the mirror.

"What are you going to do about Beth?" her reflection asked her.

"Take her casserole dish back to her and try and establish some sort of positive relationship," Maggie replied.

"It will just be Paige Taylor all over again," the reflection said.

"I was thinking the same thing."

"That's because I'm you," the reflection told her.

"No, I'm better looking than you," Maggie said as she turned around and went into the kitchen.

She found the post-it note on the electric water kettle she used every morning for her hot tea.

"Filled up and ready to go. Early meeting with docs. Good luck w/ Beth. I love you - Abner."

Maggie laughed when she saw the name Abner.

"I'm not as crazy as Gladys, bud," Maggie said out loud. Sean's reference to the "Bewitched" character made her smile. She turned on the kettle and placed a tea bag in a mug. "And I love you too, Sean," Maggie said as she pulled the note off and stood there for a moment before adding the hot water to the mug.

She went out to the patio and gazed at the waterfall as she stirred her tea. Her thoughts drifted back to high school and Paige Taylor. *I wonder what Paige is doing now*, she thought as she pulled out her phone. She had tried to "friend" her on Facebook a few years ago but Paige wouldn't accept her request. She could still read her profile page though. Nothing had changed. *Still rich, it seems.*

"Well, I'm not doing so bad myself," Maggie said as she looked down at the phone. *I wonder if you still have a convertible Mustang. Damn, I was jealous of that car. You only won the student body president election because you probably bribed everyone to vote for you. If only ten of my friends had remembered to vote that day, I would have won. But they were stoned. Dammit. Man, was I pissed when I confronted them. Didn't stay pissed though. I took several hits off of that bong and I didn't give a shit. We laughed a lot that day.*

That's what I need to do. I need to find a way to make us all laugh. I'm good at that. I wonder if Connor has any dope? Yeah, that's a great idea, Maggie. "Here is your casserole dish, Beth, and by the way, I rolled a couple of doobies. Care to get stoned?" Then I could text Sean: 'No worries, mon. No worries. Me and Beth are jammin' now!'

Shit, Maggie, concentrate. What the hell is wrong? Why are you letting this woman intimidate you? You have nothing to worry about. Connor didn't do anything but smart off to her. What is it? She is the one that acted like a child when she stormed off last night. Yeah Sean, did you see that little hissy fit? Everyone else sure the hell did. Barbara even suggested we leave. Damn, I wish I had said something about that last night.

Getting her to laugh though is a good idea, but how do I start that process? she thought as she took a sip of tea. *Well, saying "I know you're a rich bitch" probably won't be any good. That didn't go over that well with Paige, even though my friends did laugh. "Hello, Beth, I bet people don't call you a whiny little ass because your ass isn't that little and I mean that in a good way." Uh, no, Maggie. Focus!*

I know. I know! Make some of those fudge brownies with the buttercream icing. Everyone in the entire world likes those. Ok, there may be one person who doesn't, but everyone you've made them for likes them. Leave out the nuts, showing her that you are sensitive to nut allergies. Use lactose-free milk, showing her that you are sensitive to lactose intolerance. No gluten. Put them in her casserole dish. It's a win all the way around. She couldn't complain about that. I think that would give us a starting point for a conversation and she'll see that I'm trying to be contrite. Trying to make things better. Great idea, Maggie. Great idea.

Be prepared though. You may have to take the first "volley" of venom when she sees you. She looks like the kind who would be thinking all night of what she was going to say to me when she saw me again. You can stand there and be quiet and just listen to it. Let her get it all out. Then you can apologize. Even an insincere apology will work; she'll never know. You're an expert at making people think you are sorry when you really aren't. Because let's face it, she is wrong about the pond proposal. But remember Maggie, that doesn't matter now. You won. Let it go at that like Sean asked you to. You won't ever be her friend, but you can at least make her think you are.

As Maggie sat and replayed the conversation with Beth, other thoughts began to muddle her mind. *Was she wrong about draining the pond,* Maggie asked herself? *Sean was right in a way. Dry river beds, done the right way, with the right landscaping, don't look too bad. But that's just stupid. I bet she left out some things that the naturalist told her. He may have said the less water, the fewer snakes, but I bet he also said, he wouldn't recommend doing something like that. Doing so upsets the natural eco-system and he would have never been okay with that. She omitted that because it didn't go along with her way of thinking. She's conniving. I know she is. I can tell.* Maggie heard a "Mom" and looked up to see Connor standing in the doorway.

"Good morning, son."

"Morning. How was the meeting last night?" Connor asked as he came over and sat down next to her.

"It was good," Maggie said.

"Nice try," Connor answered. "Now tell me the truth."

She smiled at her son. He could always tell when she was lying. There was that bond between them. They could both tell when either one of them was hiding something.

"The meeting was about the pond," Maggie said. "Beth proposed draining it and making it look like a dry water bed, with rocks, flowers, that sort of thing. It was a close vote. If not for me asking Amos, she would have gotten her way and drained the pond."

"She's not very bright, is she?" Connor asked. "What she's suggesting won't do away with snakes around here. Where there are woods, there are snakes. Even water snakes would be attracted to this area because of the pools and because of Amos's waterfall pond. Does she want to drain all the pools and Amos's pond too?"

"I would be afraid to ask her that," Maggie said. "But they do have a pool. I saw it last night. Maybe I should have said something about that."

"I don't think that would've been a good idea, because I'm betting when you said, 'if not for me asking Amos,' that didn't go over well with Ms. Stevens. Am I right?"

"Were you there at the meeting, hiding somewhere?" Maggie asked as she raised her eyebrows at her son.

"No, but I know how she would have responded to you asking Amos," Connor replied. "And I saw him earlier last night. He wasn't wearing any clothes. I'm guessing he showed up at the meeting naked too."

"He really wasn't there for the meeting, I don't think," Maggie replied. "I think he was chasing deer and he wasn't completely naked. He did have some black and green paint of some sort on his face."

"I bet that was a 'thumbs up' for everybody! You just need to let things rest, Mom. You don't need to do anything else. I'm sure everything will work out just fine," Connor said and smiled at her.

She reached over and took his hand and nodded her head. "I was going to make some fudge brownies for her. As a way of saying I was sorry. That should be okay, don't you think?"

"Yes, I think that would be just fine."

Emiliano drove by the Circle K later than usual that morning on his way to Sycamore Springs. He had finished one beer as he entered the code and drove into the neighborhood. He went through the bridge and parked his truck at the end of the cul-de-sac. He looked around but didn't see anyone or any car at the Thompson's or the Stevens' home. He had a purpose for driving to the end of the road today. There was a mother-in-law home on the Thompson property that was always unlocked and he wanted to go in and take a look around.

He walked down the driveway and through the yard, to the back of the secluded property where the mother-in-law home sat. He went around the back, up to the small porch, and tried the handle on the door. It opened and he went in.

He looked around the kitchen. He didn't see anything that was worth very much in the cabinets. He took his time looking around the living room and though the furniture was nice and worth some money, he wasn't sure how he would get any of that out of the home without being seen. He walked into the bedroom and he immediately found what he was looking for. On a side table next to the bed was an iPad. He could take it and get some decent money for that. He thought he should get at least $100, but he knew the pawnshop would probably only offer him half that much. He told himself he would hold out for $75 as he tucked the tablet into his pants and under his shirt before leaving.

On the way down the driveway, he saw Ms. Stevens waving to him, motioning for him to come over. *What does she want,* he asked himself. *I can't go over there right now with this iPad. But I need to say something.*

"Buenos Dias, Ms. Stevens," Emiliano hollered out to her. "I'll be right over there. I just need to get something out of my truck."

What the hell am I going to get out of my truck? He stashed the iPad on the floorboard of the passenger seat and pretended to look around. *Shit, your phone man. Just tell her you needed to get your phone.* He opened the truck door and started toward the Stevens' home. *Where did she go? She's not in the front yard anymore. Oh fuck. What if she's inside calling the police? What if she saw him go into the cabin? What are you going to do now, man? I'm not going back to jail that's for fucking sure,* he told himself as he knocked on the door. *No, I am not going to jail.* Beth opened the door and smiled at him.

"Hello, Jorge," Beth said. "I saw you over there at the Thompson's mother-in-law home. Did you lose something?"

"Yes, ma'am," Emiliano replied. "I thought I left my hand pruners back there somewhere, but I couldn't find them. I could have sworn I had them when I was trimming the red tips that are on the backside of the house the other day, but no luck."

"What do they look like?"

They are fucking pruning shears. What the hell do you think they look like? Emiliano was saying in his head but the smile on his face hid those thoughts. "They are old, but very sharp and reliable, with a red handle," Emiliano said. "I'm sure I will find them. Maybe they're behind my truck seat somewhere."

"Is that what you were looking for in your truck? The shears?"

What the hell are you, a prison guard of some sort? Cool it, Emiliano. Stick with the story.

"No, ma'am," Emiliano replied. "I left my phone on the truck seat. Need to have my phone with me all the time now. I started my own company."

Beth seemed a bit surprised by that last comment. "Is that so?" she asked. "Well, do you have time to come out on the patio and tell me about it? I can get you some iced tea or coffee or some bottled water?

"Water would be great," Emiliano said as he followed her into the house. He waited just outside the kitchen as she retrieved two bottles of water and motioned for him to follow her.

What the hell is she up to he asked himself. *Is she stalling so that the police can get here? Fuck!* He felt beads of sweat dripping from his forehead. They sat down at the table in the middle of the patio and Emiliano opened up his water bottle and took several drinks.

"I just wanted to thank you again, Jorge, for saving me and my little girl from that copperhead the other day. I have thought about that many times since then and I just thank God that you were there. I'm thinking you were supposed to be there that day," Beth said.

Supposed to be there? Divine intervention. You would get along great with my aunt. You both believe that there are spiritual events that shape your day. Bullshit, Emiliano thought as he smiled at her.

"Tell me about your new company," she said.

Showtime, Emiliano thought. "I think I can do a better job with landscaping than the company I was working for. Plus, I will do it cheaper. In fact, for your yard, I would do it for $125. That's the grass and the edging. And if you want me to do the shrubs, I'll be glad to add that for an extra fee, depending on what you want me to do," he said as he smiled at her.

Beth reached over and took hold of Emiliano's hand and squeezed it.

"Oh, I am thinking that would be a good idea. I can tell you would do a good job at cutting the grass and trimming the bushes. I bet you are really good at trimming bushes," Beth said as she let go of his hand and took a drink of her water.

Emiliano saw her tongue linger on her lips longer than necessary. *Hell, she is coming on to me,* he said to himself.

"Where are your children?" he asked.

"One of them is at Mother's Day Out at the church and the other two are at school," Beth said. "It's just you and me here discussing the terms of the new contract."

Maggie finished the brownies and arranged them in Beth's casserole dish with some aluminum foil over the top and headed down the road toward the Stevens' home. She saw the blue Chevy truck parked at the end of the cul-de-sac and wondered who it belonged to. *I'm sure Beth knows,* she thought as she walked up and knocked on the door. She waited for about a minute and tried looking inside but could not see anyone. *Maybe she's in the backyard.* As she walked around to the back of the house, she looked over at the patio and saw Beth and a black-haired man sitting at a table. All she could see was the back of his head as it covered up Beth's face.

What the fuck? "Shit!" she yelled as she dropped the casserole dish and watched it break on the stone walkway.

Both the black-haired man and Beth ran over and looked down at Maggie who was trying to pick up the broken glass.

"I was returning your casserole dish. With some fudge brownies. I, um, tripped on one of the stones and dropped the dish. I'm so sorry. If you want to give me a broom, I'll be glad to clean everything up and I'll get you a new dish today. The brownies didn't have nuts and were lactose-free," Maggie added as she saw Beth frowning at her and stood up. She hoped the fact that what lay on the ground was nut and lactose-free would still score her some 'brownie points 'with Beth and as she thought about that pun, it made her smile.

Beth wasn't sure what Maggie had seen, but she knew she needed to say something about Jorge. She didn't like the way Maggie was smiling at her.

"Maggie," Beth started. "This is Jorge. The gentleman who saved me and my daughter from the copperhead that I was speaking about at the meeting. We were just talking about the new landscaping company he has started. He's going to start doing our yard. Cheaper and better, right, Jorge?"

"Yes, ma'am," Emiliano replied. "Shall I start tomorrow? I don't mind that it's Saturday."

"Yes, that will be great, Jorge. See you tomorrow. And thank you for getting that little speck of pine straw out of my eye."

What a fucking load of bullshit. How stupid does she think I am? Maggie asked herself.

"No problem, Ms. Stevens. I'll see you tomorrow," Emiliano said as he left, making sure he stepped over the broken glass and brownies. He walked around the edge of the house and waited. He wanted to listen to what was said.

"I'll clean up the mess you made," Beth said looking down at Maggie. "And you don't need to get me another dish. I appreciate your gesture."

It was all Maggie could do to restrain herself as Beth accused her of making a mess. *It won't be as big as the mess you made when I tell your husband about your new landscaper,* she thought. *That little thank you at the end was so I wouldn't say anything, wasn't it? Well, maybe I don't need to say anything. Not just yet.*

"Sure," Maggie smiled. *And, I think this is the perfect time to talk about those homeowner's fees.*

"Beth," Maggie started. "I wanted to discuss our homeowner's fees with you. $200 a month seems like quite a lot. What exactly does that pay for?"

"It pays for the landscaping at the front of the subdivision, around the pond, and ensures we have enough money for any road repairs," Beth replied. "Since this is a private road, we are responsible for repairs. We've already had to do some repaving, and it's not cheap, especially with that covered bridge and pond."

"It sure seems like a lot." *I wonder what Darrin would say about the landscaper sticking his tongue down your mouth,* Maggie wanted to say but she held back as she waited for Beth to respond.

"We can bring it up at the next meeting," Beth said. "I'll make sure the new president is aware of your concern."

"What new president?"

"Oh, we held a vote via email," Beth replied. "Have you not checked your email? Jim wanted to step down and I offered myself up to do that job since I was basically doing it anyway, as well as the treasurer and secretary's job. It just makes things so much easier. I have already gotten ten votes for that proposal, so effective immediately, I am the new president of the homeowner's association. And treasurer and secretary."

"You have got to be kidding me!" Maggie replied with a disbelieving smile.

"No. I'm not kidding you," Beth replied. "And I'm sure that pond issue will come back up again too."

Goddamn you. Paige Taylor, all over again, Maggie said to herself. *Problem is, Paige, that Mustang of yours is just an old blue Chevy truck this time. And I don't think the neighbors are really going to like seeing it around. Especially one neighbor, a Mr. Darrin Stevens.* But before she said anything else, Maggie heard her son's voice.

"You just need to let things rest, Mom. You don't need to do anything else. I am sure everything will work out fine," she heard him say and she knew he was right. At least for now. *I know what I saw and I know you know, Beth Stevens.* She bent down and picked up a brownie and wiped the dirt off it.

"A little dirt never hurt anybody," Maggie said as she took a bite of the brownie and stared back at Beth. "Sorry about the casserole dish." She turned around and started walking back toward the front of the house and saw the blue truck pulling away. *You should be leery of women carrying casserole dishes in the future, Jorge,* she thought as she took another bite.

Chapter 8

A thorn in her side

Emiliano's heart was racing. He had broken into a house and escaped clean, came up with an idea for his own company, and had a very good-looking woman hitting on him. *A very rich good-looking woman* he thought as he opened a beer and went straight to the pawnshop.

The successes of the day did not stop at the pawnshop. He got more than he thought for the iPad. Miguel paid him $80 and told him he would rent a tractor and edger to him for $40 a day, provided he brought them back to him each evening in good condition. Emiliano worked out a deal so that at least $40 a week of that money would go toward owning the tractor and edger if he rented the equipment for five days each week. If he was smart and hustled, he could own that equipment in several months and have some spending money for him and his aunt. *Things were looking up. Firing me, Doug, was a good thing* he thought as he shared a beer with Miguel and signed the paperwork for their deal.

After he loaded the tractor and edger into the back of his truck, he headed to the lake. He was hoping what he had seen there the other day was still nearby. That woman that saw him and Mrs. Stevens needed to be warned to not say anything about what she had seen. He knew the perfect way to do that and he knew where she lived. He had seen her several times before. She lived across the road from the crazy man with the waterfall. He wondered if that crazy man had replaced those fish as he drove up past the empty Emiliano's Park guardhouse and threw a penny into the fee box.

He parked next to the picnic tables and got another beer. *Yep, they're still here.* He smiled and walked along the edge of the water while thinking about what a good day it had been. He was anxious to show Mrs. Stevens how well he could trim her bushes. After all, he would need her recommendations to build up his new business.

Beth swept up the broken glass and brownies and wondered exactly how much Maggie had seen. Then she remembered what she had said as she looked up at them. "A little dirt never hurt anyone." *She saw us, me and*

Jorge kissing! She stared up at the patio from where Maggie had been standing as she recalled the image of Maggie's face when she was wiping the dirt off the brownie. *But from that perspective, she could have only seen the back of Jorge's head. She could only assume we were kissing, but she could never be completely sure. But did she mean she was okay with that? Was she telling me that my secret was safe with her?*

It was probably not a smart idea to antagonize her with the pond issue now. She would have to gauge what Maggie was thinking and how this might play out over the next few days. Perhaps she could take her some more food. Or some of her hydrangeas. She could tell she liked plants. *Yes, I'll take her some hydrangeas* Beth decided as she dumped the final pieces of glass into the trash. Her face lit up as she considered something else. *I'll make her an officer of the homeowner's association! I can't think of a better way for the two of us to become friends,* Beth thought as she placed the broom and dustpan back into their proper place in the garage. *And if not friends, I can't think of a better way to make sure she doesn't become a bigger thorn in my side than she already is.*

Maggie simmered with anger, fueled by the interaction with Beth and aggravated by the heat and humidity that surrounded her. *I'll be damned if I let her do anything about the pond knowing what I do now. But you have to be smart, Maggie. You can't just win one hand of poker. You need to win the entire pot. Boy, that really pisses me off that so many people already voted and elected her president. She sure knows how to get things done around here. She's been living here for years and she knows everyone, or at least it appears so. But nothing is certain yet except that you know she likes kissing men other than her husband. And that's a good thing to know.*

What a crock of shit! Maggie remembered how strict and proper Beth presented herself when she brought over that macaroni and cheese. *Are you going to be strict with Jorge?* Maggie wondered as she started to laugh. *Should I tell Sean? No, I don't think he needs to know yet. Perhaps if things start to go in a direction I don't anticipate, I'll tell him, but for now, there is nothing to say. You'll just have to think about me and what I might say each time you see me, Beth. Wondering if this is the day I spill the beans. I like that. I like that a lot. In fact, I don't see that pond ever being dry as long as we're living here,* Maggie said to herself as Connor walked into the kitchen.

"Well, it looks like things went well," he said.

"Better than I expected."

"See Mom," Connor shook his finger at her. "I told you things would work out."

"Yes, you did, son, You're almost always right."

"Almost?"

"Yeah," Maggie replied. "And considering that this is the Friday before the Monday when you have to go back to school; what do you think about going to see the new 'Jurassic Park' movie? I think if we leave right now, we can just about make it to the matinee. We may miss the previews, but we would be there for the start of the movie for sure."

"What are we waiting for then?" Connor asked.

"Just let me change my shirt and spritz myself with something that smells a little better than sweat. Just walking up here from the end of the road soaked me."

"Ok. I'll start the car!"

Within two minutes, Maggie was opening the door to her Ford Explorer and Connor backed out of the driveway. "Where is the theater?" he asked.

"It's someplace called Riverwatch Luxury Cinemas. They're supposed to have leather recliners – all the comforts of home," Maggie sighed.

"Cool," Connor replied.

"Go to the front of the subdivision and turn left. We'll get on Bobby Jones and turn onto Washington Road before we turn onto Riverwatch Road," Maggie directed as she looked at the Google map on her phone.

"Hmmm…Old Firecracker Bob may have been right," Maggie commented.

"What are you talking about?"

"Our realtor told us everything leads to or off of Washington Road when he was bringing us out here to see the house," Maggie said. "I called him Firecracker Bob because he told us he had firecrackers going off in his head."

"What?"

"Your father told me not to say anything about that so just keep that between us, but that's what he said. I wasn't sure he should be driving but he said he was fine," Maggie explained.

"Yeah, I suppose so," Connor replied. "As long as they weren't M-80's, but the little firecrackers should be fine. With those M-80's, I think some of his brains would have leaked out of his ears."

Maggie laughed at her son. He was just like her in so many ways. He had her sense of humor, which at times, was considered being a smartass, and she knew he would have to learn when to tone things down. He was very smart, even smarter than her. He never seemed to forget anything he read. And he loved sweets and chocolate. And like her, they both had the ability to eat them without appearing to gain weight.

And because they loved science fiction and horror, the "Jurassic Park" books and movies were some of their favorites. They both thought the books by Michael Crichton were better than the movies, but they could still watch the movies over and over again. She loved those times with her son. Eating popcorn, Reese's Pieces, and watching movies. She looked at him as he got out of the car. He was almost six feet tall now. Bigger than Sean. Her son was getting older, but she knew they would always love going to the movies together. She was sure of that.

They reviewed the movie on their way home and both gave it 3.5 stars. Good, but not great. Worth watching. They agreed they would watch it again when it came out on pay per view and they also agreed that going to the movies had gotten much more expensive.

"Oh, what the hell, Connor. You're about to start school on Monday. Sixty dollars is worth it to spend some time with my baby boy!" she exclaimed.

Connor looked at her like she had two heads. "That cost sixty dollars?"

"Yes, it did."

"Why didn't you get a senior discount?"

Maggie tried to suppress her smile but she couldn't. "Funny, funny, funny. I won't be a senior for quite some time and with talk like that, you may not even make it to your senior year."

Connor smiled. He enjoyed going to the movies with his mother. He liked being around her. He thought she was funny and smart. And they shared a lot of common interests now. *I bet I can even get her to touch a snake by the end of the summer* he thought.

They got back to the house around 5:00. Maggie pulled into the garage and told Connor that she was going to go get the mail before she came in. She walked down the driveway and smiled as she looked over at the pond and covered bridge. *That never gets old.* She reached in the mailbox and pulled out the mail. There were two old brown leaves on top of the envelopes. She picked them off and threw them to the ground. *How did those get in the mailbox?*

She felt the stinging in her hands right away, as if a swarm of bees had attacked her. Her hands started to redden and burn and she knew something was wrong. She glanced down and noticed those brown leaves were now moving. She ran up the driveway as fast as she could; the stinging and burning intensifying with each step she took. She threw the mail down and rushed into the kitchen to put her hands underneath some cold water.

"Damn, this hurts!" she yelled.

Connor heard her cries and ran into the kitchen to see what was wrong. She showed him her hands and told him about the brown leaves in the mailbox.

"I think there was some spider or something on them," Maggie said. "They were moving."

"You need to keep your hands under the cold water and try to wipe them with some soap if you can. Then you need to put some antibiotic cream and aloe on them and take some anti-histamine," Connor said.

"Did you get a medical license online that I wasn't aware of?" Maggie winced as she asked.

"No, but I can tell you're having a reaction to what stung you. Let me go see if I can find out what it was," Connor said as he walked out the garage door.

"Be careful!"

Connor found the old brown leaves on the ground by the mailbox. He flipped them over with a stick and then took out his phone. He googled "poisonous caterpillars in the south" and identified the picture of what lay on the ground. They were puss moth caterpillars. The information on them said, "Envenomation causes intense throbbing pain, burning, and a rash with erythematous spots. Nausea, abdominal pain, headache, and respiratory distress can be realized."

"Shit," he said as he ran back to the kitchen. His mom was still at the sink cleaning off her hands. "Are you feeling nauseous or have a headache or any trouble breathing?"

"No, my hands are just burning and stinging, but it's getting some better," Maggie said. "Why?"

"Because those leaves you saw were not leaves. They were puss moths. The hairs on their body inject you with poison."

"Well, how lovely. What a nice name for a moth. Perhaps we have some vomit bugs crawling around the house too."

When Connor heard his mother say vomit bugs, he knew she was going to be okay. "You'll be much better in about an hour, I think. Just clean off your hands the best you can," he added as he began to think about what had occurred.

He knew those caterpillars didn't just crawl into the mailbox. They were put there. Probably by someone who was trying to send a message. He didn't know what kind of message but as he thought about Amos's fish and now these puss moths in the mailbox, he began to see that message was a warning of some sort. He knew that this was not a coincidence and that concerned him. He was afraid that whoever was doing this, didn't realize that they were playing with fire. A fire that may be difficult to extinguish once it started to burn.

Chapter 9

Deer repellant

Just like Connor said, within an hour, Maggie's hands were much improved. They were still red but the stinging and burning had subsided and now there was just a dull ache. Maggie checked her watch and saw it was a little after six. She wasn't hungry after all the snacks she and Connor had at the movies, but she knew Sean would be home soon and asking about dinner.

"Are you hungry?" she asked Connor.

"Not that much."

"Neither am I," Maggie replied. "Would you mind calling your father and tell him that if he wants something to eat to grab it on the way home? Maybe he could stop by Subway and get y'all some sandwiches. I think I'll just have a salad later."

"Sure," Connor replied. Sean was glad to hear from his son. He had been so busy he hadn't eaten all day and a Subway sandwich sounded good. About thirty minutes later, Sean walked in with the sandwiches and tossed one to his son. He noticed Maggie's hands immediately and asked what happened.

"Puss moth caterpillars. Did you know those lived around here, Sean? A little heads-up would have been appreciated," Maggie said sarcastically.

"What the hell?" Sean asked as he sat down and examined her hands. "What are puss moth caterpillars?"

"Well, according to Connor, they are things that look like dead leaves and crawl up in your mailbox," Maggie said. "If you see any dead leaves in the mailbox, be careful and don't grab them."

"How in the hell did they get in the mailbox?"

Connor just listened to their conversation. He didn't want to say they were put there by someone until he was sure. There was no sense in throwing a match onto a fire without any proof. He had learned that as he got older.

"I have no idea," Maggie said. "But the damn hairs on those sweet little caterpillars are poisonous. Who would have thought with a name like puss moth that they would be harmful, huh?"

"I can show you what they look like," Connor told his dad.

"Are you telling me you didn't send them back into the flaming pits of hell once you realized what they did to your mother?" Maggie asked.

"I didn't do anything about them except find out what they were," Connor said. "I wanted to make sure you were okay. I doubt they've gone far. And I can dole out retribution with Dad," Connor said as he looked over at his mother and bowed his head.

"That's more like it," Maggie replied. "Subservience and obedience is all I ask. Is that too much?"

"Come on, son," Sean said. "Show me what you're talking about while the Queen Mother here rests."

Connor and his father searched around the mailbox for one of the puss moths. They had crawled off but Connor knew what he was looking for and he had a keen eye when he was out in the woods.

"There's one!" Connor yelled. He picked up a stick and flipped it over to show his dad the tiny hairs on it that injected venom.

"I read where some people compare the sting to that of a jellyfish and some folks can have a severe reaction that puts them into anaphylactic shock," Connor said. "Nasty little things, aren't they? I can't find any value in them except as part of the food chain."

"Yes, they are nasty looking," Sean said as he stepped on it and twisted his foot into the ground.

"Want me to set them on fire now?"

"Don't say stuff like that, Connor. Even when I know you're joking," Sean answered harshly and turned to go back to the house.

Connor nodded his head at his father's reprimand and held his head down as he looked at the ground. Sean knew he had responded inappropriately and he needed to let his son know he wasn't really mad at him.

"Don't worry. I'll find out tomorrow what kind of insecticide will be best to keep them away. And I'm sort of surprised the caterpillar hurt your mother."

"Why do you say that?"

"Most of those types of things are afraid to hurt a witch," Sean quipped.

"I'll tell her you said that," he said as he elbowed his Dad and laughed.

"I just bought you a sandwich and you're going to sell me out?"

"Well… since you bought me a sandwich," Connor said and smiled as he and his father went back into the house.

The next morning, Sean slept in until about 7:00 and got started on his run a little later than usual. At the end of the cul-de-sac, he saw Beth outside talking with a young man. They seemed to be having a conversation about her yard and when she noticed Sean, she waved at him, motioning for him to come over to her. *Shit,* he thought as he started walking her way. *She's going to say something about Maggie and Amos. Just smile, Sean. Try and make things better. You know how to do that.*

"Hey, Sean," Beth said.

"Good morning, Beth. What's up?"

"I just wanted to know if you would ask your wife something for me."

Here it comes, he thought. "Sure Beth. Be glad to."

"Would you mind asking her if she would help me with the homeowner's association? You know, serve as the secretary/treasurer?"

" You want her to help you with the homeowner's association?" Sean repeated, trying not to sound shocked.

"Yes. I've come to realize that she cares about the way things look around here and I can't fault anyone for having the same passion I do for our neighborhood."

"Okay," Sean replied hesitantly. "I'm sure Maggie would be happy to help. And you're right. She is passionate about the way things appear. I'm glad you can see that. I'm sure she will do a good job."

"Thank you, Sean. Just tell her I'll get in touch with her later today or tomorrow."

"Yeah, no problem." Sean turned and started walking back toward the road. He watched the man get the lawn tractor out of the blue truck and start it up. *I wonder what service they use. Don't see any name on the side of the truck. Their yard is very nice though. I'll ask later* he thought as he started jogging back toward the house.

What had Maggie done to get Beth to change her opinion of her he wondered. She didn't mention anything to him. *Could Beth have just had a change of heart? Damn. I can't wait to tell her.* He picked up his speed and ran as fast as he could up to the entrance gate and back to his house. Maggie was in the kitchen when Sean came in, heating water for her tea.

"How is the hand today?" he asked.

"Doesn't hurt. Just red and a little itchy."

"Good." Sean got a bottle of water from the refrigerator. "Guess who I saw on my run this morning?"

"Bill Clinton," Maggie said.

"Nope."

"George Bush."

"Maggie," Sean said as he held up his hand to stop the other responses that were lined up ready to come out of her mouth. "Beth."

"How can you be sure it was her and not a puss moth? They're very similar. Only difference is in the spelling of moth. Beth's has a 'u' in it."

Sean just shook his head as he rolled his eyes. "She wanted to know if you would be interested in helping her with the homeowner's association. She wants you to serve as secretary/treasurer. I'm so proud of you and whatever you did to mend the fences. You didn't tell me you did anything. How did you get her to change her opinion?"

Well, catching her with her tongue down Jorge's mouth helped the most I think, Maggie wanted to say but she didn't. She just smiled at Sean and told him that she took her some fudge brownies and that they had a real good talk.

I'm impressed, Beth. You're keeping me close, aren't you? Good idea. That way you can try and control me, right? Wrong. But it is a smart plan. We can work together. You will just have to learn who is in control, but I'm sure you will over time. This is good. Very good. I'll go down and say hello to my "bestie" later. Maggie smiled again at Sean as she took her cup of tea out on the patio.

Sean soon joined her with some oatmeal and English muffins. "Want any?"

"No, I'm good," Maggie said, "but thanks."

Sean nodded his head and began to eat his breakfast.

"I love coming out here each morning and listening to the waterfall as I have my tea," Maggie said. "You did good, husband. I am pleased."

"Even with the puss moths?"

"Yes. 'Cause I know you will be doing some spraying today to kill those damn things. Right?"

"Right," Sean said as he smiled and reached over and rubbed his wife's thigh.

"Need some help with your shower?" Maggie asked as she responded by reaching over and grabbing Sean's crotch. "It appears you do. Follow me, Spongebob Tightpants."

For a few minutes they both disappeared under the water until their bodies released them back into the shower. "I'm glad you needed some help with your shower," Maggie said with a smile.

"I'm glad you were there to help me," Sean said as he kissed his wife.

Sean was dressed in minutes and told Maggie that he was going to Lowes to get some pesticide. Maggie still had a towel wrapped around her body and said that she thought she would walk down the road this morning.

"Going to see Beth?"

"Yeah, if she's out in her yard," Maggie said.

"Good idea." He thought about getting Connor to go with him and checked the time. It was almost ten and Connor was still not up. He started to go wake him, but then remembered it was the Saturday before his son went back to school so he just turned around and left. *Let him sleep,* he thought.

Maggie spent some additional time in the bathroom getting ready. Her hair was short but she wanted to make sure that there wasn't any gray showing. When she looked into the mirror, she examined more than her hair though. She was somewhat vain, she admitted it. She liked what she saw in the mirror and she wanted to continue to like what she saw as she dropped the towel and took a visual inventory of her body.

If Barbara's breasts were cantaloupes, she would have to say hers, using the garden analogy, were very large tomatoes, which in her opinion, were more appealing. Her stomach was still firm and though she thought her ass was a little less round than she would like, it was also firm and muscular. A good 8 she thought and maybe on a good day with a little wine and my sparkling personality, a 9.

"You are a narcissist," the image in the mirror said to her.

"I am not," Maggie replied.

"Oh really. How many people do you know who talk to their image in the mirror?"

"Hundreds," Maggie said as she smiled and then looked away from the mirror. When she looked back, the reflection began talking again.

"Hundreds? You really want to stick with that story?"

"I don't know for sure. It's not like I've asked everyone I have ever met. But I'm guessing a lot."

"And if you're correct, then they are narcissists like you," the image replied.

"So?"

"What are you going to do when your looks start to fade?"

"Plastic surgery is always an option."

"Then you would be a fake," the image replied. "How could you live with yourself?"

"Pretty well after I got rid of all the goddamn mirrors."

"Time will tell."

'Yes, I suppose it will." Maggie said as she continued to comb through her hair, and seeing that everything looked appropriate, applied her makeup and got dressed.

It was a quarter of eleven when she walked into her kitchen. Connor was at the kitchen bar eating cereal. "How's the hands?"

"Good," Maggie replied.

"You look nice this morning. Where you headed?"

"Well, thank you for noticing. I thought I'd go for a walk in our neighborhood and meet and greet our new neighbors."

"You mean go door to door?" he asked.

"Not exactly. But it is Saturday," Maggie said. "And it is before noon, so I imagine a lot of them will be out in their yards, pulling weeds, planting flowers, you know."

"Don't most of these folks have people that do that for them?"

"Yes, a lot of them have lawn services, but I think many of them like to work in their yards and gardens too," Maggie replied. "At least that's my opinion from what I've seen."

"Well, they do call this the Garden City," Connor replied somewhat sarcastically.

"You are correct," Maggie laughed. "Your dad is at Lowes. He should be back in just a bit. Maybe you can help him spray for those puss moths and any other dangerous creatures that might be lurking out there. I'll see you later."

As she walked down the driveway she smiled when looking over at the pond and the covered bridge. *I wonder if I'll ever be able not to do that* she asked herself. She walked toward the marsh side of the pond and spotted the dark purple and yellow swamp irises. They looked beautiful against the green reeds that seemed to blend in with the leaves of the irises. She noticed the pitcher plants too. They had a woodsy feel about them. Not as spectacular in color as the irises, but they were unique and still very pretty.

She turned to go down the street. She passed the Skye home first. It resembled a lodge nestled in the mountains of Colorado or Montana and was separated from Amos's home by a ravine of thick woods. The front yard consisted of large boulders, mulch, trees, and ferns. The wooden porch appeared to wrap around the entire house and as she walked by it, she could just make out the large back deck that seemed to disappear into the woods. She thought she saw a small waterfall or rock fountain next to the deck along with several large iron sculptures. "I bet that house is gorgeous inside," she mumbled as she continued to walk.

Next to the Skye's home was a ranch-style house that looked like it might have been built in the 50s but there was no way it could have been considering the age of this subdivision. It was a dark yellow stucco with three large picture windows along the front of the home. Maggie wondered who the builder was and then saw the two large women in the front yard working in their flower garden. *Must be Frances and Jennifer,* Maggie said to herself. Their house was set at the bottom of the hill on which the Skye home had been built. There were woods all around the home with the driveway bordered by large trees, azaleas, abelias, and hostas.

"Hello," Maggie called out. *Good lord! They look like Swedish models. One blonde and one with raven black hair. What was the name of that woman that played Red Sonya,* she started asking herself as she smiled. *Brigitte Nelson. Shit. I am looking at two Brigitte Nelsons.*

"I'm Maggie," she said as she walked over to the black-haired model. "I love the way your builder married the different styles. The 50s ranch with the modern yellow stucco. Very pretty."

"Hello, Maggie," the black-haired model responded as she removed her work gloves and shook her hand. "I'm Jennifer and this is my life partner, Frances. You moved into the hobbit house, didn't you?"

"The hobbit house?" Maggie asked with a surprised look on her face.

"Oh, don't take what I'm saying in the wrong way," Jennifer said. "It's just what Frances and I call it because it looks like it's built into the side of the hill. Like the hobbit home. There are a lot of beautiful homes in this neighborhood but yours is one of our favorites. When it came on the market, we thought about buying it for a moment, but we decided it was just too much trouble to move. And we do like our home. I'm impressed you caught the vibe we wanted it to generate. You have a good eye."

"What happened to your hands?" Frances said as she walked up to Maggie. "I'm an RN, but don't spend much time in the hospitals anymore. Spend more time in Washington fighting for the people that work in them. It looks like you were stung by something and had a reaction to it."

"I was and did. I was stung by a puss moth," Maggie replied.

"A what moth?"

"Puss moth. They live around here. If you see anything that looks like a dead leaf with hairs on it, don't touch it with your bare hands. It will sting the shit out of you. But mine are doing much better now. Just still a little red and itchy."

"We've never seen them and we've been here for three years," Frances said.

"Well, they are around here, for sure," Maggie replied. "My husband is at Lowes looking for something to spray around the yard to kill them. If you want, I could tell you what he finds."

"Yes, let us know, but we only use organic materials on our yard and plants."

"That must be why your hostas and azaleas are not all eaten up by the deer that roam through here like it's their own personal cafeteria. I love hostas and the ones along your driveway and around your house are so beautiful. What do you use on them as deer repellant?" Maggie asked.

Frances smiled and walked over to the side of the house that was fringed by thick woods. Maggie watched as she removed her pants and bent down and proceeded to pee on the hostas. Her eyes widened as she watched Frances do that on several plants before she pulled her pants back up.

"And I would have thought that a house as nice as yours would have had indoor plumbing," Maggie commented.

Jennifer started to laugh. "Like we said – organic. Dog poop works well too. We save all of our dog poop and put it among the plants. As you've noticed, it works."

"Yes, yes I can see that!" Maggie laughed. "Well, It was nice meeting both of you and I'll let you know what Sean picks up from Lowes."

"By the way," Jennifer said as Maggie turned back around. "I think you'll do a great job for the homeowners association working with Beth."

How in the hell did she know that already? Shit. Beth is a witch. But let's see how well this communication channel of hers really works.

"Thanks," Maggie replied. "Speaking of the homeowners association, I'd like your opinion about something, since you happened to mention it. What would you ladies think about painting the guardhouse? Maybe a deep forest green?"

"With some cranberry accents?" Frances asked. "That would match the color of the tiles on the roof."

"I hadn't thought of that, but sure," Maggie replied.

"I think that would be tres chic," Jennifer replied and threw her a kiss of approval.

Tres chic? Jesus, Maggie said to herself as she continued to smile. "Great. Thanks for the input," she said as she left.

But that deer repellant you ladies use, Maggie thought. *I would be very careful squatting down over a bunch of hostas and mulch. I don't think you want a puss moth caterpillar getting up into those bushes. That wouldn't be so tres chic, I promise you.*

Chapter 10

Renaissance Fair

The house next to Jennifer and Frances belonged to Ulf and Agathe. Maggie thought it had a Norwegian flair with its white brick gables and many sloping rooflines. Tall pine and pecan trees dotted their front yard and a very large sycamore tree stood at the entrance of their driveway.

As she continued walking, she soon saw the yellow corvette parked beside a lovely beige stucco house with an inviting front porch made of river rock. *That's Phil and Barbara's* she said to herself. She could make out at least two levels of porches behind the house and their front yard was a lush carpet of dark green grass, accented with colorful pockets of roses and azaleas. *I wonder if they use the same type of deer repellant as Frances and Jennifer. Hell, I bet they bottled it and gave it away as Christmas gifts last year to their neighbors,* Maggie snickered to herself.

The last four homes at the end of the street belonged to the Stevens', Thompson's, Bartholomew's, and Mrs. Cayman. Besides the Stevens' house, Maggie wasn't sure which of the other three belonged to which family. Beth's yard was freshly mowed. Maggie could smell the cut grass and could see all the fine lines that had been edged clear around the driveway and sidewalk. *It appears Jorge has done a good job,* Maggie thought as she walked down the driveway. *I wonder if she will be recommending him to the rest of the neighborhood. You won't be able to use the selling point of his tongue to your neighbors, Beth. At least I don't think you will. I don't really know them that well yet. Maybe you can with some of them.*

Before she could even get to the sidewalk that led to the front porch, Beth came out of the front door waving at her.

"Good morning, Maggie," Beth greeted her. "It hasn't even been two hours since I talked to your husband about working with me on the homeowner's association board and you are already coming up with ideas. How awesome!"

It hasn't been ten minutes since I told the Swedish models either Maggie thought. *You need to work on that 'how awesome.' It could be mistaken for 'how awful' if someone wasn't listening carefully.*

"'It's not too much, is it?" Maggie asked. "The guardhouse does need some work, don't you think?" *By the way,* Maggie was thinking. *This is just the beginning.*

"Yes, it does," Beth replied. "I'm not sure I would have thought of forest green, though."

"Nor I of the cranberry trim to match the tiles," Maggie said as she smiled at Beth. "But I have to admit as I think about it, it does work."

You think you saw something, don't you? Beth thought to herself. *I can tell. You're testing me. Trying to push me. Well, be careful Maggie Brodie. People that push me often find themselves looking up to me from the ground.*

"I'll tell you what," Beth said. "Let me check with a painter friend of mine and get some quotes. And then we can talk. Would that be okay?"

"Sure. I could ask around too if you like. I don't want you to have to do the work for my idea."

Yes, you do. But that's okay for now. "It's no problem. Really," Beth replied.

"Okay, then. By the way, which house is the Thompson's, and which is the Bartholomew's and Mrs. Cayman's? I have all of them figured out except for these at the end of the road."

"Oh, my! What happened to your hands?" Beth suddenly noticed the redness of them as Maggie pointed toward the other homes.

Like you give a shit. "Puss moth stings," Maggie said.

"Ooooh, those can be painful."

"So, you've heard of them?"

"Oh yes. You need to be careful around them. We have our yard sprayed to keep them away."

"Maybe you sent them our way because of the spraying. It's interesting because Jennifer and Frances said they had never seen the nasty little things in the entire three years that they've lived here."

What are you trying to insinuate, Beth asked herself. *Just keep things civil. She is testing you. Just remember that.*

"You know, that makes me think we should send out an email to the homeowners and warn folks about them. Maybe even add that in the realtor brochures somehow. Some folks have quite a reaction to them. Are you okay now?"

"Still stings like hell." She was lying but that's what she wanted Beth to think.

" I'm sorry to hear that," Beth replied. "I'll send something out to everyone today."

"Good idea."

"What were we talking about before?"

"The homes," Maggie reminded her.

"Yes, yes," Beth said. "The one right next to us is Renee and Jim Thompson. Beside them is Caleb and Jasmine Bartholomew in the black and white brick. Lots of granite and marble inside. It's just beautiful. And then the small green stucco is Mrs. Cayman's. She barely meets the housing requirements of 3000 square feet. Nice inside though. An old country-looking kitchen filled with antiques. It's a nice home and she's such a lovely lady. But the smoke and the mothballs. The odor just permeates the house. She only has one family member that I know of who still visits with her. Her niece, Savannah. And she only comes around about once a month. Mrs. Cayman is over 90 years old. I know we'll miss her."

"Did she pass away?" Maggie asked.

"No. But she's always sick. Has Stage 4 COPD and is on oxygen and still smokes. It's just a matter of time, I'm afraid," Beth said matter of factly.

Yeah, I can tell you are all broken up about it. My God, you are a piece of work, Beth Stevens. You are just a replica of a real person, aren't you? No, I forgot, you belong to a coven. Ask her, Maggie. Ask her.

"I'm just curious. You remind me of someone we knew in Florida. Their last name was Montgomery. You weren't a Montgomery, by chance, were you?" Maggie stood there smiling and then she heard Sean calling her name over and over.

"Are you okay?" Beth asked. "You were staring at me and weren't saying anything. I was afraid you were having a seizure. That can happen with those puss moth bites."

Damn it. I thought for sure those words were coming out of my mouth but you stopped me, Sean. I remembered what you said. How you told me to act. Your warning worked.

"I'm fine. Anyway, thanks, Beth. Look forward to working with you. I can't wait to see those prices on the paint. And if it's too much, Sean and I wouldn't object to painting it ourselves. We're pretty good painters. The neighbors might even help. If they like the idea."

"Yes, perhaps. I'll be in touch," Beth said as she smiled and went back to her house.

A puss moth curse and an illicit love affair. Yeah, I think we'll get along just fine Maggie thought.

Sean was outside spraying the yard when she got home. She glanced over at Amos's house and saw him down by his waterfall pond, but she noticed that the waterfall was not flowing. She called out to Sean and suggested they go over and check on him. As they approached him Maggie could see that Amos was draining the pond.

"Hello, Amos," Maggie said. "This is my husband Sean. We just wanted to come over and say hello."

Sean held out his hand but Amos just looked up at him and then back down at the pond.

"What are you doing?" Sean asked.

"What the hell does it look like I am doing?"

"Uh… draining the pond," Sean answered and smiled.

"You sure that boy is yours?" Amos asked. "He seems to be quite a bit smarter than you."

Maggie couldn't contain herself as she burst out laughing. "Can we help you with anything, Amos?"

"Find the son of a bitch that killed my fish. And I still haven't ruled out anyone." He glared up at Maggie and then Sean.

And then within seconds, Maggie recognized that faraway look. Amos squinted his eyes again as if he was looking into the sun, but when he spoke, Maggie realized he wasn't looking into the sun. At least not the sun that was up in the sky today.

"Where the hell have you been, Sergeant?" Amos asked.

"What?" Sean replied.

"I said where the hell have you been, Sergeant? Clean the wax out of your damn ears. Didn't you go out on reconnaissance? Anything that we need to be aware of? How many clicks out are they?"

Sean looked over at Maggie and this time he knew what Maggie was telling him without her having to say anything out loud.

"We're good, sir," Sean said. "Everything is clear."

"Good news. Damn good news," he said and turned back toward the task of draining his pond.

Maggie walked over and touched Amos on the shoulder. He looked into her eyes and nodded his head. She grabbed Sean's hand and heard Amos yell out to her as they were leaving.

"They'd better not drain the neighborhood pond," Amos said. "Don't let the sons of bitches do that."

"I won't," Maggie called back.

" I see what you mean," Sean said. "He's there and then he's gone. We need to make sure that Connor doesn't hear anything about draining the pond."

Maggie just nodded her head. She wasn't going to tell him that she had already told Connor.

"That's been stopped, right?"

Again, Maggie nodded her head. "Yes, for now, but I think Beth still has it in her mind to do it."

"Well, with you working with her and us getting to know the people around here better, I think we can make sure that never happens. It was such a close vote anyway. We just need to make sure Connor doesn't know anything about this. He doesn't need to get upset and do something stupid and reckless," Sean said as his voice trailed off.

"We're good," Maggie said as she rubbed her husband's arm. "By the way, what are you spraying around the yard to kill the damn caterpillars?"

"Something that has bifenthrin in it," Sean replied.

"I was going to suggest that," Maggie said as she smiled. *So much for organic.*

"Yeah, I bet you were," Sean said as he grinned. "Oh, by the way. While you were getting to know Beth, Phil drove by and suggested we go with him and Barbara to the Renaissance Fair tonight. He says it has great beer and food. They're leaving around 2:00 and said they would drive. I said I'd ask you but I thought it sounded like fun."

"Does it say on that insecticide bottle that the fumes may affect your ability to think? A Renaissance Fair? Are you kidding? Where is it? If you say Europe, I might be persuaded to go."

"It's in Columbia, South Carolina," Sean replied. "That's only about an hour away. Good food, beer. C'mon. It will give us a chance to get to know Phil and Barbara better. You like them. I know."

"Okay, Okay," Maggie gave in. "Since you are slaying the dragons around the yard and since I was successful in redirecting the witch's spell from down the street, I'll go."

"What do you mean you redirected the witch's spell?" Sean said. "No. Don't answer that. Just tell me she's upright and breathing."

"Upright. Not breathing too well."

"Funny," Sean said as they walked up their driveway.

After he was paid for mowing Beth's yard, Emiliano took the tractor and edger back to Miguel. He made the $40 payment and said he would see him Monday. Emiliano felt great. He had spent $6 for gas for the equipment which gave him $79 for the day's work. He called his aunt and announced that he had some good news and would like to celebrate by buying pizza for the family tonight. She asked him if he had gotten a new job and he told her it was even better than that - he had started his own company. She couldn't believe what she was hearing as he told her that he would explain everything later tonight.

He bought a twelve-pack of Budweiser at the Circle K and started for Emiliano's Park. On the way there, he calculated in his head the money he could make from taking care of lawns. He knew he could do three to four big yards a day in the upscale neighborhoods. If he managed to do four yards, he could clear over $300 a day. He wouldn't have anyone bossing him around, besides the homeowner, but they never really said much, unless you missed a spot in the yard. And he knew that he could cut their yards better than Forest Landscapes because he would be paying attention now. Because it was his company. His company. He liked the way it felt to say those words.

It would take him a while to get the business going but with Beth's help and recommendations, he thought he could get a lot of work pretty quickly. He just needed about twenty nice homes. Beth could help him get those, provided he took care of her needs and he was positive that he would be able to do that. He only drank a few beers at the park and ate a peanut butter sandwich he had brought from home. He didn't want to smell like beer when he went back to see Beth. He stopped on the way back to Sycamore Springs and bought some mint Listerine and some cheap cologne that he thought smelled good. At least it smelled better than sweat.

Emiliano reached Sycamore Springs around 2:00. He waved at the nice Lexus SUV that was exiting the neighborhood as he was going in. Maggie and Sean were in the back seat of the Lexus and they both noticed the blue truck. Sean asked Phil if he knew who drove that truck and Phil said he didn't. Sean said he had seen it earlier and that the driver took care of the Stevens' lawn. Maggie quickly spoke up and added that Beth had just switched to this guy. His name was Jorge and he owned his own business. Phil remarked that if Beth Stevens was using him, he must be good and she probably got him for less money than what he was paying the Forest Lawnscape company. Sean asked Maggie if she would find out more about him from Beth and she said she would be more than happy to do that.

Barbara turned around and looked at Maggie with a surprised look on her face. "When did you get to be buds with Beth?" Barbara asked. "I would have never thought that possible considering what happened at the meeting the other night."

Maggie smiled. "Beth and I are working together now. I'm the new secretary/treasurer of the homeowner's association. You must not have read your email from her. You'll need to be better about that in the future so you don't miss anything vitally important that the new secretary/treasurer sends out. And if you must know, I won Beth over with my passion and personality."

"I will and I'll be damned," Barbara said as she reached over at poked Phil. "We have royalty in the car. We will have to make sure Agathe and Ulf know that when we get to the fair,"

"Shit," Maggie said and they all laughed.

I wonder what Emiliano is doing back here this afternoon, Maggie thought as everyone continued to talk. *If only I could drop in on her 'accidentally' on purpose. Oh well. Knowing what I do about Beth now, I am sure there will be other opportunities.* She smiled and started to listen to Phil and Barbara talk about the fair.

Beth was out in her front yard when she saw the truck coming down the road and stop in her driveway. She could hear Darrin in the back with the children and she greeted Emiliano as he got out of the truck.

"You did a terrific job, Jorge. But I think you missed one spot," she said as she looked around before running her hand over her crotch. "You can get that later, though. Now, what can I do for you?"

"Would you make some recommendations to the other homeowners for me?" Emiliano asked. He still wasn't ready to tell Beth his real name.

"I'd be glad too. I know the Thompsons and Bartholomews next door would jump at my recommendation. As will Mrs. Cayman. The Gillespies will too. Phil will do anything to save a dollar. Not sure about the others. But I know some folks in other neighborhoods. You may have to trim a few hedges. Have you got a big hedge trimmer you can use?" Beth asked.

Jorge looked at Beth and grinned. He knew what she meant by that question and he was sure he could meet her expectations.

"I take that as a yes. What's your phone number?" Beth asked. "You never gave it to me. And what's the name of your company?"

Emiliano gave Beth his cell phone number as he tried to come up with a name for the company. He should have done that earlier. He knew that. *Shit,* he said to himself, and then he thought of the park. *Emiliano's Park.*

"El Parque," he said.

"What does that mean?"

"The park."

"Wow. How poetic. I like that," Beth replied. "I'll text you some numbers after I talk to my friends. Next week, when you come to mow my lawn though, you need to come after 9 a.m. Understand?"

" Yes, I understand."

"Ok, I'll see you later, Jorge," Beth said as she turned and went to join her husband and children in the pool.

This was a very good day Emiliano thought. He found a scrap of paper on the seat of the truck. He wrote today's date and the words "El Parque" on it and smiled as he put the piece of paper in the glove compartment. He would look at it each day as he started work. He didn't mind hard work, especially now that he was working for himself. The paper would be a reminder that on this day he became El Jefe.

It was about 3:30 by the time the Gillespies and the Brodies arrived at the Renaissance Fair and found a place to park. Maggie asked Barbara how long they usually stayed because she had told Connor that they would be home by eleven. "Oh, we're usually home by ten, because Phil can only consume so much ale and turkey legs," Barbara said and they all laughed.

Phil handed them tickets – courtesy of Ulf and Agathe, he said – and they entered the fair, greeted by someone wearing a period costume and juggling daggers. They watched him for a few moments and clapped when he stopped and bowed and held out his hand. Phil gave him a dollar and the juggler said, "Thank you, my lord," and then went off to find the next group of customers.

"Does this happen all day long?" Maggie asked. "Because that really wasn't too bad. I was fearing the worst coming here, I have to admit."

"You'll have fun," Barbara replied. "Just stick with me and I'll make sure you have a good time. Speaking of which, how about a glass of wine?"

"Sounds good!"

"I'm taking Sean over to the turkey leg place and then we'll be in the ale tent," Phil said. "Meet us over there after you get your wine."

"C'mon, Maggie," Barbara said as she looked for a sign to point them in the direction of the wine.

Following the signs, they passed many people in period costumes. Some of them were working on various leather goods; another was a blacksmith making iron works of art. Several people on stilts came walking by and one stepped over Maggie as she stood there looking up at him.

"I'm glad he didn't have a third leg as big as his other two. That would have been scary to see dangling down in front of my face."

Barbara laughed as they soon found the wine tent and both got a glass of wine.

"I can't help myself anymore. So, I'm just going to ask," Barbara said. "Are your hands okay? Is that some sort of psoriatic flare-up?"

"Puss moths," Maggie answered.

"I've never seen one of those in the entire time we have lived out in Sycamore Springs. But I know of them. They are nasty little things. What happened?"

"I thought they were dead leaves in the mailbox and just pulled them out. Won't make that mistake again. Sean has sprayed the yard now so, hopefully, they are all dead."

"Glad to hear you're okay. Some folks have a bad reaction to them. And speaking of reactions and third legs, wait until you see Agathe," Barbara teased.

"What are you saying?" Maggie asked. "Don't tell me she is a man. And it's pronounced Ah-get, not Ah-ga-tha, right? The spelling confuses me when I keep seeing how it's written in my email."

"Yes, Ah-get, and no, no, nothing like that," Barbara said. "She is a sorceress at these events. Ulf is usually at the archery tents or sometimes even does sword fights. But what you'll remember today, and this is a promise, is Agathe."

"Well, you have most definitely piqued my interest," Maggie said as she took a sip of her wine. "The wine is good. Pretty sweet though. Almost like grape juice."

"Yes, everything here is good," Barbara laughed. "But you're right. This wine is sweeter than I expected. I don't think I'll get this one again. Let's go explore a little before we look for our Viking husbands. There are some really good craftsmen here."

They strolled down a path with tents on both sides filled with people selling hand-made crafts: jewelry, candles, soaps, baked goods, and stained glass.

"These candles are very nice," Barbara said as she picked one up. "Oh, this one smells like pine," and she held it out for Maggie to inspect.

"Oh, that is nice. I think I need this one for Connor's bathroom," she said.

"Why do you think I stopped here?" Barbara asked. "After Phil has eaten his way through the Renaissance Fair, you'd think the septic tank exploded at our house." Maggie laughed again. *I do like her!*

" Do you see anything else you might be interested in?" Barbara asked as they viewed the remaining vendors.

"Maybe later. I'll get a little ale in Sean and bring him back to look at the jewelry. Never can have enough jewelry."

"I agree. Don't you think we should get another glass of wine before we venture on yon quest for our men?" Barbara asked.

"Oh yes," Maggie agreed.

While choosing their next glass of wine, Barbara heard someone call her name. They both turned around to see Agathe smiling at them. She was wearing white leggings with a black leather vest and some sort of dark green bra, but that is not what Maggie saw. All she could see was the necklace hanging from her neck. *Those can't be penises* she thought as she heard Agathe welcome them to the fair.

"Hello, Agathe," Barbara said. "You remember Maggie, don't you?"

"Of course. Welcome, Maggie. How are you enjoying the fair so far?"

"It's more than I expected," Maggie said as she stared at Agathe's necklace.

"I make them myself," Agathe proclaimed.

"I'm glad to hear that," Maggie replied. "I'd be very concerned if they were real."

Agathe laughed. "They represent power for me as a sorceress. I make them out of clay. I add a new one for each year of the fair. Here's the one that I made for this year." Agathe held one up close to Maggie's face.

"Very nice," Maggie said as she stepped back. "Very life-like."

"Well, enjoy the fair," Agathe said as she saw someone she knew in costume and went off to join her.

"Told you," Barbara gloated.

"Yes, you did. Well, that's something I can't un-see," Maggie said as she turned toward Barbara. "Wine. I need more wine."

Barbara nodded and ordered merlots for both of them.

"Ummm," Maggie said as she took a drink. "This is good. Much better than the first one."

On their way toward the ale tent, Maggie suddenly saw a "Fortune Teller" sign.

"Oh – I have to go in there!" she cried.

"That's fine. I'll just go on over to the ale tent and hold down the fort with the guys until you get there."

Maggie pulled back the canvas door and upon entering she saw a table in the middle of the tent with five candles in the center. A woman sat behind the table, her face half-hidden by the flickering candle lights and a scarf that was accented by the darkness surrounding her.

"Welcome. What do you wish to know?" she asked as she held out her hand and pointed at the empty chair.

Maggie sat down but wasn't sure what to give her as there was no sign denoting the price so she put a twenty-dollar bill in her hand. The woman took the money and informed her that would allow her two questions. Maggie thought for a moment before responding.

"What's the name of the person living in my neighborhood who doesn't like me?" Maggie asked in a sarcastic manner knowing the person would come up with a name that she would try and make meaningful, probably saying it was some dead ancestor from five hundred years ago that she had never heard of before.

"Liz," the woman answered immediately.

Maggie looked at the woman and leaned back in her chair. *What the fuck? Is that supposed to mean Beth? Liz is short for Elizabeth, but I have never heard anyone call her Liz. But what a strange coincidence. Out of millions of names, she said Liz. That's kind of creepy* Maggie thought.

"Liz," Maggie repeated. "Interesting." *Might as well play this out.*

"Will this Liz try to hurt me in any way?"

"The red sand will be a warning," the voice said.

"Wait a minute," Maggie said. "What the hell does that mean? That's not an answer to the question I asked. Answer the question. Yes or no?"

"Only two questions requested. Only two questions can be answered. That is all," the voice said as it disappeared into the shadows.

Maggie sat in silence for a moment and then picked up one of the candles and held it up toward the chair but she found that no one was sitting there. She stood up and looked around the tent with the candle and saw the exit at the back. *Ahhh. Slipped out the back.* She threw back the cloth and walked outside. She expected to see someone standing there, smiling at her, and then together they would both laugh about the trick, but no one was there. It was just her holding a candle in the sun.

God damn it. "I think I'll just burn down the fucking tent," she said out loud. *That should get the attention of the person that was in here,* she told herself. And though she did see a lot of people staring at her with puzzled looks on their faces, no one came forward.

"Just kidding," she said as she blew out the candle and went back inside to replace it. "What the fuck," she said as she blew out the rest of the candles.

As she walked toward the ale tent, she thought about what the fortune-teller had said. *The red sand will be a warning. What the hell does that mean? And the name. Does Liz actually mean Beth?* Sean could see that his wife looked troubled when she walked up and he asked her if everything was all right. Maggie knew she didn't want Sean worrying about this. He always overreacted, so she smiled and nodded her head.

"Agathe has the nicest necklace, honey," Maggie said. "I told her to make one for me."

Barbara and Phil laughed and Sean looked confused. "What's going on?" he asked.

"Dicks," Maggie said. "Agathe has a thing for dicks. Has a bunch of them on a necklace she wears. She says they give her power. Don't you think that would be something that would look good on me? I doubt it would ever go out of style. They were so cute and tiny. What do you think? Can we get her to make one for me?"

Sean looked at Phil and Barbara and then back at his wife. "You aren't kidding, are you?"

"Oh, I don't kid about things regarding things," Maggie said and when she did, Barbara and Phil laughed even more.

"Oh, good Lord," Sean said as he got up and got another glass of ale.

"Where can we get something to eat? Preferably not a hotdog or something on a stick," Maggie said.

"C'mon," Barbara grinned. "I know of a good hamburger place. But just to let you know, they do sell corn dogs."

"As long as they aren't on a necklace, I'm good with that."

While they waited in the food line, Maggie asked Barbara if she had ever been to one of the fortune-tellers at the fair.

"No, I'm afraid they would look like Agathe," and Maggie smiled. "How did you like that meditation tent you went into?" Barbara asked. "Did they have some nice incense burning?"

Wait a minute. She said meditation tent, didn't she? I went into a fortune teller's tent. She knows that. Why is she asking me about a meditation tent?

"Uh, yes," Maggie said. "It was fine. Would you get me a cheeseburger and a Pepsi? I need to go to the lady's room."

"Sure," Barbara said.

Maggie turned and tried to move as fast as she could without running toward the location of the fortune teller's tent. She found it but the sign that said "Fortune Teller" was gone. Maggie put her hands up next to her ears and closed her eyes. *Oh shit,* she said to herself as she opened her eyes. *It's happening. Here at the Renaissance Fair, it's happening.*

Inside the tent she found some people sitting around a table, with a heavy scent of incense. They all had their eyes closed and some were chanting. *A meditation tent! What the hell is going on?*

Maggie raced out of the tent and back to Sean. She looked pale like she was ready to throw up.

"What is it?" Sean asked. "Bad food, drink, what?"

"I saw something that wasn't there," Maggie said. "And I talked to a person that wasn't there."

Sean looked at Phil and took Maggie's hand and led her away so they could talk more privately.

"You're obsessing. And having a severe panic attack. Did you take your meds today?"

"No, I was feeling good and I thought I may have some wine so I didn't take any."

"Take two now, Maggie. You know better than to skip a day. You're obsessing over something and when you do, your mind never shuts off. I wouldn't be surprised if it didn't have something to do with Liz. But you know better than to let this happen."

"Why did you just say 'Liz'?" Maggie asked.

"What are you talking about?"

"You said that this probably had something to do with Liz."

"I didn't say Liz, I said Beth." Sean tightened his hand around her arm. "You know what happens when you get stressed out over something. Now take your pills and then come sit down under the tent, out of the heat. I'll get you some water." He led Maggie back into the ale tent and helped her sit down.

"Is Maggie okay?" Phil asked.

"She will be," Sean said. "Just some heat issues and she forget to take some medicine for her stomach. I think there was something in that homemade wine that made her ill. She'll be okay."

Within a few minutes, Barbara was back with the food that Maggie had ordered. She saw Maggie looking pale and drinking some bottled water. "What's going on?"

"Stomach issues," Sean said as Maggie looked up at Barbara and managed a weak smile. "But she has taken some medication now and it should help."

Though Sean would not want her to ask, she knew she had to. She needed to know. She had been doing so much better since they moved. She didn't want to have a setback. Not now.

"Didn't you see the sign for the fortune teller?" Maggie asked as she looked at Barbara.

Phil looked at his wife and raised his eyebrows as he suspected there was something more going on with Maggie. He spoke before Barbara could.

"They got you. They do that. They often change up the fortune teller's tent and make it look like something different when you go by it again. They do that to mess with you. Like there is real sorcery within the grounds upon which we walk. Na na na na, Na na na na," he said as he tried to imitate the Twilight Zone music.

"Damn," Sean said. "I could see where that could mess with people's minds."

"Yes, it can," Barbara said as she looked over at Maggie. *Perhaps she had only seen the words "Fortune Teller" in small letters under the "Meditation Tent" sign,* she thought.

"Would it be okay if we left?" Sean said as he looked over at Phil. "I'm afraid the medicine she took will make her real drowsy and she just won't feel like doing much."

"Sure," Phil said. "Whenever you're ready. I've only had two ales, so I'm good to drive. I'm going to get some water and you tell us when you're ready to leave."

"Thanks."

Maggie felt the calming effects of the medicine course through her body. *They shouldn't do that kind of shit to people. Would have been nice for a little warning,* she thought as she looked over at Barbara and tried to smile.

"Sorry, Maggie, I should have warned you," Barbara said. "They have fooled me and Phil before too."

The comments from Barbara made Maggie feel better than the two pills that she had just swallowed.

"It's okay," Maggie said. "I just hope Agathe doesn't run into Snow White later today."

"Why?" Barbara asked.

"She would be pretty pissed seeing all the dwarf's dicks wrapped around her neck."

Barbara laughed. "Yes, I imagine she would. I know I would be pretty pissed living in a home with seven men that couldn't satisfy me."

"Well, they still could. They would just need some guidance from our neighbors who live in the yellow stucco," Maggie mumbled.

"Oh my God," Barbara gasped as she laughed and watched Maggie lean her head against her husband's shoulders and close her eyes.

Chapter 11

Bait

On the way back from the fair, Maggie rested her head against the window of the car. The cool air gently blowing from the air conditioner felt good on her face. She didn't participate in much of the conversation, but she could hear what everyone was saying. She heard Barbara ask Sean when Maggie had met Frances and Jennifer. Sean didn't know but he assumed it was earlier that day when she had taken a walk through the neighborhood. Maggie then heard her ask Sean what kind of stomach problems she had and she heard Sean lie. He told her that she had irritable bowel disease and severe diverticulosis. "Tell them the truth," she heard herself say, but she failed to hear the words come out of her mouth as she closed her eyes.

She heard Barbara say she knew several other people with severe stomach issues and understood how awful they could be. She looked at Maggie and then over at Sean as she thought about the "Fortune Teller" sign. Even though she knew the fair changed out those signs, she sensed there was something else that neither he nor Maggie was telling them. She remembered Sean saying how changing those signs could mess with someone's mind and to her, it didn't appear that he was speaking in general terms. His tone reflected a sound of familiarity with that type of issue.

Maggie felt Sean's hand on her arm as he leaned over to let her know they were back home. She raised her head and wiped her hand across her eyes as she watched the gate go up at the front of the neighborhood. Barbara saw Maggie stir and smiled at her.

"Feeling any better?" she asked Maggie.

"Yes. I'm sorry about ruining the fair for you guys."

"You didn't ruin anything," Barbara replied. "Just the fact you got to see Agathe was good enough for me. And what you said about her was about the funniest thing Phil and I have ever heard."

"I have my moments," Maggie said as Phil pulled into their driveway.

"Thanks, Phil. We'll do something again sometime soon," Sean promised.

"You bet," Phil replied.

"Goodnight guys. Again, sorry," Maggie said as she walked into the garage. Sean followed her and hit the buttons that closed the garage doors.

They heard the television on and found Connor on the couch with a half-eaten pizza sitting in front of him. Maggie plopped down in one of the big leather chairs and smiled at her son.

"What are you two doing back so early?" Connor asked. "It's only seven."

"Your mom wasn't feeling too good, stomach-wise, so we left early. But, she's better now. Right, Maggie May?"

Maggie raised both of her thumbs but didn't move any other part of her body.

"I didn't eat that much at the fair. Mind if I have some pizza?" Sean asked Connor.

"Help yourself, Dad. You paid for it."

Sean picked up a slice and sat beside Connor. "What are you watching?"

"'Alien Covenant.'"

"Have I seen that?"

"Not sure."

"Yes," Maggie said. "But you probably don't remember it. You never do."

"Well then, I think I'll just go watch the Braves in the bedroom," Sean said. "You okay, honey?"

Maggie repeated the two thumbs up signal and Sean headed for their bedroom.

Connor had been watching his mother since she had gotten home. He hadn't seen her like this in some time. Something was going on besides a stomach ache. "What's up with you, Mom?" he asked tentatively.

"I don't really know." She began to think of a more definitive reason to give her son, whom she knew was going to ask more questions. "I think maybe a migraine. Severe headache, nauseated. It couldn't be a delayed reaction to those puss moths, could it?"

Connor understood that question was asked to stop him from inquiring further but he knew she wasn't reacting to the puss moths. Now he was sure there was something else going on. She was obsessing over something. That's what caused the current condition he saw with his mother.

"Did you have a panic attack?" he asked.

"Little bit of one," she admitted.

Connor knew his mother still was not telling the complete truth. "You didn't take your medicine today, did you?"

There was no sense in lying about it. He would know. "No," Maggie replied.

"Hmmm," Connor said. "I wonder what you would tell me if I didn't take mine?"

"That we would be giving you back to the adoption agency."

Though her eyes were still closed, Connor knew by his mother's response, she was feeling better. "Oh, I long for the day," Connor replied and he could see his mother smile.

Maggie opened her eyes and looked at her son. "I'm sorry, Connor. I promised you I would and I didn't. I apologize. You forgive me?"

Connor nodded his head yes. "Was there anything good about the fair?" he asked.

"I did see a very interesting necklace that one of our neighbors was wearing. It appears that Agathe pretends to be a sorceress at these events. She wears a necklace with seven little penises hanging from it," Maggie said.

"Was she fighting with Snow White or something?"

Maggie laughed and winced as the laughter caused her head to hurt. "I know, that's the same thing I said," Maggie replied.

"So, I think it's safe to say that Amos is one of the sanest people in this new neighborhood, wouldn't you agree?"

"Appears so. Him and your Dad."

"What about Dad?" Sean asked as he came back into the living room.

"Mom and I were just discussing who was the sanest person in the neighborhood. You edged out Amos."

"Hold that thought," Sean said. "Since school starts back on Monday, what do you think about going fishing tomorrow? A friend from work told me a great place to go. It just means getting up a little early. We can have a picnic lunch out there. Even do a little evening fishing, if things are going well, and then come home and do whatever you guys want to do for dinner. Or just come home after lunch and chill out around the pool."

"Ok, this next response is very important," Maggie said as she looked over at Sean. "How early?"

"Around six."

"And Amos it is," Maggie concluded.

"Ah, come on, Mom," Connor said. "You love to beat Dad by catching the biggest fish."

"There is that," she agreed. "Well if we're getting up at six, I need to go to bed now. I'm exhausted."

Maggie didn't even bother to brush her teeth. She was asleep before Sean got into the bed and wasn't even aware that he watched tv for a little longer before he turned off the lights.

While she slept, the thoughts in Maggie's mind kept moving around in her head like a gerbil on a wheel in its cage. She kept seeing the necklace of penises around Agathe's neck. She could see the words "Montgomery" and "Liz" in dialogue balloons coming out of her and Sean's mouth as they were talking to Snow White, who was yelling at the dwarves while they were lined up in their chairs with their pants off. She saw her pull out a meat cleaver and chop off their penises and tell them she might as well make jewelry out of them since they were of no use to her any other way. She saw the tent again but this time the sign said "Fortunes Not Told." The people were laughing at her as she ran out the back of the tent with the candle in her hand. She watched as Connor took the candle from her hand and said he knew what to do to stop the laughing. He set fire to the tent and she screamed "No!" and bolted upright in the bed.

The red numbers on the clock indicated it was 4 a.m. She closed her eyes and tried to sleep but she kept thinking about the dream and what happened at the fair. Still awake an hour later, she knew she wasn't going to get any more sleep so she got up and took a shower. She thought about the fishing trip Sean had planned and it made her happy that he wanted to do that for their son. She told herself that she even felt like going fishing and she smiled at the image in the mirror as she got dressed.

Within minutes she had a cup of tea in her hand and headed to the patio to listen to the waterfall. It was that moment of the morning when the sky looked like an etch-a-sketch which was losing the black picture that had been painted the night before as the particles of black disappeared, leaving a light gray unpainted palate. She hadn't seen this picture in a while and it was calming to her. She took a sip of her tea and heard the door open behind her.

"You're up early," she said as she smiled at Connor. "I'd fix you some breakfast but we're going to stop and get something on the way to the lake. Can I get you something to drink?"

"No, I can wait. How are you feeling this morning?"

"Good. Real good." She wasn't going to say anything about the dream or the encounter with the fortune teller. It would only upset him and she wasn't going to do that.

"Ready to go fishing then," Connor said as his father joined them.

"I like to hear that. Let me load up the Explorer and we will be off." Sean quickly packed up the car and they drove out of the subdivision while the day was still gray. As each minute passed, Maggie watched the light begin to emerge from the sky and bring color to the world around them. They stopped at Popeye's for some breakfast and then headed for the lake.

"Where are we going to fish?" Connor asked.

"Over in South Carolina. Clarks Hill Lake. Somebody at work told me about this place. The Essie May Washington Branch State Park. Very underutilized and a really good place to fish off the bank. I think we could catch some crappie or bluegill or maybe a catfish if we're lucky," Sean replied.

"Who the hell is Essie May Washington?" Maggie asked.

Connor looked on his phone and replied within seconds. "She was the daughter of someone named Strom Thurmond. Damn. He was 100 years old and still serving in the Senate. Six months after he died, she came forward and told everyone he was her father. The story is that Strom had sex with the family maid. He never acknowledged her but paid for her education and gave her money. It also says he was against segregation. What a hypocrite."

"Another name for this lake we're going to is Strom Thurmond Lake. I guess this was some sort of atonement by him to get this part of the lake named for his daughter," Sean said.

"Your very first lesson about the deep south, Connor," Maggie said. "It is still trying to dig itself out from the past. You just remember to always do the right thing, even when it's not that popular."

"Yes, very nicely said Maggie," Sean said. "We should remember that as we deal with our neighbors."

Maggie rolled her eyes at Sean and finished her chicken biscuit as they were crossing the Savannah River into South Carolina. They stopped at a place in Modoc for some bait before they saw the sign for the park. The guardhouse was closed, but there was a sign requesting money if you were in a car or camper. Sean stuffed several dollars in the box and drove into the park. It was empty of cars and people. There was only a little park within a small peninsula surrounded by the water of Clarks Hill Lake.

" Let's go catch some fish," Sean said as he got out to unload the gear. He took the large cooler, Maggie got the picnic basket, and Connor grabbed everything else. Sean put the cooler next to an old wooden picnic bench close to the water. He then hung a hammock between two cedar trees by the bench.

"Your mom may need that later," Sean told Connor.

"Ha!" Maggie replied. "You'll be in that before anyone else."

"That's why I brought another one," Sean replied proudly. He pulled another hammock from the pack and hung it near the first.

"Bring the bait, Connor," Sean said as he headed down to the water with the fishing rods. "Okay, the minnows are for the crappie and bluegill and this bag of chicken from Popeyes may land us a catfish. I think the best place to cast is over there in those reeds. That place over there", as he pointed to his left, "where there are some saw palmettos and old deadwood out in the water might be a good place too, but let's try here in the reeds first."

They hooked the minnows and cast their lines into the water while Maggie watched. It wasn't long before Connor felt a bite and reeled in a good-sized bluegill.

"Nice fish son! That's a big fish! I bet it weighs almost a pound. That's a good sign," Sean said as he felt a bite and pulled in a fish of his own. "One to one!"

"Yeah, but mine was bigger," Connor bragged.

"Yes, his was bigger," Maggie chimed in. "I'm going to try my luck over by those palmettos." She grabbed her fishing rod and a cupful of minnows and donned her snake boots.

"Be careful over there, mom. Don't go into the water above your knee, okay?" Connor said.

"Got it," Maggie replied as she went off toward the marsh, baited her hook, and threw it into the water. The sun was up now, but this part of the peninsula was still covered in shadows. She heard Connor and Sean catch several more fish before she even felt a nibble. She retrieved the line and the minnow was gone so she put another one on the hook and re-cast. After a while, the only sounds around her were those of the birds and she thought the marsh looked beautiful and untouched in this shaded light. There was no trash, no signs of other human beings, and it made her forget everything else. Though she kept losing minnows, she didn't care. She was happy. She wasn't even aware of the time when Connor came to check on her.

"Aren't you getting hungry?" he asked.

"A little bit," Maggie said. "Why - what time is it?"

"A little after 11."

"You're kidding!"

"Nope," Connor said. "Doesn't look like you're having much luck over here."

"No, but I'm good. It's so pretty and peaceful out here. What's for lunch?" Maggie inquired as she reeled in her line and came out of the water.

"Not sure. Dad hasn't said."

"How many fish have you guys caught?"

"I've caught 6 bluegills and a crappie, and Dad has caught 9 bluegills," Connor reported.

"I bet you still have the biggest fish so far, so we are good," Maggie said as she winked at her son.

The picnic table was now covered with a paper polka dot cover and filled with several large plastic bowls.

"Here's some hand sanitizer for you two," Sean said. "I have iced tea, Pepsi, and some other drinks. In the bowls are potato salad, chicken salad, and a fruit salad. I've got some pita chips and for dessert, chocolate cake."

"Who the hell are you?" Maggie asked as she looked at her husband. She put her fishing rod down and cleaned off her hands. "You made all this?"

"Of course," Sean replied straight-faced.

After the looks of disbelief, he confessed. "Okay, okay. Once you said yes to fishing and went to bed, I hurried off to the store. Impressed?"

"You're a horrible liar. But I am indeed. C'mon then, let's eat! And I hope you have a hard lemonade in that cooler," Maggie said as she filled up her plate. "This is good, husband. I didn't realize fishing made you so hungry."

"Well, you haven't had much to eat in the last two days," Sean smiled and handed her a lemonade.

"Yeah, now I'm very impressed. So, Connor? Dad did pretty good this time, didn't he?"

"Yeah, this time," Connor admitted.

Sean just smiled. "Hiding the cake from you two was a challenge. One of the cooks at the hospital made it. I was just waiting for the right time to bring it out. Supposed to be delicious."

"Well, we will see about that. Hand me some more of that chicken salad. What store?" she asked Sean.

"Publix made all the salads," Sean said. "They're pretty good, right?"

Maggie nodded her head as she ate and tipped her drink toward Sean. They reminisced about some of the different places that they had been fishing together while they finished lunch. Minnesota. Tennessee. Alaska. They talked a long time about the trip to Alaska and Maggie finally cut a large piece of the chocolate cake for herself.

She closed her eyes and sighed at the taste. *Oh my God. This is the best chocolate cake I have ever had* she thought. "The person who made this cake works at the hospital?"

Sean nodded his head yes.

"You should lose your job if you ever let her leave. This is amazing. No, check that. I doubt if you two would like it, so just leave it here and I'll take care of it. I'll give some to Amos and the other neighbors when we get back."

They laughed as Maggie got another piece of cake and climbed into one of the hammocks.

"She won't be awake long," Sean smirked as he glanced at Connor and cut them both a slice of the chocolate cake. "Mmmmm…she's right. I do need to be fired if she ever leaves."

Sean told Connor he was going to close his eyes for just a minute too as he got in the other hammock. Connor didn't mind. He told his father that he was going to explore the marshy area where his mom had been fishing. Sean reminded him to put on his snake boots and Connor just nodded his head.

He walked over to the marsh and began looking around. He wasn't sure what he would find but he wasn't surprised when he saw a rat snake curled up under one of the saw palmetto plants. A good place for a rat snake, Connor thought as he continued to explore.

Emiliano received a text from Beth on the way to his park that morning. She said they were leaving for church but she had already lined up both the Thompsons and the Bartholomews as clients. She had given them a price of $125, the same as her home, and hoped he was okay with that. Their yards were similar in size to hers so she just thought that would be the appropriate rate.

Emiliano didn't appreciate her setting the price, but he knew he could not negotiate with Beth now. It was too early in their relationship to do anything like that. He just agreed that would be fine. Beth sent him a smiley emoji and said she was working on some other people she knew in Evans and that he would also be doing Mrs. Cayman's yard as soon as she was out of the hospital. He would probably need to charge her a little less since her lawn was much smaller.

Emiliano asked her which house belonged to Mrs. Cayman and she explained it was the small green stucco across from hers. She then reminded him to not come before 9 a.m next week and he said he remembered. She ended by saying she looked forward to seeing him. There was no sexual innuendo in the messages and Emiliano knew better than to insert any in his responses. He knew she wanted to control that part of the relationship and he would allow her to do that. At least for now because he needed her more than she needed him, and both of them understood that.

It was early afternoon when he pulled into Emiliano's Park. He threw a penny into the box by the guardhouse and drove down the road. He saw the red Ford Explorer in the parking lot and slowed down. There was food on the picnic table and he saw people in hammocks. He thought he recognized that car as he drove by it and then turned around and headed back toward the entrance. Yes. He remembered where he had seen that car before. It was the lady in Sycamore Springs. The lady who saw him and Beth. *Shit,* he said to himself as he drove by their parked car and looked over at them one more time. *They cannot come to Emiliano's park without my permission* he told himself as he stepped on the accelerator and sped away.

Maggie thought she heard someone driving down the road but she didn't bother to look up. until she heard the engine accelerate. She thought she saw the back end of a blue truck driving away and she closed her eyes again. *That can't be who I think it is. It's not him,* she said to herself several more times. *He is not following you. You are still rattled a little bit from the fair incident and the dream. Get your mind on something else. Like fishing.* She got up and grabbed her fishing rod and some chicken and headed back to the marsh. She put the meat on the hook and threw her line in the water. Within a few minutes, she heard a branch snap behind her and she jumped. She turned around to see Connor standing there.

"You scared me," Maggie said.

"Why? Am I scary?"

"Of course not," Maggie replied. "But I thought I heard someone drive through here and then I heard someone walking behind me and so I was just startled."

"You did hear someone drive through here. Someone in a blue truck."

"What shade of blue?"

"I don't know, blue. Does it matter?"

"Light or dark blue?" Maggie asked and by the way she asked it, Connor could tell that it did matter.

"It was light blue."

Maggie suddenly felt a big tug on her line and her rod was bent down toward the water.

"Shit, Mom," Connor said as he went over to her. "You've got something big on that line."

Maggie started to reel as fast as she could and pulled on the line but it wasn't moving much.

"Need some help?" he asked.

"No. I'll get the son of a bitch," she said as she thought about the blue truck which made her angry and more determined.

Sean heard the commotion and came over to find them standing there with Maggie's rod bent down toward the water.

"That looks like a damn big catfish," Sean said. "Keep it on there, Maggie. Don't let it get away!"

She pulled some more and reeled more line in and they all started to see the shadowy image on the other line. It was a large fish of some kind. Sean helped steady Maggie's shoulders as she strained to hold onto the fish. He helped her move back out of the water each time she reeled the line in and they soon saw the fish on the end of the line.

"Wow! That's about a twenty-pound channel catfish! Whoo-hoo!" he yelled. Maggie reeled the fish into the shallow water. Sean grabbed its tail and moved it onto the sandy shoreline.

"Connor, get a picture," Sean said as he pulled out his pliers and held up the fish between him and Maggie.

"Got it!" Connor said and as soon as he did, Sean placed the fish on the ground and began removing the hook from the fish with the pliers. Maggie stood unmoving as she saw the blood from the fish wash over the sand and remembered the words of the fortune-teller. "The red sand will be a warning."

Shit. This can't mean anything. It's just blood from a catfish. It can't mean anything. Not for you or for Connor. If you told him what you saw, he would become very suspicious and you can't have him acting that way. He's in a good place now and you can't disrupt that. Hell, he's going to a new school. Trying to meet new friends. He'll be the outsider as he always is. You can't create other problems for him to worry about. You want him to fit in. He can do that here. You know he loves the new house. And Sean is thinking of getting him a car. No Maggie. You can't say anything to Connor about any of this.

She had to remain strong. She told herself again that the light blue truck, the red sand, and the name "Liz" meant nothing, even though she couldn't block out the image of Connor setting fire to the tent in her dream. She closed her eyes and told herself that he could never know how all those things seemed to connect in her mind. Sean couldn't know either. She promised herself that she wouldn't say anything to either of them about it. After all, this was just a coincidence.

There was also a part of her mind telling her that she needed to be careful. A part of her that suggested she needed to be more suspicious of Jorge and Beth and to be more cautious of what she said and did around them. A part of her that told her to be very wary of accepting any accolades from Beth or any help from Jorge. A part of her that told her that as long as she understood and did that, everything would turn out fine.

Chapter 12

A familiar Island

"Well folks, I think the show is over," Sean said as he watched the catfish swim away. "I don't think we will get a better or bigger fish than that. What do you guys think?"

"I think I caught the biggest fish," Maggie replied.

"Yes Maggie, you did. I think I said that already."

"I just wanted to hear it again."

Connor smiled. "Yeah Dad, I'm good with leaving. This was fun, but let's go back home and veg out by the pool. It's getting really hot."

"I think it's supposed to be close to a hundred today," Sean replied as they all walked back to the picnic table.

"A hundred!" Maggie repeated. "Shit, get me in the AC and then the pool. And another hard lemonade for the road. After all, I did catch the largest fish."

"This may go on all day," Sean whispered to Connor as they loaded up the Explorer.

"I think you can count on it," Maggie said as she took a drink. "Tell me when you two have the car packed. I'll be glad to get in the car at that point."

"And you married her why?" Connor asked.

"She makes me laugh," Sean replied. "I overlook all the outer blemishes and her looks. After all, they are just superficial."

"I heard that," Maggie said. "I will overlook it. Seeing how I caught the biggest fish."

"Hell-o-fire," Sean said as he put the cooler in the car and bowed to Maggie. "We are ready to go now, your majesty."

Connor loved listening to his mother and father have fake fights. They made him laugh and for some reason reminded him how lucky he was. They had forgiven him for his mistakes and had never dwelled on them. He knew that not all parents were like that. *Yeah*, he thought, *he was pretty lucky.*

It had been a really nice day, but there was something that troubled him as he heard his mother say goodbye to Essie May Washington branch park and wave at the sign. The way she asked him about the blue truck. She seemed upset about it but he also knew she was trying to hide the way she truly felt. *Why was she worried about the blue truck?*

He remembered she also seemed to go into some trance-like state for a moment when his dad was taking the hook out of the catfish's mouth. It was as if the blood upset her. He knew she wasn't bothered by the sight of blood. She had tended his scrapes and bruises countless times without even flinching. *What was it about the blood from the catfish?*

He had also discovered about a half-dozen puss moth caterpillars around the lake as she and his father slept. He knew better than to bring that up but something was going on. He was certain of it. Perhaps he could find out something more on the way home. She seemed to be in a good mood due to the hard lemonade and the fact she had caught the biggest fish. Maybe she would say something else about the truck.

"We should have saved that catfish for Amos's pond," Connor said.

"Oh, I wish you'd mentioned that before your father let it go. But now that I think about it a little more, I don't know if that would've been such a great idea. Every day, your father would have to drive by that pond and see the big fish his wife caught. I'm not sure he could handle it."

Sean just smiled listening to Connor and Maggie talk. She seemed to have forgotten about yesterday at the fair and that was a good thing.

"Dad, did that truck wake you up too when the driver hit the accelerator? He didn't look like a redneck even though he was trying to make sure that we heard him. He looked thirty-ish. Latino. Dark black hair."

Maggie took a drink of her hard lemonade and waited for Sean's response.

"Yeah, I heard something," he replied.

"It was a light blue truck. A Chevy, I think," Connor continued

Shit, Maggie said to herself.

"Really? I wonder if that could have been Jorge?" Sean asked as he turned to Maggie. "Sure sounds like him by that description."

"Who is Jorge?" Connor asked.

"A landscaper," Sean replied. "He takes care of the Stevens 'yard. Your mom is supposed to be asking Beth about him doing ours. I wish he had stopped if it was him so we could have talked. But it couldn't have been him. That would have been too much of a coincidence, don't you think, Maggie?"

Connor waited for his mother to reply but he heard nothing. *She is afraid of that blue truck for some reason. That's why she pauses, But I need to be sure. I don't want anything to happen to the wrong person.*

"What do you think, Mom? Think it could've been Jorge's truck?"

Shit, Maggie said again to herself. *Shit, shit, shit. He won't let up until I answer him. And he'll know if I am lying.*

"Yeah, I guess it could have been," Maggie said.

She's scared of him for some reason. She thought it was him and jumped when she heard me come up from behind her. Wait a minute. The puss moth caterpillars. Could those two things be related? Jorge and his blue truck and the caterpillars? I knew someone was sending a warning for some reason. Why would the Stevens landscaper do that to mom? I need to be more alert. And I need to let her know that too without freaking her out.

"I'll keep an eye out for him," Connor said. "When I see him, I'll let him know you're interested in talking to him about the yard."

"Thanks, Connor," Sean replied. "Maggie is supposed to get his number from Beth so I don't think that will be necessary."

"No problem. I'll still keep an eye out for him just in case."

Message received loud and clear, son. I hear what you're saying. Maggie, tell him everything is okay and he doesn't need to worry. Tell him.

"He's kind of shy, I think," Maggie replied. "So, he may be a little standoffish if you approach him so just be aware of that. It doesn't mean anything except I don't think he feels comfortable around people. But don't worry with it. It's really not necessary."

Sean picked up on that warning from Maggie and added to it. "Yeah. Just remember that. You know how shy people can be especially when strangers come up to them. I'm sure your mom will get his number tomorrow from Beth."

"We're cool," Connor replied.

I hope so, Maggie thought. "How about getting me another one of those lemonades?"

"Coming up," Connor said as he handed her one from the cooler.

" Thanks, Connor. It will be so nice to relax by the pool."

"Yes, it will," Sean agreed. "What do you want for dinner tonight, Connor?"

"Chocolate cake will be good enough for me."

"This day keeps getting better! I won't even have to cook!" Maggie exclaimed.

"Like that was going to happen," Sean said as he looked over at Maggie. She tipped her drink to him and smiled. "You know me well, husband."

"Yes, and each day I become a little more frightened," Sean replied.

Connor burst out laughing. And even Maggie had to acknowledge that was a good zinger. She wasn't going to think about the fortune teller. No today was just going to be a peaceful day with her family. Sean pulled onto

Lavender Lane and she smiled as they drove through the covered bridge and over the pond.

They spent the rest of the afternoon at the pool and it was 7:00 before they knew it. Sean announced that he was hungry and was going to make some sandwiches from the leftover chicken salad. Maggie and Connor agreed that sounded good and to let them know when everything was ready. Sean acknowledged their request and went into the house. Connor decided to take advantage of this time alone with his mom to ask a few more questions.

" Are you okay, Mom?" Connor asked. "Medications good?"

"Yes son," Maggie replied. "Everything is fine. Don't worry. You just need to think about school and how you are going to wow everyone at Westminster. It's one of the best schools in Augusta, you know."

He didn't completely believe everything she was saying but he also heard the "don't worry" signal again so he decided not to push that line of questioning any further.

"Why am I going there instead of the high school around here?" Connor asked.

"Very poor ratings. The schools we are zoned for have some issues. They probably don't get the funding they need or the right teachers. We don't want you in that environment. You wouldn't get the individual attention like you will at Westminster. I think you'll like it there."

"But you or Dad will have to drive me every day," Connor said.

"Well, maybe not for too much longer," Maggie said. She looked at Connor and put her finger to her lips. "That is a surprise. But if you do well the first semester, I think we might look at getting you a car. Don't you dare tell your father I said anything."

"I think I can keep a secret and I will do good. I promise you," Connor replied.

"I know you will Connor," Maggie said and then jumped into the pool. The cold water sobered her up a little. *I wonder how many of those hard lemonades I drank? Enough,* she thought as she swam a couple of laps and then got out.

"Coming inside?" she asked.

"Yeah, I guess so," Connor said as he got up and followed his mother into the house.

When Maggie went to bed that night, she found Sean asleep with the computer still in his lap. She smiled as she took it and placed it on the bedside table. She looked at what he was doing. *Good Lord, that's way too many emails,* she thought as she turned off the computer and kissed Sean on his cheek and whispered, "Thank you for the day."

She turned off the lamp and closed her eyes but she couldn't fall asleep. Because of the medications she took and the alcohol she drank, she knew she shouldn't take any more of her medicine to help her sleep, but she went looking for some of Sean's and found the bottle of Triazolam and took one. She closed her eyes again and after about an hour of reliving the events of yesterday and today, she finally slept.

Emiliano wasn't happy about the people at his park that afternoon. They hadn't asked his permission to use it and they hadn't paid him to use it. Their neighborhood would have to pay for the use of the park and he knew the best way to make that happen. Rob the old lady's home at the end of the cul-de-sac. He remembered Beth telling him the owner was in the hospital and surely there would be some nice things in there he could steal. He drank only a few beers the rest of the day in case he was stopped by the police on his way to the subdivision. He went to bed early and set his clock for 2 a.m. Getting into Sycamore Springs around 3:00 in the morning would be a perfect time, he decided.

Maggie woke up and stared at the clock. 3:00. She knew her body wasn't going back to sleep and she knew better than to take any more medication. A walk would do her good, she thought, so she quietly got up, put on some jeans and tennis shoes, and walked out the back door. All she had for a light was her phone and the streetlights, but that was sufficient. She liked the way the streetlights provided just enough light from one to the other so that there were intermittent moments of complete darkness. She embraced those moments. She pulled the black covers of the night around her and just stood there listening to the frogs around the ponds and the occasional rustling in the leaves. Probably an opossum or maybe a large toad. She had learned from Connor that snakes made very little sound as they moved through the night so she wasn't scared of the noises in the woods. She convinced herself the snakes wouldn't be on the road either. After all, there was nothing for them to eat there. No, she felt safe walking down the road that night.

Emiliano parked in a dark corner of Lavender Lane just before the entrance to the covered bridge where no one in the neighborhood could see his truck. He got out holding an LED pen flashlight, a small crowbar, and a backpack that was empty except for the small .38 revolver he had purchased from Miguel on his release from prison. The serial numbers on the gun were gone and Miguel had been very anxious to get rid of it. Because of Miguel's anxiety regarding the gun, Emiliano knew that it had some bad history, but he didn't care. All he knew, was that he wasn't going back to prison and this gun would help ensure that didn't happen.

Maggie enjoyed looking at the houses in the dark. The decorative lighting accented different parts of the landscape that weren't as noticeable in the light of day. Amos's waterfall was lit up showcasing each level of the water as it fell. *I'm not sure if it's prettier in the daytime or at night.* Lights were hidden behind boulders and shining up on the Japanese maples in the Skye's yard. There were even lights hidden in some big ferns making them look like something from an "Outer Limits" episode representing plant life from a distant planet. There were lights under each of the three picture windows and at both ends of the yellow stucco ranch. *I really do like that house*, Maggie thought as she walked by it and lifted her nose in the air. *Nope, can't smell the deer repellant. Thank God.* Ulf and Agathe's driveway was lined with lights and there were also several on the large sycamore tree that looked very nice. Much nicer than she expected.

At Phil and Barbara's house, only their front porch was lit. *I wonder what those plants are in those large urns on the porch.* She pulled out her phone and turned on the flashlight as she walked across the yard. When she got closer, she realized they were various colors of poppies. *I might want to do that for our back patio.* As soon as she turned back around, she saw someone passing beneath the streetlight between the Skye's and Frances and Jennifer's homes. The image frightened her and she ducked down into the thick row of red tips next to Barbara and Phil's front steps.

Emiliano proceeded along the road. His night vision was excellent and he studied each house for movement as he went by. He wasn't afraid because he was confident that everyone in this neighborhood was sound asleep and unconcerned with what might be happening outside at this time of the morning. He passed Beth's house and saw the stucco home on his left tucked away in the woods. As he walked down the driveway, dimly lit by small solar lights, he quickly searched for signs indicating the house had an alarm system. There were none that he could see so he moved around to the back door. He took his flashlight out and examined the windows and doors. He didn't see anything that suggested they were wired so he started to work on the back door. There were two locks on it, one of them a deadbolt, but Emiliano knew neither would be a problem. He had opened many like them numerous times. He pulled out a small metal pick and was inside within minutes.

Maggie watched as the man went to Mrs. Cayman's house but instead of calling the police, she moved closer to get a better view of the thief. She went behind Beth's house and came out on the side of the Bartholomew's and hid behind the large children's slide and playhouse. She could see a small light bouncing up and down in the Cayman house like some sort of fluorescent butterfly moving around and she pulled out her phone. She dialed 9 and 1 and then hung up. *What are you doing? Wait and watch* she heard herself answer her own question.

As soon as he got in the house, Emiliano smelled the smoke. Smoke and some strange sweet-smelling perfume. The sweet smell was not pleasant in any way. Emiliano felt nauseous and covered his face with a bandana from his knapsack. That helped, but he knew he needed to get out of there as soon as possible.

Emiliano went straight to the mahogany vanity table in the bedroom. He opened a dark wooden box that was filled with jewelry. He didn't have time to sort through the box, so he closed the lid and picked it up. He immediately felt a presence behind him. He looked around and though he couldn't see anyone, he sensed someone was there, staring at him, telling him to leave the jewelry alone. It sounded like an old woman with just a whisper for a voice that he recognized.

"Is that you, Abuela?" Emiliano asked hesitantly.

The presence didn't answer him but he knew it was still there. Watching.

"I miss you, Abuela. I will listen to your warning," he said as he put the jewelry box back on the table. He then opened each drawer of the vanity, and soon found the origin of the sweet, sick smell that permeated the house along with the smoke. There were little white balls in each drawer sitting on top of the clothes. He wasn't sure what they were, but their smell told him they shouldn't be handled.

Finding only clothes and those little white balls, he turned his attention from the vanity and looked at the bed. He pulled the sheets back, lifted the mattress, and there between the mattress and the box springs was a brown folder. He couldn't believe people still used the bed as a hiding place. *Old people never learn*, he thought when he opened the folder and started counting the hundred-dollar bills. There were twenty of them. "Gracias, Abuela," he said. He remade the bed so that it looked like it hadn't been touched and he felt the presence once again behind him. This time he heard the voice in a more distinct manner. It was a woman's voice, old like his abuela, but without the Spanish accent. She told Emiliano that she hoped he used the money to turn his life around and then he felt it leave the room, though he knew it was still in the house.

He told himself that he needed to leave because of the fumes and the fact that he now had $2000 but that was not the main reason. He wanted to leave because of the presence of the old woman in the house. He knew it was still there. Watching him. He opened the kitchen door and stepped outside. He took several large breaths of the fresh air, locked the door, and hurried down the driveway.

He kept looking behind him as he hurried down the road, almost afraid of what he might see when he turned around. Though he looked back often, he never saw the person trailing him as she stayed within the safety of the shadows. By the time he got to the Brodie house, he was feeling much better about the night. *I will use this money to pay off Miguel for the equipment and I will be the owner; El Propietario,* he thought and smiled. He looked up at the house on the hill and pointed to his backpack. "This is the price of using Emiliano's Park," he said. He didn't see the person follow him into the bridge or watch him get into his truck. He turned the truck around making sure he didn't leave any tracks in the grass and then drove out of the neighborhood.

At the sight of his truck, Maggie knew for sure it was Jorge. She suspected it was him as she caught glimpses of him under the streetlights, but seeing the truck confirmed it. She turned around and walked back home thinking of what she should do. She decided she would use this information as additional leverage with Beth and let her know she was sleeping with a thief. She wasn't sure how she would make Jorge pay back whatever he took, but she would do something. Perhaps he would be cutting Mrs. Cayman's yard for free for the next several years. Yes, she liked that idea. She would suggest that to Beth tomorrow since that would be such a friendly gesture for a sick woman in the neighborhood. They would tell everyone they were paying for it out of the homeowner's association funds, but she and Beth would know that wouldn't be necessary.

She also thought about the home that Jorge had just robbed. The little stucco house surrounded by the woods where the elderly person resided, isolated and lonely most of the time. A niece who came by once a month wasn't much interaction with the outside world. *How much of a life could that be?* No one from the neighborhood visited her because she smoked and everyone knew smoking around oxygen was not safe. The owner of the house knew it too. Mrs. Cayman sat there every day wondering if this was the day she ran out of oxygen or whether the flame that was inches from the oxygen would be accelerated by its presence and set her and her house on fire. Maggie was certain Mrs. Cayman didn't care as she sat there alone in a house full of smoke. She was living on an island. An island separated by trees, fear, loneliness, and indifference. A place prone to accidental fires.

Funny, she thought. Sycamore Springs had more similarities to the last neighborhood they lived in than she expected.

Chapter 13

Hourglass

The next morning, Maggie was already sitting on the patio with her usual cup of tea when Sean got up. He walked outside and asked her if everything was okay.

"Everything is fine," Maggie replied. "Just didn't sleep that well, so I got up and walked around the neighborhood. It's almost as pretty at night as it is during the day. I'll get a nap sometime later today, probably out by the pool. I want to get Connor to school and then I think I'll go by and see Barbara and apologize. Perhaps ask them over. What do you think? Would that be okay?"

"Sounds good," Sean answered. "I'm going for a run. See you in about thirty minutes."

Maggie sat for a while longer and then went to make sure Connor was up before going into the kitchen and toasting a couple of bagels. Sean grabbed one and some coffee on his way out the door and said he would be working late tonight. They were prepping for a division visit and he would be spending a lot of time today making sure the hospital was as spotless as possible. She nodded her head and knew that meant he would be home anytime from seven to midnight.

Connor came into the kitchen, took one of the bagels, and devoured it in three bites, washing it down with a glass of milk as if he hadn't eaten in weeks. His mother looked at him incredulously.

"Had to eat quick so I could brush my teeth again," he explained as he went back to his bathroom. Within a minute he was back and ready to go.

As Maggie and Connor drove toward the school, he asked why his father hadn't taken him. The school was just a few miles down the road from the hospital.

"It's the mom in me, I guess," Maggie replied. "I remember taking you to school for the very first time and I wanted to take you to this new school for the first time."

"You do know when I go to college, you will not be walking me to class on the first day, right?"

"Who says I won't?" Maggie asked.

"Uh, me."

"Do you remember when your dog went to school after we moved to Ocala and you were in the fifth grade? She would wait for you outside the door of the school the first couple of weeks and I would have to come get her because she wasn't leaving without you," Maggie asked.

"I remember. Cindy was a good dog."

"Yes, she was a real good dog," Maggie replied nostalgically.

"You're not going to cry now, are you?" Connor asked.

"No," Maggie said as she somehow managed to reabsorb the tears that were beginning to form.

She pulled in front of the school and looked over at her son. "Don't beat the shit out of anybody on your first day and don't smoke in the bathroom," she instructed.

Connor laughed. "Good advice," he replied as he got out of the car.

Maggie knew he wasn't going to look back and wave. It wouldn't be too cool for a junior in high school to do that, but she waited anyway. She waited until she saw him disappear inside and then she let the tears she had been able to suppress, escape from her eyes and fall to her cheeks. *Get it together,* she told herself as she wiped her eyes and drove away.

What she had told Sean was true. She was going to see Barbara this morning and apologize again. But what she had failed to tell him was that she was also going to see Beth too. She was looking forward to that conversation. She wondered how she would let Beth know that her new boyfriend was a thief. She didn't think she would come right out and say it but that would depend on Beth. She was also going to make sure that Beth understood that the decision-making process and the neighborhood hierarchy had changed.

Later, when Sean brought up the subject of Beth's new lawn service, she would have to tell him that they would not be using them. She would just say that he said he was too busy for the time being but she would inquire about using them later.

She knocked on Barbara's front door and also pressed the doorbell and then heard someone yell that she was in the back. She walked around the side of the house and saw Barbara trimming some of her rose bushes.

"How did you hear me knock on the door from back here?" Maggie asked.

"I heard the doorbell," Barbara said as she took off her leather gloves and hugged Maggie. "How are you feeling?"

"Well, that's why I'm here. I wanted to apologize again for making us leave the fair early on Saturday."

"Think nothing of it. Would you like some iced tea or water or some coffee?"

"Iced tea if you're going to have something."

Barbara held up her Yeti and smiled. "I was going to get some in just a few minutes so you came by at the perfect time." She pulled out a pitcher from the small refrigerator on the patio.

" That's very convenient," Maggie said as she took the glass from Barbara.

Barbara pointed to the table on the patio and Maggie sat down across from her.

"It is. Very," Barbara replied. "I think Phil thought he would just fill it up with beer for parties, but we find we use it for so much more."

Maggie hesitated and looked down for a moment before she began talking. "Well, I wanted you to know that Sean wasn't telling you everything when we were at the fair. Yes, I do have stomach issues, but the real problem, is uh…" she said as she stopped and took another sip of tea. "Well, I had a nervous breakdown, several years ago. I used to battle depression and it got really bad. Debilitating as a matter of fact. But I saw a good doctor. Talked through a lot of things and now, with medication, I'm the wonderful, funny, witty, intelligent, and humble person you see sitting across from you now."

Barbara laughed. She knew there was more going on that night at the fair and now that had been confirmed. And then she remembered her own struggles with depression.

"Thank you for sharing that with me, Maggie. I'm sorry it happened. I did talk to Agathe and she said they were moving the fortune-telling tents around all through the fair. I bet you felt like you were seeing things, didn't you?

"Well, honey," Barbara said as she leaned over and patted Maggie on the hand. "I've been there. Two years ago, almost to the day, I was diagnosed with ovarian cancer. I was in a bad place when they told me. But Phil, God bless him, wouldn't allow me not to fight. I was a lucky one. When they did the surgery, they found that it had not spread and the doctor told us the long-term survival rate was over ninety percent. And even though I knew that, and should have been happy, the smallest of things would just make me weep. Facing your own mortality changes things. I understand how hopeless you feel when it doesn't seem like you are in control anymore. But you know something that really helped me? Some advice from my counselor. She reminded me that we can only control what we can control. We will never know the grand plan and though that sounds like I am preaching, I can tell you it certainly helped me. I don't have to do anything but live in the moment. I can control the moment and how I react in that moment. And that's all I can do and what I try and do. A good bottle of wine and a good roll in the hay doesn't hurt with keeping the mind focused either."

Maggie laughed and Barbara smiled at her. "And by the way, Agathe told me that they heard some woman come out of those fortune-telling tents yelling that she was going to burn the fucking tent down if she didn't get some answers. So, you see, there was someone else at the fair that night who was a bit upset with their trickery."

She's talking about me, Maggie thought, *and though she knows it, she didn't say it was me.* "I wish I could've seen her," Maggie replied, and then she and Barbara laughed until they had tears in their eyes. Tears that reflected humor and sadness. Maggie realized she had found a friend and a confidant.

"Do you have children, Barbara?" she asked.

"Yes, two girls. Both of them grown and married. The oldest, Katherine, lives in Atlanta and has two kids and my youngest, Joanna, is getting ready to have her first. She lives in Austin, Texas. I'm going out there when she's ready to deliver but that won't be for several more months. And because I know you're going to ask, here," she said as she pulled out her phone to show Maggie pictures of her daughters and grandchildren.

"That black-haired little boy, Samuel, is something else," Barbara said. "He is into everything. His brother, Eli, is the total opposite. Can sit there and just read a book all day long and never hear a word out of him."

"You look like you have a wonderful family." Barbara could sense there was something else Maggie wanted to say but hesitated.

"I do. Very blessed," Barbara replied. "How old is your son? 16?"

"Yes, Connor. I took him to school today. He's going to Westminster."

"Good school."

"Yes, we did a lot of research. We wanted a place where Connor could get one on one attention. He's very bright. Way smarter than me or Sean. But his mind, well, uh, I think the acorn didn't fall too far from the tree, unfortunately. His mind never seems to shut off. Like mine. And he can become very defensive. Especially if he hears things said about me."

No telling what he heard them call his mother when she was suffering the way she was, Barbara thought. *Children can be very cruel about those types of things.*

"But he's such a good kid. He takes medication too and it has worked wonders. He was really shy and stayed to himself. Didn't really like being around other kids. Well, really, other people," Maggie said.

"Sounds a little like the neighbor that lives across the street from you," Barbara said.

"Yes, in a way, he and Amos are a lot alike," Maggie said. "Only Connor doesn't take his clothes off and run around the neighborhood. But about being anti-social, yeah, he was a lot like that."

Barbara was looking at her with concern so she explained further. "With everything you see in the paper today about these young kids and the shootings, I have to admit, it worried us too when Connor was acting the way he was. But Connor hates guns. Wants them outlawed. Says the only way to stop this type of thing from happening is to get rid of the guns. He and his dad have these second amendment arguments all the time. I think Connor realizes now that you can't just get rid of all the guns, but he doesn't even like being around them.

"And he won't kill a thing that he finds out in the woods. Gets mad when I spray the ants. Says it's our own fault. But he knows, it doesn't matter what he says, I am killing those damn ants," Maggie said and then paused to sip her tea. Barbara just nodded her head and laughed.

"He loves the woods. And the neighborhood pond? Well, he could stay down there looking around for hours. Loves it. I'm not sure if he's going to be some sort of biologist or naturalist, but I do know it will have something to do with animals. Might even be a vet. If it walks, crawls, slithers, hops, or flies, he wants to know what it is and everything about it. He's the one that told me about the puss moths. He always says as long as you understand what you're dealing with, you have nothing to worry about when you're out in the woods. I disagree, but he is quite adept when he's out there. Fearless and smart.

"And like I was saying, he is just so much better socially now," Maggie added. "Doesn't feel anxious around new people anymore. In fact, he was looking forward to going to school today. And that has never happened."

"He sounds like a good kid. I can tell you two are very close and you should be proud of the way you've helped him grow up and through his struggles."

"I am," Maggie replied. *You don't need to tell her about the fire. Not now. Maybe later when you are much better friends, you can tell her about the fire. But not now.*

"Well anyway, I didn't mean to take up your entire day. But I did want to come over and apologize and explain what happened. And invite you and Phil over for dinner. Seeing how Phil loves turkey legs, I can get Sean to do one of his turkey loins out on the grill. They're delicious."

"We'd love it, but only if you allow us to bring the wine."

"Deal," Maggie said as she stood up. "By the way, your yard and roses are so pretty. You don't use any of your neighbor's deer repellant, do you?"

Barbara looked confused.

"You don't know, do you? Your neighbors down the road use their own urine and dog poop for deer repellant."

"Agathe?" Barbara asked.

"Yeah, that's who I would've guessed after seeing her at the fair the other night but no, not her. The two Swedish models in the yellow ranch."

"Oh, my God," Barbara gasped.

"I'm surprised you didn't know that," Maggie said. "They weren't at all bashful about showing me how things are done."

"Are you kidding me?"

"No ma'am," Maggie said. "Though after I told them about the puss moths, I think they'll be less inclined to expose the shrubbery, so to speak."

"Maggie, you are awful," Barbara said as she leaned over laughing.

Maggie smiled. "Thanks for the tea, Barbara, and thanks for understanding. I'll see you later." Within a few moments, she was at Beth's house, and just as she expected, before she could even get to the door, Beth came outside to meet her.

"Hey, Maggie," Beth said. "How are you?"

"I'm good, Beth. I didn't sleep that well last night though, so I got up and took a walk and it was great. Felt much better when I got home. The neighborhood is almost as pretty at night as it is during the day. The lights around your house are very pretty. I love the Skye home at night. The way they have those lights around the rocks and trees is just beautiful."

"Thank you, and you're right," Beth replied. "The Skye's house is very pretty at night. And so is Amos's waterfall."

Maggie was taken aback to hear Beth compliment Amos, considering what had just happened regarding the pond vote. *Interesting* Maggie thought and before she could say anything else, she saw the blue Chevy truck coming down the road. *Holy shit. This could not be better timing.* The truck pulled into Beth's driveway and Jorge got out.

"Jorge is just coming by to talk to the Thompson's and Bartholomew's about doing their yards," Beth said as she looked at Maggie.

"I bet he appreciates your help in making that happen."

"Well, I'm just happy to do it. He's such a hard worker," Beth replied.

"Good morning, Mrs. Stevens." Emiliano touched the tip of his hat and tilted his head slightly towards hers.

"Good morning, Jorge," Beth replied. "You remember Maggie Brodie, don't you? She lives in the house on the hill across from Amos, the one with the waterfall."

"Si, good morning, Mrs. Brodie," Emiliano said as he repeated the finger to the hat gesture.

"Call me Maggie, Jorge. So, Beth is going to help you try and get some more business for your company today."

"Yes, ma'am," Emiliano replied. "She is introducing me to the Bartholomews and the Thompsons today. I am grateful that they will give me a chance. I will do a good job."

"I was thinking," Maggie said. "Seeing how we have a very sick neighbor down here in this cul-de-sac, and since you will probably be working around here anyway, it would be so nice if you did Mrs. Cayman's yard too. For free. I hear she is a frail sick woman and I just thought that would be a nice gesture on your part. I'm sure that would impress the other neighbors."

"She is no longer frail and sick," Beth said. "I got word she died last night. Around three in the morning, I'm told. I was going to send out an email to everyone but just haven't had a chance yet."

Maggie studied Jorge's face. He looked pale. Almost sick.

"Dios mio," Emiliano said as he made a cross over his chest with his finger.

"You may not believe this because I'm not sure I really believe in the supernatural myself," Maggie started. "But I think I may have seen Mrs. Cayman's spirit going through her house one last time last night. I was out here right around three this morning and I saw a white light flickering through the house for a moment and then it disappeared. Isn't that the strangest thing? It kind of gives me goosebumps."

Emiliano knew Maggie was referring to his flashlight but he also knew he felt the presence of the dead in that house. After all, he had grown up in that world. A belief system where the spirits of the dead often interacted with those of the living. And though he knew Maggie didn't see Mrs. Cayman's spirit or that of his grandmother, he was convinced he had been guided by both of them. He had followed their directions regarding the jewelry and had received approval for taking the money. So, he wasn't concerned with being haunted by an unhappy spirit. What worried him was that the person across from him talking about seeing those spirits was lying. She knew he was there and that he broke into the house and she was making sure he understood that.

"Wow, that's crazy," Beth said as she looked at Maggie and then Jorge. She could tell he was startled but she wasn't sure if it was because of Mrs. Cayman's death or from what Maggie said about seeing her spirit in the house earlier that morning.

He knows, Maggie said to herself as she looked at the expression on Jorge's face. *He knows I saw him in Mrs. Cayman's house. This is better than I could have hoped for.*

"You know, Jorge, Mrs. Cayman's death is all the more reason for you to take care of her yard. That would be such a kind thing to do. Especially now that she has passed on and her house will be on the market. Beth said she only had a niece who came to visit her occasionally and I'm sure that would be a load off her mind, knowing that the yard would still look nice. And Beth, I'm planning to send out an email about painting the guardhouse and mention the colors we talked about. So, you won't have to do that. I bet we get a lot of feedback on it and I am sure we can do it even cheaper than we thought because we can just do it ourselves. You know, provided the neighborhood wants to," Maggie added.

What are you doing, Maggie? Beth asked herself. *What do you know? You must know something else that makes you think you can just do as you please. Something else about Jorge. I can tell by the way both of you are acting. You think you have the upper hand now, don't you? Well, we will see about that.*

"What a wonderful suggestion," Beth replied. "You would do that for Mrs. Cayman, wouldn't you, Jorge? And Maggie is right, the Thompson's and Bartholomew's would be very impressed that you agreed to do that as a friendly gesture."

Emiliano nodded his head yes. He felt like he was back in a prison for a moment. Agreeing to things that he didn't want to do but had no choice except to do them. And it was making him angry. But as he had learned in prison, the women in front of him could not know what he was thinking or how angry he was. He had learned to conceal what he was thinking very well.

"Great," Maggie said. "It was nice to see you again, Jorge, and thanks Beth for being so understanding about the guardhouse. Let me know what you find out regarding the arrangements for Mrs. Cayman's funeral. I'd like to donate to a charity if her will or her niece specify one and I think the neighborhood should send flowers for her service. Oh, and can you send me everyone's email address?"

"Sure," Beth said. "And I agree about the flowers. You are so thoughtful."

Maggie just nodded her head and smiled and started back home. As soon as she got out of earshot, Beth looked at Emiliano and shook her head.

"I don't know what you did or what Maggie saw you do last night, but I can tell it was something. I don't even want to know but it's clear Maggie thinks she has something on the both of us and can tell us what we can and cannot do and I don't like that. I need you to send her a warning of some kind. Something that lets her know she can't boss us around and that she is not in control of things around here. Do you think you can handle that?" Beth asked angrily.

Emiliano nodded his head without saying anything to Beth about already doing that once. But, the less she knew about what he did, the better.

"Good. Now, let's go next door and I'll introduce you to the Thompsons and the Bartholomews and get that business straightened out and then I want a big hard one to play with," Beth said with a tone that suggested she was more demeaning than seductive.

Beth introduced Emiliano to Renee and Jasmine and told them he would be mowing all their lawns on Wednesday and had also agreed to take care of Mrs. Cayman's yard at no cost, as she broke the news of her passing. Both of the women were very impressed with Emiliano and anxious to have him take over their yardwork. Beth then took Emiliano back to her home. She pulled off his pants and grinned when his body revealed he was eager to make her happy. She took hold of him as if he was some sort of inanimate object and walked toward the couch.

"Put it in me now, Jorge," Beth said as she took off her pants and bent over the couch. "Put it in me hard," she said several times and Emiliano did as she requested. She reached back and clutched his hand and put it over her mouth just before she let out a muffled scream of pleasure.

"That was even better than I thought it would be," Beth said as they got dressed.

Emiliano smiled. He didn't question what he was doing with Beth. Nothing people did shocked him anymore. He had met women like Beth before. For a moment, he did wonder whether she would have come on to him the way she did if he hadn't stopped her from stepping on that copperhead. Maybe, maybe not, he thought, but now it didn't matter. Now they were connected in a way that he could use to his advantage. He would do whatever Beth told him to do. At least for now. He wasn't sure what fantasy she was fulfilling when she had sex with him, but he would make sure she was kept satisfied.

" I look forward to seeing you and that big boy again Wednesday," Beth said as she reached over and grabbed his crotch. "But, be careful around here, Jorge," she said as she closed the door and went upstairs.

As he walked back to the truck, he thought about Beth's warning and the words Maggie had spoken. Maggie reminded him of his sister. She was strong, cunning, unafraid to say what was on her mind, and dangerous if threatened. Emiliano's sister lived in California and had already killed one boyfriend. It was ruled self-defense, even though he died from a tent stake that she drove through his eye and into his head after he had beaten her badly. He broke her arm, several ribs, and her jaw and she was still able to take his life. But Emiliano wasn't surprised when he heard about what had happened. Anger can empower you to do things you wouldn't think were possible. He knew that. He wasn't sure Beth did though and he was positive that Beth didn't know how difficult Maggie would be to intimidate.

But he had learned a lot in prison. It would have to be a much stronger warning this time than the puss moths. Something that would send a very serious message to her that she couldn't ignore and told her to stop sticking her nose into other people's business. He was in a very dangerous position and would have to be very careful. He was already a two-time offender and if Maggie called the police on him, he would probably be going to jail for the rest of his life. And he wasn't going to allow that to happen. He wasn't going back to prison. Not because of her, or Beth, or anyone.

He started his truck and drove downtown to the stone and rock center that he had visited many times when he worked for Forest Lawnscapes. He had seen something there several weeks ago that he thought would be the perfect warning. The large boulder was still there, untouched and unmoved. He was in luck. He found what he was looking for and coaxed it into a jar and drove home.

Late that night, he drove back to Sycamore Springs and passed Maggie's house, checking to see if anyone was home. The lights were on in the house and there were cars in the garage. One of the garage doors was open but the garage was dark. He drove to the end of the cul-de-sac and parked in the shadows away from the street light. He got out and walked along the edge of the road, trying to stay away from the light as much as possible.

He could see into the kitchen from just outside the garage and he stared into it for several minutes before moving. He crept toward the door to the kitchen and set the jar next to the steps and the women's sandals. He backed out of the garage and into the driveway before he turned around and moved closer to the cover of the trees. He turned around one more time to see if he could see anyone, but no one was there. Sweat was pouring off his forehead by the time he got back to his truck and he opened a beer. He finished it off with several big swallows and started his truck. As soon as he drove onto Peach Orchard Road, he opened another beer and smiled. Tomorrow he would pay off the lawn equipment and celebrate the birth of his new company out at Emiliano's Park. He was proud of what he had accomplished so far and believed he had done everything necessary to make it a success.

Just before going to bed, Maggie went to check that the garage door was closed. It was still open so she stepped outside to hit the door closer and noticed something next to her sandals. She flipped on the garage light and picked up the jar.

"What the hell is this?" she screamed and dropped the jar. Answering her scream, Sean and Connor both came running and found her pointing down at the black spider that was motionless within the shattered glass.

"Is that what I think it is?" Sean asked.

"Yes," Connor said as he quickly grabbed another jar from the pantry and ran outside. *Fuck*, he said to himself. *Who the hell is doing this?*

Maggie hadn't moved an inch and watched while Connor trapped the glistening black spider inside the jar.

"Sorry, mom," he said as he held the jar up for her and his dad to see. "I shouldn't have left it there."

Maggie recognized the well-known red hourglass shape on the spider's abdomen as it crawled around inside the jar. She wasn't sure if she was more afraid of the spider or the red hourglass that reminded her of those words. The words that the fortune-teller said: "The red sand will be a warning." Regardless of what anyone else told her, she was now convinced that the words were not arbitrary. They were prophetic. She didn't know how the person in that tent knew, but they did. Twice now she had seen the words revealed to her. Twice now she had been warned, and this time, she saw the flames burning in the background as she looked at her son and she was frightened.

Chapter 14

Princess

Elizabeth Ann Oglethorpe Stevens was born a princess. Not a fairy tale princess, but a little baby who from the first day she took a breath, was adored and doted on by her father and her father's father. Nothing could be good enough for this little girl. Though her mother or grandmother might disapprove of some of the things she requested, all she needed to do was to ask her father or grandfather, and her wish would be granted. Normal families would look at the little girl and say she was spoiled rotten. They might say that amongst themselves, but they would never say that in the presence of the little girl, or her father or grandfather.

She was born in Mobile, Alabama; a fourth-generation Oglethorpe. Her great-great-grandfather made millions during the Civil War profiting from smuggling anything and everything to both sides of the war. After the war, the smuggling industry became a legitimate shipping industry and the wealth of the family continued to grow until five-figure discrepancies were dismissed as mere rounding errors.

The privilege that extreme wealth provided to those in the south was like that of European royalty or that of the Mafia. Within their domain, no was never an option. Everything that they needed, they were able to get. Everything they didn't even know they wanted, they got. That is the world in which Beth lived.

She attended the University of Alabama, joined the Kappa Kappa Gamma sorority, and became the first freshman ever to hold an office. By the time she was a sophomore, she was the president of the sorority and presided over it as if it was her own small kingdom. The entire sorority house was renovated due to her grandfather's generous donation and to the people within the sorority, Beth was indeed royalty. She was smart, beautiful, and rich. But that wasn't enough for Beth.

She enjoyed manipulating the people around her and she loved to catch them in a lie. And when she did, she took great satisfaction in humiliating them in front of as many people as possible. Over time, the girls of the sorority learned not to cross Beth. It also didn't take too long for the administrators of the school to learn that same lesson. Large sums of money shortened their learning curve.

Hazing within sororities or fraternities was often known as "Hell Week," and in Beth's sorority, it was a more than an appropriate name. During this process, Beth realized that she became aroused when she saw the young women with their hands tied behind their backs, waiting to endure the next indignity. And regardless of whether they made it through the selection process or not, those who participated in the activities came away with an understanding of who Beth was and what she thought was gross or embarrassing.

The pledges were forced to eat large earthworms or roaches, sometimes both. Even the girls with no chance of being selected were forced to eat Oreo cookies with dog shit as the filling. The smart ones declined and left. The unfortunate ones followed instructions and threw up before being rejected. Their hair was washed in a combination of shampoo and dog urine, which was far more urine than shampoo. Their hair was dyed lime green, pink, neon orange, or yellow, which at the time this was done, brought tears to the young women whose beautiful well-coifed hair was ruined for some time. They could elect to have their hair shaved into Mohawks instead of undergoing the dye, but the results were the same for the young women: intense embarrassment.

But Beth pushed things too far her senior year. Two young girls died during the hazing incidents from alcohol poisoning and the university could not hide what happened, even with all of Beth's money and influence. She was removed as the president of the sorority and expelled. She returned home to Mobile and though everyone in the elite social circles knew what had occurred, no one mentioned anything around Beth or Beth's family. Away from the Oglethorpe family, they wondered how Beth avoided criminal charges but the words in those discussions were hollow and had no meaning. Anyone who participated in them already knew the answer to the questions they asked.

Still, Beth suffered some repercussions, if not being invited to parties or not having calls returned could be considered repercussions. Over time, Beth felt alone and abandoned and began searching for something else. She researched colleges in Alabama and found the University of Mobile. She visited the Christian school and informed her parents she wanted to enroll there. Her mother and grandmother were ecstatic to see Beth interested in changing her life and focus, but her father and grandfather had their doubts about whether this was the right school and path for Beth. However, they did not interfere. Beth enrolled and graduated from the University of Mobile with honors and she felt like she had turned her life around.

Her mother believed that attending the Christian school would be a life-changing event for her daughter and when Beth graduated, she could see the change. Beth even apologized to her mother for her past actions. She realized how wrong she had been and asked for her forgiveness. Her mother accepted her daughter's apology and hoped she was not fooling herself like she had done so many times with her father. She had accepted the apologies of Beth's father for years and she still often ended up crying or drinking after learning they were lies. She hoped it would be different with Beth. There was good reason to believe that because Beth believed it herself. She thought she had really changed. But she hadn't. She had just been successful in discovering a detour around the deformed bridge of neurons that had and would always shape her behavior.

She met Darrin at the University of Mobile. He was a senior enrolled in the five-year MBA program. They married when he graduated with a Master's in accounting and he began working at Beth's father's business as a financial officer. Beth loved being married and was overjoyed when she became pregnant with their first child. When given the chance, Beth would tell anyone and everyone how the University of Mobile had transformed her life. She bragged about how she had changed and many of her old friends believed her. And things were good for several years. But when her grandfather became sick, the moral synapses disengaged.

She stayed by her grandfather's bed the entire time he was ill. He had end-stage COPD and was drowning in his own mucus. Though he was on oxygen, he still struggled to breathe and Beth prayed again and again for relief, but none was provided. None, until he took his last breath. That breath provided relief in this world but his wife and Beth's mother doubted there would be any for him in the next one he encountered. They were all there to witness him take his last breath. His chest rattled for a moment and his eyes opened wide. They saw the fear within his eyes until it disappeared, and all that remained were glassy marbles resting in a wrinkled and ashen face.

The misshapen bridge within her mind reconnected on that day as Beth looked at her dead grandfather. The cruel nature of his death gave birth to the feelings of malice and callousness that had been hidden away but were now uncovered and much more familiar to her.

"He shouldn't have died like that," she screamed at her mother and grandmother. She couldn't understand how all their money could not provide enough medical care to prevent this from occurring. "He shouldn't have died that way," she screamed at the doctors and nurses and berated them for their ineptitude.

When she heard Amos yell out his vote that night at the homeowner's meeting, Beth was reminded of the day her grandfather died and heard herself screaming at the nurses and doctors. She looked at Maggie and saw someone she was jealous of from the first day she had met her. She thought she and her son were disrespectful and she didn't like the way Maggie looked. She was pretty and not afraid to speak her mind and she didn't like that. There had been girls in her sorority like that and she made sure they were always given the shit jobs regarding the planning of parties or events. She knew how to deal with women like Maggie. Even as she said the name in her mind, it made her angry. Maggie. What kind of name was that? Hell, it sounded more like a dog's name than that of a woman.

Maggie embarrassed her but it was her grandfather, Amos, who embarrassed her even more. It was his vote that had ruined her plans. She would make sure that both of them paid for that indignity. She hadn't felt this way since she had been expelled from the University of Alabama and the change within her that night at the meeting was brought forth like an ember which was stoked into a raging fire by a gust of wind. The people on the patio got a glimpse of it as she abruptly ended the meeting and left them feeling surprised and confused. But her husband witnessed the entire transformation and it shocked him.

He had seen his wife act coldly with him many times before. He had seen her get angry, even furious. But he had never seen the way she looked that night when he followed her into their bedroom. She sat on the edge of the bed with her fists clenched on her knees and rocked back and forth without saying a word. She didn't respond to him when he talked to her and when he sat down next to her, the look in her eyes told him not to come any closer. The only thing he could do at that point was to go back outside and apologize; making up a story about a migraine headache. No one believed what he was telling them. Everyone had seen the way Beth looked and understood it was best if they left.

Beth never liked Amos. Amos was her mother's father and when he embarrassed her that night, all the feelings of animosity between them resurfaced and burned within her stomach like an ulcer.

Amos was the first one who called Beth "Princess." It wasn't done out of love. He said it in a fit of rage as he confronted Beth's father about his affairs and the way he was hurting his daughter and his family. She remembered him pointing at her and telling her father that she had become a spoiled little princess and he would regret the way she was growing up one day. Because of that encounter, Beth would have nothing to do with her mother's father from that day forward.

In her young eyes, she couldn't understand how anyone could talk that way to the man who gave her everything. The man who bought his little girl clothes and jewelry, a horse, and later even cars and vacations. The man who built her a dollhouse the size of a small trailer when she was just six years old. She still had the newspaper article about it from the Mobile Press Register framed in her bedroom. The reporter said "Little doll gets dollhouse of every girl's dreams," and she loved reading those words and the attention it brought her.

It was a defining moment in the little girl's life. A moment when the twisted belief that love meant always hearing yes and having everything given to you and done for you was embedded in her mind. The man yelling at her father and who knocked him to the ground couldn't love her. He had never given her anything. That night would alter the way she thought and acted toward him and many others in her life. She never saw Amos again. Not until he moved into Sycamore Springs.

An unbiased observer that night might have thought that Beth had been hurt by seeing her mother crying. A woman pleading with the two men to stop fighting as her little girl stood there watching it all. But she had seen her mother cry many times before and that night she only saw a person who had told her father on numerous occasions to stop buying her so many things. Beth's twisted way of thinking only became more distorted as she watched her mother try to help the man who had knocked her father to the ground and was saying so many mean things about them.

Beth became convinced the woman who was married to her father was jealous of her. No matter how she tried, her mother could not persuade her daughter that what she mistook for jealousy, was really fear. Fear that her daughter would live an immoral life like that of her father and her father's father.

Beth had seen her father with other women. She didn't know these women were having affairs with her father until she heard that word uttered by Amos when he and her father got into a fight. Even when she heard the word, she didn't understand what it meant until she asked one of the housekeepers. Even then, she shrugged it off as if it meant nothing. Those women seemed to make her father happy and she could see nothing wrong with that. As she grew older, she realized that she received more money and more things from him when she kept quiet about any discretions she discovered.

She didn't welcome Amos when he moved into the neighborhood. She never visited him. As far as she was concerned, he was just a homeowner who lived down the road from her. Perhaps years of therapy with a counselor could have revealed the issues and aberrations that were manifested in the self-centered and cruel manner in which Beth acted, but that was never done. So, no one would ever know the true reason for her malicious behavior or what lay beneath a surface of civility and insincere kindness.

This wasn't Beth's first affair. After the third child, she became bored with Darrin. Sex with him seemed like a chore and she didn't want another chore to do. She wasn't sure what attracted her more to Jorge; the fact that he looked like a model in work boots and jeans or that he seemed fearless by picking up that copperhead and putting it away in the woods. She could tell he was attracted to her by the way he looked at her and she knew he wouldn't be afraid of having sex with a married woman. It didn't seem like much of anything would scare him.

She also knew he would satisfy those sexual fantasies that she was afraid to share with Darrin; those sexual cravings that arose during the time she was hazing all the young pledges. To Beth, Jorge was just another one of those pledges who would do as she asked. Like them, she had something he wanted. The pledges wanted to be a member of the sorority and the elite social benefits that provided them. He wanted access to the people that Beth knew and the financial benefits of that access. The status and the gender of the willing participant were different, but the willingness to do what Beth said would be the same.

Emiliano arrived on Wednesday morning promptly at 9:00, just as Beth had requested and she took him into the den. She instructed him to shower and then come back out with no clothes on. He did as she ordered. She then told him to tie her hands behind her back with the scarf she handed him and to do what she said. With her hands behind her back, she knelt in front of him and began the ritual. Emiliano's size challenged her oral appetites, but once satisfied, she stood up and leaned over the couch, and told him what to do, before her screams were muffled by the pillow in which she buried her face.

Afterward, she told him to untie her and to get dressed and Emiliano again followed her directions. Once dressed, she told him that he had work to do and smiled.

"Just think, Jorge," Beth said, "You have this to look forward to every Wednesday. But I need something else from you."

"What is it?" Jorge asked.

"I need you to keep yourself clean. No nasties. You understand?"

"I understand."

"I hope so. If you do, I promise that you'll have the best sex and more money than you've ever had in your entire life. But if you don't, well, then, I'm not sure how well you'll be able to pee without big Pedro. Oh, and by the way, I have three more homes that are interested in your services. Here are the addresses and the phone numbers and the names of the people you need to speak with. They're expecting your calls," Beth said as she handed him a slip of paper before she turned and walked away.

Emiliano nodded his head and stood quietly for a moment before he left. He had to admit the sex he had just experienced was some of the best he had ever had, but he wasn't sure Beth understood everything yet. He knew she still thought of him as something less than herself but that would change. Not now, but once he got what he needed from her, things would change.

It took him almost six hours to mow and trim the landscape of all four of those lawns in Sycamore Springs that day but he never felt better from working so hard in his entire life. As he loaded the tractor into his truck, he glanced at Beth's house and smiled as he placed the slip of paper she had given him in the glove compartment and patted the closed door with his hand. *See you next week, Princesa,* he said to himself as he started the truck and drove down the road.

Chapter 15

A new belt

"Connor! What the hell are you doing leaving a black widow spider next to the steps?" Sean yelled. "You know your mother hates spiders. And a damn black widow? What the hell are you thinking?"

"Sorry. I'm so sorry, Mom. I found it the other day in the woods and was going to take it to school. To the biology teacher. He seems like a cool guy. I told him about the puss moths and then I found this."

Maggie studied her son. She told herself she always knew when he was lying but as she listened to him, she wasn't so sure anymore. The interactions with Beth and Jorge and the prophecy from the fair were all coming together and starting to make her suspicious. She didn't want to doubt what her son was saying, but the past and the present were starting to converge again and that would require her to be more cautious and watchful of his actions.

"I'll put it outside. It can't get out of the jar. And I will have it out of the house tomorrow. I promise," Connor said as he took it out of the garage. He looked at the black widow in the jar and it concerned him. Not because of what it was, but because of why it was there. Someone was pissed off at his mother and had sent a message to her not once, but twice. And as he thought more about it, he remembered Amos and the dead fish. *Was that another sign meant for mom? And the catfish at the lake. The way she looked at that catfish.* It was the same look he had seen tonight when she found the black widow.

Somehow, everything is related. He was beginning to see his mom becoming the distrustful person that she had been not that long ago. The familiar signs were starting to return. *But why? What is causing this? What did she do? What happened to her? She hasn't done anything except go to that fair. That's it. Something happened at the fair. That had to be it. Things will get out of hand soon if I don't intervene. Whoever is doing this doesn't understand what will happen. But they will.*

"Why did you leave it out here by my shoes?" Maggie asked.

"I don't know," Connor replied as he tried to think of what to say. *Just like the video game, Connor. Anticipate.*

"Just thought that would be a good place so I could get it on my way out to school tomorrow. I put it there as I sat on the steps to take off my boots. I just didn't think it would be a problem."

"Knowing how I feel about spiders, you just put it by my shoes and forget about it?"

"Mom, that's what I said," Connor replied. "Are you saying you don't believe me?"

There is the all-or-nothing question Maggie thought as she looked at her son. *Now, what are you going to say?* She saw the garage burning from her backyard within her head so she tried to redirect the conversation as she replied.

"I'm sorry. I do believe you. I'm just a little on edge. First the puss moths. Now the black widow and the thought of that cotton mouth down there in the pond."

"Wait just a damn minute," Sean said. "What cottonmouth?"

"The one in the pond," Maggie said. "Connor has seen it several times."

"Shit, Mom," Connor whispered in an exasperated manner. "What the hell are you doing?

Protecting you, Maggie said to herself.

"Don't talk to your mother like that Connor," Sean reprimanded.

Connor hung his head. *It won't work this time Mom*, he thought as he looked up into his mother's face. *I know what you're doing. You think you can throw me under the bus and I'll be distracted by this. But I won't let that happen. Not this time.*

" It won't harm anyone," Connor said. "Unless you get in its way or it feels threatened by you."

"Connor, young children are living around here. That damn snake won't know if the kids are threatening it or not. I know you don't feel like it's a danger but it is. Tomorrow afternoon you and I are going to catch it and, if we can't catch it, I'm going to kill it. We can't have it in the pond. And don't even think of arguing about it. That's just the way it's going to be," Sean said.

Maggie saw the hurt on Connor's face. She wanted to tell him she was sorry but she knew she couldn't do that. She thought that would be like admitting to him that she needed his help. Letting him think that would only create problems she wasn't sure she could handle this time. And she knew if she couldn't fix whatever happened, she would lose her son for a very long time. Perhaps forever.

"Let's just all go to bed and get a fresh start tomorrow," Sean said. "I'll be home around 3:30, Connor, and you and I will get that snake. "

Sean closed their bedroom door and looked into Maggie's eyes. She could tell he was mad and was trying his best to control his anger.

"You knew there was a very poisonous snake in the pond and did nothing about it?" Sean asked in a controlled monotone voice. "What were you thinking? And before you try and answer that, I know the answer already. You didn't want Beth to know. That was more reason for her to drain the pond and you didn't want her to know that. But think, Maggie. Just because Connor is okay around those damn things, doesn't mean everyone else is. Little kids could get hurt. Even die. Do you want that on your conscience?"

Sean was right, but she also knew what she had seen and what had been told to her. She couldn't ignore either of those warnings. Sean would never believe her if she told him that Beth was going to try and do something to harm her or her family, but she now understood it was a strong possibility. And Jorge. He was a thief. What else was he capable of doing?

No, if she told Sean about Beth or Jorge he would think she was obsessing over something that was not real. Imagining things, especially if she related it to what she heard at the fair and the red sand warnings. *Well, I didn't imagine Jorge and Beth kissing and I didn't imagine Jorge breaking into Mrs. Cayman's house but that will all come out eventually.* Right now, she just had to make sure Connor did nothing harmful and that her family was safe.

"You're right, Sean. I'm not sure what I was thinking. Thanks for being there for me to lean on when I need you." She reached up to kiss him and then pulled him close and laid her head on his chest.

"Maggie, Connor gets his cues from you. If he sees you anxious, scared, obsessive, or just acting weirded out, well, you know what can happen. And that can't happen again. It just can't. We won't survive it all if there is a next time."

"I know, Sean. I get it," she said again as her voice trailed off. She knew Sean was right. She couldn't let Connor know about the signs or any of her concerns. She knew that he would react and like Sean, she feared how that reaction would manifest itself.

The next morning, Connor got up early to make sure his dad could take him to school. He didn't want to upset his mother again by seeing the spider. He walked slowly to the school doors after his dad dropped him off wondering what he was going to do with the spider.

He didn't even know the biology teacher and though he was pretty sure he would be interested in seeing the spider, he also worried that he could be labeled as the weird kid by bringing in a "show and tell" during the first week of school. He couldn't risk that type of attention and possible ridicule from the students so he went into the bathroom and flushed the spider down the toilet. He threw the jar away and then went back outside to wait for school to start. His parents would probably never even ask about it again, but if they did, he was prepared for that. He would tell them he dropped the jar and had to kill the spider. *Again, just like the video games. Always stay one step ahead* he told himself. That was very important now.

Maggie didn't wake up until eight that morning and hurried out of bed thinking that she was going to be late getting Connor to school, but she discovered Connor and Sean were already gone. She followed her morning ritual and went out to the patio with her cup of tea. She felt bad about what happened and how she handled things with her son last night. She had hurt him, and knowing that it was necessary didn't make it feel any better.

Maybe I could pick him up early and we could go buy some fish for Amos's pond this afternoon. He would understand it was an apology. Plus, he needs to be here anyway. Because of the snake. It might even be better if he caught it without Sean around. Sean won't be that much help anyway. Unless Connor used him as a decoy, she said to herself and started laughing. *I'll tell Connor that. He'll get a kick out of that. But first I need to do a little work on the computer.*

She found the message from Beth in her email with all the neighborhood email addresses. She sent out a note asking for their ideas about painting the guardhouse. She relayed the suggestion to paint it green with cranberry accents to match the roof tiles. She said they could do the job for under $200 if they did the work themselves and added that she and Sean were willing to tackle the project. She ended by saying she looked forward to their input and then thanked Beth for her willingness to consider this renovation. She knew that would piss Beth off and smiled as she imagined her reading it.

She took a shower and headed down the road to Beth's house. She wanted to see her face when she told her about the black widow. She stopped to admire the flowers around the pond and as she walked over toward the tall water lilies, she glimpsed something moving in the water. She stood still for a moment before she spotted a large bullfrog swimming toward her. She smiled for just a second before she saw the large gray snake reach out and grab the frog in its mouth. Ten seconds later the bullfrog was gone and the snake swam away into the marshy grasses.

"Shit!" she said out loud as she continued to Beth's. She was glad that Sean told Connor to get the cottonmouth out of the pond. Though it had probably just eaten its breakfast, one less snake in the pond sounded pretty good to her. Reaching the cul-de-sac, she noticed how nice all the lawns looked. She could see that Mrs. Cayman's yard was mowed and she smiled. *Muy Bueno, Jorge* she thought, as she turned toward Beth's house.

She was surprised when she had to knock on the door because usually, Beth met her out in the yard. *Maybe I caught her doing something else, although I don't see the blue truck anywhere.* Within a few minutes, Beth came to the door with her youngest child in her arms. She opened the door and smiled at Maggie.

"Sorry. Summer had a big ole poop, and we were just cleaning it up," Beth said as she kissed her on the forehead. "I never have understood why baby poop smells so bad, do you?"

"Uh, no," Maggie replied. *Who will blink first, Beth?* she thought as she smiled at her. *Who will blink first?*

"I sent out the email this morning about the guardhouse," Maggie said.

"Okay," Beth replied nonchalantly.

"I really appreciate your support on this."

"Sure."

Okay, I've had enough of the Stepford wife act. "Tell Jorge he did a great job," Maggie said. *That should get things going.*

"I will," Beth replied.

"Don't you want to know what I was referring to?" Maggie asked, somewhat perturbed by Beth's lack of concern.

"Mrs. Cayman's yard, of course. What else could you be referring to?"

God damnit, Maggie thought as she gazed back at the innocent face staring at her. *You are a conniving, cold, little bitch, aren't you? I can't be the only one that knows that, but you are very good at hiding things, aren't you?*

"All the yards," Maggie replied. "He did all of them back here in the cul-de-sac, didn't he?"

"Yes, he did. He's very good at what he does."

Yes, I bet he is, Maggie said to herself as she smiled.

"Well, I didn't want to take up much of your time this morning," Maggie replied. "Just wanted to come down and let you know about the email."

"Sure."

"I'll see you later," Maggie said and started to walk away.

"Okay," Beth replied.

Maggie took several steps before she stopped and turned around. "By the way, you won't believe what my son found the other day."

"What was that?" Beth asked.

"A black widow spider. Puss moths, black widow spiders. What else is around this neighborhood that I need to be worried about?" Maggie asked.

"Goodness," Beth replied. "I haven't seen a black widow since I've lived here. But I'm sure they're out there."

I'm not so sure about that, Maggie said to herself. *You didn't send Jorge out looking for one, did you? And you are avoiding answering the question? Is that your plan? Feign ignorance?*

"Well, I'll let you know what the neighborhood says about the guardhouse," Maggie said. "Oh, and have you heard anything about the services for Mrs. Cayman?"

"No, nothing yet. And Maggie," Beth started, "regarding your question about what else to be worried about in the neighborhood. I suppose that all depends."

"Depends on what?"

"On your awareness," Beth replied. "If it hadn't been for Jorge last week, I would have stepped on a copperhead. In these woods, you just have to be aware that some things can hurt you. I know I've learned an important lesson."

"Yeah, I think I've learned that same lesson. I'm a lot more aware now of what to be looking for. Goodbye, Beth."

"Have a good day, Maggie," Beth said as she turned around and walked into the house. She looked down at Summer and kissed her head. *Black widow spider.* She said the words several times in her head. "We're going to have to be careful when we go outside, Summer. A lot of nasty things are out there," she said as she smiled at her daughter.

Maggie stopped in the middle of the road and looked back at Beth's house. She saw it burning and she put her hands over her eyes and shook her head. *Connor can never know* she told herself over and over and took a deep breath. When she got home, she opened her computer and had already received comments from Barbara, Frances, and Jennifer saying they were in favor of painting the guardhouse and would all be willing to help. *Off to a good start,* she thought.

She then did a google search for koi in the Augusta area and found a place she could buy them - Bob's Tropical Fish store. She wrote down the address and went outside and sat beside the pool and thought about her conversation with Beth. She had to be even more careful now. She was certain that Beth was somehow responsible for that black widow in her garage, even though Connor said he put it there. *He was lying because of the way I've been acting. He knows it was a warning too and he is thinking that he has to protect me. And that could be dangerous for everyone.*

She would have to start changing his perception and eliminating his concerns which wouldn't be easy. She jumped into the pool and swam until her muscles ached before getting out and falling asleep in one of the Adirondack chairs. She didn't dream. She just slept and woke up at noon.

A few hours later, she entered the office of Connor's school and told them she needed to pick her son up a little early for a dentist appointment. In a few minutes, Connor came into the office and Maggie started speaking before he could ask why she was there.

"I bet you forgot you had a dentist appointment today, didn't you?" Maggie asked.

Connor smiled and nodded his head.

Maggie looked over at the secretaries and shrugged her shoulders. "Teenage boys," she said. "They'd forget everything except where they left off in the latest video game."

The secretaries smiled and nodded in agreement as they watched Connor and his mother leave.

As soon as they got outside of the school, Maggie started to apologize. "I'm so sorry. I didn't mean to hurt you by talking about the cottonmouth, but your father is right. It needs to go. It could hurt someone."

"It's okay Mom. I get it."

"Are you sure? There's nothing more to any of this Connor, I promise you."

"I know," he replied.

"No, you don't," Maggie replied. "I am fine. There is nothing you need to worry about and you shouldn't feel like you need to do anything. I just forgot to take my medicine for a couple of days and I got like I do when I don't take it. I get forgetful and worry about things that I make up in my head."

Connor wanted to tell her he didn't think she was making things up in her head this time, but he knew better than to do that now. She would become even more suspicious. So, he just listened. He knew she would keep talking, trying to explain things.

"I'm a little anxious, I admit it," Maggie said, "but I'm taking my medicine now and have reached out to start therapy again. It couldn't hurt to do that. I really enjoy it, actually."

"That's good, Mom," Connor said. *But you aren't fooling me. I know you could easily go into that dark place with a little more prodding and when that happens, I'll need to be there. To provide the light you need to get out; to burn away the illusions.*

" So, you're okay, right?" Maggie asked. "You're not stressed out about me or concerned about anything going on with me?"

"No, I think you're doing all the right things."

"Good," Maggie said as they got in the car. "I wanted to go by Bob's Tropical Fish store and get you to help me pick out some koi for Amos's pond. I think he'd like that. And, I thought it might be better if you caught that snake without your father being there. Unless you plan on using him as a decoy."

Connor laughed as she knew he would. *So far so good. Mission accomplished, I think. But I still need to be cautious.*

They bought five koi of various colors for Amos and headed home. Maggie pulled off to the side of the road in front of Amos's waterfall, and as luck would have it, Amos was there working on the pond. She and Connor brought the fish to him and Amos looked at them suspiciously.

"Hello, Amos," Maggie said. "Remember me telling you that I would buy you some new fish the other day?"

"No," he answered.

"Well, I said I would," Maggie said as she held up her bags. "Is it okay if we put them in your pond?"

"If you don't, they'll die pretty soon in that bag."

Connor and Maggie laughed as they bent down and released the fish. They began swimming and Amos smiled. Maggie elbowed her son and Connor nodded his head as he watched Amos's reaction.

After a few minutes, Amos went back to what he was doing before they got there; cleaning out leaves and branches from the water. Connor bent down beside him. "I hope these live a long time, Amos."

"Yeah, me too. Why aren't you in school? You do go to school, don't you?"

"I got out a little early," Connor replied. "Mom and I wanted to get you these fish and then I'm going to go over to the pond and catch a cottonmouth that's made its home over there. Take it out to the lake so no one gets hurt."

"That sounds like a nice thing to do."

Connor smiled.

"But sometimes acts of so-called kindness can be deceiving. Sometimes they only hide the demons that are hiding in the barn. Waiting for you to let your guard down. Seen it way too many times to not believe it," Amos said.

He stood up and looked up and down at Connor and then over at Maggie. "Is this the sergeant's son?" he asked.

Maggie nodded her head yes. *He has the past and the present all there in his mind, connected somehow.*

"Well, tell the sergeant it appears that he didn't raise a thug," Amos said as he turned back to working on the pond.

When they got home, Connor gathered the things he needed to catch the cottonmouth. After putting his boots on, he and Maggie started for the pond.

"You did hear that I'm not a thug, didn't you?" Connor asked.

"Yeah, I heard it," Maggie said and rolled her eyes.

Maggie looked at her son. He was calm. Unafraid, as he put the plastic aquarium on the ground and walked into the marshy reeds with his snake grabber in front of him. Connor methodically peered into the reeds. With her sight focused on Connor, she failed to see the other eyes in the pond which were watching her son. Eyes that neither she nor her son had ever seen before. Eyes that had traveled from a very large pond on a hundred-acre farm about a mile down the road. These eyes were not friendly and were moving in her son's direction.

Connor pushed the reeds away with his snake grabber and found what he was looking for. *Lucky,* he thought as he reached in and seized the snake near its head with the grabber and started backing out of the reeds. Maggie could see that he had captured the snake. It scared her but she had confidence in him and let out a sigh of relief as she glanced toward the middle of the pond. It was then that she saw the eyes attached to the floating log that was quickly approaching her son.

"Oh shit!" she screamed. Connor turned around and saw the eyes coming toward him. He was looking at a good-sized alligator and didn't have much time to act. He looked over at his mother but he knew he didn't have time to reach the side of the pond and, even if he did, that would mean nothing to what was stalking him. Plus, that would put his mother in danger. *I've got to get the snake in front of me and hope that gives me enough time to get out.* He started to swing the snake around when he heard four loud shots. One of the alligator's eyes exploded and the blood spurted from its head. When he looked up, he saw Amos on the side of the bank with a .45 automatic service revolver in his hand.

"Hold on to that snake," Amos said as he stepped into the pond and started walking toward the alligator. He put two more shots in the animal's head and then smiled.

"Never can be too careful with these sons of bitches," Amos said as grabbed the alligator by the tail and started backing out of the pond. "I'd say a little over six feet," he said. "Just big enough to be interested in what was in the pond. Probably about 200 pounds, I'd guess. I can get it over to the side of the bank all right, but not sure I can get it out of the pond on my own. Can one of you help me with that?"

Maggie and Connor were speechless. They watched Amos tug on the alligator's tail while moving backward in the pond. He got the tail and the back legs of the alligator onto the ground and then got back in the water and pushed on the upper torso until it was completely out of the water.

"I'll be damned. Stronger than I thought I was," Amos said as he got out of the pond and rolled the alligator onto its back before walking back to his house. Maggie watched Connor place the snake in the aquarium and close the lid and then she ran to him. She grabbed him in her arms and hugged him with tears running down her cheeks.

Connor told his mother over and over again that he was okay as he felt her body shaking against his. He was pretty sure that she wouldn't find it funny knowing that his pants weren't just wet from being in the pond. So he said nothing, other than he was fine, as they continued to hold each other. Looking over Connor's shoulder, Maggie saw Amos coming back with a large knife in his hand.

Amos kneeled down and began carving away at the underbelly of the animal. He looked at Maggie and grinned. "Don't say anything to that woman down at the end of the road about this. She wouldn't like this at all, but by God, I'm getting me a new belt!"

Chapter 16

Murky Water

Maggie thought she saw a man on the other side of the pond butchering some type of animal but she wasn't sure if what she was looking at was real or not. A large snake slinked along the ground but she thought it looked more like some sort of reptile mime moving up against imaginary walls. It crawled up those walls and back, but never forward.

She felt confused, angry, and relieved all at the same time. She felt like she was being crushed and she pushed out with her arms and grasped at air. She tried to remember what she was supposed to be doing but it was hard for her to focus on the words that were swirling around in her head and running down a drain deep within her body.

The words "Connor" and "snake" were floating in the air and she remembered seeing a snake just a moment ago. She looked up to see Connor throw a match at the snake and then it burst into flames. It slithered to the pond and as it entered the water, the pond caught fire. Through the flames, she could see the outline of some being on the other side of the pond. She couldn't make out who it was, but she could see that it was cutting up the body of an alligator. Then she remembered.

She saw her son's face. Right in front of her. Amos was slicing away at the alligator's underbelly. She recalled him shooting the animal as it was moving toward Connor. He had saved her son's life. *A fucking cottonmouth. Connor was in the fucking pond trying to save a fucking cottonmouth and then this thing comes along out of nowhere.* "Goddamn alligator!" she screamed.

She wanted to slap her son as hard as she could and tell him he was stupid. But she didn't because she knew she would lose the connection she had with him if she did, regardless of how angry she felt. She had to subdue her anger and just concentrate on how good it was to have her son in her arms. He had caught the snake and was safe. It didn't go exactly as planned, but he was safe. All because of that crazy son of a bitch who was kneeling next to the damn alligator.

Sable was on her back porch when she heard the gunshots. She feared the worst but cautiously moved down her driveway. She saw Connor and Maggie standing beside the pond.

Oh my God. What has Amos done? When she got closer to the pond, she saw Amos on the other side kneeling on the bank. And then she realized what he was kneeling over.

"Are you okay?" she asked when she reached Maggie and Connor.

"Careful," Connor said as he pointed down at the aquarium.

The cottonmouth was squirming around in the clear plastic box and Sable felt Maggie's arms around her before she could say anything else. The composure that Maggie was beginning to acquire, disappeared when she saw Sable. Another mother; and as she hugged her, she started crying again. Sable felt Maggie's body trembling against hers and she pulled her close.

"It'll be okay," Sable said several times as Maggie continued to cry. As she held onto Maggie, she studied Connor and he appeared to be unhurt. Amos didn't even seem to be aware she was standing there.

Maggie took a couple of deep breaths and wiped her eyes as she let go of Sable. She stepped back and managed a weak smile.

"I'm not sure what happened, but just before I say you could use a drink, can one of you tell me if everyone is okay and that I don't need to call 911?" Sable asked.

Maggie shook her head as she looked over at her son. *He is standing there as if he is guarding me,* Maggie thought. *Even though he was the one in danger. Because of a fucking snake. A fucking poisonous snake. Goddamn it.* She screamed the words in her mind one more time before she closed her eyes and took another deep breath. When she opened them, she had once again steadied herself and started to explain what had happened.

"We're fine, Sable. Well, I'm not sure fine is the right answer, but we're not hurt. Amos shot the alligator as it was coming toward…" Maggie was unable to finish the sentence. Tears welled up in her eyes again and Sable grabbed her hands.

"Oh, honey. I'm here, your boy is here. Everything is okay. Right this moment. Right here. You and your son are okay. It's okay," Sable said.

Maggie listened to Sable's words and she thought about what Barbara had told her. *Sable is telling me the same thing. Control what you can control right now. Be there in the moment.* She tried to calm her breathing and nodded her head.

"Connor was getting the cottonmouth out of the pond. He saw it a few days ago and we were going to get it out of there so it didn't hurt any of the young kids, or really anyone, I guess. And yes, Connor. Before you say anything, I know what you want to say, but let's just not go there right now. Anyway, he was in the pond and we weren't aware there was an alligator in there, and well, before we knew it, it was coming after Connor and if not for Amos…" Maggie said as she looked over at him. "Well, if not for Amos, I'm not sure what would have happened."

By now, Amos had removed the belly skin and most of the internal organs. There was blood all over the bank and the edge of the pond. If someone had just walked up, they would think someone had been badly hurt or even killed. But that didn't happen, Maggie reminded herself. Amos paid little attention to anything other than the dead alligator. He finally saw her and looked up.

"Careful, don't step on that belly skin. That's the good stuff. Gonna be my new belt. You're not going to say anything to that woman down at the end of the road about this, are you?" Amos asked.

Maggie shook her head no several times.

"Beth," Amos said as if a light had come on and illuminated the name on an unused projector screen that was hidden away in a dark corner of his mind.

"Her goddamn name is Beth. Damn spoiled little princess." He jabbed the knife into the alligator and cut away the last remaining part of the organs from the hard armor. He tossed them into the pond.

"The turtles will like that," he said as he looked up at Maggie.

Maggie touched Amos on his shoulder and kissed his forehead. "Thank you, " she whispered into his ear.

"You're the mother of that boy, aren't you?" Amos asked. "The boy that's not a thug. Smart boy. Likes to hunt for snakes. You're his mom, aren't you?"

Maggie nodded her head.

"What's your name again?"

"Maggie," she said as she felt tears on her face.

"Yeah that's right, Maggie," Amos replied. He had turned back toward the alligator when she heard him add, "Thanks for the fish."

"You're welcome, Amos," Maggie answered with a trembling voice

He continued to work on cutting off the alligator's limbs and tail. Maggie took a deep breath and spoke to Connor. "Are you going to be okay with all of this?"

"Yeah, I'll be fine. I'm just going to wait on Dad and then we'll take the snake out to the lake and let it go."

"Sable, this is Connor, Connor this is Sable," Maggie said as Sable came up to join them. "We're going to her house and drink some wine. Tell your father he can find me over there."

"Nice to meet you, Connor," Sable said, "I'll take good care of your mom."

Connor watched them walk away for a moment and then picked up his snake grabber and the aquarium. Just before he left, he called out to Amos, knowing that he probably would not even acknowledge him. "See you later, Amos!"

"See you later, Connor."

He smiled when he heard his name. Amos was looking right at him and waved. "Would you like a new wallet?" he asked.

"Yeah, a wallet would be great."

"Have it for you in about a month," Amos said as he continued disassembling what remained connected to the alligator's body.

"Thanks again, Amos."

Connor looked at the snake in the aquarium on his way home. "You got me into a little trouble today, friend," he said to the snake. "That could have been a bit of a problem, and I don't think you would've survived if I had put you out in front of that gator's mouth. He would've taken a big bite of you and the snake grabber. Probably wouldn't have cared what he swallowed. I think that would've given me enough time to get out of the water. Yeah, I'm pretty sure that would've given me time to get away. But I learned a very important lesson today.

"I would've lost the game today because I didn't stay one step ahead," he said as he looked down at the snake. "I wasn't thinking and I didn't see the potential danger. But that won't happen again," he said as he leaned the snake grabber against the aquarium and went in the house to change clothes.

As they walked up the driveway to Sable's house, Maggie was once again reminded of the mountains when she saw the large timber lodge. "I just love your house," Maggie said. "It seems like it belongs in the Colorado mountains. And your front yard is like a forest. It's like a cabin in the forest!"

"Yes," Sable replied. "Red and I love the mountains. The south just gives us more time to do things outdoors. Fewer winter issues, you know. We love to visit the mountains in the winter but being stuck inside for weeks on end due to a blizzard or twenty feet of snow, well, Red may have wanted to try it, but I sure as hell wasn't going to."

Maggie laughed.

" Come on," Sable said as she took Maggie by the arm. "Come see the backyard."

Sable opened one of the two massive wooden doors and led Maggie into a large great room with wooden timbers going from one side of the ceiling to the other.

"Love it!" Maggie said as she looked up. They walked through the kitchen, which was open to the great room, and down the hall to several sets of French doors. Sable opened one and Maggie followed her onto the back porch that appeared to have no end.

"It just disappears into the woods," Maggie said without even being aware she was talking out loud.

"Yes, Red designed it that way. He wanted the house to just be an extension of the woods. He made the little waterfall feature too. Got the rocks out of Brevard, North Carolina. If you haven't been there, we need to go sometime. Surrounded by mountains and the most beautiful waterfalls." Maggie looked at the little creek that ran along the edge of the deck and then disappeared into the woods.

Sable walked over to a circular bar made of river rock. When she turned around, she had a bottle of wine in her hand. "You like Riesling?" she asked.

"Oh, yes," Maggie replied.

"Then you're going to love this. It's called 'Poet's Leap' and it's one of our favorites."

"Delicious," Maggie replied after tasting the wine. "Hope you have a lot of it!"

Sable filled her glass. "We should be ok!"

There was something interesting to see wherever Maggie looked, whether it was a metal sculpture of some kind, or a tree or plant that she had never seen before, or just the beauty of the log home.

"It's so lovely out here." Maggie walked over to examine an S-shaped metal sculpture that glistened when the sun reflected off its shiny red metallic color. "Who made this?"

"I did," Sable replied.

"What is it?" Maggie asked.

"Do you like it?"

"I love it."

"Then it's whatever you want it to be," Sable said. "I could stand here and say something snooty like 'it is a piece that represents the beginning and the end' or something stupid like that, but it isn't anything except metal shaped like an S painted with some bright red paint. I just liked the way it looked as I started making it."

Maggie laughed. "I think I want it to be a red S."

"You are very astute," Sable said as she smiled.

Sean didn't bother to glance at the pond as he drove out of the covered bridge. He turned toward his house and saw Connor waiting for him. He looked down and saw the snake in the aquarium and wondered what was going on. He opened the door and before he could even ask the question, Connor began providing the answer.

"Mom came and picked me up early from school. We bought Amos some koi for his pond and then I went in and got this little girl. I'll be ready to go when you are."

"Your mom?" Sean said. "Your mom helped you get the snake?"

"No. I got it by myself. I don't think she would go near it."

"No, she definitely wouldn't have done that," Sean agreed. "Did you have any issues, problems?"

Connor was ready for that question. "No," he replied. He wasn't lying. He didn't have any trouble getting the snake. He could tell from the question that his father hadn't seen Amos on the way in. He would make sure he saw him on the way out. And be ready for the questions.

"Where is your mom?"

"She's with a person called Sable. I think she's the neighbor next to Amos."

"Yeah, that's Sable Skye. Why is she over there?"

"She came by the pond after we had gotten the snake out."

"Ok, give me five minutes and we'll be ready to go," Sean said as he went inside.

Sean sensed that something was a bit off. Something didn't seem to be quite right about the way Connor was talking and acting. He seemed a little nervous. But Sean knew better than to pry right now. He felt that his son had more to tell him and he had learned from the past, that it would be better to just allow it to occur. And if things still didn't seem right by the time they got back, he would ask Maggie what was going on.

Connor loaded the snake in the back of the SUV. When Sean came out he was carrying his shotgun case and put it in the back seat. On a different day, Connor would have said something to him about bringing the gun, but he wasn't going to say anything today. As they drove down the driveway, Connor pointed at the pond. "What is Amos doing over there?" Sean asked.

"Carving up an alligator. About six feet long. He shot it today."

"When today?" Sean said as he looked over at his son.

"Right after I got the snake." *Again, not a lie* he told himself.

"Shit," Sean said. "The alligator was in our pond?"

"Yeah."

"Damn, Connor," Sean said. "You're lucky you weren't in the water. Holy shit."

Connor wasn't going to reply to that comment. He wasn't about to tell his father that he was in the water. He wasn't sure if his mother would but he was ready for that if she did. He would tell his dad that he was never in any danger. He would say that he didn't tell him earlier because he would've just worried about something that was already over and done.

But as a precaution, he would be more careful in the future. If he was going to get in the water, he would first make sure that there weren't any undetected alligators. He knew how to do that. All he needed were some cherry bombs or m-80's from the fireworks store. Alligators were very sensitive to vibrations within the water and those explosions would cause them to surface. And carrying a 10-inch blade that could pierce alligator hide would be the backup plan. *Yeah,* he told himself. *I'll be ready next time.*

"Shit," Sean said again as the image of the alligator flashed in his mind. He was beginning to think that draining the pond wouldn't be such a bad idea. A dry river bed might be much safer after all.

"Essie May Washington Branch State Park?" Sean asked.

"Yeah," Connor answered, "That will be a good spot for her."

Chapter 17

Red

"What's going on out here?" Red asked as he walked out onto the porch.

"We're celebrating life. And I must tell you, your house is beautiful. This back porch is amazing. And your wine selection is outstanding. And regarding that; please note my glass is empty," Maggie said as she handed Red her glass.

"It is always good to celebrate life, Maggie Brodie," Red said as he retrieved another bottle of the Riesling and refilled her drink. "Thank you for celebrating life with us today."

"You talk like we are in some western movie," Maggie said.

Sable laughed as Red smiled. "I have told him the same thing so many times," Sable said. "That's just the way he talks. It gets even worse after he's been drinking. Then, oh my God, you would think he was Wes Studi in the 'Last of the Mohicans' movie. He starts explaining what every little thing means, what life and death mean, and what nature is trying to tell us. Sometimes I just want to say that the tree is just a damn tree, but then I realize his version is better than mine. And, I love that about him. He never forgets who he is or what it is that surrounds us. He is one hell of an artist. And one hell of a husband. So I just go along with the way he talks. You should too. He'll keep your wine glass filled and keep you entertained all night."

Maggie held up her glass and peered at Red. He was smiling at her and his wife. *He was almost beaming* she thought. *They are very much in love.*

"Wine glass filled and entertained all evening?" Maggie asked suggestively. "Hell, I may never go home." Maggie walked over to inspect a metal sculpture close to the bar. "What is this?"

"It's a sunflower," Red answered and poured some whiskey over ice in his glass.

" A scotch man, huh?" Maggie said, reading the label on the bottle in his hand. "Glenmorangie, 18-year-old, single malt."

Red nodded. "Do you or Sean like scotch?"

"Tape, yes," Maggie said. "The brown liquid in $100 bottles, not that much."

Red and Sable laughed.

"A sunflower, you say?" as Maggie turned back toward the metal sculpture. A breeze came up from the woods as if it had been cued by the special effects department. It turned the large metal concave petals around the hubcap-shaped head that looked like it had been pelted by a hammer many times. Maggie walked over to the sunflower and felt the six-foot metal stem.

"Did you make this?" Maggie asked as she looked over at Red.

"I did," Red said. "Sable said it was too tall but I think it may not be tall enough. What do you think?"

"It's tall enough," Maggie said as she took a sip of wine.

"Issue settled," said Red as he smiled. "Where is your husband, Maggie?"

"Somewhere between home and the lake. My guess is the Essie May Washington State Park. They're releasing a water moccasin that Connor found in the pond last week. Sean suggested we get it out of there before it hurt someone. Sean would have just shot the thing, but Connor wouldn't go for that. He said we just needed to relocate it. So, he caught it today and they're taking it out to the lake to let it go."

"Your son caught the water moccasin?" Red asked.

"Yes, he strolled in the water as if it was nothing and grabbed it, and then uh…." Maggie said as she stopped to take a drink. "And then, well he got the snake and put it in an aquarium to take it out to the lake."

"Your son has the soul of a warrior."

"My son has the soul of someone that likes snakes. He likes all animals. He knows all about them and what he doesn't know he'll find out. There is no fear in that boy at all concerning things that I don't want to have anything to do with. By the way, do you know anything about puss moths or black widows?"

Sable was very aware that Maggie didn't mention the alligator. She noticed her pause as if she was going to bring it up and then didn't. *I wonder why she did that* she asked herself.

"I've never heard of puss moths, but, yes, very familiar with black widows. Have seen several of them before. Why?" Red asked.

"There were some puss moths in my mailbox," Maggie said. "Nasty little things. They have poisonous hairs and they sting and burn. Had them on my hands and arm. Luckily, I wasn't allergic to them, because some people are. Then Connor caught a black widow. I didn't know it was in a jar out in the garage, and when I went to pick it up, I dropped the jar and broke it. My son didn't hesitate. He went right in, got another jar, and captured it before it even thought about moving.

"It's funny, I've mentioned those puss moths to several people and no one from Barbara's house on up has ever seen them. Barbara knew what they were but she said they've never been in her yard. Beth was quite familiar with them. Said she had even seen them before. I think she may have put them in my mailbox," Maggie said.

Sable and Red looked at each other and then at Maggie. They were both thinking the same thing. Did she just accuse Beth of trying to hurt her?

"Damn guys. Lighten up. I was just kidding. I know Beth wouldn't do anything like that," Maggie said as she took a drink of wine and smiled. *She may not have done it, but I am not sure her big Spanish chew toy didn't.*

"And then Amos killed an alligator today," Maggie said as she poured more wine.

Red looked at Sable. She nodded her head yes to let him know Maggie wasn't bullshitting him again.

"How big was it?" he asked.

"I think Amos said it was about six feet. He's cut it all up by now. Going to make a new belt out of the skin. If you have a desire for some alligator leather items, I would suggest you get your orders in soon. He was carving that thing up pretty well when we left him. Where is the restroom?"

"I'll show you," Red said. "Sable, would you get out some cheese and crackers, maybe some fruit, while I show Maggie the way?"

"And then you're going to show me the rest of this fabulous house," Maggie said.

After she was done, Red gave her a tour of the house and explained to her how different things were made and the many types of wood that were used throughout the house. Native American rugs and blankets and art dominated the decorations.

"Everything is so beautiful," Maggie said. They stopped in front of the large picture windows that overlooked the front yard.

"The sun sets on this side of the house," Red explained. "It is quite majestic when the light comes through the windows. At the very top of the windows is stained glass. A different color over each window. Just wait," he said.

Maggie hadn't noticed the stained windows before but as the sun started to filter through them, the room was lit up by orange, red, and yellow hues.

"Wow!" Maggie exclaimed. She was suddenly startled by a thud against the window. Red caught her as she moved back so she didn't fall.

"What was that?" Maggie asked as she stared at the small drops of blood on the window.

"A blue jay that was destined to die," Red said as he looked at the dead bird on the porch and then over at Maggie.

"Something is troubling you, Maggie," Red said. "Nature has provided you with a sign. There is an obstacle in your life that you will need to overcome. Come sit down." He led her back to one of the leather chairs in the great room.

Maggie sat and took a sip of wine as she thought about Red's words. *He said there was an obstacle in my life that I needed to overcome. How many more signs do I need?*

Did he say a blue jay? A blue jay that was destined to die? He sure the fuck did. Ok, I get it, world. I get what you are telling me. I'd have to be crazy not to. Does this sign have anything to do with a blue truck driven by a person whose name starts with J? Sean will think I need to be institutionalized to believe all of this, but there are no more coincidences in my way of thinking. No, I get it now. Our destinies are intertwined somehow.

"Are you okay? You look pale." He put his hand around her wrist and looked down at his watch. "Your pulse is a little high. Do you have heart problems? Do you need me to call for medical help?"

Maggie only heard fragments of what Red was saying. She shook her head no as she thought about Beth and Jorge and tried to calm her breathing.

"I'm okay," Maggie said. "The dead bird bothered me a little bit and then what you said."

"It means something to you, doesn't it?"

"Yes, but it's personal. I hope you can respect that."

"Of course."

"Thank you," Maggie replied as she thought about Beth. *What has she actually done, Maggie? You think she, or her boy Jorge, placed puss moths and a black widow in your yard. What else has she done? The puss moths were just an irritation and the black widow was in a jar and couldn't have really hurt me. So what is she saying? Wait a minute. Amos's fish. Did she kill Amos's fish? There is something there. He is afraid of her. Fuck her. She killed his fish and sent me several warnings. I get it, Beth. You're telling me to stay the fuck away from you and don't get in your way or your business, huh?*

Well, you made some mistakes, Beth, and making Connor suspicious of you is a big one. That could be very bad for you and your family. I saw the snake and the pond burning earlier when I looked at my son. I have to make sure I keep that under control as I deal with you; you petty little bitch. God damn spoiled little princess. Good description, Amos. Good description.

The sound of the doorbell ringing brought Maggie into the present. "I'll bet that's my husband," Maggie said. "I'm fine now. Thank you. And can you keep this just between me and you?"

"Sure," Red agreed.

Maggie smiled and asked Red if she could answer the door. He just nodded and Maggie hurried upstairs and yelled through the door.

"Who is it?" she asked.

"Is that you Maggie?" Sean replied.

"Maggie, Maggie who?"

"Maggie," Sean said in an exasperated manner.

"Okay, okay." She opened the door.

"You've been drinking," Sean said when he saw the attempt at a look of seriousness on her face.

"Yes, I have and I encourage you to join me," she said as she turned around and started toward the back porch. Red was in the hall and greeted Sean.

"Welcome," he said as he shook Sean's hand.

"Be sure and look up," Maggie said as she walked through the house. "Beautiful isn't it?"

Sean agreed as he gazed at the room. "I love the exposed timbers and all the different woods."

"Thank you. All of the wood is reclaimed."

"That's pretty amazing."

Red smiled. "What can I get you to drink?"

"A whiskey and water would be great."

"Crown Royal or George Dickel?"

"Crown would be good. Just some ice and water," Sean replied as he followed Red outside.

Maggie and Sable were sitting on the edge of the porch near the waterfall. Sean followed Red to the bar. "Some porch you have here."

"Thank you," Red replied. "I hear you and your son released a water moccasin into the lake?"

"Yeah, we did. I'm not sure whether that's a good thing or not."

"It is a good thing," Red replied. "That snake has a purpose. A reason for being here. You gave it a chance to fulfill that purpose."

"I hope that purpose isn't biting some unaware skier or someone swimming in the lake."

"It could happen," Red said. "But it's very rare. They don't want to confront humans. They would prefer to go away from them."

"You sound like my son."

"He appears to be very attuned to nature," Red replied.

"Yes, he is, but, I'm a little worried about that pond. Amos killed an alligator that was in it today. The same pond my son was in just moments before, catching a damn water moccasin. And then Amos kills an alligator. Maybe we don't need that pond," Sean said.

Sable watched Maggie listen to Sean talking about the alligator. *Her son didn't tell his father what actually happened. He didn't say that he was in the water when Amos killed it and Maggie isn't going to say anything either. She's doing that for her son. It scares her but she is doing it for him.*

"That's not the first alligator or water moccasin that has been in that pond," Red informed him.

"What?" Sean asked, alarmed.

"I've also had to kill an alligator in that pond. It was not afraid of humans. I'm not sure who was feeding it but it was drawn to humans when it saw them. And that is never a good thing. When an alligator associates food with humans, it becomes very dangerous. I could not release it into the lake like you were able to do for the water moccasin. I had to kill it. Getting rid of the pond, however, will not get rid of alligators or water moccasins, or other poisonous snakes or creatures that exist in the woods," Red stated.

"Well, it sure as hell might reduce the likelihood of them being around. Especially alligators."

"To some degree, yes. But what about Amos's pond? Your swimming pool? The other pools in this neighborhood or nearby? It will not eliminate their existence nor the fact that you may still encounter one."

Maggie wanted to shout "Hell yes!" but she knew she couldn't do that. Not now. *If Sean knew the alligator was in the water with Connor, he would go ape-shit crazy. I need to steer this conversation in another direction* she thought as she got up and walked over to the bar.

"Do you come here often?" Maggie asked, sitting down next to Sean. "I'd like another glass of Riesling, bartender. And don't worry, I am not driving. I'll call an Uber to get me home. Where do you work, stranger?"

Sean shook his head. "How many of those have you had?"

"Not enough," Maggie said. "I can still see only one of you."

"Did you know about that alligator?"

"Of course," Maggie answered. "I was there."

"Don't you think it's pretty damn scary that it was in the same pond that Connor was in?"

" Yes, it was very scary. But Connor is safe. He is fine. And you won't keep him from going into ponds, even if you drained this one. He'll always find another. And I know he'll be more careful in the future. I know our son."

Sean knew Maggie was right about finding another pond even if they drained this. He also knew Red was right. He nodded his head and then looked back at Red.

"Do you let anyone into this place?" Sean asked.

"No, not anyone. Only those who like to celebrate life," Red laughed.

That shitty little princess at the end of the road can't come here then. Just thinking about it made Maggie smile. *And even better, she won't get her way with draining the pond.*

"And… CUT," Maggie said. "Cue the people walking down the road, holding each other's hand as they walk into the sunset. Excellent, Red. Excellent."

Chapter 18

Several hundred drinks later

The movie reference made Sable and Red laugh. Sean was used to his wife's humor but wasn't ready to acknowledge it.

"Hey Red, can you get me another drink and call this woman sitting beside me an Uber?" Sean asked.

"I can but I think her name is Maggie."

"All right, Red!" Maggie said as she high-fived him.

Sean just shook his head again. Maggie could tell he was still worried. He seemed to acknowledge the fact that Red was right about the pond and that she was right about Connor. And he did try and make light of everything by suggesting an Uber. *So was he just saying that to end the conversation or was there something else bothering him?* She reached over and put her hand on his and he didn't even acknowledge it. *Something else is bothering him* she told herself. *I guess he'll tell me when he's ready.* She walked over and sat by Sable at the table.

" Maggie, try this merlot cheese and the garlic goat cheese. I think you'll really like them. They both have a very unique taste," she said.

The taste of the cheeses made Maggie even hungrier and she began to sample everything that was on the table. "Mango? Really? Who keeps mango in their house? Who does that?" Sable just smiled while Maggie took several bites of the sweet fruit.

"I'm sorry, Sable," Maggie said. "I know it looks like I haven't eaten in days, but everything tastes so good."

Wine and stress relief. Good motivators for hunger Sable thought to herself as she told Maggie to eat as much as she wanted.

"Can I have some too?" Sean said as he joined them.

"If you hurry," Maggie replied.

Sable laughed at Maggie hovering over the fruit while Sean reached for some cheese and crackers.

"Do you folks like barbeque?" Red asked.

"Yes, we love it."

"Why don't I order some racks of ribs and some fixings from Sconyers? It's a good restaurant, right up the road. I could get it and be back in about thirty minutes. How's that sound?"

"I've heard of that place. The people at work tell me that everyone needs to try Sconyers at least once," Sean replied.

"Yes, it's good. And even better, it's close by."

"Please let me pay for it," Sean said.

"I cannot allow you to do that. You are guests in my home. It is an honor to have you here with us."

"Don't argue with Wes Studi, Sean," Maggie said. "If you do, he may feel like he has to cut off a finger or something because you have dishonored him. And look at who you're talking to. You can tell he's the type of man that would do just that."

Sable burst out laughing as she looked at her husband. "Maggie, you are not right in the head!"

"If you only knew," Sean replied.

"Wes, I mean, Red," Maggie started. "Would you at least let us pay for something for our son? I'm sure he hasn't eaten and is expecting us to come home soon. But I'm envisioning a late night here. One of those hundred drink nights."

"Hundred drinks?" Sable asked.

"After four glasses of wine, anything I drink after that becomes a factor of ten. Sometimes during one of those nights, I may cross over into the shadow world, so just be aware of that," Maggie answered.

Sean looked at Maggie. "Some of us have to work tomorrow," he said.

"Yes, true. And we salute those that do," Maggie said as she took a drink of wine.

Sean smiled. *Ah,* Maggie thought. *A real smile. He'll open up. Just give him a little more time.*

"Why don't you invite him over here for dinner?" Sable asked.

"Thank you, Sable. That's a good idea. I'll ask him." She pulled out her phone and called him.

"How's it going over there?" Connor asked.

"We're having a good time," Maggie replied. "Thinking of getting some barbeque and wanted to know if you would like some? Come over and eat with us."

"Sounds good, but I just ordered a pizza. I thought you and Dad might be over there a while."

"You are a very clever boy."

"I bet you say that to all your sons."

Maggie laughed. "Not all of them. Just the ones who know how to get in and out of a pond safely."

Connor knew what his mother was doing. Saying that so his father heard those words. She hadn't told him about what happened with the alligator and she wasn't going to.

"Thanks, Mom."

"Yeah. See you later," Maggie said as she ended the call.

"Our son has taken care of himself. He's already ordered a pizza thinking that Sean and I may be out late," Maggie reported. Sean nodded his head and finished off his drink.

"Well, at least take me with you, Red," he said. "I'd like to see the place."

Sable poured Maggie another glass of wine and toasted to a hundred and together they laughed. Maggie bombarded Sable with questions and then apologized for doing so and blamed it on the alcohol. Sable didn't care. She enjoyed talking about her art and how she met Red in Montana. She talked about her first marriage and how they were still friends and had two grown children, both of them working in health care. One was a nurse and one was a physical therapist. They both lived in Montana and she said that she and Red try to visit them at least two to three times a year.

She asked Maggie if she had ever been to Montana and Maggie told her no, just as they heard Red and Sean return from the restaurant.

"You need to go with us sometime. It may be the most beautiful state in the country."

"Which one?" Maggie asked.

Sable laughed. "I guess I didn't say. How many glasses of wine have we had?"

"I think about sixty," Maggie replied and Sable laughed.

Sable got some plates and silverware and placed them around the table while Red put the food out on the bar. "The buffet is now open," he announced.

"You don't have to tell me twice," Maggie said. She picked up a plate and went along the bar taking a little bit of everything. "It smells delicious."

When they were all sitting down at the table, Red held up his glass of scotch. "To new friends, new experiences, and to finding new ways to celebrate life."

New ways to celebrate life, Maggie repeated in her mind. *It's as if he's saying, avoiding death is a reason for celebration, but I didn't tell him about the alligator almost killing Connor. It's like he knows though. Maybe it was the bird. Perhaps Red Skye, aka Wes Studi, is really an Indian Shaman. Even if he isn't, he sure as hell sounds like one.*

"Everything looks really good. Thank you," Sean said, tipping his glass to Red and Sable.

"You are welcome. Here let me freshen up that drink."

After dinner, Sean told everyone about the argument that he had to mediate earlier in the day between two of the directors at the hospital. As was the case with most arguments, this one was due to poor communication which led to a misunderstanding. But something interesting happened during that argument. Something he had never seen before. One of the directors starting yelling and when she did, the other one bowed her head and started to chant. He had never witnessed anything like it.

"Well, you aren't a chipmunk or a lizard, so I'm guessing the chant wasn't from a wizard," Maggie said as she took a drink of wine.

"Very astute observation," Sable said as she grinned.

"What was she chanting?" Red asked.

"I'm not real sure," Sean replied. "But I think it was something like OM, MANY, PADME, HUM, over and over."

"You have a good ear," Red replied. "That is a Buddhist chant. A mantra for the dissipation of negative energy or ghosts."

"Ghosts?" Sean asked.

"More likely, in this case, negative energy," Red replied.

"Good to know," Sean said. "I would hate to tell the CEO that we needed to call the 'Ghostbusters.'"

Sable laughed at Sean's comment but Red and Maggie didn't. Red smiled at the reference, but he thought back to the bird crashing into the window. He glanced at Maggie. She wasn't laughing and appeared to be concerned about what Sean had said. *She is thinking about the bird's death and the meaning of the chant. I can see it in her face and eyes,* Red said to himself.

Indian folklore, Buddhist chants. What else do you know, Red Skye? Maggie asked herself as she looked over at him. *It's really kind of creepy when you put it all together. Shit, just thinking about it all is going to bother me the rest of the night.*

And then there's the woman at the end of the cul-de-sac. The spoiled little princess, as Amos would say. And her Spanish minion that drives the blue truck. I'll have to ask Beth if he is a filet minion, Maggie thought and smiled. *She won't find that funny, but I do. Even funnier when I see the look on her face. He put the puss moths and the black widow in my house for you, didn't he? At a time when I am worrying about Connor capturing a goddamn poisonous snake with a fucking alligator stalking him. Fuck. Everything is going to shit.*

No, goddamn it. I won't allow all of this to grow into something it isn't. Connor is okay and I need to keep him from becoming concerned. He is already suspicious and trying to protect me. And you know that's how it begins. How it grows into an obsession with him and how things start to happen. Where accidental fires happen.

You can control all of this, Maggie. But tonight, you need to do what Red suggested. Celebrate life. Connor is safe tonight because of that crazy sweet man that lives across the street from you. You are safe. Sean is safe. That's all you need to think about right now. Steady the nerves and the anxiety with a little more liquid courage tonight. Let it help you find the switch that turns off all of the thinking.

"You don't have another bottle of that wine, do you?" Maggie asked as she looked over at Sable.

"Of course we do," Sable said as she got up. "We've only opened up two. We have a whole case of it."

"Then Sean was right," Maggie replied.

"Right about what?" Sean asked.

"About calling me an Uber," Maggie replied.

Chapter 19

Horoscope

Sean poured Maggie into bed when they got home. She was asleep by the time he took her shoes and pants off. "See you tomorrow," he said after he brushed his teeth and headed toward the guest bedroom. He didn't want to wake her up in the morning when he got up to run.

For several hours, Maggie didn't move. She didn't think. She didn't dream. She just lay there and breathed. And at times snored. Early in the morning, the images of yesterday started to appear like a kaleidoscope; at times distorted and at other times, clear and distinct pictures.

She saw the pond and then saw Connor standing in the water. She felt the water on her body and looked down. She was standing in front of Connor in the pond with the snake grabber around her neck. She could feel Connor pushing her backward in the water as he held onto the snake grabber with both of his hands. She reached up and tried to remove the clamps from around her neck but she couldn't. She tried to speak but no sound came out. The clamps were so tight around her neck that she could barely breathe. The alligator was coming up behind her. Connor had let go of the snake grabber and was now swimming toward the edge of the pond. She turned around to see the alligator's jaws open wide as she yelled, "No" and woke to find herself sitting on the side of her bed with a pillow wrapped around her head.

"Shit!" She put the pillow down and sat there for a moment, trying to catch her breath. As soon as she lay back down and closed her eyes, she was asleep again. The images faded in and out, but she found herself walking back toward the pond. As she got nearer, the image of her son standing in the water came into focus.

She saw the alligator to his right and ran to the edge of the pond. When she reached for him, his arm changed into a cottonmouth. She fell back onto the bank to avoid it as it lunged toward her. Connor said, "Get out of its way and you'll be fine," and she rolled over as the snake slithered past her. She saw Connor walking back to her and she yelled at him to hurry because there was an alligator in the water.

She then saw Amos pointing the gun toward her. She was waving her head no and pointing at the alligator when she heard the shots. A woman screamed and Maggie looked behind her as Beth fell backward to the ground. A knife was in her hand and both of her eyes were gone with blood spurting from the empty eye sockets. Maggie kicked Beth's body and as she did, Beth lifted her head and screamed. Maggie opened her eyes and saw that she had kicked all the covers off the bed. "Thank God," she whispered and told Him that she just wanted to sleep. As soon as she closed her eyes again, she heard a voice beside her.

"Why are you screaming?" it asked. "It's all your fault you know. I told you we needed to drain the pond."

She opened her eyes and saw Beth. She was laying beside her, on top of Sean.

"And by the way, if you're just going to come home and pass out, there will be others who will take care of your man for you," she heard Beth say as she watched her start to go down on Sean.

" No!" she cried and sat up. She looked over at the other side of the bed and saw neither Beth nor Sean and she shook her head.

"What the fuck?" She got up and drank some water before getting back in bed. *Just sleep* she said to herself and she thought about Sable and Red's art and tried to focus on that. "An S is just an S," she heard herself say over and over before she drifted off to sleep.

It was almost 9:00 before she woke up. She knew Sean and Connor were long gone so she just laid in bed for a moment and thought about the evening before and all the wine that she and Sable consumed. *It was a hundred-drink night for sure*, she thought as she rubbed the back of her head.

She remembered bits and pieces of the evening after Sean talked about the fight between the directors. She remembered Sean asking Sable about her red S and her asking him what he thought it was, just like she had asked her. Sean said that, for him, it represented the ebb and flow of the world. Red commented that was an interesting observation and she remembered how Sable told her that she got mad at Red because sometimes a tree is just a fucking tree. Maggie thought she preferred the way Red viewed the world. Maggie remembered kissing Sean on the cheek when he said that because she liked the way he viewed the world too, even though she didn't agree with him some of the time. And then she remembered the nightmares and shivered for a moment before she got out of bed.

She walked into the bathroom and looked in the mirror and heard the image that was gazing back at her.

"I'd advise you not to look in the mirror this morning," it said.

"Good advice." Maggie opened the drawer and pulled out her hand mirror. She suddenly realized what the hell she was doing.

I am looking at a mirror with a mirror in my hand because the mirror is telling me not to look in the mirror. How screwed up is that? That should be a good thirty minutes for a therapist, which by the way, I told Connor I was seeing. And that's not technically the truth. I did talk to Barbara about things though. I really did do that. I'll ask her for a recommendation for a therapist since she's been down that road herself and I don't want to lie to you, Connor. I never want to lie to you.

As she continued to look in the mirror, she blew into her hand and winced due to the smell. *Even though no one is here, you need to brush your teeth. Now. Wow, that's a lot of cheese and wine. And comb that stuff on your head that looks like hair and then you can go fix yourself some tea. That's a good plan.* She stuck out her tongue at the image in the mirror.

With a cup of tea in her hand, she sat outside by the waterfall. *It's as nice as Red's and in some ways even nicer* she thought as she admired the sight and the sound of the moving water. *I do like his little creek, but ours has more rushing water. More cascades. But they are both pretty.*

The longer she sat there and looked at the waterfall, the more she began to consider the things she wanted to avoid. She didn't want to think about her son down at the pond or the nightmares she had last night, but they were both at the forefront of her mind; swirling around in her head like leaves going toward the skimmer of the waterfall.

She saw her son in the pond with the snake and the alligator approaching. For the first time since it happened, she saw the blood spurting from the alligator's head when Amos shot it. She closed her eyes and saw the blood of the bird on the window and the dead blue jay on the porch. And she remembered what Red had said it represented: an obstacle in her life that she needed to overcome.

What does that mean? Maybe it meant allowing Connor to get the snake out of the pond. She hadn't wanted him to do it and it became a nightmare that she would never forget. But Connor was safe and she had been there with him, allowing him to do what he loved. *But how many more times will something like yesterday happen? There are a lot more ponds out there with alligators in them* and just the thought of it made her body shake. *And am I going to tell Sean what really happened?* She was afraid of what he would say or do but she didn't want to keep things from him. *A fucking obstacle. Check.*

Maybe it had something to do with Jorge. He was a thief and screwing someone who wasn't his wife. And the omen. The blue jay. That can't be a coincidence. It has to have something to do with him and Beth. Remember the words of the fortune-teller? The person in the neighborhood who doesn't like me. She said her name is Liz, short for Elizabeth, i.e. Beth. And that little bitch doesn't like me, that is for sure. And the other thing the fortune teller said. "The red sand will be a warning." There's a blue truck at the lake and the blood from the catfish is on the sand as it drives by. Then there's a black widow in my garage. Hello, red hourglass. Red sand warning.

Hell, Maggie, do you need one of them to come hit you over the head with a hammer? She remembered last night's dream with Beth coming at her with a knife. Her eyes gone; shot out by Amos. She couldn't get that image out of her mind. All she could do was say, "Obstacle. Yes. Check."

But were these truly obstacles, she asked herself. She wasn't sure. And she knew she needed to be one hundred percent sure. There could be no misunderstandings. Not this time.

"No misunderstandings and no mistakes," she said out loud. *And you must overcome these obstacles without getting Connor involved. You can't let him get involved. Not again. He must see you control your impulses. Control what you can control, Maggie. That's what you need to do and what Connor needs to see you do. That starts today.*

Maggie called Barbara and got the name of the therapist she used some time ago. Knowing how Maggie was, Barbara also warned her about the therapist's name - Dr. H. P. Nutt. It sounded like Maggie dropped the phone and picked it back up, laughing out loud.

" You have to admit, Maggie," Barbara said, "with a name like that, in the profession she's in, you have to be good at what you're doing or you'd never make it. Because once people saw your name next to the words 'psychiatrist,' they would just assume it was a joke."

"Truer words have never been spoken," Maggie said as she began to get her laughter under control.

Maggie was able to get an appointment with Dr. Nutt for the same afternoon, due to a cancellation and mentioning that Barbara had referred her. She opened her laptop and found her mailbox full of emails from her neighbors. With each one she opened, the smile on her face grew. There was only one dissenting vote, but even she said if the neighborhood agreed to paint the guardhouse, she would at least prefer a more neutral color.

Fuck that, Maggie said to herself as she framed her reply.

Sycamore Springs Homeowners:

Thank you for your input regarding painting the guardhouse. It looks like we are going to do some painting! I will get the paint this week. The weather for next weekend looks like it will be dry so we will start painting next Saturday. Thanks also to everyone who volunteered to help. And special thanks to Jennifer and Frances for the great color scheme. Looking forward to seeing everyone next Saturday at 9 a.m.   Maggie

She took her time getting ready for her appointment with Dr. Nutt. She had at least an hour and a half before she needed to leave so she poured some organic salts into the bathtub and relaxed in the lavender and jasmine-scented bubbles. She was reading about drought-tolerant plants in a new gardening magazine when she saw an advertisement for organic deer repellant. She laughed when she read the ingredients. Unified dog urine was the first on the list. *I don't know what unified dog urine means but I think it's just a fancy name for dog urine mixed with water. I really need to talk to Frances and Jennifer about going in together on a new product* and she laughed even more. She put down the magazine and closed her eyes for a moment, taking in the scent and the relaxing nature of the water. Her mind, however, could not relax and she was soon fretting about her meeting with the new doctor.

You need to be honest with her, Maggie. But how honest? I don't think we need to go into the fortune teller's predictions or the blue jay omen. Not at first. She'll think you're a complete nutcase. I guess that now I'm her patient, I am a nutcase. I wonder how many times she's heard that. But seriously, what do I say? You can talk about Connor if you need to but only if she brings him up. He saw a therapist and he is fine now, so you don't need to introduce that subject. But you do worry about him and you can tell her that. Yes, that should be okay.

Don't talk about Beth or Jorge either. At least not in this first session. Just talk about your depression. And your anxiety. That's all you need to focus on this first time. Yeah, that will be enough for today.

She had no trouble finding the University medical buildings and walked into the office with twenty minutes to spare. The receptionist was very friendly as she asked for her insurance card and the payment and then told her she would let the doctor know she was there. Maggie thanked her and sat down. She picked up a newspaper and glanced at the headlines before flipping to the comics and crossword puzzle page. She checked her watch and decided she wouldn't have enough time to complete the crossword puzzle. She turned the page to the jumble and the daily horoscope. *Well, stars and seers, what do you have to tell me today* she asked herself as she perused down the page and found her sign.

"Gemini – This is an important day for the twins. Don't dismiss the strange advice from a friend or the friendly advice from a stranger."

Well, that's pretty weird she said to herself as she read it and then read it again. *Here I am in the psychiatrist's office for the first time and you're talking me to about taking advice. Damn. Is Dr. Nutt my friend or a stranger? Oh shit. Now I'm going to be wondering about this the whole time I'm talking to her.*

"Hello, Maggie," she heard and looked up at a very attractive woman with her hand held out.

Maggie hadn't even seen her walk up as she was too busy thinking about the horoscope reading. Everything in her mind seemed jumbled now. *Stand up, Maggie. Hold out your hand* she heard her brain telling her.

Maggie managed to get up. "Hello," she said as she held out her hand.

"It's a pleasure to meet you, Maggie. I'm Dr. Nutt. Let's go into my office and get to know each other."

She seems very nice. What a nice way to introduce herself Maggie thought. Dr. Nutt offered her a chair in front of her desk. Maggie sat down and Dr. Nutt sat across from her.

"Hello, Dr. Nutt. My name is Maggie. Oh, wait a minute, you already know that, don't you?

'Yes, I do. But that's okay. Tell me about yourself. Maggie."

Think, Maggie. Remember what you can talk about and what you shouldn't talk about it. You are meant to be here. The horoscope suggested that. Yeah it did, didn't it?

"Well, I am 42 years old. Been married for twenty years. Got married right out of college to my husband Sean. We have a son, who is 16, soon to be 17, Connor. Born on October 31st, Halloween. Sean and I were going to a Halloween party that night and I was dressed up as the ventriloquist's dummy. It was a really cute costume, but we never made it to the party. On the way there, my water broke. We need to do that again sometime. The Halloween party part, I mean. Anyway, we just moved here about three weeks ago. I drive a 2016 Ford Explorer that I love. My favorite food is pizza. As is my son's. I like to make it as well as order it. Still trying to find the best pizza in town, but like I said we've only been here three weeks. Moved here from Florida. My husband is a hospital administrator. I love our new house. The neighborhood is so beautiful. We have a covered bridge and a beautiful pond right there at the entrance. We have a beautiful pool. I love spending time out there and by the waterfall. We have a waterfall right off the patio. I go out there each morning and have a cup of tea so I can listen to it. It's so peaceful. I like to stay in shape. I like good wine. I love having a good time with my friends and my family. Have met some really nice people in the neighborhood. In fact, one of them recommended you and though I know you can't talk about her, her name is Barbara. You can take it from there. So, there's that. And then there is the fact that I sometimes get depressed and have taken Zoloft in the past to help me with that," Maggie concluded.

"Maggie," Dr. Nutt said gently.

"Yes?

"You're not applying to be a game show contestant. You're here because you find that therapy has helped you in the past. I don't need to talk to the doctor who prescribed you Zoloft. I don't care what he or she may or may not have thought about you. What is important to me and what will be important for you should we go forward, is that you just come in here and talk to me about the things that are troubling for you. Things that you think you need help with. We all need someone to talk to sometimes and being in a new place can be difficult. You said you sometimes get depressed. Let's start there. When you say you get depressed, what does that look like?"

"I uh, get worried. Anxious. Afraid. Angry sometimes. Unwilling and not wanting to do things sometimes," Maggie replied. *Don't say obsessive. Don't go there yet. Think before you speak.*

"I think about things that are depressing and they worry me and I can't get them out of my mind," Maggie said. *Sounds sort of like I'm obsessive, but I avoided saying the word. Good, Maggie.*

"Like what?" Dr. Nutt prodded.

"Like dying or getting very sick. Debilitating sick. My son getting sick or hurt."

"You don't worry about your husband getting sick or hurt?"

Maggie looked at a picture of an autumn landscape on the wall as she thought about the question.

"No, I don't," Maggie finally replied. "Sean never gets sick. He's always there for me. Has always been there for me and Connor."

Dr. Nutt smiled at her.

"Well, thank you, Dr. Nutt. It didn't take long for that breakthrough. You are very, very good. It was a pleasure meeting you. Now, if you'll just give me that prescription for Zoloft for those times when I worry about myself or my son and get in a funk, then I'll just head on back home. Otherwise, I don't need it. Cured and ready to tackle the world." Maggie smiled.

Dr. Nutt chuckled as she looked at her. "Maggie, first of all you know it doesn't work like that. It's very comforting to hear that you have someone you can depend on and whom you've come to realize is always there for you. But Zoloft is not a pill that you can just take when you're feeling depressed. You take it all the time. That's how it works. The fact that you said what you did, tells me even when it was prescribed, you didn't take it as you should have," Dr. Nutt replied.

"Wow," Maggie said. "The horoscope was right and I don't believe in that stuff. Never even read it. But today. BOOM. I read it and then you tell me all this stuff that is so true about me. Like you are there looking into my soul. You don't have that ability, do you?"

"What did the horoscope say?"

"To not dismiss the strange advice of a friend or the friendly advice of a stranger."

"Sounds a bit like a fortune cookie to me."

"Yeah, it does now that you mention it."

"Did your previous doctor ever mention the word bipolar?" Dr. Nutt asked.

Maggie noticed the other pictures in Dr. Nutt's office. Lots of landscapes. All depicting a different time of the year. A different season. *I wonder if that was intentional* Maggie asked herself.

"The pictures on your wall represent the different times of the year. Did you choose that on purpose?" Maggie asked.

"Yes, I did. That's very astute of you to notice." Dr. Nutt replied. "We all go through change in our life. The seasonal pictures represent that to me. And remind me of it. I am not the same person I was in my twenties. Nor the thirties. Or the forties and we will just stop there on the timeline. You get the picture - no pun intended. I'm not the same doctor I was when I first started my practice. Back then, you couldn't tell me anything that I didn't know. But now I understand that I don't know everything. I learn something from someone every day. Every day. Isn't that amazing that we all have that gift? The ability to learn something every day and to grow from that?"

"Yes."

"Yes - it is amazing that we all have that gift to learn each day or that your previous physician discussed what the effects of having a bipolar personality meant?" Dr. Nutt asked.

"Both," Maggie agreed.

"Thank you, Maggie," Dr. Nutt said as she looked at her and smiled. "One last question about your previous physician and that will be all I ask about him. How often did you meet?"

"At first once a week, then it went to twice a month," Maggie answered.

"How about you and I see each other once a week for a month and then go from there?".

"Yes, that would probably be a good idea."

"And I'll write a prescription for Zoloft, but you have to promise me to take it every day. Agreed?"

Maggie nodded her head as Dr. Nutt wrote the prescription.

"And I will know. I do have the ability to look into your soul. I am a psychic as well as a physician."

Maggie's eyes opened wide and then she laughed as she saw Dr. Nutt stand up and smile. "Just set up a time with the receptionist that is convenient for you."

"Thank you for today," Maggie said.

"I look forward to seeing you again."

"Just before I go," Maggie started. "I need to ask one thing. Did you ever think of changing your name? I mean, come on. You had to be kidded mercilessly as you were growing up. And then when you became a doctor. A psychiatrist, no less."

"It's funny but I never did," Dr. Nutt answered her as she walked over and opened the door. "I found it made people laugh when they heard it and I was okay with them laughing. Even at my expense. It never bothered me, I just laughed along with them. It started many a conversation with people who may never have even bothered to talk to me otherwise. I bet it had something to do with you coming to me today when your friend told you about me. Didn't it?"

Maggie nodded her head. Though she had only talked with Dr. Nutt for thirty minutes, she was becoming quite impressed with the perception and demeanor of the woman.

"I'll see you next week, Maggie." Dr. Nutt then looked at her receptionist. "Just work with her calendar, Janice."

"So, what kind of schedule did you and Dr. Nutt want to set up?" Janice asked.

"Once a week for a month and then we'll go from there."

"Okay, how about Thursdays at 1:00?" Janice asked but Maggie didn't hear her as she read the diplomas.

"Damn you, Barbara," she whispered as she shook her head.

"Excuse me?" Janice said.

"Oh, I'm sorry," Maggie said as she looked down at Janice and took the appointment reminder. "I was just thinking of my friend Barbara and something she told me, or should I say neglected to tell me. On purpose, I may add. I'm fine, I'm fine," Maggie said as she turned around and walked out.

She couldn't stop laughing as she thought about Barbara and the name she had read on the diploma. *H. P. Nutt. Hazel Penelope Nutt. Hazel Nutt. Damn you, Barbara,* Maggie said to herself as she laughed. She sat for a moment in the car and retraced her meeting with Dr. Nutt. *It was a good meeting. She seemed very perceptive and friendly. And I didn't say anything that would raise a red flag about Connor. I protected him.*

It was interesting how she made me aware of how I think about Sean. She's so right. I never worry about him. I just think he will always be there for us but that's so unfair. I sort of take him for granted. I'll do better with that. Which means I have to tell him about the alligator. I'll do that tonight. We'll get to the other obstacles at other sessions but I feel like I can share stuff with her and she won't judge me. She just wants to help me. I can talk to her about Jorge and Beth, provided I don't make things up about them. You aren't a hundred percent sure that they have done anything to you so you need to keep that to yourself for now. All you know about them for sure is that Jorge is a thief and Beth likes to screw around and is a control freak. Everything else is just conjecture. But you will know. You'll soon learn everything you need to know about both of them. Then you can tell everyone.

Thank you for the advice and the referral, Barbara, she thought as she backed out of the parking space and headed home. *And thank you for the surprise - the name. I think I may have peed on myself.* "Hazel Nutt, psychiatrist," she said out loud and laughed again.

Chapter 20

Buffet

Connor had called right around three and told his mother that a friend had invited him over to hang out after school. When she wanted to know more about this new friend, he told her that he had a green iguana and several snakes that he wanted to show him. His name was Sam Nixon and he met him in science class. He told her that he lived in Pepperidge subdivision, which wasn't too far away from them. As he started to hang up, Maggie asked, "How are you getting home?"

" His dad said he'd bring me. He drives a Chevy truck." As soon as he said those words, Connor realized that his mom's mind would go into overdrive and he needed to provide some more information. Fast.

"It's a red Silverado with black interior," Connor added. "They're big Georgia fans. They have a University of Georgia license plate and get this, a 'Hunker down Dawgs 'sticker on the rear window."

"I'm not sure I can allow him to park that truck in our driveway," Maggie replied. "You do understand I went to Auburn and that your father went to Tennessee?"

"Yeah, but is Georgia really worse than Florida? You know the place where we lived and just moved from?"

"For me, yes, for your father, no. Okay, you dodged a bullet on that one." Shit. *Gators. Amos. Bullets. The nightmare about Beth. Impossible to suppress that imagery I suppose.*

"What did the teacher say about your black widow that scared the shit out of your mother?" she asked.

"He didn't get to see it. I dropped the jar on the way to class and the only thing I could do at that point was kill it. If it had jumped on someone, or if anyone had seen it, I would have been labeled the weird kid or something even worse."

Maggie heard the words and she wanted to reach through the phone and hug her son. She could still hear the pain in his words from his past. He was still holding on to parts of it or they were holding on to parts of him. She wasn't sure which was true, but she knew she needed to say something to make him think about something else.

"I haven't told you this, and I don't know why, but guess what my therapist's name is?"

"Freud," Connor answered quickly.

Maggie laughed. "Good one, but nope. It's Nutt, spelled with two t's.

"I don't think the two t's matter. Really, a Dr. Nutt is your therapist?"

Maggie could hear him laughing. "It gets even better. It's Dr. H. P. Nutt."

"Peanut. Now you're just making things up," Connor said as he continued to laugh.

"Nope. And here's the kicker, the H is for Hazel. Dr. Hazel Penelope Nutt."

"Hazel Nutt. Shit, mom. With a name like that, she has to be the best therapist in town."

Just what I said Maggie said to herself. *He thinks just like me. He is so much like me.*

"She is good. We had a very good session today. I'm looking forward to seeing her again."

"That's great Mom," Connor said. "I'm proud of you."

Maggie felt the tears welling up in her eyes. "See you later, son. Have fun." Maggie said. "And Ditto." She stood there with the phone in her hand crying. Connor wouldn't like her telling Sean about the alligator but she wasn't going to lie to Sean anymore. Connor would have to just work through it. After the initial shock, she knew Sean would let it go. Especially when he heard that she was seeing a therapist again. *Even if her name does sound like a cartoon character* she said to herself as she wiped away the tears and smiled.

The next day, Emiliano received a call from Beth to let him know she had eight more people interested in talking to him about caring for their yards. The lawns were smaller than those in Sycamore Springs, but he could probably still charge $100 for each of them. Emiliano thanked her several times and Beth said that she expected a big gift when he came to see her next week. He said he would bring her one and she replied "Yes, I know you will."

He began calculating the money he could make from the eight new customers. With those new yards and the yards he was already doing, he figured that he would have about $1400 per week in cold hard cash. *Cold hard cash, hombre* he thought and pumped his fists into the air. This was the most money he had ever made. And he didn't have to share it with anyone. Not even the government, since as far as they knew, El Parque didn't exist. He wanted to celebrate. And he knew exactly how he was going to do that.

That weekend, he went to Emiliano's Park. This time as he drove by the guardhouse, he threw a quarter instead of a penny into the empty box.

"We need to make some improvements around here," he said as he drove by the empty building and laughed. He parked his truck in one of the many empty parking spaces. He carried his cooler, two large Subway sandwiches, and a bag of Jalapeno-spiced potato chips over to one of the picnic tables. He popped open a beer, looked up into the sky, and said, "Salud!" as he took a long drink. He looked around at "his park," took another long drink and the first of many Budweisers was empty. He got another beer from the cooler and began eating one of his sandwiches.

The potato chips weren't spicy enough for him, but they would have to do for today. He told himself that in the future, he would need to bring the jalapeno dip that his grandmother made. He thought he remembered how to make it but if he didn't, he was sure Luna did. Perhaps he would even invite Luna and her children to his park. *Perhaps.*

The Italian sub with the hot peppers tastes good he thought *and complements the wonderful nuances of the beer.* He laughed as he imagined Beth and her snooty friends saying something like that as they lay next to their pool drinking wine and snacking on different kinds of cheeses that were probably imported. *Fuck that shit. I know fancy words too, Princesa.*

"I am not the idiot that you think I am," he said out loud as he took a drink.

Emiliano thought about his life and the way his luck had changed. The anger inside of him had subsided since he had lost his job. He felt different now. The bag of briquettes within his gut was still present, but the bag was over half empty now and the combustible material on what remained, was becoming less and less volatile.

He liked coming and going as he pleased. He liked being his own boss. Setting his own time. Owner of his own company: El Parque. It even sounded like a real landscape company and he was proud of the name and his work. He was free. Out of prison. When you have spent over half of your life in prison, being out meant something. He knew that now and had never appreciated his freedom more than this moment in time. *Look around you, Emiliano. You even have your own park,* he thought as he laughed.

He was working hard but he enjoyed it because he was doing it for himself. He was going to be making enough money to get his own place soon. *You were in the right place at the right time, this time. You saved the Princesa and her Nina Pequena and you were rewarded with $2000 and your own company. Free and clear.*

With the thought of the words "free and clear," he hesitated. He heard Maggie talking to him and Beth about seeing the spirit of the woman's house he was in that night. He remembered the presence now. At first, he thought it was the spirit of his grandmother. But he knew it was not his grandmother when she told him that she hoped the money would help him. The voice he heard did not have a Spanish accent. She may have guided him out of the house, but he knew that wasn't what Maggie saw. She saw his flashlight. She saw him and she wanted him to know that. For the first time since he had been released from prison, he felt unsure of his actions and his behavior.

You cannot go back to prison. You say you don't want to go back to prison, but what you are doing is saying something else he thought as the argument took place in his head. *You know that. Your luck will run out sooner or later. And when it does, you will have two choices, and neither of them will be good ones.*

Do you really want to kill someone now, like Beth is suggesting? Maybe when you were younger. You were angry and stupid then and could have killed someone without thinking twice about it. You were lucky it didn't happen. Maybe when you were in prison. Yes, you could have killed someone while you were in prison, but you didn't have to. Again, you were lucky. You know if you kill someone now you'll be looking over your shoulder for the rest of your life or you'll be dead. Dead and buried or a dead man living in a 6 x 9 cell. Living in a tomb with bars for the rest of your life.

The world owed me and it still owes me, he said to himself as he sneered and took another swig of beer. Then he heard another voice, the stronger voice inside of him now, asking a different question. *Why does the world owe you anything? Just because you were born poor? Your parents came here to give you a better life and they got killed for doing so. They told you to work hard so that you could make it. But they were killed by people like you. People who were angry like you. People who thought the world owed them something. The kind of person that is still inside of you and still angry. The person that now scares even you.*

Think, Emiliano. When your parents died, your grandmother and your aunt tried to help you but you didn't listen to them. You were too angry and thought you were too smart to listen so you pushed back. But they loved you anyway. Luna still loves you. She wants to see you succeed. You know that. Deep down, you always knew that. But you haven't shown her that you know that. You've never thanked her or told her that you care about her.

Buying pizza one day for the family doesn't cut it. But do you remember seeing the look on her face when you paid for the pizza? She was proud of you. And that made you feel good, didn't it? She thinks you're turning your life around but you're just fooling her. And you're fooling yourself too if you don't really change.

You killed the old man's fish because you think he got you fired. You put puss moths and a black widow in the woman's yard. Quit calling her 'the woman.' You don't like it when people refer to you as 'the Mexican.' Use her name. It's Maggie and you've done things that could have harmed her. In fact, they did harm her. But they didn't kill her. You got lucky again, Emiliano.

You did those things because you were angry and thought you needed to send a message. And then you do things because Beth is telling you to. Why are you doing everything Beth tells you to do? She doesn't give a shit about you. The only thing she's done is given you access to people who would not have even looked at you otherwise. She opened some doors for you. But she will close them too if given the slightest reason, even if that reason didn't make sense to anyone but her. She lives in her own world. You've pulled back the curtain on just a small part of it and you already know that in that world, she has her own rules.

Think about it, man. She makes you shower before you touch her. And she makes you fuck her from behind. She doesn't want to see you. She just wants to live out some fantasy she has in her screwed up mind. She wants control of you. Wants? Hell, she has control of you. She tells you to tie her up and fuck her because she knows she can say whatever she wants and you will do it. You are just a faceless dick that she wants up inside of her.

"Chingate, la puta!" he yelled as he drained his beer. He got another one and sat down on the shore, continuing to consider all the things going back and forth in his head.

After you've taken care of these eight new yards for a while, and they can see your work, you need to get away from Beth. Because she is no different than the guards in prison. In her heart, in her mind, she is no different than them. And just like the guards, it will not be easy for you to get out from under her control.

He saw something moving out of the corner of his eye. A snake was swimming toward him. He jumped away from the shore as its body zigzagged in a straight line across the top of the water. He watched it go right past where he had been sitting without even giving him notice. It swam into a dark corner of the shore and disappeared into the grasses and reeds that were growing there.

"Serpiente de algodon. She doesn't care what is in her way or if you are here or not. It appears I must share the park with you," Emiliano yelled out as he pulled another beer out of the cooler and walked back over to the water.

"That's okay. I'll stay away from you, but you must stay away from me. Comprendes?" Emiliano removed his shoes and walked back down to the shore and waded out into the water up to his stomach. He held his hand up as he sank into the water until it covered his head.

He climbed out of the water and went back to his truck for his cousin's sleeping bag and his .38 revolver. He put the sleeping bag on the ground at the base of a big oak tree and then walked back to the shore and continued to drink his beer. He carried the revolver with him.

"I stay away from you and you stay away from me." Again and again, those words echoed within his ears and off his eardrums as if they were drum sticks.

"Idiota!" *The words meant more than just sharing the park with the snake,* he thought as he hit his forehead with the palm of his hand. It was then that he smelled something familiar. The same sweet smell that made him nauseous the other night. Though he couldn't see anyone, he knew the old woman was there.

Before he could say a word, he heard a voice in his head that he recognized. It was not the woman's voice that he heard before. This voice had a familiar Spanish accent.

"Idiota es verdad," the familiar voice said.

"Abuela?"

"Si, su abuela and su amiga. Estaba contigo la otra noche. Se llama Sarah. Sarah Cayman. Le debes muchas gracias por el dinero and la senal."

Emiliano shivered as he felt a breeze come up out of the water and seem to encircle him. He listened to his grandmother tell him that she and Sarah Cayman were there. It was Mrs. Cayman who was with him in the house. His grandmother said he owed her many thanks for the money. And for the sign that she just sent him.

"Si Abeula, si. Many thanks, Senora Cayman. I now have two voices that I hear inside of me, eh? Espero no estar loco," he said and paused for a moment.

"No, I'm not crazy" he continued and smiled. "I hear both of you and I see it now. The Princesa. The serpiente. They are sisters, eh? I understand now."

He felt the presence of his grandmother and her friend leave, but he was okay with that. He now understood what he needed to do. He no longer needed to argue with himself. He knew what Beth would do when he told her that he would not see her anymore. She would be angry; she would show her fangs just like the cottonmouth. She would call her friends and make up some reason for them to fire him. Or something worse.

Will you also tell them that I was fucking you and that I wanted to stop it? Will you tell them that I put poisonous bugs in a neighbor's yard because you didn't like her? No, I don't think so, Princesa. Because you are much more devious than that, aren't you? If I ever brought that up, you would say that I raped you. And who would they believe in your world? Of course, it would be you. Because there are rules within your world and you control them.

I understand, Princesa. I know what you'll do but I have seen you now. I know where you are over there in the weeds. I know if I go near you, I will need some protection. Something that will prove to everyone that I'm telling the truth. I'll record us the next time we're together. And then we'll have our talk. When I'm ready to get away from you and have a real chance to reclaim my freedom.

He sat down with his back up against the trunk of the large oak. The sun was hot but there was a breeze coming off the water and it felt good in the shade of the old tree. He placed his head against the rolled-up sleeping bag and put the revolver in the middle of the bag. *A few more beers before a siesta Emiliano, and then you can watch the sunset. Yes, that will be good,* he thought and then closed his eyes.

He did not dream. He was asleep but still aware of his surroundings. Prison had taught him how to do that. It was a necessity in there if you were going to stay alive and uninjured. Twice he had awakened just in time to keep someone from harming him. The fact that he beat the shit out of the person who was trying to hurt him, both times, was also significant. The display of that kind of awareness and power within prison was very important. In fact, it saved his life.

When Emiliano awoke, the sun was starting to set. Bueno, he thought as he looked at the beautiful orange and creamy blue sky.

"It will be a beautiful sunset tonight," he said as he looked down at his hand. It was still holding the half-empty beer that was there when he went to sleep. He poured it out because he had plenty more in the cooler. He had brought enough for the entire day because he hadn't planned to drive home that evening. He could not risk getting a DUI and he knew that he would be too drunk to drive after consuming an 18-pack. No, tonight he would watch the sunset, eat another sandwich, and finish his beer before he put his sleeping bag in the back of his truck and turn in for the night.

He opened the cooler and got out another cold beer. "Muy hermosa," he said and raised the beer toward the sky. He wandered over to the shore again to get a better view of the sunset and paused for a moment to take off his shoes. The grass felt good on his feet and he smiled as he edged closer to the bank.

When he looked down at the water, he dropped his beer. There was a dead body halfway out of the water and resting on the sand. The other half, still in the water, served as a decomposing buffet for the bluegill, perch, and sunfish that were swimming around it, tearing away at the pieces of flesh that were clinging to the bones and resembled small, discolored, and enticing thread-like worms.

As his eyes scanned the body, they soon came to where the head should be. There wasn't one; only shoulders and a neck. An eel swam out of the neck and back around the body as it disappeared into the green water. He glanced around the lake and back at the park. He didn't see anyone but he knew he needed to leave. If he was drunk, it would only be detected by blood alcohol percent. From any other aspect, he was now visibly sober.

He left his shoes off. He instinctively understood it would be better if they found a footprint rather than a shoe print. He packed everything back in the truck and used a large branch to wipe away as much of his footprints as possible as he walked backward toward the truck. He checked once more before he left and saw nothing that would indicate he was ever there. He started the truck and drove away thinking that he would never be coming back to Emiliano's Park again.

Chapter 21

Moonbeam

As he drove back to his aunt's house that evening, Emiliano remembered the other dead bodies he had seen in his lifetime. Two of his friends had been shot dead in an alley; both of them with several bullet holes in their bodies and one in the middle of his forehead. While he was in prison he had seen an inmate have his throat cut from ear to ear. He thought he had become immune to seeing dead bodies but the one he had just seen unnerved him.

It looked like something from a horror movie. A blueish-black-white monstruo made up by the special effects department and sprinkled with fish food to encourage the fish to swarm around it. He couldn't get the image out of his mind as he tried to concentrate on the speed limit and make sure that he wasn't doing anything to attract attention with his driving. He had driven in worse shape before and it was the image of the headless body that was much more distracting to him tonight, rather than the eight or nine beers that he had consumed earlier that day.

The dead bodies he had seen before were all meant to send a message to those that found them. He couldn't help but wonder if this body wasn't a message too. Telling him what his future would look like if he didn't find a way out from under Beth's control. He broke into a cold sweat and pulled into the nearest convenience store parking lot to gather himself.

"Dios mio," he said as he looked up into the rear-view mirror. *Was the body even real,* he asked himself, *or something he imagined? An image of the future? A future where he killed Beth and cut her head off and dumped her body in the lake? I am talking to spirits. Spirits of the lady in the house and of mi abuela. They tell me things. Tell me that the serpent is Beth. And then you see the dead body. What is happening?*

"Espero no estar loco," he whispered as he dropped his head to the steering wheel. He repeated it several times before he glanced back to the rear-view mirror. His heart stopped for a moment and he sat up straight.

The Richmond County police car pulled up behind him and the officer walked into the store. Emiliano knew that he looked suspicious just sitting in his truck. He needed to do something.

Think, Emiliano. Think. He kept his eyes focused on the rear-view mirror. *Maybe he didn't see me when he went in. If I lay down, out of sight, he'll just see a parked truck. The owner in the store buying something.* He surveyed the parking lot. There was his truck, the police car, and a couple of other cars. *It's possible.* He locked the truck doors and slid down into the seat until he was not visible.

He would be in trouble if the policeman came over and looked in the truck. He needed an excuse and just hoped that he wouldn't be able to smell the alcohol. He pulled out the jalapeno chips and shoved them in his mouth as fast he could. And he waited.

He kept listening for the police car to start but he didn't hear anything. *Maybe he's still in the store drinking coffee or chatting with the store clerk*, he told himself. *I need another plan. This isn't going to work.* Then he heard the tapping on the driver's window and saw the policeman standing there. One hand was on his revolver and the other on his flashlight that he shone into the truck.

"Un momento," Emiliano said as he started to feel around on the floor.

" Got them," he said as he held the keys in his hand and put the bag of chips on the seat next to him. He rolled down the window and smiled as he looked at the officer.

"Evening sir," the officer said. "How are you doing tonight?"

"Fine, fine," Emiliano replied.

"What were you looking for?"

"My keys – I dropped them."

"What have you been up to this evening?" the officer asked.

"Just got back from fishing at the lake."

"Really? Did you catch anything?"

"No, not this time."

"Where were you fishing?"

"In a little cove, just off the bank. Not sure what the name of it is or if it even has a name. Just right off the road," Emiliano replied.

"Do you have a fishing license?" the officer inquired.

Fuck. If he lied about the license it would only lead to more questions. He needed to tell the truth and hope for the best. Fishing without a license wouldn't put him back in jail. He hoped.

"No sir, I don't," Emiliano admitted. "I was just going to release if I caught anything but all I got were little nibbles."

"Can I see your driver's license?"

He pulled out his license and handed it over. The officer focused his flashlight on it and then back at Emiliano's face before giving him back his license.

"Well, you need to have a fishing license even if you catch and release, Mr. Martin," the officer said. "You'll get one before you go fishing again, won't you?"

"Si, yes sir," Emiliano replied.

"Next time try Wildwood Park. You'll catch some fish there, I promise you. Have a good evening now," the officer said as he turned and walked back to his car.

Emiliano watched the officer drive off with his heart pounding in his chest. Though he didn't feel the spiritual presences with him while he was talking to the officer, he knew a miracle had occurred, because he didn't shit all over himself. He wiped the sweat off of his head with his arm and slowly pulled out of the parking lot.

On any other night, he would have been going to jail. He was legally drunk. He didn't have a fishing license but told the officer he was fishing. If he had asked him if he had been drinking or asked him to open the cooler, it would have been all over. If he had asked him to get out of the car and then conducted a drunk test Emiliano knew he would have failed. The officer didn't even check his name for prior arrests. *What is going on,* he asked himself.

He called me Mr. Martin. He didn't treat me as just another drunk illegal alien. He didn't act like I was a felon who had just gotten out of jail. Tonight none of that mattered. He just asked some questions and told me to have a good evening. He asked himself how that happened over and over as he shook his head. *The world is telling you something, Emiliano* he said to himself as he pulled into his aunt's driveway. His aunt and her two children were just finishing up dinner when he walked inside.

"I didn't expect you back so early," his aunt said. "I thought you were going to spend the night at the lake."

He just shrugged his shoulders. He wasn't sure what to say considering everything that had occurred earlier.

"Are you hungry?" Luna asked. "I can fix you something."

"I have a sandwich in the car," Emiliano replied. "I forgot to bring it in, but I'm not very hungry."

Luna sensed there was something wrong and she told her children they could finish their dinner in the den and watch tv because she wanted to talk to their cousin. She was only ten years older than Emiliano but when he looked at her now, she seemed to be much older. More like her mother; his Abuela.

Just like her mother, Luna had her children late in life. She was thirty-seven years old and Emiliano's cousins were now thirteen. He had been in jail since they were babies, so they had never had much of a chance to get to know him. He had been fine with that up until now, but tonight as he watched them get up from the table, he wanted to reach out in some way.

"I've got that sandwich from Subway out in the car. Would either of you want it for your lunch tomorrow? I'm not going to eat it. It would make a good lunch," Emiliano offered.

"Sure!" Charles replied enthusiastically.

"Good, I'll put it in the refrigerator for you." He smiled as he turned around to go get the sandwich. "And thanks for letting me use your sleeping bag, Charles. I only used it to take a nap. It made a very good pillow," Emiliano said as he walked out the door.

When he came back in the children were gone and Luna was waiting for him at the table.

"Sit down, Emiliano. What is wrong, Sobrino?"

"Nothing."

"I can tell when you're lying. I inherited that ability from your grandmother. You know you were named after her, don't you?"

"What?" Emiliano asked.

"Your father was very close to our mother, your grandmother. She raised me and your father, pretty much on her own. She couldn't depend on your grandfather. He was gone much of the time. We found out much later that he spent a lot of time in jail for various crimes. Drugs. Theft. Drunk and disorderly. The list goes on and on. Unfortunately, you inherited a lot of his blood and it worried your parents and your grandmother in an awful way. And the way you were living your life when you were younger," she said as she looked down and shook her head. "Tus anos mas jovenes fueron horribles, Emiliano."

Luna leaned forward and placed her hand on her nephew's cheek. "But you also inherited the blood of your grandmother, Emilia. She was a very strong woman. Una mujer muy fuerte. Always working or taking care of us. She didn't have many material possessions in her life, because she spent all her money taking care of me and your father. She was a good soul. Your grandfather, amigo con el diablo," Luna said.

Emiliano had never known that. His father had not told him and he had never thought of his grandmother as anything but his Abuela while he was growing up. And by the time he was in the fifth grade, none of his family meant much to him anymore. He was too busy doing things with his friends that he didn't want to share with his family.

"Did you lie about having your own company? Is that what you want to tell me?" Luna asked. "Please don't tell me you stole that money. Are you hiding from the police? Whatever it is, tell me now, Emiliano. Tell me the truth so that I can help you."

Emiliano wasn't sure what to say. He wasn't sure what he had seen today. If that body was real, he would be the prime suspect if he told anyone about it. That scared him because he wasn't sure if anyone would believe him. Then he remembered the policeman at the store. He believed him. For the very first time, a policeman had given him the benefit of the doubt. But even when that occurred, it happened when he wasn't telling the officer the whole story. Because he understood what would happen if he told the truth. He would go to jail for a very long time, maybe even the rest of his life.

Now he was sitting across from his aunt as she asked him what was wrong and he still didn't know what to say. He knew what he should say, but he couldn't bring himself to do it. After all, he still wasn't sure if he had seen a dead body. Or the serpiente de algodon. Or had talked with dead people. He wasn't sure if he was just scared or crazy. He felt like he was perhaps both at that moment and telling his aunt that he found a dead body at the lake didn't sound like a very good idea. Not then. Maybe later, when he was sure of what was happening.

But he had to say something. The longer she looked at him, the more his skin felt like it was burning as if she had thrown boiling water on him. His skin was hot and he wasn't sure he could withstand the way it felt for very much longer. If he didn't say something he would just start screaming. And then if he started screaming, the image of the mad man would be complete. Neither one of them would have to wonder anymore as to what was happening.

"Who is Sarah?" Emiliano asked.

Luna sat back in her chair when she heard the question. She seemed stunned and sat there speechless. Eventually, she got up and retrieved a picture from her bedroom. She placed it on the table in front of him.

"Look at the picture, Emiliano," Luna said.

He picked it up and saw two older women with their arms around each other, standing in front of some rose bushes. His grandmother died while he was in jail, but even though he hadn't seen her for a long time he still recognized one of the women in the picture as his Abuela. The rose bushes looked familiar too.

"Do you recognize your Abuela?"

Emiliano nodded yes.

"The woman standing next to her is her best friend. Your grandmother worked for her for thirty years and though she was her employee, that woman treated your grandmother like she was part of her family. She gave me enough money to buy this house. She protected your grandmother from the police because she was never a legal citizen. Her name was Sarah Cayman. She died just days ago. Her niece is arranging a memorial to scatter her ashes at Lake Thurmond. She and my mother spent a lot of time up there. Picnics and such. Your father and I often went with them."

Emiliano's eyes widened as he looked at Luna and then back at the picture. He said nothing but the tears streaming down his face told his aunt more than words ever could. She put her arms around his neck and let him rest his head on her shoulder.

"I want to change," she heard him whisper. He couldn't see her face, but she was crying too. Crying and smiling as she hugged him. Hearing those words changed both of them that night. Luna was never more proud of her nephew than she was that night and a bond was formed between them. Luna now believed that her nephew had a real chance for a good life.

Chapter 22

Ashes

Luna wiped away her tears as she looked into his face. What she couldn't see but knew she felt was that a different Emiliano was sitting across from her. "Why did you ask about Sarah?" Luna asked.

Even though he now trusted his aunt more than ever before, he still wasn't comfortable telling her about the spiritual encounters at the Cayman house or the lake. He couldn't bring himself to tell her that he had gotten that money from breaking into Mrs. Cayman's house either. Or say anything about the dead body. No; encounters with ghosts and headless bodies were not something he was ready to discuss with anyone. Even his aunt.

"I mow her lawn," Emiliano said. "I do not charge anyone for it. The neighbors in her subdivision asked me to do it for a sick lady." As he started to talk, Emiliano realized there was a way to discuss this with his aunt.

"They told me her name was Mrs. Cayman," Emiliano started, "and I didn't think anything about the name, but as I was going around the house, mowing, edging, I felt something strange. As if there was someone there - watching me, smiling at me. I had never felt anything like that before."

Luna made the sign of the cross across her chest and smiled at her nephew. And before she could ask, Emiliano continued with a version of a story he was comfortable sharing.

"I felt that same presence out at the lake today. As I was sleeping. I even thought I was talking to Abuela. She said she was there with her friend, Sarah. That's why I came home early. When I woke up I remembered everything, like they were both there, sitting and talking to me. I thought I might be going crazy. Talking to ghosts is not something you share with many people. When I was out on the streets or in prison it would have gotten me killed. In those places, people who talk with the dead, end up dead. It frightens the people around you. And even though I didn't feel threatened by hearing their voices or feeling their presence, it still scares me to talk about it with you now. The things you learn in order to survive, are not something you are quick to give up."

"They are with you, nephew," Luna replied. "They are with you now for a reason. You told me that you wanted to change. That is because of them.

They are telling you that you need to change and for the first time, you are listening. I wouldn't be surprised if they didn't send you a sign of some sort, telling you what to do or that will mean something to you."

Emiliano could see the image of the headless body and the snake. He saw the eel crawling out of the body and he wanted to shut his eyes to block out the image, but he knew he couldn't do that without prompting more questions from his aunt that he didn't want to answer. So, he just nodded his head as if he understood what she was saying.

"How about some bunuelos?" Luna asked. "You said you weren't hungry but perhaps something sweet would taste good? I learned how to make them from Emilia."

Emiliano smiled. His grandmother's bunuelos. He hadn't had those in twenty years. "Con un gran vaso de leche?" he asked.

Luna smiled. "Yes. With a big glass of milk, my Emiliano." She liked saying those words, "my Emiliano," and she repeated them several times in her head while she prepared the dessert and milk for her nephew.

The next morning, Emiliano got up early so that he could have breakfast with his cousins. He chatted with them about school and what their favorite subjects were. Charles and Angela enjoyed talking with their older cousin and Luna smiled as she listened to them. She reminded them that they needed to leave soon and hurried them off to brush their teeth.

"What do you plan to do today Emiliano?" Luna asked.

"I have eight new clients to call on. A woman in the Sycamore Springs neighborhood has been very helpful to me. She lived across from Mrs. Cayman. I stopped her from stepping on a copperhead and ever since, she has wanted to help me build my business," Emiliano said.

"Is she married?" Luna asked.

Emiliano knew that wasn't really the question she was asking. She wanted to know if he was sleeping with her. "Yes, she is married. Has tres ninos," Emiliano said as he smiled at Luna and continued to talk before she could ask any more questions about Beth.

"With these eight new yards, that is if they are willing to hire me, I will have 16 yards that I am taking care of. I will earn over $1400 each week, Luna. That's money we can use to find a better place to live," Emiliano said as he stood up and took his cereal bowl over to the sink.

Luna smiled at Emiliano. "Oh, wouldn't that be wonderful? But you know you can stay here as long as you want to."

"Si, yo, si, but you and your family deserve more and I want to help." Luna hugged her nephew and told him good luck as he walked out the door.

The eight prospective clients were all in the North Ridge subdivision in Evans. When he drove into the neighborhood Emiliano realized that although the homes were large, they were very close together, in some cases, not more than twenty to thirty feet apart. Their lawns were small, but they all had beautiful shrubs and flowers so he knew they cared about the landscape. Beth said he should be able to get $100 for each yard. He wasn't sure that was possible unless he promised to make sure their shrubs and flowers also looked good year-round.

He knocked on each of the eight doors and complimented the homeowner, telling them how attractive their house and yard were. He explained that he was in the lawn-care business and had been given their name by Beth Stevens, who could vouch for his work. He would do his best to keep their yard immaculate all year. Seven of the eight agreed to his price of $100 per week and two of them even asked if he could start that day. Emiliano said he would be glad to do so.

He worked very hard on those two yards, making sure the lawn was cut and edged perfectly. He hand-pruned the hedges, spent time pulling up weeds from the flower beds, and raked the mulch so that it was neat and orderly around the trees and shrubs. When he was finished, both women were very complimentary and said they looked forward to working with him for a long time. Emiliano was happy as he drove back to the pawnshop to look at some more equipment. There was a hedge trimmer there that he wanted to buy and he began to think about how he could get more work without relying on Beth. *I need to advertise somehow. Maybe Luna could help me make some flyers that I could tape on the mailboxes in the subdivisions. Yes, that's a good idea.* When he got back to Luna's he began sketching out a design of how he wanted it to look.

He texted Luna and asked her if he could take them all out to a Mexican restaurant this evening to celebrate the seven new yards he got today. Luna sent a happy face emoji to him along with the words: "Estoy muy orgullosa de ti." Emiliano smiled when he read that she was proud of him.

She also said they would have to go out another time since it was a school night and she would be getting home late, but if he wanted to pick up some food for everyone that would be great. They loved the food from Veracruz on Peach Orchard and she asked him if he could find it. He didn't bother to remind her that his company was formed all because of a neighborhood off Peach Orchard and he was sure he could find it.

When the children came home from school, Angela spotted Emiliano's crude drawings for his flyer idea on the kitchen table. She asked him what he was doing and he explained his idea to her. She surprised him when she said she could help. She turned on the computer and asked what he wanted on the flyer.

"I want a picture of a home with a beautiful landscape, like one you'd see on tv, a million-dollar home."

Within a few moments, Angela found what he was looking for by searching on Google and the HGTV website. 'Now, what do you want the flyer to say?"

" Beautiful yards need beautiful work."

She looked up at him and shook her head and laughed. "The first part is good," she said, "but you need something else to say at the end. What about: 'Beautiful yards don't happen by accident. They require hard work. Let...' What's the name of your company?".

"El Parque," Emiliano answered.

"Let El Parque do the hard work for you. Call 706-830-0205 and ask for Emiliano," she typed. As soon as he saw his name in print he knew he needed to remove it. At least for now. For now, he was still Jorge.

"Just put the phone number," Emiliano said. "We'll go from there."

"Sure. Mama always says not to give out too much personal information – you can't be too careful! I think you should get some colored paper to print these on," she added.

"Can you show me where to find some?" he asked.

"Sure," Angela replied. "Walmart or Target would have some," Emiliano remembered seeing a Walmart on Peach Orchard.

"Good, then why don't you and Charles come with me and we could stop by Veracruz on the way back and pick up some dinner?"

"We love Veracruz!" Angela exclaimed.

"Yes, your mother might have told me that," Emiliano chuckled.

When they got back home, they ate dinner and then Angela printed off a hundred copies of the flyer for Emiliano on bright orange paper.

"Es perfecto! That should get people's attention!" Emiliano said as he hugged his cousin. When Luna got home a little later, he showed her the posters and told her how much Angela had helped him. He warmed up dinner for her and she and Emiliano talked as she ate. She told him stories about his father and mother that he had either forgotten or had never known. She also talked to him about Emilia and how much she meant to her and his father. There were many times that she heard Emilia tell his father that he needed to be patient with his son and that he would turn out okay.

"When she died and you were in jail, it broke my heart. But I always remembered her telling your father that," Luna said. "It's why I let you move in with us after you were paroled. You were angry when you got here, but you have changed. You have changed because of su Abuela. She still looks out for you."

He went to sleep that night thinking about how nice the flyers looked and how things had changed. He looked forward to tomorrow and the growth of his company, but when he dreamed, the monsters returned. He saw the body at the lake again. He saw himself drop his beer and rush to load up the truck. As he looked around the park one last time before he drove away, he heard someone tell him everything looked fine.

When he turned back, the body was there in the cab with Beth's head on the wrinkled blue shoulders. He collapsed against the door when he saw the head fall into the lap of the dead body and heard Beth say, "Oops!" The eel crawled out of the neck and dropped onto his lap and he fell out of the truck. He found himself on the floor next to his bed, with his arms flailing at nothing but the dark. He looked at the clock on the table beside his bed. It was 4 a.m. He got back in bed but he didn't close his eyes. He wasn't going to be able to sleep anymore so he just waited for the sun to come up so he could go to work.

He wasn't looking forward to going to Sycamore Springs this week but at least he now had a plan for what to do about Beth. He wished he could just tell her goodbye today but that wouldn't be smart. He still hadn't actually cut all those new lawns and he needed them for his company. The money was too important for him and his aunt. He couldn't have Beth stopping him before he got started. He wouldn't let her do that to him. He arrived at Beth's a little after nine. She was waiting for him in the downstairs den. Naked.

"What do you think, Jorge?" she asked.

"Muy hermosa," he said as he smiled and felt for his phone in his pocket. He had set the video function key before he got out of the car so it would capture everything from the beginning.

"Very beautiful is the right answer," Beth replied. "Shower is on. Ready for you and me. Today we take a shower together, only we might use our tongues more than a washcloth. What do you think?"

I think that is a load of shit he thought but he just smiled as he hoped the phone was capturing the audio. He knew he would not be able to take any pictures today. They went into the shower and he did everything Beth told him to. And just like women had told him for years, his dick had a mind of its own and it went into every place Beth wanted it to go.

When they were getting dressed, Beth smiled as she admired his firm body.

"You know with that body, you could be a porn star," Beth said. "Did you ever think about doing something like that instead of mowing yards?"

"Remember, no nasties," he said as he pointed down at his groin.

"I did say that, didn't I? Well, maybe one day," she said as she started to go up the stairs.

"Beth," Emiliano said as she turned back toward him. "What do you know about Mrs. Cayman?"

"I know she smoked a lot and she's dead," Beth said in a disinterested way. "I didn't like her and I don't think she liked me. Why are you asking about her?"

I'm sure she didn't like you Emiliano thought but he didn't say anything as he tried to think of an answer for Beth's question. Before he could answer she stepped off the stairs and came over to him. "You did something to her house. I knew it!" Beth said. "You robbed the old bitch, didn't you? Show me how you do that! Show me how you break into houses."

"I didn't break into her house. I just remembered that woman, Maggie I think was her name, mentioning the funeral. That's all. I'm cutting her yard for free. I just wanted to know about her."

"That's a lie. You just want to know when would be a good time to break into the house again. When most of the neighborhood is gone to a funeral; would that be a good time?" she asked.

Emiliano smiled. He said nothing and hoped the smile would be a sufficient answer for Beth. It was.

"The funeral is tomorrow. Her niece is doing a memorial for her at two o'clock out at Thurmond Lake. And if I see your truck over there tomorrow at that time, I'll be coming over to watch you work. Even though I don't want to smell all that damn smoke," Beth said as she turned around and walked away.

He listened to the recording when he got back to the truck but it was garbled and very difficult to even hear Beth's voice. "Fuck!" he yelled as he deleted it. *Next time, Princesa.* He sent a text to Luna telling her that the memorial for Mrs. Cayman would be tomorrow at 2:00. She answered him saying she knew that and asked how he found out. He reminded her that he cut her neighbor's yards and some of them were talking about it.

Luna replied that she planned to attend and asked if he wanted to go with her. He told her that he would like to and would see her later. He didn't get home until almost seven that evening as he added several of the new North Ridge yards to his schedule. He had realized he didn't have anything appropriate to wear to the funeral and was about to get cleaned up and go out shopping when Luna came home. She took him upstairs and showed him one of his father's old suits that she had hanging in her closet. "He always thought he looked fly when he wore this suit!"

Emiliano laughed at the thought of his father saying something like that. He tried on the suit and it fit perfectly.

"Just need to get you some shoes tomorrow, but after that, then you'll be looking fly too!"

While driving to the memorial service Luna told Emiliano about going to the lake with Sarah and Emilia. As they got closer to the lake, Emiliano didn't hear much of what Luna was saying. When she turned into the Essie May Washington Branch State Park entrance, he felt himself getting sick to his stomach.

"I can't tell you how many times we came out here," Luna said as she drove her car up the road and to the guardhouse.

This time someone was there and he asked them if they were attending the memorial and Luna told them they were. Emiliano was sweating heavily as Luna pulled in to park. "Are you okay?" she asked. She handed him some napkins from the glove compartment.

Emiliano nodded his head yes and wiped the sweat off of his forehead.

They got out of the car and headed toward the group of people gathered in the middle of the park.

"Thank goodness they're in the shade," Luna said. There were about twenty folding chairs lined up in rows, with one chair at the front beside a small table that held the urn. Emiliano noticed several men in maintenance uniforms acting as if they were working. He knew they weren't maintenance men. He could spot a policeman a mile away and he knew those men had to be cops. They were there looking for the killer to return to the scene of the crime. He hadn't heard anything on tv or the radio about the body, but he knew they must have found it.

Luna walked up to the young girl at the front of the chairs and hugged her as she told her how sorry she was about Sarah. Luna introduced Emiliano to Sarah's niece, Savannah.

"You're the nice man taking care of my aunt's lawn, aren't you?" she asked.

Emiliano nodded his head.

"Thank you so much for that," Savannah said as she took Emiliano's hand in hers.

As soon as he touched her hand, he smelled the sweet sickening smell of the little white balls, and he tried to not get sick.

"I'm sorry for your loss," he said quietly as he stood and listened to Luna and Savannah talk about her aunt and Emilia. He concentrated on not getting sick as he listened and then Luna took him by the arm and led him to the chairs to sit down.

He looked around at the other people there and saw many people from the Sycamore Springs neighborhood but he didn't know their names. He recognized the Bartholomew's and Maggie and her family. When he saw Maggie, he looked away quickly and didn't dare look up until he and his aunt sat down. Emiliano knew he needed to leave as soon as the service was over because he didn't want his aunt talking to her or anyone else from Sycamore Springs and asking who Jorge was. He wasn't ready to discuss that with his aunt.

Maggie was startled to see Jorge and wondered what he was doing there. *Who is that woman he's with? Why were they talking to Mrs. Cayman's niece?* She looked around to see if Beth was here and wasn't surprised when she didn't see her. *Maybe he isn't who I think he is* Maggie thought. *Maybe he really does have a conscience, even though he is screwing Beth. That lady he is with seemed to know the niece and they appeared to be friends. I'll find out some more after the service* she said to herself.

At exactly two o'clock, Savannah sat in the chair beside the table and placed an iPod into a wireless speaker that no one had even noticed. The sounds of Aretha Franklin singing "Think" soon filled the air, followed by "Natural Woman," and finally, "Amazing Grace." After that song, Savannah stood up smiling.

"My aunt loved listening to Aretha Franklin. I think she had every album she ever made and she made a lot of them. I bought this iPod when she was having trouble getting around so she could have it right by her bed and believe it or not, she would put her earbuds in and she'd go where she could go, listening to Aretha Franklin. She loved this lake too. She had a lot of good memories of this place. She loved coming here and having picnics with her best friend, Emilia Martin, and her children. She was a simple woman who enjoyed simple pleasures. Unfortunately, two of those simple pleasures happened to be tobacco and scotch and she wasn't going to ever give either one of them up. She was a generous person and gave hundreds of thousands of dollars to charity. Always anonymously. In fact, she would not be happy with me sharing that information today. She never wanted anyone to know. She thought everyone deserved dignity and respect and the ability to enjoy the simple pleasures of life.

"She never suffered from not having her loved ones around her, and to Emilia, Luna, and Jorge, I wish to thank you for that. You were like family to her. She wasn't one for long speeches and she didn't want a lot of fuss at her funeral. She told me to just cremate her and put her out in the trash with the other ashes that were all over her house. She said the body wouldn't mean anything to her then and she would enjoy that smell one more time. Well, Sarah, I don't smoke but I am willing to light one up for you today and if anyone else wants to, feel free, as I take her ashes to the lake and scatter them into the water she loved." Savannah pulled out a pack of Camel non-filters and lit one up as she picked up the urn and walked toward the shore.

Everyone else got up and picked up a cigarette and though most of them didn't light it, they carried one with them as they followed Savannah. Emiliano was still sweating as they reached the very place where he had seen the body even though he knew it wouldn't be there. He watched Savannah open the urn and toss the ashes onto the water. They swirled around in the air before falling onto the water and floating for a moment before they dissolved and disappeared.

Savannah tossed the cigarette into the urn and Luna laughed at what many would have considered irreverent if they didn't know Sarah.

"She would have liked that," Luna said approvingly when Savannah rejoined them. Beads of sweat were on Emiliano's head as he stood next to his aunt and Savannah told Luna that she needed to get him home because he didn't look well. Luna agreed and told Savannah that they would be in touch and Savannah said, of course, they would.

Maggie watched Jorge and what she assumed to be Luna walking away. *Well, I guess now isn't the time to ask him about anything. Must have been named after his father*, she thought. Maggie began to consider the possibility that he may not have been breaking into Mrs. Cayman's house that evening. *Perhaps he had a key.* She had never thought of that. *But he didn't turn on the lights. If he had a key and was supposed to be there, why wouldn't he turn on the lights?* She didn't know but told herself she would find out.

Luna looked at Emiliano and asked him again if he was okay. He nodded his head that he was as he wiped his brow one more time.

"Did you light up your cigarette?" Luna asked as she started the car.

Emiliano shook his head no.

"Goodness, I sure smell smoke in here," Luna said as she rolled down her window. "Must have been that cigarette that Savannah and a few others smoked. Or maybe just from Sarah's ashes."

Emiliano didn't smell smoke, but he detected a faint whiff of the sweet-smelling white balls, and this time it didn't smell that bad.

Chapter 23

Savannah

The color started to return to Emiliano's face and the cold sweat that enveloped his body disappeared as they headed back toward town. He had never expected to return to Emiliano's Park and was trying to piece together in his mind how all of this had happened. His park was the very same place that his grandmother and father and aunt had come to when they were young; their favorite place. *How could that just be a coincidence? It can't be* he told himself. *It can't be.*

"You look like you're feeling better," he heard Luna say and he nodded his head.

"Yes," Emiliano replied. "I don't know what happened but all of sudden I just got a sick feeling in my stomach."

"Lo se sobrino," Luna said.

Emiliano turned and looked at her.

"Tus padres funerals."

Luna was right. He hadn't been to a funeral since his parents died and he had never even given another thought to that day until now. Memories of that day were like old cans of paint, dumped in a corner of the garage and forgotten about. But now he began looking for those cans of paint and as he found them and pried the lids off, images of the service came back to him.

He had stood between Luna and his Abuela as people came over and offered their condolences. His silence and lack of response to their nice words were excused because they all knew he was distraught over his parent's death. But they were wrong. The silence and expressionless look on his face were due to the fact his parents were killed and he was afraid more people would also die. Perhaps he would even die, but that had always been a possibility with the criminal lifestyle he had chosen. He just never thought it would kill his parents, but then he reasoned, in their neighborhood anything was possible.

He remembered there was so much food after the service and then he remembered those rose bushes. The buffet table was set up in front of those rose bushes. All of the food, all of the people; they were there in Mrs.

Cayman's back yard after the funeral. The rose bushes were much bigger now and there were more kinds of roses but he remembered them. The roses had glowed with color and filled up his nose with their scent. He now remembered the nice house and all of those people eating, while he went off into the woods and smoked a joint. Perhaps the enhanced color and smell of the roses were influenced by the marijuana that day. Maybe. But it didn't matter. What mattered is that he remembered. He had been in that yard half a dozen times since he had gotten out of jail and he had never recognized it. It had been just another lawn to mow, but he now knew it was a place that mattered.

His aunt watched her nephew as she continued to drive. He seemed to be lost in thought after she mentioned his parent's funeral. *Maybe he is remembering something about that* she thought. *But wait a minute. He said he was taking care of Sarah's yard. And that he felt strange when he was there. As if someone was watching him. There is more going on here than just pure coincidence. How does all of that just happen?* And then it hit her. *It doesn't.*

"Today, at the lake, where we went, that is the same place where you always go, isn't it?" Luna asked.

"Yes," Emiliano replied.

"La madre, Mary y Joseph," Luna said as she made a cross over her chest.

"Emiliano," Luna started. "Do you understand what is happening? You are being guided by el espirito. I told you they were with you for a reason and I'm more convinced of it than ever. You are taking care of Sarah's house. You come to the lake at the same place where Sarah and su abuela came with me and your father. This is not a coincidence. There is a spiritual connection you cannot ignore. No estas loco. There is a reason they are with you, guiding you. And I know you are trying to listen to them. Do not ignore what they are telling you, sobrino."

Emiliano nodded. He wasn't sure about the degree of sanity that he currently possessed because of everything that was going on, but maybe Luna was right. *Maybe, I'm not crazy and the dead body in the lake was not real, it was just a sign. That had to be what happened because if there was a dead body out there yesterday, that place would have still been a crime scene today. They wouldn't have let us in there to have a memorial service.*

They wouldn't have wanted people in there destroying potential evidence. But if all of that was true, then why were the police there disguised as maintenance men? It doesn't make sense. They were there waiting. Watching. Looking for signs that someone there knew something about the body. That someone there was maybe the killer.

Damn this. Being paranoid sucks, but paranoid keeps you alive. Kept you alive on the streets and in prison. So, man, you just have to work through this. Help me, Abuela.

As they pulled into the driveway and Luna parked the car, she turned and looked at her nephew and took his hands in hers.

"I know you are still trying to understand what is going on. But you're being given another chance at life, my Emiliano. Do not waste what is being given to you. The spirits forgive you!" she said as she reached over and kissed him on the cheek.

She deserves to know everything, he thought as he followed Luna into the house. *She accepts spiritual presences and influences as normal. Just a way of life. But he wasn't ready to tell her everything. How could you be rewarded for the bad things you have done? Are still doing. The voices you hear. It appears you've developed a conscience since you got out of prison and it will haunt you forever if you don't make changes. The voice of the old woman and su abuela. They will not be your friends if you don't change.* He saw an image of himself standing over the dead body that was bent over the couch in Beth's house. Her head was again on its shoulders, except this time it was on the body backward, smiling at him.

"I really liked that idea of the black widow. Nice touch, but next time, don't use the jar. Now fill me up," Beth's head said as it twirled around several times like the girl in the Exorcist movie. He hated that movie. *Stupid fucking movie* he thought as he went to his room and laid down. Luna looked in on him once and then closed the door. She knew he had a lot to think about and she didn't want Charles or Angela bothering him when they got home.

After the service, Maggie watched as Jorge left with that woman who seemed to know Savannah very well. Sean was talking to Phil and Barbara when Barbara noticed that Maggie was focusing on something else besides the conversation.

"Isn't that the guy that cuts the yards in our neighborhood?" Barbara asked.

"Yes. His name is Jorge," Maggie replied.

"Jorge?" Barbara asked. "Do you think…" and before she could finish her thought, Maggie completed it for her.

"Yes, I'm pretty sure the woman he was with is the same person that Sarah's niece referred to as Luna," Maggie said. "And I'm guessing that Jorge was named after his father and that Emilia that she spoke of was their mother. So that would make Luna his aunt."

"Small world isn't it, Inspector Holmes," Barbara said.

"Sometimes too small," Maggie said as she watched them drive away and look back at Barbara. She didn't even respond to the Inspector Holmes reference and Barbara wondered what was bothering her. She received the answer as soon as Maggie spoke.

"Where is Connor?" she asked to no one in particular. She was just speaking out loud as she looked around the park but didn't see him.

"He's over there by the shore," Sean replied. "Looking around in the weeds as he likes to do."

"For God's sake, this is a memorial service, Sean."

"Yes, it is, Maggie, but Connor isn't doing anything wrong."

"He should be over here with us. He should give his condolences to Mrs. Cayman's niece."

"Calm down, Maggie. I'll go get him. Excuse me Phil, Barbara," Sean said as he walked away.

"Why didn't the Thompsons come?" Maggie asked as she looked at Barbara and Phil and everyone else that was standing in line to talk with the niece. "Did the niece ever mention her name? I don't recall her doing that."

"Her name is Savannah," Barbara replied. "Very nice girl, well, young woman. I think she just graduated from the Medical College. I believe she is a nurse."

Maggie nodded her head as she saw the Bartholomews talking to Savannah. "I see Jennifer and Ulf and Agathe and Red and Sable, but I don't see the Thompsons or the Stevens family," Maggie said. "I should have asked Amos to come with us," she said as she continued to look around.

Barbara looked at Phil and shrugged her shoulders as Maggie appeared to be taking the attendance roll for the neighborhood. "I'm not sure, Maggie." Barbara wasn't going to speculate on why anyone didn't come. She didn't feel it was necessary and she could tell it would only make Maggie more agitated than she already seemed.

"Are you okay, Maggie?" Barbara asked.

"Yes, I'm fine. I just think the neighborhood should all be here. I knew Beth wouldn't come and it's my fault for not asking Amos to attend, but…" she said as her voice trailed off.

"Sorry, Mom," Connor said as he walked up. "Hello, Mr. and Mrs. Gillespie."

"Hey, Connor. Why don't we go speak to Savannah now?" Barbara asked and took Phil by his arm. Maggie, Sean, and Connor followed behind them.

Sable stopped to talk to them as they passed each other. "Beautiful ceremony," she commented. Everyone nodded in agreement and smiled except Maggie. She was watching Jennifer, who was talking to Savannah.

" Savannah is a sweet girl," Jennifer said as she met her neighbors in the receiving line. "I wish Frances could have been here. But she's in Washington and just couldn't get away. She liked Sarah very much. She used to check in on her. Made sure she was clean and didn't have bed sores. Tried to stop her from smoking but that was like telling someone to stop breathing."

Yes, she should have been here, Maggie thought. *And why in the hell didn't the Thompsons come,* she asked herself again. *Oh, wait a minute. Beth knew Jorge was going to be here. She couldn't be here with him and her husband both. I see that now.*

Ulf and Agathe said hello to everyone as they walked by them and Maggie was glad to see Agathe wasn't wearing her penis necklace. *Thank God she doesn't have one of those for all occasions* she thought. Or maybe she did and had it hidden under her blouse. She made a mental note to ask Barbara about it later. Maggie listened to Barbara and Phil talking to Savannah and heard them tell her goodbye as they turned and walked away. She heard Sean introducing themselves to Savannah and Maggie knew she needed to regain her focus. She looked into Savannah's face and smiled.

"I'm very sorry for your loss," Maggie said as she took Savannah's hand. "She sounds like she was quite the independent woman."

"She sure was," Savannah replied. "Right up until she went in the hospital. She didn't let an oxygen tank hold her back. If she wanted to go someplace, she would. Frances was so nice to her. Took care of a lot of her medical needs. And Luna, what a saint."

"Was that Luna and her nephew?" Maggie asked. "Earlier. Right after the service. Talking with you?"

"Yes," Savannah replied.

"How well do you know them?" Maggie asked.

Sean looked at Connor and nodded toward the car. Once his wife had that answer, he was going to make sure they were turned around and walking back to the car.

"I've known Luna since I was a little girl. I just met her nephew today."

"It was a beautiful service, Savannah," Sean said. 'Your aunt would have been proud of you. We wish you peace and comfort. I'm just sorry we never got a chance to meet her."

Savannah nodded. "Thank you for coming."

"Savannah," Maggie said as she felt Sean squeeze her hand. "Do you know if there were any break-ins at your aunt's home since she's been in the hospital? Have you noticed anything missing?"

Sean couldn't believe Maggie's questions and was becoming embarrassed. He looked to Connor for some help, but Connor also seemed interested in what his mother was asking. *Shit,* Sean said to himself. *She's putting thoughts in his head that he doesn't need to have. God damnit, Maggie.*

"No, not that I am aware of. Why do you ask?"

"I just couldn't sleep one night and went out for a walk. I thought I saw someone in her house."

"Oh, no! Did you call the police?" Savannah asked.

"No, I didn't."

"Why not?" Savannah asked.

Maggie hadn't anticipated that question. She was expecting Savannah to tell her that her aunt's home had been broken into. And then Maggie would tell her that she saw Jorge in it. But now, how was she supposed to respond?

"Would Luna's nephew have had a reason to be in there?"

"Maybe. Luna had a key and she may have asked him to check on things. Is that who you saw?"

"Yes, I'm sure it was," Maggie replied.

"Then I'm sure it was something that Luna asked him to do," Savannah said as she smiled.

"Was Emilia Luna's mother?" Maggie asked.

Sean could do nothing now but just watch his wife. He knew he couldn't stop her. He had been in this type of situation before.

"Yes. She and my aunt were friends for over thirty years."

"Wow, that's a long time," Maggie replied. "I wonder why you never met her grandson before now?" Maggie asked.

Sean raised his hand and covered his eyes. *What in the hell are you doing* he wanted to scream but he knew he couldn't. It would only make matters worse now.

Savannah just smiled as she looked into Maggie's eyes. "I'm not sure, but thank you for coming," she said as she picked up the urn and headed for her car. When they saw her leaving, the men who Jorge thought were policemen began folding the chairs and loading them into a truck. They worked for the funeral company.

When they got in their car, Sean turned to Maggie. "What in the hell was with all the questions? You complain about Connor but what you were doing was much more inappropriate."

Maggie wasn't going to respond. She would just sit and silently allow Sean to chastise her. By the time they got home, he would have everything out of his system and they could talk again. She could tell that the Zoloft that Dr. Nutt had given her was helping even though she was still analyzing Savannah's responses while he talked. But at least she wasn't arguing with him. *That's an improvement* she said to herself.

Why was that the first time Savannah had met Luna's nephew if they were such good friends? She was avoiding answering the question. I bet she really knew the answer but didn't want to say. Luna's mother was Sarah's friend for over thirty years and she never met her grandson? Seems unlikely. Plus, it doesn't make sense for him to have been in Mrs. Cayman's house without turning on the lights. It's not like there wasn't electricity to the house. She was still in the hospital. She wasn't dead yet.

I still think Jorge was in there looking for something to steal. He's not an honest person. Savannah doesn't know much about him because he's the black sheep of the family. Probably just got out of prison or something like that. That would certainly be a good reason why she hadn't seen him. Prison. Of course, that's it. And I'm going to find proof of that. I bet there's a website where you can get that information. I'll ask Jennifer about it. She's a lawyer. She would know.

I bet he killed Amos's fish, too. And regardless of what Connor says, I still think Jorge put the puss moths and black widow in our yard. To frighten and to hurt me. Hell, he is screwing another man's wife. I know I am right about him. I know I am. You'll see, Sean. One day you'll see what I have known for some time. The predictions from the fair. The omen of the dead blue jay. And I hear you, Sean. Connor hears you too, so be careful of what you're saying.

I wonder if Savannah was named after the river or the town. She's a pretty girl. I bet she's a good nurse too. Seems to have the right demeanor to be a nurse. Caring. Sensitive. Level-headed. Good communicator. She seemed nice too, Maggie thought as she heard Sean in the background listing all the things she shouldn't have said at the funeral.

Chapter 24

Listening

Connor listened to his father argue with his mother but it was a one-sided argument this time. She wasn't responding to anything he was saying. He understood why his mother had asked Savannah those questions. She was suspicious of Jorge, the man who drove the blue Chevy. It frightened her when she saw him in the neighborhood and again at the lake. How much of this was just an obsession and how much of it was a true concern, he didn't know. But someone put a black widow in the garage and it wasn't him, no matter what he told his mom. Someone put salt in Amos's pond and killed his fish. And he was pretty sure that the puss moths didn't just crawl into their mailbox on their own. *But what does all of this have to do with the talk? Remember she changed after the fair. You need to keep searching for the answers, Connor.*

"Dad," Connor started. "Don't you find it somewhat odd that Savannah had never met Jorge until today if Luna and her mother were such good friends with Mrs. Cayman?"

Maggie wanted to smile when she heard him ask the same question but she knew she couldn't. Sean would become even more annoyed. She also knew hearing Connor asking that question was a double-edged sword. She knew what he was capable of when he felt she was threatened. So did Sean. And the question from Connor rattled him. She could tell by the look on his face as he tried to explain away his son's question.

"There could be all sorts of reasons," Sean answered. "Family reasons that we aren't aware of. Just because she was meeting him for the first time today doesn't mean something sinister was going on."

"Yeah, I know, but did you notice how he looked?" Connor asked.

Where are you going with this? Maggie asked herself. *What did he see that I didn't see?*

"What do you mean?" Sean asked.

"He was very sweaty and looked kind of nauseated. And when he saw mom, he looked away, like he didn't want to be seen," Connor replied.

He saw that Maggie said to herself. *He saw it too. I should have known. He becomes more aware each day. More like me.*

"It was a funeral service," Sean replied. "Some people never feel comfortable in those situations. It isn't easy especially if they were very close…"

"But," Connor interrupted. "She said she had never met him until today."

"You didn't let me finish," Sean said. "What I was saying was if they were very close, or something bad happened to them in the past, or they are even going through a tough time now for some reason. It doesn't have to have anything to do with Mrs. Cayman. Perhaps something traumatic happened to him as a child. Or to his parents. Jorge's father wasn't there so something might have happened to him. The thing is, we just don't know. People are very good at hiding things that have happened to them. Bad things. I've seen it over and over again at work. You wonder how the employee was even making it to work each day considering what was going on at home. It's really sad sometimes."

Maggie knew Sean was right and she should say something to support what he was saying. To keep Connor from becoming even more suspicious.

"Your father is right," Maggie said. "I shouldn't have asked those questions at the funeral. It wasn't appropriate."

Connor knew that was his mother's way of telling him to let it go, so he did. He didn't ask any more questions, but he was determined to be even more vigilant when he saw that blue truck in the neighborhood.

The next day, Maggie sent an email reminder to the neighborhood about the guardhouse painting project on Saturday. She had the paint and she asked people to bring paint brushes and rollers if they had them. They would start at 9:00 in the morning and there would be a cook-out at Jim Thompson's house later that evening, beginning at 6 p.m. She also thanked everyone for attending Sarah's memorial service and said she wished she could have gotten to know Mrs. Cayman before she died and that she was sure she was looking down on everyone there yesterday, probably smoking a cigarette. She placed a smiley face emoji with a halo over its head at the end of the sentence and sent the message.

She closed her laptop and smiled as she thought about Beth fuming when she read that last little comment. *Serves her right. She should have been there at the memorial service, but you knew she wouldn't come. She doesn't respect the living. Why would you think she would respect the dead? I wish I could've seen how she interacted with Jorge and his aunt though. That would've been fun to see. Perhaps another day* she said as she changed into her swimsuit and went out to the pool.

She tried reading the gardening magazine she had bought last week but her mind kept wandering. She kept going back to her last session with Dr.

Nutt. They had talked a lot about her family, particularly Connor. How smart he was. How he was fascinated by all the creatures that walked or slithered through the woods or water. How he had captured the water moccasin and released it at the lake. Dr. Nutt asked her if she was scared when he did that, and Maggie remembered smiling and looking around the room as she tried to think of how she should respond.

She nodded her head yes as she told her about the alligator. She was terrified at first but later, when Connor was safely standing in front of her, her fear turned to anger and she wanted to slap the shit out of him for risking his life over a damned cottonmouth. Dr. Nutt told her those were normal feelings considering what had just taken place and then asked Maggie how Sean reacted when he heard about it. Maggie sheepishly admitted she hadn't told him. At that moment she realized Dr. Nutt wasn't like her previous therapists. She didn't politely chastise her for not telling Sean or even ask her why she didn't tell him. She just sat and waited for Maggie to continue talking.

As Maggie proceeded to tell her about Amos and going to Sable and Red's, she soon realized she needed to steer the discussion back to Sean and the alligator. She preferred talking to Dr. Nutt about her reluctance to tell Sean about the alligator than share with her what Red said when the blue jay flew into the window. So, she said she had only told Sean that Amos had shot an alligator in the pond – not that it was going after Connor when he shot it. She knew he would overreact and want to drain the pond right away and he even mentioned doing that very thing that night when they were at Red and Sable's house. Even though she thought Sean realized you can't put a protective bubble around the pond, she knew he would go ape-shit crazy when he learned Connor was in the pond and if Amos hadn't been there, she wasn't sure what would have happened. She then heard Dr. Nutt's questions as if she was sitting there next to her at the pool.

"Do you think Connor would have been killed?" Dr. Nutt asked.

Maggie hesitated for a moment and then replied. "I don't know," she said as tears welled up in her eyes again.

"Maggie," Dr. Nutt said, "You trust your son. That's evident because you allowed him to get in the pond. He was retrieving a dangerous snake. Not many people can do that. From what you tell me, he is very smart and confident about the animals in the wild. You said he was the one that told you what to do with the puss moths, which, by the way, will make me go home and spray my yard, thank you very much. I would have been happy in my ignorant bliss without ever hearing about those nasty things, but you have ruined that now."

Maggie remembered laughing when she heard that.

"But the key here is that you trust your son," Dr. Nutt continued. "I would imagine your husband does too and because you both do, I think it would be good for everyone to discuss this as a family. I'm sure you don't want to keep secrets from Sean and I'm sure Connor doesn't either. It's unhealthy for both of you and unfair to both Connor and Sean."

Maggie heard herself telling Dr. Nutt she was right and thanking her for her advice. She had left the therapy session knowing that she was going to tell Sean about the alligator, with Connor present to answer any concerns that Sean was sure to have. She would be happy to get that "obstacle" out of the way.

Dr. Nutt was wrong about one thing though. She did need to keep some secrets from Sean and even Connor. They didn't need to know about the signs she had heard and witnessed. Neither of them needed to know about the dead blue jay. She was doing what both Dr. Nutt and Red told her to do. Removing an obstacle from her life. She still needed to work on the other obstacles in her life. She needed to gather all the correct information before she took any action. She could not allow herself to be wrong this time. She was too afraid of what she would lose if she made an error in judgment.

Maggie cooked one of Sean and Connor's favorite meals for dinner that night – chicken smothered in shallots. She enjoyed making it. It was one of those dishes she had perfected and it always turned out well. Sean recognized the smell as soon as he walked in the door from work. The aroma made him smile and also feel a bit curious.

"What's with the special dinner?" he asked as he got a beer from the refrigerator.

"I haven't made anything nice since we've moved in," Maggie replied. "One thing after another has seemed to come up, and well for whatever reason, it just seems like I haven't had time. So, I had time today and… Voila!"

Sean smiled. He believed there were other reasons for the dinner that evening but he wasn't going to mention it. *Why spoil it by suggesting that the therapy sessions and medication were helping?*

As they sat down to dinner, Sean said a blessing thanking the Lord for watching over them during their move to their new home and especially for watching over their family as they had encountered some unique and difficult issues which had all been overcome with His help. All of them chimed in with an "Amen" and Maggie smiled as she looked over at her husband and son.

During their meal, Connor entertained them with stories of his new friend Sam's unusual pets. He had a green iguana that was a little over three feet long, which required very specific amounts of light and heat in order to thrive. He also had a Corn snake that he had caught in his yard and a California King Snake. He informed them the Corn snake often gets mistaken for the copperhead but the dark-colored hourglass shape sideways on the snake's back lets you know it's a copperhead. He also raved to his parents about the color of the King Snake and asked if they'd like to see it. He was sure that Sam would let him borrow it for the night if they were interested.

Sean waited for Maggie to respond because he knew she hated snakes. But he was surprised by her response when she told Connor that she'd be happy to see it, but maybe he could just borrow it for a little while and they could take a look at it in the garage before he took it back to Sam. *Good compromise* Sean thought. Connor said sure and promised to arrange it for next week.

Maggie then looked at Connor and took a long drink of water. When he saw the look on his mother's face, he knew what was coming. She was going to tell his father about the alligator. But he had known that was always a possibility and he was ready for it.

"Sean," Maggie started. "I didn't, and neither did Connor, but the other day, when Connor caught the water moccasin, and there was that alligator in the pond. Well, uh….oh hell. We didn't tell you the whole story. Connor was in the pond with the alligator coming toward him," Maggie said as she took another gulp of water and waited for Sean to blow up. But there was no explosion.

After a long pause, Sean asked quietly, "Did you ever feel like you were in danger?"

Connor knew he couldn't lie. For a moment, he was scared shitless when he saw that alligator coming toward him, but he knew he needed to frame that feeling differently this evening as he replied to his father.

"For a minute there," Connor started. "But I knew if I could get the snake out in front of me and in front of the alligator, he would be preoccupied with it and the snake grabber. I was pretty sure I would be able to get out of the water then and I doubt he would have even been interested in me once he got hold of the snake and the grabber. They would've given him a fight as he tried to bite into them, so I felt pretty good about my chances.

"But I did learn one thing. I didn't anticipate things as well as I should have. You always need to be one step ahead when you're in those types of situations and I wasn't. Next time, when I'm getting in the water, I'm going to make sure there aren't any alligators in there first."

"How are you going to do that?" Maggie asked before Sean could speak, though he was going to ask the very same thing.

"First of all, I won't go in the water in the evening. That's when they're the most active. Second, I'm going to throw some firecrackers, large ones, like cherry bombs or m-80s in the water before I get in. That will bring them up from below the water if they are there. Sam told me about a place off I-20 going toward Aiken. The first exit once you go over the Savannah River. It's called Wacky Waynes. He said they have everything I would need like that. And third, I'm going to get a big blade. One like Amos had the other day. I think it needs to be about ten inches long and thick enough to go through alligator hide. Gators don't like to have to fight for their food. If someone fights back with something that can hurt them, they'll back away. I think I'll be fine if I have those things. I'll be more than one step ahead of the game, so to speak, and that usually makes you a winner. I won't be caught unaware again," Connor finished.

Maggie couldn't hide her admiration for her son as she listened to him. She was almost beaming. *He is so smart. He's given this a lot of thought. It scared him but he's learning how to overcome those fears by coming up with a plan of action. We can't keep him from seeking out dangerous things but we don't need to worry. He'll be as safe as he can be and he'll be doing what he loves. We can't deny him that desire to learn about everything that's out there, even though we find it unnerving.*

"I should have said something that day," Connor added. "But I didn't want you to worry, especially seeing how we were going to take the water moccasin and release it into the wild. I know you're not real thrilled about doing that type of thing and would've been just as happy to shoot it. So, I really appreciate you doing what you did. I'm sorry I didn't say anything sooner."

Even more impressive. I need to learn from him she said to herself as she smiled at her son. *He took ownership of the issue even though I'm the adult. I'm the one who should have said something. But he places the burden on his back. He always has.*

"Thank you, Connor, for your honesty. And thank you, my wife, for having a guilty conscience. It sounds like you have things worked out, son, and you're right. I don't like you fooling around with animals and insects and other creatures out there that can hurt you. But I have to admit, you're not impulsive and rash. You plan things out. You research things. You find out about whatever it is you are working with or interested in and I don't know how I'm supposed to tell you not to pursue something you love. I don't think either your mother or I can do that. And though I know it won't be easy, you're just going to have to spend some time continuing to educate me and your mother."

Maggie wasn't sure if she was prouder of her husband or her son that evening. It didn't really matter. It wasn't a contest. She was proud of both of them and even a little proud of herself. She had after all listened to that blue jay and given his death some meaning. She was happy about that.

Chapter 25

Cook-out

Saturday morning, most of the neighborhood came out to help paint the guardhouse. Saturday evening, most of the neighborhood saw an alcoholic set himself on fire and saved by the swimming pool.

At 8:30 in the morning, Maggie was at the guardhouse preparing everything they would need for painting. By 9, everyone else had arrived. Sean and Connor began sanding and painting the interior. Jennifer and Sable were in charge of the cranberry trim around the windows and door jambs. Maggie, Barbara, and Phil were taking care of the exterior. Maggie put Ulf and Agathe to work cleaning up any litter in the common areas and killing the weeds that were growing up around the road and the pond.

As a surprise, Red showed up with two stained glass windows that would replace the plain transoms over the doors. Everyone admired them and Maggie asked if the design had a meaning.

"Yes, the windows are symbolic of friendship and a good life," Red told the group.

"Did Beth help you design those?" Maggie asked sarcastically. At the same time, she felt Barbara's elbow nudge her arm as Beth and Jasmine approached.

"Did I hear you mention my name?" Beth asked. "Something about helping with a design?"

Red looked at Sable for some direction, but she couldn't give him any before Maggie spoke up.

"We were just talking about these stained glass windows that Red made. I asked if you helped him with the design. They reflect, no pun intended, friendship and a good life," Maggie said as she smiled.

You know god damn well I had nothing to do with those windows, Beth said to herself. *But you're testing me, aren't you, Maggie? Just like the pretty little girls used to do in the sorority before they knew who I was. And what I was capable of doing to them.*

"No, I didn't, but they are beautiful," Beth said as she looked over at Red. "Thank you."

You won't embarrass me again in front of everyone Beth thought as she looked at Maggie. *But I need to be careful. Subtle. Non-threatening. You thought you and your friend Barbara would have a good laugh at that comment, didn't you? That's not going to happen.*

"I wish everyone in the neighborhood could see these pieces and understand what they mean," Beth replied. "It's a shame that they can't."

"What do you mean?" Maggie asked.

Come along little fly, Beth said to herself. *I'm here waiting for you.*

"Over there - Amos," Beth said as she cocked her head toward his house. "His poor mind is just not capable of comprehending those concepts. He is so reclusive and paranoid about most everything, as you know. He just won't be able to appreciate the thoughtfulness behind these windows. But that doesn't diminish the beauty of the windows nor the kind intentions they represent."

God damn you, Beth Maggie said in her mind several times and just before she said it out loud, she felt Barbara grab her arm.

"Amos understands more than you think, Beth," Barbara replied. "He may not know or remember what they mean when he sees them, but he will see them and I bet he'll like them. He loves color. Just look at his gardens and the beautiful koi in his pond. The windows will not be lost on him."

Beth smiled at Barbara. She was ready for a response from her or Maggie. She was hoping it came from Maggie but she could see that her anger was being kept in check by her friend.

"Yes, he'll probably enjoy the color. He does like color. Not sure if you are aware of it or not but he is a very good painter," Beth informed them.

Maggie could see that Barbara was as surprised as she was as Beth continued.

"He paints the sunrise and sunset every day. I'm sure he could make a living selling the pictures. They are that good. But unfortunately, he can't."

"Why is that?" Maggie asked.

"He burns them as soon as he paints them," Beth said as she smiled. "I asked a therapist friend of mine about that once and she told me it probably either meant that he didn't believe he had made anything of value or that he was trying to reconcile some traumatic experiences in his life. The world he created on canvas; destroyed by the fire he created in this world."

Maggie and Barbara stood there trying to process what they heard. Beth smiled. *Mission accomplished* she told herself. *They have learned you pay a price when you try to embarrass me or make me the butt of your jokes.*

"Would you make one of those windows for me, Red?" Beth asked sweetly. "Those symbols are exactly what I would like for people to see as they came into my house."

Red nodded and said, "I'd be glad to. I can have it for you in a couple of weeks."

"Oh, no rush," Beth said. "I'm sure we aren't going away anytime soon."

Did you hear that, Maggie? Beth said to herself. *That last little line was for you.*

I wonder if I can convince Red to include something in the design that suggests the woman who lives in this house is a bitch, Maggie thought as she continued to stare at Beth.

Jasmine walked over to Maggie and held out her hand. "I'm Jasmine Bartholomew. We only met once and I wasn't sure if you remembered me."

The voice made Maggie aware that she was still staring at Beth and she turned around and smiled at the pretty young red-head. "Of course, I remember you. It would be hard to forget your beautiful red hair. Is that natural? I am so envious."

"Yes, all natural," Jasmine smiled as she blushed. "Well, I am here to help. What would you like me to do?"

"Would you help us with the exterior?" Maggie asked. "I see you brought your own paintbrush."

"Come on," Barbara said as she took Jasmine's arm. "I'll get some paint for you."

"And what would you like me to do?" Beth asked sweetly.

Leave was the first word that entered Maggie's mind but she knew she couldn't say that.

"Would you mind helping Ulf and Agathe with killing the weeds?" Maggie asked. *Maybe you can just wave your hand over them and they will die.*

Beth hated doing yard work. *How did you know that?* Beth asked herself. *You are fucking with me again, aren't you? You think you wield the power but I'm sorry, Maggie, you don't. I know why you said that. This is about Jorge. You think me killing weeds is some sort of perverted justice. Well, fuck you. You still don't get it. But I'll show you again as I'm not about to start killing weeds for you. I doubt I'll ever do another damn thing you suggest. Let's just see how that works out for everyone.*

"Why don't we just hire someone to do this?" Beth asked.

Before Beth could continue Maggie interjected. "I suppose you mean Jorge?'"

Beth smiled. "Well, he can get the job done. I can promise you that and he would be more than happy to have the extra work. The neighborhood can afford it. I know how much money we have in our account. I don't think we should be wasting our time killing weeds. It could even be a little dangerous. There are things out there in the weeds and woods that can hurt you. You more than anyone else should know that, Maggie."

What a bitch! Your lewd reference to your little boyfriend is disgusting. And I heard your not so veiled threat. Fuck you and him. Both of you need to stay the hell away from me and my family or you will regret it. You will regret it.

" You are right, Beth. There are things out in the weeds and woods that can harm you," Maggie said. "So please be very careful."

"Well, everyone is working so hard. I think I'll go to the Mennonite bakery and get some pastries and some coffee from Starbucks for everybody. Be back in a little while."

Maggie watched Beth walk away. *Shit,* she thought. *The little Princess thinks she is going to keep her hands from getting dirty this morning. But I've got news for you, Beth. Your hands will never be clean. No matter how many times you try to wash them.* Maggie picked up her brush and continued painting. She didn't even bother to look up as Beth drove past them and beeped and waved.

By the time Beth returned with the pastries and coffee, the inside of the guardhouse was finished and Red already had one of the windows installed. Two sides of the exterior and all but one of the trim areas were also done. Beth handed out the refreshments and then took some to Ulf and Agathe who were down past the covered bridge spraying weed killer. Within an hour the guardhouse was completed and everyone stood back to admire the job.

"It looks wonderful, Maggie," Barbara said admiringly. "The colors and those windows, Red. Wow, such a nice touch. Good choice on the color palette, Jennifer."

"I just recommended the accent color. I think Maggie had the true vision. It's really beautiful," Jennifer commented.

Sean hugged his wife and said that he and the guys were going to go help Ulf and Agathe finish with the weeds.

"I don't think they need our help, do you?" Barbara asked Maggie.

And though Maggie wanted to show everyone how selfish Beth was by not helping, she heard the "not wanting to do that" voice in Barbara's question.

"No, I think us girls are done for the day," Maggie said. "Thanks for everyone's hard work. Hope to see all of you at the party tonight." She picked up the empty paint cans and other trash that had accumulated.

"I'll get Red's truck and load the ladders and everything else," Sable said.

"Okay, see everyone at Jim and Renee's later," Beth said as she got in the car and drove away.

Maggie thought it was odd that she didn't offer Jasmine a ride but she didn't seem bothered by Beth's lack of consideration. She was smiling and seemed happy as she walked along the road with Jennifer.

Barbara came up to Maggie and asked if she was okay. "Don't worry about Beth. Everyone knows how she is," Barbara said. "We have a saying around here. You can't spell "Bitch" without a B and a T."

Maggie smiled at her remark.

"We all see her true side or at least most of us do. Maybe not Ulf and Agathe. Don't know about them sometimes, but anyway as I was saying, we all see her for what she is. She doesn't fool us. You should be proud of what you got accomplished today. The guardhouse looks great. It's the first time we've all come together for the benefit of the neighborhood. And now there's a party tonight at the Thompsons and believe me, there will be plenty to drink. You did good, controlling yourself and dealing with her. I was impressed." Barbara gave her a quick hug.

" Shit, you stink," Maggie said.

"Yeah you do too," Barbara replied as they laughed again.

As they were getting ready for the party that evening, Maggie asked, "Do we really need to go tonight?"

"Yes," Sean replied. "Don't even start."

"Don't even start," Maggie repeated in a mocking whisper. She wasn't sure if Sean heard her or not, but he was not biting. He ignored her as he finished getting dressed.

"I'll be downstairs waiting on you," he said.

Maggie looked at herself in the mirror while she applied her lipstick and brushed her hair.

"Well, what do you think?" she asked her image.

"I agree," she replied. She took hold of her breasts and repositioned them into her bra. "That's more like it. Not bad, not bad at all." She smiled as she turned around and walked down to join Sean in the kitchen.

"Where's Connor?" she asked.

"He's outside," Sean replied. "Waiting on you."

"Well, aren't you going to tell me how good I look?" Maggie asked seductively. She took the beer out of his hand and rubbed the tip of the bottle around her lips.

"You won't be doing that at the party, will you?"

"Maybe, maybe not," she teased.

"Remember - your son is going to be there," Sean said.

"Then I will just have to be very discreet," she retorted and pulled Sean's head down to kiss him. "Are you sure you want to go? I'm beginning to feel something else that tells me otherwise."

Sean just shook his head. "You, discreet? I'm looking forward to seeing that."

Maggie followed him out the door and they met up with Connor at the edge of the pond and the three of them walked down the road toward the party.

The Thompsons had the biggest home in the neighborhood. One of the best features of the three-story brick house was a huge outdoor kitchen with two stoves, a pizza oven, several grills, and a bar that was stocked to the hilt. They entertained quite often and their house reflected the ability to do so.

The party was being held out by the pool and as they approached the house, the Brodies could hear music coming from the back of the house. There were no cars in the driveway or parked along the circle of the cul-de-sac.

"It looks like everyone walked here," Connor said.

"Good reason for it," Maggie said as she looked up at Sean and he told her not to say what she was thinking with his eyes.

"I mean, it's such a beautiful night, who wouldn't want to walk?" Maggie replied as she mouthed the word "discreet" to Sean. He nodded his head and replied, "We'll see," in the same silent manner.

They found everyone on the large flagstone patio. The pool and hot tub were separated by a generous wall of rocks that created a waterfall flowing into the pool. Stained concrete tables were placed around the patio with wicker chairs for seating and the massive curved bar anchored everything at the center. At the other end of the patio, a pergola covered with clematis, climbing roses, and trumpet vines provided a natural contrast to the concrete and stone.

"I thought this was a house, not the Ritz-Carlton at Lake Oconee," Maggie whispered to Sean as they smiled at the people who had begun to notice them arriving.

"He has a lot of money," Sean said as he waved toward Phil and Red. "I'll catch up with you later. I need to talk to Red."

Maggie looked over at Connor. "This may not be much fun for you bud, but I bet there's a lot of good stuff to eat," she said as she placed her hand on his arm.

"I'll be fine," he replied. "You and Dad have a good time. There's a tv over there next to the bar and there are a lot of woods I haven't explored out behind us."

She smiled at her son and together they walked over to the bar. *Shit, they hired a damn bartender*, Maggie said to herself as she heard her name and turned around.

"Maggie will have the Poet's Leap," Sable said to the bartender. "Hello, Connor."

"Hey, Mrs. Skye."

"I was hoping you would bring that wine," Maggie said, "but I thought it would be a little too forward of me to ask."

"Heavens no," Sable replied. "I have a few bottles left that I was hoping you could help me finish off so I brought them along."

Maggie and Sable tipped their glasses together and started over to join some of the other women. "Will you be okay on your own for a while, son?"

"Sure, I'm going to check out the food. Don't worry about me."

" Look who I found over at the bar," Sable said as she nodded her head toward Maggie.

"Good evening ladies." Maggie continued to look around, taking in the luxurious place. "Good Lord! How much are the rooms here?"

Everyone laughed except Agathe, who seemed puzzled. "What does that mean that you said?" she asked.

"Don't you think this place looks more like a hotel than a house?" Maggie replied.

"Ahhh," Agathe replied. "Sarcasm is good, huh?" she said as she smiled and lifted her drink.

Maggie nodded her head at Agathe and could see that she appeared uncomfortable in this social setting. It was hard to understand how someone who wore a necklace of penises in public could be nervous around people but Maggie realized that at the fair, she was someone else. She wasn't Agathe. She was the sorceress of the mystical lost dicks or whatever she called herself.

She turned her head and saw her husband standing next to Jim Thompson, Caleb Bartholomew, and Ulf under the pergola. Jim and Caleb looked like they were working on their golf swings and even from where she was, she could tell Ulf was not comfortable in this type of setting either. Perhaps if they modified their swing just a tad, to reflect that of swinging a scythe, he would be able to participate in their conversation, understanding that the action they were demonstrating was something that he was familiar with in his home country.

Beth and her husband were talking to Renee and Jennifer and Frances next to the pool and Maggie began to wonder if she could go the entire evening without having to talk to Beth. *If I'm lucky* she thought as she took a sip of wine. Beth caught her looking at her though and smiled. When Maggie saw that devious grin on her face, she looked away quickly as if she had stared into the face of Medusa.

"So what's the deal here?" Maggie asked the women.

"Deal?" Agathe asked. "Yes, would love to play the cards. What game do we play?"

Maggie looked at Sable and crossed her eyes and Sable smiled. "Would anyone like some more wine?" Sable asked. "I have a lot of this Riesling for everyone to try."

Thank God and thank you, Sable, thought Maggie.

"I'm not sure we will play cards right now Agathe," Barbara said, "but maybe later. She then turned toward Maggie and began answering her question.

"It's about 12,000 square feet, living quarters. It has ten bedrooms and each bedroom has its own bathroom."

"You're kidding me!" Maggie exclaimed.

"I don't kid about bathrooms," Barbara said as she grinned. "Jim made a ton of money in real estate and Renee came with a lot of money. I think her family owned most of Burke County before they sold it all and they owned and sold a lot of land around the lake too. I think the house cost about 3 million to build when they built it six years ago.

"Damn. Didn't know we were living so close to the Vanderbilts. I don't know about y'all but I'm starving. Let's see what's on that delicious-looking food table."

"That's a great idea," Barbara said. God only knows when we will be having dinner. Jim and Renee like to eat late," she said sarcastically.

Hearing Jim and Renee's names reminded Maggie that she needed to greet their hosts. *But not before I get another glass of wine* she told herself. With a refill in hand, Maggie walked over to Jim, who was still discussing golf swings with Caleb and Ulf, and thanked him for having the cookout.

"Glad to do it sweet cheeks," Jim said as he ogled Maggie.

Did I just hear him call me sweet cheeks? He couldn't have said that! Can he really be that big of an ass? That was just a joke. Surely he can't be that drunk and that obnoxious this early into the evening. Let's just pass it off as a joke and play along.

"The Cheeks are my cousins and live in Missouri. I didn't know you knew them, but my name is Maggie," Maggie replied.

Jim laughed out loud as he took a big swig from the large glass of whiskey. "Beth told me that you were a feisty one!"

Beth told you I was a feisty one, huh? A feisty one what, she asked herself. *Calm down, Maggie. Remember your son is here. You've only been here thirty minutes. Just leave. Add him to the "avoid" list for the night.*

"Yes, well, you have a beautiful house, and thanks again for having this party," Maggie said as she turned around and walked away.

"Damn, just as good going away as it is coming toward you," Jim said.

Maggie stopped in her tracks and then walked right back toward Jim. He was a large man, probably a couple of inches taller than Sean, but he wasn't as fit as her husband. He had a large barrel chest, blonde hair, and dark blue eyes that she thought was the only redeeming feature on his face. His nose was large and wrinkled and his skin was dark brown and leathered from what she determined was probably long hours on the golf course and even longer hours trying to ensure that the bottles of liquor on the shelves behind his bar never got old.

She could tell Caleb was embarrassed by what Jim had said and was trying to avoid eye contact. *You're afraid of him, aren't you,* Maggie thought. *For some reason, you are afraid of him.* Ulf was clueless about what was going on and just looked at Maggie and smiled. *He reminds me more of Ichabod Crane than Lurch. Tall, skinny, awkward, shy, and unaware.*

"I hear that you're a big golfer so let me put this in terms you will understand," Maggie started. "I'm not sure what you meant by IT, but if IT refers to me in a sexual manner, or if you say anything else to me with any kind of sexual connotation, I will show you why I never succeeded at golf. My golfing instructor told me I gripped the putter way too tight. Said it looked like I was strangling it and if I gripped it any tighter, I would break the damn club." Maggie stared straight into Jim's eyes.

As she walked away Maggie hoped she wouldn't hear him say anything else and was relieved when she didn't.

"You should try this crab dip," Barbara said as Maggie rejoined them. "It's out of this world and the shrimp and cocktail sauce are excellent."

Barbara didn't hear Maggie respond and when she saw her face, she knew something had happened. "What's wrong?"

"Jim Thompson," Maggie replied. "He's a ...." and before she could finish her thought, Jasmine finished it for her.

"He's an alcoholic asshole," Jasmine said. "And I hate being around him and his wife, who if I didn't know was a mean drunk, would be worried about her. But they deserve each other. Caleb says Jim is okay with just the guys around and he tells me they always have a good time playing golf, but I refuse to go out with them anymore. The only reason I came to this party was that I knew there would be a lot of people here and I wouldn't have to interact with them."

Jasmine's response stunned the other women. Everyone except Maggie. She remembered the way Jasmine looked when Beth didn't offer her a ride back to her house earlier that day. Jasmine wasn't offended, she seemed happy. Jasmine and Beth weren't friends. *And I bet she thinks Beth isn't much different from the Thompsons.*

"Well, what do you think of your other neighbors?" Maggie asked as she looked at Jasmine.

Barbara and Sable looked at Maggie as if she had asked Jasmine to reveal the codes to a nuclear silo hidden in their neighborhood, but there was nothing that they could do now. The question had been asked. And when they realized that, they were glad Maggie had asked it. They wanted to hear the answer too.

"Darrin is a nice guy. We even dated in high school. He was the first," Jasmine said quietly as she drained her wine glass.

"Would you like some more wine?"

"Honestly, I'd prefer some Wild Turkey with a little ginger ale," Jasmine said as she looked over at Sable.

"Not a problem," Sable said. "I'll be glad to get you one."

"When you say first, what you mean first?" Agathe asked.

"He was the first person I had sex with," Jasmine replied.

"Ahhh, I remember that," Agathe replied as if she was there. "That was very good, huh?"

"Yes, it was then," Jasmine replied as she looked at Agathe and then at Barbara and Maggie with a confused look on her face. "But that was a long time ago."

Sable returned with her drink and Jasmine drained it all in one swallow and slammed the glass down on the table as if she was participating in some drinking game and was waiting on them to tell her she won.

"I think Beth has tried to seduce my husband," Jasmine said as everyone but Agathe noticed that she was beginning to sound drunk.

"For some reason; hell, for many reasons, I feel like she has a problem with the fact that I had sex with her husband. A long damn time ago, but that doesn't matter. She just wants to have sex with Caleb like it's some power thing with her. She doesn't care that he's married to me. She just wants him to say she had him and I've told him that. It pisses me off so much that I want to just go up to her and pull her hair out of her fucking head," Jasmine said.

"Uh, you might need to eat something," Barbara said as she looked at Jasmine with concern. "I'll get a plate of food for you."

Jasmine nodded at her as Barbara patted her shoulder and told her she'd be right back.

"Perhaps we should do an intervention and get Jim into AA," Maggie said.

Jasmine looked at Maggie with an air of bewilderment. "He would never go to Alcoholics Anonymous," she said.

"I didn't mean Alcoholics Anonymous," Maggie replied. "I meant the group of people you referred to earlier: Alcoholic Assholes."

Jasmine and Sable laughed so hard that tears were rolling down their faces. When Barbara got back with the plate of food they were still laughing.

"Okay, what did she say? What did Maggie say that I missed?" Barbara asked.

"You had to be here. She was just making Jasmine feel better. I'll tell you later," Sable said.

Maggie smiled as Jasmine began to eat. She thought Jasmine looked like the flower that shared her name and had many of the same attributes. She was pretty, thin almost vine-like, but not a fragile vine. A vine with a strength that was very tough and hardy once it was grown. And like the flowery vine, she appeared to be clinging onto something. Something that she felt was slipping away.

Without warning, Jennifer was standing by their table and Maggie asked if she wanted to join them. She answered, "Gladly!" so emphatically that it made Maggie anxious to hear what she had to say. *I know this has something to do with either Renee or Beth. I just know it.*

Jennifer pulled up a chair and sat down and started talking.

"I don't know how Frances can stand it," she said as she looked at everyone at the table. "I'm sorry. That was very rude for me to just come over here and start bitching. I know everyone here, but I'm being a bigger ass than our hostess and her good friend. Sorry. Let me start over. Hello everyone. I hope you're all doing well." She picked up a napkin and wiped her eyes.

"Welcome to the table of awareness," Maggie said as she looked over at Agathe.

Agathe reached up and moved her hand around her neck. Just the reference to something magical made her wish for her necklace of penises. Maggie smiled as she glanced at Agathe, knowing what it was she missed having with her at this moment.

"What's wrong, Jennifer?" Maggie asked.

"Nothing, really. Well, it wasn't supposed to come up at the party. Frances and I had a little tiff earlier. When I was walking back from the guardhouse this morning, I began to think what a shame it would be to drain our pond and I said that to Frances. But she wouldn't listen to me. She said it would still be better to drain it and listed all sorts of health reasons, as she usually does when she gets into an argument. She is very good at being able to do that sort of thing. And so, we just agreed to disagree and not bring it up tonight. But there she is, joining right in with Beth and Renee when they started talking again about draining the pond and how they would have to get whoever moved into the Cayman house on 'their' side. She promised me," Jennifer said as her voice wavered for a moment.

"But say they get whoever buys the Cayman house to agree to that, if you vote against, it would still be a deadlock vote," Maggie said.

"They plan to negate Amos's vote. They want to have him declared mentally incompetent to vote. And when I heard that, I just couldn't stand to be around any of them. Amos is rough around the edges for sure, but deep down, he's got a good heart. He gets confused sometimes, I admit that, but he's a good person and I think he's battling demons from the war that we should respect. He needs our support, not our pity and certainly not our antipathy."

Connor was walking over to the appetizer table to get something more to eat and overheard Jennifer talking about the pond and Amos. He stopped as if he was watching tv so that he could hear what they were saying. When he had heard enough, he went back to his seat by the woods and began thinking of how he could stop everything that Jennifer referred to from happening.

Before Jennifer could continue, a chef appeared at their table in a colorful hat and pastel apron to ask everyone how they would like their filet cooked. They gave their preferences and after he walked away, Jasmine announced, "I'll change my vote too. Then it won't matter what they try to do with Amos, though I'll fight that too. I know the bylaws of the HOA. To change them, you need eighty percent of the neighborhood to agree and Beth and Renee would never get that."

"Thank you, Jasmine," Maggie said. She began to think about the subject of their conversation. *Why is Beth so obsessed with draining the pond? Don't we all have better things to do with our lives than to be concerned with something that appears so trivial? It is after all just a fucking pond. I voted against draining it just because I thought it added beauty to the subdivision but it's not like it's the Gaza strip for God's sake. And I voted against it because Connor likes it. Don't deny that, Maggie.*

But it's all about power isn't it, Beth? All about the way you grew up. You're not used to hearing someone tell you no. You are dismissive, manipulative, and condescending. And an adulteress liar. Okay, you started all of this and you think you'll get your way, but that's just not going to happen. You've threatened me and my family and I know it was you pulling the strings with Jorge. You meant everything to be just a warning. To ensure that I knew who was the boss in this sick little world of yours. But what you did could have hurt my family. I won't struggle with the why of this issue anymore. Nor question myself or my actions. And believe me, I won't let you do anything to Amos either. I just hope I can protect you from Connor.

"Jennifer. Do you know of a way to check if someone has a felony record?" Maggie asked.

"Sure, there are lots of websites that provide that information. Statewide. National. Why?" she asked.

"I have the name of someone that I need to research," Maggie replied. "I want to see if he is dangerous."

"Who is dangerous?" Beth said as she walked up to the table. "How is everyone doing? Did you get your steak orders in? Isn't the appetizer table something else? I mean a little cheese and some fruit would have been fine, but you could make a meal just with all the appetizers."

Maggie looked up at Beth. "What is Jorge's last name Beth?"

"Martin," Beth replied. "Is there something wrong? Oh, don't tell me. You think Jorge is dangerous? My God, Maggie. You really have this conspiracy theory mentality, don't you? Jorge takes care of all of our lawns and is the nicest person, isn't that right Jasmine? He's even cutting Mrs. Cayman's yard for free. I don't think someone dangerous would do that."

"Thank you, Beth," Maggie replied. "Can you check that name for me, Jennifer?"

"Sure," Jennifer replied. "I'll check it on Monday."

"Will you let us all know what you find out?" Jasmine asked.

Jennifer nodded her head as Beth turned and leered at Jasmine.

"Well, I'm going to go to the bar and get another drink. I think the steaks and lobster tails will be ready in about ten minutes. Could I get anyone anything while I'm over there?" Beth asked.

Everyone said they were fine and Beth smiled and started to walk away before turning back around.

"I knew there was something else I wanted to tell y'all when I came over here," Beth started. "Did you hear about the body they found out at the lake? They haven't identified it yet, but I hear it didn't have a head. Isn't that awful? Oh – and It was found there in the Essie May Washington Park part of the lake. It had to have been near where Mrs. Cayman's memorial service was."

Beth knew it would make everyone think about the fact they were just there in the same location as a horrible murder. A place where someone's head was cut off and where they had spread that old hag's ashes. *How awful* she thought as she hid the smile that was trying to emerge across her face.

"Beth," Barbara said. "I know this isn't very Christian-like, but why don't you go fuck yourself?"

" I'm not sure this is that kind of party," Beth replied as she smiled and walked away.

Everyone stared at Barbara with their eyes wide open and started laughing. Even Agathe.

"I wasn't aware that you had such a command of the English language," Maggie said as she held up her glass and tipped it toward Barbara.

"I had to say something to get her to leave before you got up and created a scene," Barbara replied.

Maggie laughed and squeezed her friend's hand. Within a few minutes, dinner was being served and all of the husbands came over to join the women.

"What do you guys want?" Maggie asked.

"We thought we'd sit down and have dinner with our wives," Sean replied.

"There's a table right over there. Feel free to sit there. This is the table of awareness and delicate language. I'm afraid there isn't room for you here," Maggie said as the women laughed.

"Is ok if I eat with Ulf?" Agathe asked cautiously and Maggie smiled at her. *How can someone so naïve and reserved change so much and walk around with a necklace of dicks? I just don't get it.*

"Of course, Agathe," Maggie replied. "We're just kidding with the old farts."

"Oooh. Not good the men and the farts. Understand that very much," Agathe replied.

The steaks and lobster tails were cooked to perfection. The conversation was lively and the women got to learn a lot about Jasmine and realized what a nice relationship she appeared to possess with Caleb. Maggie had misjudged her. As they continued to eat and talk, she realized she had misjudged Caleb too. He was a nice man and Maggie could tell he was very much in love with Jasmine, by the words she used to describe him. She could understand how they could be corrupted by Beth and her manipulative behavior that went unseen by most or was mistaken for goodwill.

Beth sent a text to Jorge during dinner asking him if his name would be found on a felon search through the internet. Emiliano sent back a quick "No" reply. He didn't have to ask why she asked and he was glad he had not shared his real name yet with any of his clients. He knew he would have to eventually, but he just couldn't do it now. He told himself he would make things right but he needed just a little more time.

Maggie wondered if that body found at the lake had anything to do with the snake that Connor had released there. *It couldn't* she told herself. *Beth said the body was headless. It was gruesome but neither the snake nor her son had anything to do with it. Beth just mentioned it because she wanted to throw a scare in us. Nothing is sacred to her. She didn't care about Sarah Cayman or her niece or probably anyone in the neighborhood. At least no one she couldn't control.*

At the end of the meal, Jim stood up and thanked everyone for coming and hoped they enjoyed everything. He announced that the bar would be open for as long as people wanted and Beth held up her drink and said, "A toast to Jim and Renee," and everyone clapped. *Everyone had to clap,* Maggie thought. *It was indeed one hell of a dinner.*

"Any of that wine left?" Maggie asked Sable.

"Should be one bottle, I think."

"Well, I'm going to check that out." As Maggie waited at the bar, Renee came up next to her. Maggie thanked her for the dinner and told her how delicious it was and Renee just smiled at her without saying a word. She picked up her Moscow mule that was very much more "Moscow" than "mule" and walked away. *Perhaps vodka makes her deaf* Maggie said to herself as she walked back to her table. *Considering the number of drinks she's had, she probably can't hear a thing.*

Over the next hour, everyone continued to drink and eat the different desserts that were brought out. Sean suggested to Maggie that they should probably leave. It was getting late and he was sure that they all had enough to drink and eat. Maggie said she was going to have one more glass of wine so Sean agreed to "Just one more" and ordered another Crown Royal.

"After all, we aren't driving," he said and Maggie smiled at him and shook her head. As she stood there at the bar, Renee came back up to her and glared.

"Again, wonderful party," Maggie said as she got her drink from the bartender and started to leave.

"You're one of those people who think they know everything, aren't you?" Renee asked angrily.

Everyone moved closer to the bar at the sound of her loud incensed voice. Sean put his drink down and walked toward his wife. He knew they needed to leave and told Connor, "Let's go."

"Excuse me?" Maggie asked.

"You're one of those smartass know-it-alls," Renee said. "Think you can move in here and tell us how to do things. Well, we were the first in this neighborhood and you aren't going to tell us a damn thing."

"I bet you meet a lot of those kinds of people," Maggie answered smartly.

"What kind of people?" Renee asked as she slurred her words.

"Those know it all kind of people. Because I'm guessing most everyone you meet knows more than you."

Renee hurled her drink in Maggie's face and Maggie calmly asked the bartender for a towel. *I guess she can hear a little* she thought. While she was drying her face, she heard Jim's voice.

"She's a nasty little cooch, that one."

Connor put down the plate of food he was holding and marched over and shoved the fat man, whose skin was the color of a fire truck, into the pool. He then picked up the plate of food without saying a word, took his mother by the arm, and walked out with Sean following them. They heard Renee say something belligerent and loud and referenced their ancestry in a foul manner as they walked away. But the words meant nothing to them. They heard them but none of them turned around to acknowledge what she was saying.

"What's with the plate of food?" Maggie asked Connor.

"It's for Amos," Connor replied. "I wonder how long it's been since he had filet and lobster."

Maggie pulled her son close to her and hugged him and then wrapped her arm through her husband's. He looked down at his wife and she heard him whisper that he was proud of her.

She asked him why.

He replied that he had never seen her be so discreet.

Chapter 26

Door Stop

"I believe that may be the most interesting way we've ever left a dinner party," Sean said as they walked home.

"You're right about that," Maggie replied. "Why don't we watch a movie when we get home? You can pick it, Connor."

"Sure, right after I get back from taking this food to Amos."

" Don't stay too long…" Maggie started to say and then stopped. "Stay as long as you want. We'll be waiting for you."

"Okay, I won't be long," Connor said as he went through the covered bridge.

"You think that's the first time he's heard the word cooch?" Maggie asked Sean.

"Tonight may be the first time he's heard a lot of different words."

"Well, you should never stop learning," Maggie said and Sean pulled her close to him and laughed.

Maggie changed into some sweat pants and a football t-shirt as soon as they got in the house. A t-shirt that was just a little too tight on her in all the right places. She knew how Sean would react but before she could even get to the door of the bedroom, he was standing there.

"I don't think I need this shirt," she said as he picked her up and carried her to the bed. She watched him as he removed his pants and then hers.

"Nope, didn't need it," she said as she saw his reaction and felt him on top of her. Ten minutes later, they were lying next to each other on the bed.

"I'm ready for round two." Maggie smiled suggestively.

"Let's wait," Sean said. "I don't want to be in here with you screaming and hollering like you do when Connor gets back."

"Well, you could put something in my mouth that would stop that," Maggie replied.

Sean smiled. "I will, later," he promised.

"May not want it later."

"That's a risk I'll just have to take."

"Ok, Ok," Maggie replied. "I will want it later. You know me too well."

" I am not sure exactly what was going on earlier," Sean started while they were getting dressed. "But I didn't see you do anything to deserve what happened at the party. I didn't even see you around Renee or Jim the whole time we were there."

"I only talked to him once," Maggie replied. "I told him thanks for having the party and he called me sweet cheeks."

"Sweet cheeks?" Sean asked incredulously.

"Yeah, and I told him to never refer to me in any sexual terms again and left. Didn't see him again till he called me a nasty old cooch. And Renee. I saw her at the bar one other time. I was getting a glass of wine and she was getting a glass of vodka and I mean, a glass of vodka, and I thanked her too. She didn't even answer me. Said nothing till you saw her at the bar telling me I was a know-it-all and then threw her drink in my face.

"And you should hear what Jasmine says about them," she continued. "Raging alcoholics. Won't even go out with them anymore because of it. Says Renee is a mean drunk and I think we saw evidence of that tonight. And then get this. Jennifer comes over and tells us about how Renee and Beth were talking about draining the pond and trying to come up with some way to negate Amos's vote. Concocting a story saying he wasn't mentally capable of voting on neighborhood business. Both she and Jasmine said that they would vote against doing anything to the pond. Jasmine said she knew they couldn't change the bylaws without eighty percent of the homeowners agreeing to it and with her and Jennifer voting against that change, they would never have the votes."

"Good Lord," Sean replied. "What is wrong with them?"

"Well, as I said, Jim and Renee Thompson are rich snobs and alcoholics. But I think the real problem is Beth. Jasmine said she's had numerous affairs. She's even been trying to seduce Caleb. And I haven't told you this, but I'm pretty sure that Beth is having an affair with that guy who does their yard. Jorge."

"Maggie - are you sure?" Sean asked. "You know how you sometimes see one thing and think it's something else. This isn't one of those times, is it?"

"No," Maggie replied adamantly. "I saw them kissing. She's just a real bitch. Came over to our table and said something nasty about Sarah Cayman. Started telling us that the place where Savannah spread her ashes was the same place that the police found a headless body just the other day. She had no reason to say that except to just be a bitch. Barbara told her to go fuck herself."

"Barbara said that?"

"Yep," Maggie replied.

"You don't think…" Sean started to say before Maggie stopped him.

"No," Maggie said. "I know what you're thinking but there is no way that snake you released into the lake killed that person. Beth said it was a headless body. Something else happened, and it had nothing to do with you or Connor."

Sean nodded but it still concerned him. Maggie was thinking about how Connor had pushed Jim into the pool. That worried her. She was hoping that didn't suggest that more aggressive action was intensifying within him. Hidden for now but still there, just below the surface. She needed to make sure that she kept that from getting out of control.

"You know Sean, a lot of what I've told you, we shouldn't share with Connor," Maggie continued. "I think it will just agitate him. Did you see his face after what he did to Jim? It was like he did that sort of thing every day. His eyes were emotionless."

Sean heard what Maggie was saying and it bothered him too. Sometimes she overreacted to what she was seeing, making it seem worse than it really was, but tonight he had seen how detached Connor acted after he pushed Jim into the pool. Maggie was probably right this time. He didn't need to hear any of this.

"I agree," Sean said. "We don't tell Connor about the Thompsons or Beth or Jorge. We'll just have to deal with it and when I say deal with it, I mean stay the hell away from them. From what you're telling me, Jennifer and Jasmine will block anything that they try to do about the pond or Amos. So we just need to go with the flow. Just be aware and watchful. Ok?"

Maggie looked up at her husband. "Yes, agreed," she said as she pulled him in tight to her.

Connor checked out Amos's pond as he walked up the driveway. He thought he saw a head swimming around just beneath one of the lights. From where he was, he couldn't tell if it was a frog, a turtle, or a snake. He wasn't prepared to find out what it was tonight but he kept looking back as he walked up Amos's front steps. When he knocked on the front door, it fell open.

"Hello," he called as he looked into the living room. "Amos, it's me, Connor. I have some food for you from a party we went to earlier. Amos?"

Then he saw the blood. Reddish-brown droplets and smears of blood led from the front door to the back of the house. Connor followed the trail, cautiously looking around. He knew he could be shot if Amos was in one of those moods and then he realized that the blood he was looking at might not even be from Amos. He just assumed it was his because it was in his house. It might not even be human blood.

"Amos!" Connor yelled out again. "Amos, it's Connor! Are you around?"

"Out on the back porch," came the reply.

Connor wasn't sure where the back porch was but he followed Amos's voice and the trail of blood to the kitchen and the back door where he could see Amos sitting outside.

Connor walked toward the open door and stopped short when he saw how the door was propped open. There was a bloody foot shoved under the bottom of it. *Shit!* Connor proceeded slowly through the door and found Amos sitting on the porch with his cooler beside his feet. Or foot, Connor corrected himself when he saw the blackened stump where his foot once was.

"What happened here, Amos?" Connor asked as ran over to him.

"Stepped in that animal trap over there." He pointed toward the trap that was beside the porch railing. "Took my foot clean off. That god damned woman at the end of the road put it out there. Next to the pond. I guarandamntee it."

"Are you in a lot of pain?" Connor asked.

"That sounds like some dumbass question the sergeant would ask. If you ever have a limb cut off without anesthesia, you'll understand what it feels like and if you don't pass out from the pain, you'll wish to God you had. Of course, if you do pass out, you'll be dead soon from the massive blood loss. Yes, it still hurts like a son of a bitch but it's getting better. Had to put my knife in the fire and cauterize the wound or it would've never stopped bleeding. That hurt like a motherfucker, but it's feeling better by the minute," he said as he took a big swig from a bottle of George Dickel and then followed it up by draining a beer.

He threw the empty can over to the side and it clinked as it bounced off a pile of empty cans. He leaned down and pulled out another beer from the cooler and looked up at Connor.

"You said you brought me something to eat?" he asked.

"Uh, yeah." Connor handed Amos the plate of food.

Amos peeled off the aluminum foil and smiled at the sight of the steak and lobster. He took a bite and sighed.

"Damn good steak. Not a big fan of stuff that comes out of the ocean though. At least to eat. Had enough of that shit in the war, but I appreciate you bringing me the steak. It's damn good."

"Amos, I'm going to go over and get my mom and dad and have them take a look at your leg."

"Suit yourself. But before you go," he said as he chewed the meat, "can you, uh, fill my cooler up with some more beer out of the refrigerator?"

"Sure," Connor piled as many cans and as much ice in the cooler as he could and put it down by Amos's chair. "Be back in a minute." As soon as he got through the front door, he ran all the way back to his house and found his parents in the den.

"What's wrong?" Maggie asked as she saw the look on Connor's face and heard him breathing hard.

"It's Amos," Connor said. "His foot is gone."

"What do you mean his foot is gone?" Maggie asked as she jumped up.

"He stepped in some sort of animal trap and it took his foot off."

"Oh my God!" Maggie cried as she and Sean ran to put on their shoes.

"Shouldn't we call 911?" Sean asked as they went out the kitchen door.

"The foot isn't bleeding now," Connor told him. "He cauterized the wound. It looks all black and smells bad, but it isn't bleeding anymore. Does that matter?"

"Sean, you call 911 anyway, and Connor, can you run down to the party and get Frances? You know who she is?" Maggie asked.

"Yes, I know."

"Just tell her she needs to come with you quickly. And don't tell everyone else," Maggie instructed.

"Yeah, I know. He said the woman at the end of the street did this to him," Connor said as he hurried out of the house.

Maggie looked at Sean and gritted her teeth. "God damn bitch," she muttered. She ran into Amos's house yelling his name. She followed the trail of blood and was startled by the sight of a foot jammed under the door.

"Fuck," she said as she went out onto the porch, giving the detached foot a wide berth.

Amos had finished the steak and was sitting in his chair drinking a beer.

"Amos! Are you okay? I mean I know you aren't okay but how do you feel?" she asked as she looked down at his leg.

"Hey, Maggie," Amos said as he reached down and picked up the bottle of George Dickel. He took a big swig, and then chased it with another beer. He placed the bottle of liquor on the floor and it was then that Maggie saw the plate with the lobster hanging off of it behind the bottle. *He ate the steak* she thought *and dropped the plate with the lobster tail and couldn't get it. I don't know how he can eat in this type of situation but then nothing should surprise me when it comes to Amos.* Before she could do anything else or Amos could answer her question, Sean came out onto the porch and almost tripped over the foot that was jammed into the screen door.

"Don't knock the doorstop out, Seargent," Amos said as he looked at Sean. "I'm going to have that bronzed or something. I am getting to where I like it. What do you two think?"

Sean didn't know how to respond to that question and Maggie smiled at him letting him know she would have an answer. She always did.

"I think once you get everything cleaned up, it will be a very unique doorstop, Amos. It will really help you manage the foot traffic," Maggie replied.

"Ha!" Amos said as he drank his beer. "Yeah, I believe you're right."

"Amos, I want you to know, that I asked one of your neighbors to come take a look at your leg," she went on. "Her name is Frances. She lives in the yellow house a couple of houses down from you."

"One of the lesbians, huh?" Amos asked. "Boy, they are a pair of good-looking women. Why do you want one of the lesbians to look at it?"

"She's a nurse, Amos," Maggie replied. "And we called an ambulance for you."

"An ambulance? What the hell for?" Amos said as he leaned forward in his chair. "I ain't dying. Seen people get their legs blown completely off and by God, they needed an ambulance. Right now, I ain't feeling too bad. Drank a lot of Dickel and had a lot of beers that helped me get rid of the pain. Reckon it will twinge a bit when I wake up in the morning, but I don't need a damn ambulance. Won't mind one of those good-looking lesbians looking at it though. No, won't mind that at all."

Connor rushed in with Frances and Jennifer. He made sure that they didn't dislodge the foot and Jennifer gasped when she saw it.

"Amos, this is Frances and Jennifer," Maggie said as she introduced them to Amos. "Frances is the nurse. She's going to look at your leg."

Jennifer covered her mouth and knew she was going to get sick. Maggie took her by the arm and led her into the yard and she threw up just as soon as they got off the porch.

"Hello, Amos," Frances said. "Mind if I look at your leg?"

"No, go right ahead," Amos said as he winked at her.

Frances bent down and held up the flashlight on her phone and examined the leg. She checked all around it, using a paper towel to move it as needed, and when she looked up at Amos, he was smiling down at her.

"What do you think?" he asked.

"I think you've done as good a job as you could in stopping the bleeding," Frances said. "It needs to be cleaned up and bandaged and you probably need some x-rays to see how much damage has been done to the bones, but I think that you'll be okay."

The ambulance had arrived and one of the EMTs tripped over the severed foot in his rush to get to Amos and knocked it out from beneath the door. It bounced off Sean's leg and Sean jumped away.

"God damn it," Amos bellowed at the paramedic. "That's my property, you know, and I would appreciate it if you would show it a bit more respect."

"What happened here?" the other EMT asked as he looked around.

"I stepped in a god damn animal trap and the damn thing took my foot off," Amos said. "I reckon you boys ain't ever seen anything like this before, have you?"

"Seen worse," he answered and started to assess Amos's foot.

Frances walked down the porch steps and told Maggie that Amos should be fine and that she would take care of Jennifer. Maggie thanked her for coming and she said she was happy to help. Frances smiled at Maggie as she walked Jennifer around the house so that she would not have to go back up on the porch.

When Maggie rejoined the others, she saw the foot had been dislodged from the door and was sitting against the side of the house like a Halloween decoration that had been put there to scare children. She thought Sean looked a little pale too and she knew she probably needed to get him away from everything. She put her arm around his as she listened to the paramedic talking to Amos.

"You seen worse, have you?" Amos asked.

"Yes sir, unfortunately, I have," he replied.

"What's your name, son?" Amos asked.

"Brian. I did a tour in Afghanistan as a medic and have done my share of car wrecks over here. But I know what I do helps people, so I keep doing it. I know I'm good at it too. Studying to be a doctor. So one day, I hope I can be someone that re-attaches that foot over there to your leg, but I'm afraid that isn't going to be possible now. That foot has been off your leg way too long. How long ago did this happen?"

"Sun was just going down. What time is it now?" Amos asked.

"A little after ten," Brian replied. "I never heard you tell me what your name was."

"Amos. Amos Morgan."

"Well, Mr. Morgan, you need to go to the hospital and have your leg cleaned and x-rayed, just to make sure there aren't any bones that need to be set and make sure that you don't get an infection. You okay with going to the hospital?"

"You driving?" Amos asked.

"Yes, why?"

"Cause your partner tripped over my foot. Don't want someone that can't see a detached foot driving me to the hospital."

Brian laughed as he turned around and looked at Maggie, Sean, and Connor. "Are you Mr. Morgan's family?"

Maggie was going to reply that they were just neighbors when she heard her son answer.

"No, we're his friends."

Yes, we are, son. Her concern about how he acted with Jim was eclipsed at the moment by his thoughtfulness for Amos. She was so proud of him.

"Can you bring that foot with us, Brian?" Amos asked. "I want them to put it in formaldehyde at the hospital so that it won't start to rot. I want to have it bronzed later. Going to use it as a doorstop."

Chapter 27

Pictures

" You okay with letting me put you in a wheelchair?" Brian asked.

"I don't suppose I can take my cooler with me, can I?" Amos asked.

"No, but while we're waiting on my buddy, Lee, to get back here with the wheelchair, I don't see why you can't have one for the road. From what I can tell," Brian said as he glanced at the pile of cans, "I don't think one more is going to make any difference."

Amos smiled and got another beer from the cooler. "Hey, Connor. There's something I want to show you. It's in the kitchen on the stove. Would you get it?"

The only thing Connor saw on the stove was a knife. A big one with a blade as long as his forearm. He picked it up and brought it outside.

"Whoa!" Brian said when he saw the knife. "You can't take that with you to the hospital, Mr. Morgan."

"Don't plan to."

Connor started to hand it to Amos, but he shook his head no.

"I want you to have that. With enough force, it will cut clear through the branch of a tree. Sure as hell will slice open the hide of a sneaky son of a bitch gator."

Connor didn't hear either one of his parents objecting. He noticed his mother grip his dad's arm real tight and knew that was the reason his father wasn't saying anything.

"Thank you, Amos," Connor said as he gazed at the knife.

"The leather sheath for it is on the table in the den. Served me well. Take good care of it and it will take good care of you."

Maggie spotted a painting over in the corner of the porch. *That must be one of the paintings that Beth was talking about. He must not have had time to burn this one because of everything that happened.* The painting of the sunset looked as real as the sky and the sun that formed it. She would have sworn it was a photograph if it wasn't on canvas.

"You can have it," Amos said as he watched her studying it. "That is if you want it."

"I would love to have it, Amos," Maggie replied. "It is amazing and I'm not just saying that. It's like a photograph. You are an artist with an amazing ability to see the world in all its beauty," she said as she felt the tears trickling down her cheeks.

"God damn," Amos replied. "Don't get all fucking weird now. It's just a god damn piece of canvas with some paint on it. I like sunsets and sunrises. Not sure which one I like best. But looking at them, I don't know, makes me think that life is good; that there's a reason to get up each day and take another breath. I don't think I've ever captured what I see in my mind, but I keep trying to. Maybe one day I will."

"Yeah, maybe one day you will." Maggie bent down and kissed Amos's cheek.

" You ready to go now, Mr. Morgan?" Brian asked.

Amos threw the empty can onto the pile. "Reckon so. Maggie, can you lock up the house as we go? There's a key in the den in an ashtray, I think. I usually put it there but if it ain't there, look in a little ashtray in the kitchen. If it ain't there, look in the little ashtray in the bathroom. If it ain't there, it may be in an ashtray out in the garage. If it ain't in any of those places, well then I fucking lost them again."

"Don't worry, I'll find it," Maggie said as they started to wheel Amos off the porch.

"The foot, Brian, the foot," Amos said.

"Lee, can you get the foot?" Brian asked.

"Yeah," Lee replied as he picked up the foot and put it in a red bag.

"Where will you be taking him?" Maggie asked.

"We'll be taking him to the Medical College ER seeing how this is a trauma," Brian answered. "Once they assess him, I'm thinking they'll probably transfer him to the VA. You are a veteran, aren't you Mr. Morgan?"

"Semper fi! Oh god damn. Here they are," Amos said as he reached into his pocket. He pulled out his keys and handed them to Connor. "See you folks later."

They watched the ambulance leave and then looked at each other. "Well this has been one hell of a night," Sean said. "You're right though. That picture does look like a photograph. He is very talented."

"He is," Maggie replied. "He is indeed."

"Can you take the painting home with you, Sean? I'm going to try and clean the place up as much as I can. Get these bloodstains up. Clean up the mess on the back porch."

Sean took the picture and leaned it against the wall.

"No. We'll all stay to clean up everything together."

Maggie didn't move a muscle until 8 a.m. the next morning. Sean was already eating breakfast when she walked in the kitchen.

"Is Connor up yet?"

"Haven't seen him," Sean replied. "Want me to fix you something to eat?"

"Some toast and bacon would be great. I'm just going to go look in on him."

At his door, she thought she heard Connor talking to someone. She put her ear to the door and listened. It wasn't a tv. It was Connor's voice. It sounded like he was telling someone about pushing Jim into the pool and that he should have thrown his drunk wife into it also.

"Connor," she said as she knocked on the door. "Is it okay if I come in?"

The talking stopped and then it was silent for a moment. So, she knocked and asked again if she could come in.

"Yeah, come in," Connor answered in a raspy voice.

Connor was in bed and looked like he had just woken up. But that couldn't be possible. She had heard him talking.

"Did I wake you?" she asked.

"Yeah," Connor replied.

"I thought I heard you in here talking to someone."

"Do you see anyone else in here?"

"No," Maggie replied as she looked around the room.

"Who are you looking for?"

"I don't know," she said. "Are you okay?"

"Yeah, I'm fine," Connor replied. "You think we can go by the hospital today and check on Amos?"

"Sure. We'll go over there this afternoon. By then they should have a good idea how he is."

"Great" Connor replied. "Do you mind closing the door? I'm going to sleep a little more. And thanks, by the way."

"For what?"

"I know you're the reason I got to keep the knife."

How did he see me squeeze Sean's arm? He doesn't miss a thing, she said to herself.

"Get some rest." Maggie closed the door and stood outside it for a moment to see if she heard anything else. When she didn't hear another conversation, she turned and walked down the hall.

That was not good. It's started. The conversations. Just like the time before. All the stress from last night. It is more than he can handle and he's not even aware of it. He is going to need to talk to someone about it. Someone professional. Perhaps I can ask Hazel. She'll know what to do. I'll call her tomorrow. Sean doesn't need to know anything about this. He'll just worry like usual. I'll handle it. And Connor will be fine. He will be fine.

She made a cup of tea and joined Sean outside to eat her breakfast. Sean had brought the painting out on the patio and leaned it up against one of the columns. "You figured out where you want to put that?" he asked.

"I want to get it framed first. And then I think I want it somewhere in the front of the house. Where I can see it every day when I look over at the pond and the covered bridge. Knowing that the painter is close by. Just out of sight."

"How's Connor?" Sean asked.

"Still sleeping," Maggie replied. "We're going over to the hospital later this afternoon. Want to go with us?"

"Yeah, I do," Sean replied. "I've got to go do some work first but I should be back around 1 or 2. Will that be okay?"

"Yes, that's fine," Maggie replied.

Sean kissed his wife on the head before he went to get ready for work. Maggie sat and looked at the painting and listened to the waterfall for a long time. She enjoyed the sound of the water and looking at the beautiful sunset. After she heard Sean leave, she got up and checked on Connor again. He was still sleeping so she grabbed Amos's keys from the bar. *I should go over there and see if there's anything we missed last night.* Moments later, she was headed out the door.

As she entered Amos's house, she didn't see any obvious signs of blood that they had missed. She realized that he must have had a tourniquet around his leg or he would have gotten blood everywhere. Not to mention, probably died. *Still no blood. Not even any on the walls. Hell, we did a pretty good job.*

She wandered into the den and told herself that she was looking for more blood, but that was only an excuse for snooping around his house. There were pictures of a young Amos in Vietnam standing next to a helicopter with some other soldiers. One of the soldiers appeared in several pictures with his arm around Amos. *They were always holding a Budweiser.*

"Bud Light wasn't around yet, was it, Amos?" Maggie mused.

An old wooden box was next to a timeworn Bible on a table in a corner of the room. Maggie picked up a Tiffany-style lamp from the table. *"Shit,"* she thought as she looked at the aged bronze base and the stamp that said 'Tiffany Studios New York.' She began to think that this might be an original Tiffany lamp. The shade looked like blue wisteria and when she looked up the lamp on her phone, she realized that she was actually holding a genuine Tiffany lamp, worth probably close to half a million dollars.

"Damn, Amos," she said as she put the lamp down carefully and picked up the old box. Inside were two medals and several ribbons. She wasn't sure, but she thought maybe they were a bronze and silver star. She looked them up on her phone too and saw that they were both awarded for valor in combat. She said, "Shit!" again, this time out loud, as she put the medals back in the box and picked up the Bible.

A presentation page on the inner cover of the Bible read: "Katherine Bush Morgan presents this Bible to her son, Amos Morgan, on June 25, 1951, in honor of his 6th birthday." *That makes you how old,* Maggie thought as she added up the numbers in her head. *You were born in 1945, so you're 73 years old. Pretty damn stout for a 73-year-old man.* And then she thought about that alligator. The one he shot and then hauled out of the pond. *How does a 73-year-old man do those things? Not just any 73-year-old could* and she realized how lucky she and her son had been that day. As she was putting the Bible back on the table, a photograph fell out.

Amos was pictured sitting on a horse with a girl who resembled a very young Natalie Wood. She turned the picture over and read the words "*Amos and Elizabeth.*" The date on the picture was 6/25/1990. *That date,* Maggie thought. *I just saw that date.* She picked up the Bible again and found it. *June 25th is your birthday and this picture of you and the little girl was on your birthday. Who is that little girl?* She held the picture closer and studied it. "Shit!" she cried again. She slid the picture into her pocket. "Holy Shit!"

Connor was in the kitchen eating a bowl of cereal. "What's up?" he asked as his mom walked in.

"Just been over at Amos's house; making sure we got everything cleaned up. We did a pretty good job!"

"Cool."

"I'm going to go over to Sable's and tell her and Barbara about what happened to Amos last night." She picked up the painting of the sunset. "And I'm going to show them this too."

"It's a cool picture," Connor said. "He's a lot better artist than he thinks he is."

"That's an understatement," Maggie replied. "Your father is at work but when he gets back, we'll go see Amos. Okay?"

"Yeah. Sounds good."

After his mom left, Connor wanted to go check Amos's property for other traps that may have been placed around his pond. It seemed kind of strange to him that there would be only one. He wasn't sure what he would find, but he had given it a lot of thought and was going to be prepared this time. He pulled on several pairs of thick socks and then went out to the garage to the free weights his father used. He unscrewed the weights from several hand-held bars and duct-taped the bars to his calves on both sides of his legs.

His snake boots fit easily over the steel bars and he figured if he did step into a trap, the strong leather boots and the steel bars would protect him from any damage to his leg. He then removed the weights from the iron bar that his father used to do chest presses and took it with him. He would use that to set off the traps, if he found any, and also use it to test the ground around him. *Gotta anticipate what you may find and stay one move ahead* he told himself. He felt good as he looked at the knife hanging from his belt. *I'm ready.*

By the time Maggie got to Sable's, Barbara was there walking up the driveway and saw the painting.

"You sounded kind of manic on the phone," Barbara said. "What's going on? That's one of Amos's paintings, isn't it?"

"Yes, it is," Maggie replied.

"Is that what you wanted to show us?"

"Yes, but that's not all."

"Come on up this way ladies," Sable called from the front porch. Red was standing next to her.

After they were all comfortably seated in the great room and had been offered some cool drinks, Sable asked, "So, what's going on?"

" You won't believe it when I tell you – and show you. Last night after we left the party, we found Amos hurt. Well, Connor found him and came and got us," Maggie started the story.

"That's why Connor came running down to get Frances, wasn't it?" Barbara asked.

"Yes. His foot was snapped off by an animal trap."

"Oh my God!" Barbara gasped.

"Is he okay?" Red asked.

"Both Frances and the paramedics that came last night said they think he'll be fine. He's at the hospital and we're going to check on him this afternoon. We found him sitting on his back porch, just sitting there as if nothing had happened. He had numbed himself quite a bit with liquor and beer by the time we got to him though. He managed to get himself back to his house and cauterized the wound with his knife. His leg had stopped bleeding by the time we got there. He even had his chopped off foot wedged into the back door like a doorstop. Says he plans to have it bronzed."

"Oh my God," Barbara repeated as she shook her head.

"He's a very strong man," Red said. "I think he has looked death in the face many times but each time he has told him he wasn't ready to accompany him on the journey."

All Maggie could hear when Red said that was "Him very strong Kemosabe. Not afraid to die," as if Tonto was speaking to the Lone Ranger.

She started to tell them that Amos blamed Beth for putting the traps out there in the woods, but she held back. She remembered what Sean had told her last night. *Be aware and watchful.* She needed to be sure that Beth had committed the deed before accusing her of it. She knew Amos could have just as easily done it to himself but she wasn't going to say that. Not yet.

"Yes, I believe he received a bronze and silver star in the Vietnam War," Maggie replied. "I saw them as I was cleaning up the house. There were several other military ribbons too but I wasn't quite sure what they represented. I think Amos might have been a helicopter pilot in Vietnam. There were pictures of him on the wall standing in front of the helicopter with other soldiers. They had their arms around each other, drinking a beer of course. Amos hasn't ever said anything about it but I think he could have been a war hero."

"And he gave me this," Maggie continued as she pulled out the painting that was next to her chair.

Red picked it up and stared at it for a very long time before he placed it against the front window and stepped back from it.

"That is amazing," Barbara said as she looked at the picture.

"More than amazing," Sable said. "Amos painted this?"

"Yes, he paints the sunrise and sunset every day. Then he burns the paintings. He didn't get around to burning this one because of everything that happened to him last night and when I saw it, I was mesmerized by it. He gave it to me when he saw that I liked it. He said he lives for those moments when he sees the sunrise and the sunset. They give him a reason for being. He doesn't think he's very good at capturing what he sees, but I think he has captured nature itself in this painting."

"You have a good eye, Maggie Brodie," Red said. "The painting has a religious quality about it. As if God was there helping Amos move the brush."

Maggie couldn't have agreed more with what he was saying and she felt as if she was going to cry again. *Get a grip, Maggie,* she told herself. *Show them the other picture.*

"And I found this too." Maggie pulled out the photograph. She handed it to Barbara and told her and Sable to look closely at the girl's face and see if it reminded them of anyone.

Sable and Barbara peered at the picture and then as if they were telepathic, they both looked at each other and then over at Maggie and said the same words. In the same stupefied tone.

"That looks like a young Beth," they both said.

"Bingo! Look at the names on the back and the date on the picture. I know that's Amos's birthday. Elizabeth, or Beth as we know her, and Amos are connected to each other in a much different way than we all thought! I am not sure what their relationship is, but I think it is more than just estranged neighbors. More like estranged family members of some sort."

"Shit," Sable and Barbara said, again in unison.

" What a bitch," Barbara said. "I know this is Sunday but I mean. What a god damned bitch. She talks about him like he's nothing. She was like that with Sarah too. What a fucking bitch."

"Speaking of bitches," Maggie said. "What happened after we left the party?"

"It ended very soon after that. We didn't wait around for Jim to change into some dry clothes. Beth tried to console Renee. I think I learned a few more cuss words last night because she didn't stop for several minutes after you guys walked away," Sable said.

"I think I know how Renee can stand to be around Beth so much," Maggie said.

"How's that?" Barbara asked.

"I think all the vodka she drinks makes her somewhat deaf," Maggie said and they all laughed.

Connor walked around the pond, checking the ground with each step. He pressed the iron bar in a semi-circle around him before he moved forward. As he got toward the side of the pond, he saw something metallic catch the sun. On closer inspection, it was obviously a trap, not well-hidden, with only a few leaves covering it. No one would have stepped in that. It looked like it had been placed there as an afterthought, not from a well-thought-out plan.

He stuck the bar into the trap and it clanged as the metal teeth slammed shut, jarring the bar in Connor's hand. He understood how this type of trap could have snapped Amos's bones. These were large animal traps, meant to catch a mountain lion or perhaps even a bear. He had to strain to pull the teeth back to get the bar out.

He picked up the chain that was attached to the trap and realized how heavy they were. Together they must have weighed fifty pounds. He didn't remember the trap on the porch being this big, but it must have been. He moved the trap over to a safe place under a tree. He hadn't walked far when he saw another trap with even less cover over it. As he engaged the spring, the bar shook again and he began to wonder if the homemade safety device he had around his legs would be enough to keep him from getting maimed. He hoped he didn't have to find out.

He had to strain even harder this time to pry the teeth back so he could remove the bar. He picked it up by the chain and placed it with the other one. He thoroughly searched around the waterfall but didn't find any other traps. He did discover the spot where Amos must have been injured though. Blood saturated the ground and he saw some small bone fragments.

He poked around with the metal bar as he walked around the pond and waterfall another time, but he found nothing else. So he picked up the two traps and headed back home. Carrying both of them, along with the free weight bar, was not easy. He examined the traps and could tell they had some wear. They weren't new and they hadn't been well hidden which suggested to Connor that Amos had possibly put the traps out there himself. And hurt himself in doing so.

He didn't want to tell his parents yet what he had found. Or even more, what he thought may have happened. They might worry and stop him from going to see Amos. But he didn't want to tell them a lie either so he decided he just wouldn't say anything for now. When he got back home, he hid the two heavy traps in the woods behind his house. *Yeah,* he thought, *there was no sense in telling anyone about them yet. Maybe, someone might even need to use them.*

"Will you let us know how Amos is after you see him today?" Sable asked.

"Of course," Maggie said.

"You're going to ask him about that picture of him and the little girl, aren't you?" Barbara asked.

"No, I don't think so. I think I'm going to show it to someone else."

"Wrong," Barbara and Sable replied.

"I think you mean WE are going to show it to someone else," Barbara said as Sable nodded her head.

"Okay, Okay, We will. Tomorrow. I'll see you guys later."

"Tell Amos we are thinking about him," Red said as Maggie walked out the door and told them all that she would.

" What are you doing here?" Amos asked as they walked into his room at the VA hospital. "How did you know I was here?"

"Don't you remember Amos? I found you hurt last night when I brought you the food," Connor replied.

"Oh yeah, the steak. That was damn good. But how did you know I was here?"

"The EMTs told us where you would be."

"The em what?"

"Brian and Lee, the two young men that drove you to the hospital," Maggie replied.

"Oh yeah, Brian and that clumsy one that kicked my foot. You don't know where they put my foot do you?"

"No, we don't."

"Well by God, they better not have lost it," Amos grumbled. "Or there will be hell to pay."

"How are you doing?" Connor asked. "How's your leg?"

"Good, they tell me. Feels like my foot is still there. That's kind of weird, isn't it?"

A nurse came in and asked Amos if he needed anything as she checked the bandage around his leg.

"Hey, what's your name again?" he asked.

"Pam," the young nurse answered as she continued her examination.

"Can you show these folks a picture of my leg? On this computer screen, she can pull up a picture of my foot, or leg I mean. You can see the bone and where my foot was."

The nurse signed onto the computer and pulled up the x-ray and turned the monitor around so that everyone could see it.

"Tell 'em what the doctor said," Amos said as he looked at the nurse.

"They went in and cleaned everything out but it was a pretty clean break. About as good as it could be from how I hear it happened. The bone will eventually heal and in about a month or so, depending on how well he's doing, he can come back and be fitted for a prosthetic foot," the nurse said. "Is this your family, Amos?"

"No, they're my neighbors. Live right across the street from me. They're the ones that found me and called the ambulance."

" Do you know of any family we can contact?" Pam asked the Connors. "Amos says he doesn't have anyone around here. Says he has a brother but hasn't seen him in over thirty years. Not sure how to get hold of him or if he's even alive."

Maggie just shook her head no as she looked at Amos.

"But we'll help him. When he's ready to go home. We'll help him," Connor said. "You can tell us what we need to do and we'll do it."

"Is it okay to share your medical information with them?" Pam asked Amos.

"It sure the hell is," Amos replied. "I've shared more than that with them probably at one time or another."

Pam wasn't sure what Amos meant by that, but Maggie and Sean did. They had seen the naked Amos.

"Well, Amos was a little anemic when he got to the ER. They had to give him several units of blood before he was transported here. He lost quite a bit of blood from the trauma, but he's doing better now. He'll need to eat well when he gets back home and then he should continue to improve," Pam said.

"Maybe you can get me some more of that steak," Amos said as he winked at Connor.

"Yeah, we can bring you some steak," Maggie said as she looked over at Sean and he nodded.

"Can the sergeant make good steak?" Amos asked Maggie.

"He makes a very good steak."

"Well, seeing how I am a cripple and need to heal, I may need a lot of steaks, ain't that right, Pam?" Amos asked.

"Yes, Amos. A lot of protein would be good for you. And some vitamins would be a good idea too," Pam said as she looked at Maggie. Maggie understood the look. She knew that Amos probably didn't take care of himself as he should and that he needed vitamin supplements.

"Is there anything else I can get for you before I leave?" Pam asked.

"A beer would be nice," Amos replied.

"Now Amos, we've had that discussion several times. You are on pain medicine and antibiotics. You cannot have a beer while you are taking those medications."

"You can take me off the damn pain medicine and just get me a six-pack of beer and I'll be fine," Amos retorted.

Pam didn't need to ask any of Amos's visitors to know if Amos was like that all the time. She knew he was. She had seen too many veterans his age. Not eating properly and drinking probably led to some of his anemia she thought and she was right to a certain degree.

But there was also something else inside of Amos that was being masked by his traumatic injury. Something that was forming blood vessels that would burst as it grew, causing a loss of blood and anemic conditions within him. Something that the picture of his leg did not show and would require another type of picture. A picture that Amos would not share with anyone else.

Chapter 28

Another sunrise, Another sunset

Maggie got up early the next morning to watch the sunrise with Sean before he left for his morning run. *It is beautiful* she thought. *You are a lot smarter than the rest of us, Amos. We should be getting up with you each morning for this.* She laid her head on Sean's shoulder and sighed contentedly.

After Sean and Connor left for the day, Maggie sat down to check her email. She wondered if she should send out a message about Amos but decided not to since most of the neighbors probably already knew about what happened. And Beth, Renee, and Jim wouldn't care even if they did know. Darrin was still a question mark. She remembered Jasmine saying that Darrin was a nice guy back when they dated, but she wasn't sure what to think about him now. The only thing she knew for sure about Darrin was that Beth controlled him. And that happened to a lot of people who encountered Beth. So she told herself she didn't know enough about him yet to form an opinion. He could be a battered spouse for all she knew.

The sound of the doorbell interrupted her thoughts. She looked down at what she was wearing and for whomever it was, the pajama bottoms and white t-shirt of Sean's seemed acceptable. She peeked through the glass on the front door and opened it when she saw Jasmine.

"Good morning," Jasmine started. "I hope I didn't wake you."

"No, not at all, Jasmine. Please come in," Maggie said. "Can I get you something to drink? Some coffee or tea?"

"What are you drinking?" Jasmine said as she looked at Maggie's cup.

"Tea."

"That sounds good if it's not a bother."

"Oh, it's no problem."

Jasmine followed Maggie into the kitchen and sat at the table while Maggie heated some water.

"I just…" Maggie and Jasmine said at the same time and then smiled. Maggie told her to go first and Jasmine took a sip of her tea and began to talk.

"I just came here to apologize. What happened Saturday night to you was wrong."

"You had nothing to do with that, Jasmine. You have nothing to apologize for."

"I thought that at first, but then knowing how Beth is, I'm not sure that just my sitting with you didn't piss her off so much that she started putting thoughts in Renee's head. She did look at me in a very mean way when she came over and talked to us. I've seen that look before and I know how spiteful she can be. And after Renee's been drinking, putting thoughts in her head isn't that hard to do. So, I just wanted to come up here and apologize in person. You and Barbara and Sable and Agathe were so nice, but especially you. Sitting there and listening to me. You made me feel welcome and you made me laugh."

Maggie looked at Jasmine and thought what a sweet young woman she was. She started to tell her she pitied her having to live beside those terrible people but that wouldn't accomplish anything nor would it help the way Jasmine already felt. She already knew what horrible neighbors they were.

"I want to show you something, Jasmine," Maggie said as she stood up. "Come in the living room with me."

Amos's painting was leaning up against the wall and Jasmine walked over to examine it. "This is beautiful!"

"It is, isn't it? Our neighbor painted that."

"Red or Sable?" Jasmine knew they were both artists.

"Neither," Maggie replied. "Amos."

"Amos? Really? It's so beautiful. I didn't know he was so talented."

"Talented and now with one less foot." Before Jasmine could ask, Maggie explained. "First of all, let me just say, he's in the hospital and he's doing fine. He's a tough old coot that's for sure. But an old coot that I've become very fond of. That's what I was going to tell you earlier," Maggie said. "After the party, we found Amos at his home. His foot got caught in an animal trap. You haven't seen any animal traps down around where you live, have you?"

Jasmine shook her head no several times. She was stunned and couldn't believe what she was hearing. But even though the words were startling to her, she understood why Maggie was asking that question.

Maggie hadn't planned to show Jasmine the picture of Amos and the little girl but she could tell Jasmine knew why she had asked about the animal traps. *She feels the same way I do. She knows Beth could have put those traps out to hurt Amos, just like he had told Connor.*

"Can you hold on for just a minute?" Maggie asked as she went into the bedroom and came back with the photograph. "I found this at Amos's when I was cleaning up."

Jasmine stared at the picture in her hand. She turned it over and saw the words "*Amos and Elizabeth*" and the date on the edge of the photograph.

"That Elizabeth in this picture is Beth," Jasmine said with no hesitation. "I would recognize that face at any age. I have looked at that face for a very long time. That face has given me nightmares as I dreamed of her doing things to my husband. It has been branded into my memory with the hot iron of her stares and angry looks."

"I believe you and that's who I thought it was too," Maggie said. "I think Beth is related to Amos somehow. Not sure how yet but I'm certain there is some sort of familial tie between them. One that Beth doesn't want anyone to know about and one I'm afraid Amos has all but forgotten."

"Why did you ask Jennifer to check on Jorge's felony record?" Jasmine asked.

"Because I am sure Beth is having an affair with him and I have concerns about what kind of man he is," Maggie replied.

"Should I be worried about him?"

Maggie paused for a moment before she replied to that question. She couldn't say she watched him rob Sarah Cayman's house in the early hours of the morning. Savannah suggested he may have had a reason to be there. She also knew she couldn't say anything about the puss moths or the black widow either. At least not yet. Several years ago, she would have told everyone about what she thought about Jorge, but she couldn't do that now. She had learned what she said impacted not just her, but also Sean and Connor. And Connor couldn't handle any additional incendiary stimulus right now.

"Jennifer is doing some research for me so let's wait and see what she turns up. As soon as I hear from her, I'll let you know what she tells me."

"Okay. I'm going to cancel our lawn care with him though. I know Caleb won't have a problem with that once I tell him about Beth. As soon as he hears the word Beth come out of my mouth, he's like Pavlov's dog, provided you exchange salivating with sweating. He'll do anything I ask after he hears me mention Beth."

There's that strong vine again. Maggie knew she didn't need to tell Jasmine to be careful with Beth. She had heard the healthy suspicion in her language numerous times when she spoke of her. Beth was about to have her legs taken out from under her when she showed her that photograph. And once Beth was put in her place, she would lose the ability or desire to do anything to Jasmine. No, she didn't need to worry about Jasmine.

On Monday morning, Emiliano couldn't sleep. Thoughts were swirling around in his head as he tried to make sense of everything. He got up before dawn, fixed himself a cup of coffee, and sat outside to watch the sun come up. The sunrise made him think about all the things Luna was telling him about this being his second chance at life. She sensed the spiritual connection that was leading him down the path he needed to follow. She was certain that if he did, he would find success, not only in his work but also in being a better man. The sunrise indicated a new day had begun and Emiliano knew it meant more than just the passage of time.

His aunt got home a little after seven and saw Emiliano sitting on the small front porch. She asked him what he was doing and he said he was just thinking and watching a beautiful sunrise. He asked if she would like for him to drive the young ones to school and Luna smiled as she put her hands on his cheeks and kissed his forehead.

"Thank you for the kind gesture, Emiliano. But I have to go to the grocery store so I might as well take them. What I need you to do is continue what you are doing. You have changed so much in the last week. For the first time in a long time, I can see you becoming successful. Continue to be successful, Sobrino. That will be a good day for me." Luna walked inside and began preparing breakfast for her children.

Emiliano checked the oil and gasoline on all his equipment and got in his truck and headed to his first job of the day. He would be working on three yards in Northridge and he figured that it would take him about five or six hours to get them all done. He was working on his third yard when he saw the homeowner standing on her porch. He turned off his mower to go over and speak with her.

"How are you this fine morning, I mean afternoon?" the elderly lady said as she smiled at Emiliano.

"Bueno, muy bueno," Emiliano replied as he removed his straw hat. "How are you, Mrs. Smith?"

"I am pretty good for an 87-year-old woman. Got a little hitch in my giddy-up, but I'm still able to get around. The good Lord has blessed me in that way, 'cause I can still drive, get to the grocery store, the beauty salon, to church, anywhere I want to. Can't say the same about some of my friends. I'm afraid for some of them, their giddy-up done got up and left."

Emiliano smiled. "I am very happy for you, Mrs. Smith."

"You know, I just heard on the news this morning about the young girl that they found in the lake."

Emiliano felt his heart racing.

"Said she apparently committed suicide. Just walked out in the lake and drowned. I don't see or understand how someone can do that. Said a boat ran over her body and decapitated it, but they don't think the fellow in the boat even saw her. They are still looking for that head. Just breaks my heart."

Emiliano crossed his chest as he looked up at Mrs. Smith.

"You look a little pale," she said with concern. "Can I get you a cold bottle of pop? Got some orangeade in the fridge. Nehi orange. Been drinking it for over eighty years and still ain't lost the taste for it."

"Si, yes," Emiliano said. "That would taste good I think."

"Be right back." Within a minute she returned with two open bottles and handed one to Emiliano. "Thought I'd have one with you," Mrs. Smith said as she tipped her bottle toward Emiliano.

"Gracias," he replied as he took a large drink of the cold soda. It did taste good. Made all the better by the information he had just been told. He wasn't seeing things and he wouldn't be charged for any murder. Luna was right. He needed to listen to the voices of the dead. They provided him guidance and he needed to take advantage of it. He knew he was still hiding some things from Luna and his clients, but he would make that right very soon. *The sunset this evening will not make me anxious. I look forward to it tonight.*

Before she left the house to meet Sable and Barbara, Maggie made a quick call to Dr. Nutt. She left a message for her to please call as soon as she was able. *I need to set Connor up with someone that he can talk to. I don't want to let things go on too long without him receiving some help.* But she put all that out of her mind as she went out the door. Sable was waiting for Maggie at Barbara's house and together they walked down the road to Beth's.

"Do you know what you're going to say?" Barbara asked Maggie.

"Not really," Maggie replied. "I think it all depends on Beth."

"Oh shit," Barbara said, thinking to herself that it wasn't a very good idea to "wing it" when it came to dealing with Beth.

There was no answer when they knocked on the door. Maggie knocked several more times and rang the doorbell, but to no avail.

"You think she's not home?" Sable asked.

"No, I think she's home. Ignoring us." Maggie turned and walked around to the back of the house with Barbara and Sable following.

They found Beth sitting on her back porch on the phone. When she saw the three women come around the corner Beth smiled. She held up one finger indicating she would only be a moment as they walked up and sat down at the patio table. They heard Beth laugh and say she had no idea but she would let her know later. Maggie took that to mean she was talking about them, but she wasn't. Beth was talking to her travel agent about a trip to Hawaii that she and Darrin had planned to take for Christmas. As she ended the call, she looked over at them and smiled.

"What brings this tribunal to my house?" Beth asked sarcastically. "You're not planning on throwing me in the pool, are you?"

Maggie ignored what Beth was saying and just pulled the photo out of her pocket and placed it on the table. "Ever seen this picture before, Beth?" Maggie asked.

Beth picked up the picture and glanced over at them while studying it. Maggie thought she was acting as if she had never seen it before, but she expected that. She wasn't expecting what Beth did next. She ripped up the picture and set the pieces on fire and then threw them onto the patio.

"Anything else?" Beth asked sweetly.

Barbara and Sable were startled, and though Maggie didn't expect Beth to burn the photo, she knew she should have anticipated better. *Destroy the evidence* she said to herself. *Deny everything and destroy the evidence. Fuck Maggie, you should have known better.*

"We know that was you with Amos, on his birthday," Maggie stated. "Why would you be on a horse with Amos? Were you celebrating your uncle's birthday?"

"Nope. Don't know what picture you're referring to either," Beth said as if the photo had never existed.

"Beth, just because you destroyed the picture, doesn't mean we all didn't see it," Barbara replied.

"Still not sure what you're talking about," Beth said.

"Do you know that Jorge's grandmother and aunt were good friends with Sarah Cayman?" Maggie asked.

"No. And I don't care if they were."

"I don't think his aunt or your husband would appreciate the fact that her nephew and the yardman is having an affair with you. And doesn't it make you mad that Jasmine had sex with your husband?" Maggie asked. As the words left her mouth, she wished she could take them back. She only said that to make Beth mad and she could see that she accomplished that. But when she saw the fury in her eyes, she knew she had just made things worse for Jasmine too.

"What do the three blind mice plan to do now?" Beth asked. "All I've heard and seen so far are fairy tales. Things that don't exist except in the mind of the little mice."

"We know what you did to Amos," Maggie said.

"Really, and what is that?"

"You put out animal traps around his waterfall, so he would hurt himself," Maggie said. Again, as she said the words, she realized she shouldn't have. Barbara and Sable looked shocked by the accusation.

"You're losing it, Maggie," Beth said. "Don't own, never have owned, and wouldn't even know how to use an animal trap. If Amos hurt himself with an animal trap, it's of his own doing. Just more proof of how dangerous he's becoming. I think I may have to call social services on him. If he's putting traps out that could hurt a dog or poor deer that walked through the woods. Well, that's just awful to imagine. Or, God forbid, hurt your son who is always poking around the pond for God knows what."

Maggie jumped up from her chair and Barbara grabbed her arm before she could do anything else.

"God damn you!" Maggie said. "If I hear or find out you did anything to harm my family, I will not hesitate to come down here and make you wish you weren't born. I know what you did to me and I will prove it one day, so be careful. Be very careful."

"If I didn't know how distraught and unstable your mind was, I would consider that a threat," Beth replied. "And it just so happens there are two witnesses to everything you just said."

"We didn't hear her threaten you, Beth," Barbara said.

"No, not at all," Sable said. "She just asked you some questions about your past. Which appears to be catching up with you. No threats. Just neighborly advice. A threat is what we heard from your friend the other night as she yelled at the Brodies and their young son. I hadn't thought about it until now, but perhaps I should call social services or the police about that. Check on their drinking habits. God only knows if they're drinking and driving through the neighborhood or the streets of Augusta."

"Good one, Sable. Well, I am so glad you all were able to drop by. Is there anything else I can do for you ladies?"

Hearing nothing, she told them to have a nice day as she walked inside and closed the door.

"Well, shit," Maggie said.

"Don't worry" Barbara said. "I think what she did proves that it was her in the picture. Why else would she destroy it? But Maggie, those comments about Jasmine and Darrin. That wasn't good. That will just make Beth hate her more knowing that we know. And are you sure that she is having an affair with the yard guy?"

"Positive," Maggie answered.

"Well it isn't surprising but I think the only people that will be hurt by that information are Darrin and her kids. I don't think that's what we want to see happen," Barbara said. "And those traps, are you sure you know Beth had something to do with that? That would be hard to prove without fingerprints or pictures showing that she did that. And I doubt you'll find either of those. You know ever since you told me about Amos's injury, unfortunately, I've been thinking a lot like Beth on that idea. He could have put them out there himself and just forgotten. If anyone else had walked over there, a person or dog, Oh, I just can't imagine."

"Someone poisoned Amos's fish," Maggie said. "That's why he put the traps out there."

Maggie shook her head as she realized what she just said: "Amos put the traps out there." She didn't want to admit it but she just had. Beth and Barbara were right. Sean was right too. *Why didn't you listen to Sean? You know better, Maggie. Now the only thing you have done is probably made things worse for Amos and Jasmine.*

"Come on Maggie," Barbara said as she took her arm. "What you did was a good thing. It gave notice to Beth that we know who she is and she showed us a perfect picture of what a bitch she is. We know she's related to Amos and treats him with disdain and wants him out of here. And we know what a lying bitch she is, having an affair with the yard guy. Which by the way, why didn't you tell us that earlier? You can't keep that type of juicy news all to yourself."

That made her laugh and feel better. As they walked home, Barbara took Maggie's hand and looked into her face. "You know before you got here, no one would stand up to Beth. Now someone has and we appreciate it. Her influence and the 'my way or the highway' attitude is gone now. We know who she is. She is not a nice person. In fact, she's a very nasty person. Without you, it may not have revealed itself until it was too late. Especially for Amos. Granted, we will need to address some things with him but we won't let him get hurt by her. I promise you that."

"What she said," Sable agreed.

"See you later? Okay?" Barbara asked.

"Yes, see you later, and thank you." She hugged them both before walking up to her house.

Maggie sat out on the patio with a cold glass of iced tea and listened to the waterfall until Connor came home. She told him to put his books down and come with her because they were going to the VA to see Amos. She handed Connor the keys and told him to drive. He got behind the wheel and smiled all the way to the hospital.

Amos was lying in bed staring at the wall. He didn't greet them when they walked in and looked like a different person from yesterday. When he heard their voices. he turned toward Connor and asked him about Hank. Connor didn't know what to say as he looked up at his mom.

"Who's Hank?" she asked.

"My pilot. I had just strafed the jungle with my 30 caliber when a mortar struck the front of it and the chopper hit the ground. Hank was hurt bad. He's somewhere in this hospital but I can't find him and no one I ask will tell me anything about him."

Maggie sat down next to Amos and held his hand.

"The skies are so beautiful here," Amos said. "You wouldn't think they would be that different over here in the jungle but they are. The sunrise and sunset. Man, that's when they are the most spectacular. When all the smoke is gone and there are no bombs or loud noises, you can just sit there and see some of the most beautiful pictures in the world. And those are precious times because you never know if you'll be there to see it the next day. I've been trying to recreate them ever since I saw the first ones, but I just haven't gotten it right yet."

Amos asked Connor if he would help him to the window. Connor lifted him into the wheelchair and wheeled him over. They both knew what he wanted and what he needed. He needed to see the sunset. Maggie whispered to Connor that she was going to find a nurse. Amos continued talking about the jungle and the beautiful skies.

The nurse, Pam, was very reluctant to tell Maggie much. She did say that Amos would be in the hospital a little longer so that they could run some more tests. She said she couldn't say any more than that due to patient confidentiality rules. Maggie shook her head and told Pam she understood and walked back into the room. She knew she wouldn't get any useful information out of Amos today and the only thing she could do for him was to be there and let him watch the sunset; his refuge from the angry world of his past and the disheartening world of the present.

Amos watched the sun go down and he tried to remember what the doctor had told him earlier in the day. He remembered him saying he needed another test and he remembered agreeing to have it but he didn't remember what kind of test it was. He didn't really care and he remembered telling the doctor that he would have one more test but after that he was done. He didn't need to have any more tests after that one since his tour of duty was over and he was going home where he could look at the sunrises and sunsets. The thought of that made him happy.

Chapter 29

Phinizy Swamp

As they were leaving the hospital, Connor asked his mother if she thought Amos was going to be okay.

"I'm not sure." Maggie considered her answer. "The nurse said they need to do some more tests. I think he may be sicker than he knows."

"Yeah, I do too," he replied quietly.

Regardless of what the tests showed, Maggie knew that Amos would be in trouble once he got home. Connor deserved to know what was going on.

"Connor," Maggie started, and before she could get any further, a text message alert popped up on her car phone. She saw that it was from Jennifer and she pushed the "read to me" icon.

"Nothing found on Jorge. Sorry. But good news. Frances is on our side. See you later."

"What did that mean?" Connor asked.

Maggie paused before answering. She remembered what she and Sean had said about keeping this information to themselves. But she had pushed the button now. Without even thinking she had pushed the button. She couldn't lie to Connor. They had agreed to not lie to each other some time ago when things were bad back in Florida. But she also remembered how her son looked when he pushed Jim into the pool. It made her concerned enough to call Hazel to find professional help for him. *So now what are you supposed to do*, she asked herself. Before she could answer, Connor made the decision easier for her.

"You think Jorge is a criminal of some sort, don't you?"

"I had asked Jennifer to check on Jorge to see if he had any felony record. She didn't find any. So I was wrong. And the part about Frances. It just means she is now on our side to not drain the pond. That is sort of what I was going to tell you before I get the text from Jennifer," Maggie said.

"Here's my phone," Maggie said as she handed it to Connor. "Text Jennifer back and tell her thanks and would she mind telling Frances that Amos is still in the hospital and doing fine."

As they drove home, Connor realized that the data bank Jennifer searched could be wrong. Maybe that wasn't even his real name. His mother didn't trust Jorge for other reasons that she wouldn't say. But he didn't trust him either. Someone put the salt in Amos's pond. And the puss moths and black widow did not get there by accident. His mother had good reason to be wary of him, even if the database didn't reveal anything. All this text did for Connor was to reinforce the need to be watchful and ready to act.

"Like I was saying, that was sort of what I was going to tell you," Maggie said. "But I think, Amos may have hurt himself with the animal trap. I think he put it there and stepped in it by accident. That makes things even worse for Amos."

"What do you mean it makes it worse for him?"

"Neighbors can put up with him walking around naked, but they can't fear walking around the pond wondering if they're going to step in a bear trap, or whatever it was. It could hurt people, dogs. You know that."

"I don't think he has any more traps," Connor said.

Maggie looked at him and wondered how he knew that. *Oh, dear God, no. He wouldn't have helped Amos put that trap out, would he?* She was afraid to ask but she knew she had to.

"How do you know?" she asked suspiciously.

"I thought the same thing you did," Connor replied. "So, I went over there to check for more traps. I found a couple and set them off. Then I took them."

"Connor, that could have been very dangerous!"

"Could have, but I was prepared. Plus, they were in plain sight. They weren't even hidden. That's when I knew for sure Amos had put them out."

"But how do you know you got them all? And what did you do with them?" Maggie asked.

"I looked all over the waterfall area and around the pond a few times and I only found two more. I can't imagine him getting out there again when he gets home and trying something like this. He'll be in a wheelchair for months. He'll be able to get around the house, but he couldn't carry something like those traps. They were heavy. Very heavy. I think we'll be fine."

Maggie wasn't sure what to say. In one way, she was impressed that Connor was able to think about that and do something about it. In another way, she was scared that he thought about that and did something about it. *He is there again. Without question, he is there again. He feels like he needs to protect me and now Amos.*

"I want you to show me those traps when we get home, okay?" Maggie said.

"Sure," he replied.

Dr. Nutt returned Maggie's earlier call as they were pulling up to the house. She told Connor she had to take the call but she wanted to see those traps as soon as she was finished. After Connor got out of the car, Maggie told Hazel that she had called to see if she could recommend a child psychologist for Connor.

"Why are you asking that?" Hazel asked.

"He's acting in a way I have seen before," Maggie said. "He thinks he needs to protect me and he does things. Scary things. The therapist he saw in Florida helped him a lot."

"What kind of things?"

"Well, he pushed our neighbor into the pool the other night at a cookout over something he said and the look in his eyes scared me. It was as if he had disassociated himself from where he was or what he did," Maggie said. "It didn't bother him at all. And then he did some dangerous stuff at our neighbor's house."

"What do you mean by dangerous stuff?"

"He was looking for animal snares, like traps, and setting them off so he could remove them," Maggie explained.

"What kind of neighborhood do you live in, Maggie?" Before she could respond, Hazel spoke again.

"I think it would be a good idea if you and Connor both come see me this Thursday. I'll set up a time for him, just after my session with you. Then we can go from there. Does that sound okay?"

"Yes, thank you, Doctor. I really appreciate your understanding," Maggie said as she hung up.

She asked Connor to show her where he put the traps. As she examined them, she could tell that he was right. It would be next to impossible for Amos to set this type of trap out by himself again. Not in a wheelchair.

"I doubt the body at the lake would have surfaced if these traps had been around," Maggie heard Connor say nonchalantly.

She couldn't believe he would say something as cold and as unfeeling as that. "You know that body at the lake - you and your father had nothing to do with it. The water moccasin didn't kill it," Maggie said.

Connor acted like he didn't hear her. He was removing himself from conversations he didn't want to have. And she knew better than to irritate or alienate him by continuing to discuss it. *That appointment with Hazel can't come soon enough.*

"Connor," Maggie said as she stood up and put her arm around him. "My therapist…"

"Dr. Nutt?" Connor asked. "Dr. Hazel P. Nutt?

"Yes, that Dr. Nutt," Maggie replied as she managed a disingenuous smile. "Well, she told me that she would like to see both of us next Thursday. She thinks that would be helpful. Are you okay with that?"

"On one condition."

"What's that?" Maggie asked.

"That you buy some prosciutto the next time you're at the store. I had that the other night at the cookout. It was great," Connor said.

"Deal," Maggie said, relieved at the simple request. "You know we need to tell your father about these traps, don't you?"

"I understand. But they sure could come in handy if we wanted to put them out in our yard. You know to protect us from criminals, rabid animals, and such."

Maggie knew he was referring to Jorge and she wanted to stop that type of thinking from going any further.

"That's not a good idea, Connor," Maggie replied. "It could hurt someone or something we don't want to hurt."

"Yeah, I guess you're right," Connor replied and smiled at his mother. Maggie knew she would have to check on those traps routinely to make sure they were still there. She was concerned about what her son had said and was continuing to say about them.

"Oh, I need you to sign a permission slip for me," Connor said as they walked back into the house. "It's for a field trip on Wednesday to a place called Phinizy Swamp."

"Well any place with the name Swamp in it, I'm sure is a place everyone needs to visit," Maggie said as she looked at the permission slip. She read the disclaimer that said there are indeed dangerous animals that live within this habitat, but the guided tours through the swamp are very educational and safe.

"It sounds pretty cool. Lots of plants and animal life there. It has wetlands and woodlands. Over 1000 acres. Home to red-shouldered hawks, ospreys, great blue herons, soras, wood ducks, and bald eagles," Connor informed her.

"Soras?" What are soras?" Maggie asked.

"Small brown birds that make their home in freshwater marshes. I bet you've heard them before. They have distinctive whistles and whinnies, but they're pretty elusive and not easy to find."

"Ok, what I just heard you say, was that you are going off the trail from everyone looking for this bird as soon as you hear it whistle to you. That is not acceptable. Did you see this disclaimer on the permission slip?"

"There are all sorts of frogs there too. Green tree frogs, bronze frogs, and bullfrogs to name a few. Lots of different kinds of butterflies that you would probably find pretty cool. There are the red-spotted purple, the silver-spotted and broad-winged skipper, the common buckeye, the cloudless Sulphur, the zebra, and the black and eastern swallowtail. There are snapping turtles, brown water snakes, and three poisonous snakes: the copperhead, water moccasin, and the pygmy rattlesnake. There are also beavers, and muskrats," Connor said as he tried to ignore the question from his mother.

"Are there alligators there?"

"It's a swamp. What do you think?" Connor answered sarcastically. As soon as saw his mother's glaring eyes, he realized he shouldn't have. "Sorry. Yes, they are there, but they are harmless unless you feed them."

"Or until you get in the water with them and pretend that you are food!" Maggie replied emphatically, even though she remembered Red saying the same thing. But it didn't matter what Connor and Red said. If you are in the water with the alligator and if the alligator is big enough, she knew it would check to see if you were part of the menu for the day.

"I am not signing this unless you promise me you don't get off the trail and go looking for the sorta or some colorful snake that comes sliding by," Maggie said as she held the paper in her hand and looked at her son.

"It's sora," Connor corrected her. "And I promise not to go off the wooden trails." He wondered if she would catch that clarifying statement.

Maggie nodded her head and signed the permission slip. "Take some pictures for me of the butterflies and the birds. Not interested in the other. Unless you see a beaver or muskrat. Not sure I even know what a muskrat looks like."

"Sure," Connor said as he took the slip. *She didn't catch it. There are a lot of non-wooden trails out there in the swamp too.* He had done some research on the swamp when he heard about the trip and realized that the most interesting wildlife would be found off the dirt trails and not necessarily along the pedestrian wooden paths. If he happened to go off of one of those, he wouldn't be breaking the promise he just made to his mother.

"It looks like a cross between a beaver and a gopher. The muskrat," Connor said as he went back to his bedroom and began playing "God of War."

How does he know all this stuff, Maggie asked herself as she shook her head in amazement. Though she tried not to, she couldn't help but think about the alligator that Amos had killed and wondered what he had done with it. *I wonder if the teacher takes a gun with them on the trip. No. I bet they wouldn't allow it. The school wouldn't take a bunch of kids into a place that wasn't safe. You are worrying too much Maggie. Take a breath. Connor will be fine.*

She pulled out a notepad and made a note to herself to ask Amos about the alligator hide he was going to make a belt out of as she started preparing dinner. She hadn't walked two steps when she turned around and wrote down 'buy prosciutto' for Connor under the question about Amos's belt. "Can't remember a thing," she said out loud, "if I don't write it down," as she pulled the chicken out of the freezer and began to thaw it in the microwave.

On Wednesday, Mr. Talbot's science class loaded up on the yellow school bus. He checked each student's permission slip as they climbed aboard. Mr. Talbot stood up in the aisle as the bus pulled out of the parking lot and began the speech that he gave each time they went to the swamp.

"Ok, ladies and gentlemen, listen up," he began. "I have been going to Phinizy Swamp long before it became a natural resource for this area. It was named after Ferdinand Victor Francois Phinizy, an Italian gentleman who first settled there in 1778. It used to be a cattle pasture and in fact, between 1950 and 1973, Gracewood Mental Institute used patients as farmhands there. The water treatment plant built in the 1960s dumped its wastewater into those wetlands and in 1993, the government told Augusta it needed to do something besides destroying the water and the wetlands. That's when the nature park was developed and the Army Corp of Engineers got very smart about finding ways for wetland mitigation. Tremendous improvement in water and land management has been made so that creatures who could not live there due to the dreadful conditions of the land and water are now beginning to thrive there. River otters have returned to Butler Creek which empties into the Phinizy wetlands and pollution intolerant insects such as mayflies, caddisflies, and riffle beetles have returned. The 1100-acre nature park, we will be going through today, is just a part of over 7000 acres of wetlands."

"Yes, Mr. Lowe - question?" Mr. Talbot responded to the raised hand.

"Will we be seeing all 1100 acres today?"

"It would take several days to do that, Mr. Lowe. We'll only be out there for about five hours today, including our lunch break. Did anyone not bring a lunch? Good. Everyone has one. I brought a couple of extras in case anyone forgot. So, we should be good. Remember, stay on the paths. We will be on wooden walkways and some well-formed dirt pathways, but there are animals out there that could hurt you if you aren't paying attention. Especially if you go off the path. I've only seen one pygmy rattlesnake and one copperhead on the trails in all the time I've been doing these trips and if you give them time and space, they'll go on their way. But again, let's be smart and safe, and enjoy what nature has provided us. It is a beautiful place and I think you'll see and learn a lot today. Does anyone have any questions?"

"What if we need to go to the bathroom?" Dennis Lowe asked.

"There are bathrooms there, Mr. Lowe. Avail yourself of them before we go down a trail. Any other questions?"

"Are there alligators there?"

"Yes, Miss Turpin, there are. Some as big as 10 feet."

"Won't they hurt us?"

"Depends, Miss Turpin. Do you plan on getting in the water with them?

"No, sir."

"Then I think you'll be okay. But do not, and I cannot stress this enough, do not ever feed an alligator. They become very dangerous once they associate humans with food. We are not on their menu and we don't want to become a menu item because they are very indiscriminate eaters. Okay, we should be there in about twenty minutes. We'll leave our lunches in the welcome center when we arrive and then one of the guides, Bill Scheuer, will take us on several trails before we come back to eat lunch. You'll like Bill. He is an excellent guide and knows a lot about the swamp and the animals in it."

Connor and Sam Nixon were sitting together and had become good friends in the short time they had known each other. After Mr. Talbot sat down, Sam turned to Connor.

"I've been out to the swamp several times. It's a great place for snakes. There are water moccasins everywhere you turn it seems. I've never seen a rattlesnake or even a copperhead. But I've seen the ribbon snake and the rough green snake, and the banded water snake. I'd like to have one of those banded water snakes but I don't have a good place to keep him."

"I do," Connor replied. "That large pond in our neighborhood would be a perfect environment for it."

"Yeah, that would be perfect. But how are we going to get it back on the bus? It would fit in my backpack but I don't think it would like being in there. We'd have to come back sometime with an aquarium and catch one."

"But would the rangers and guides at the park allow that?" Connor asked. "I saw on the website, there is no hunting and fishing within the park itself."

"In the park, that's right," Sam replied. "But there are about 6000 acres not in the park."

"We'd have to camp out," Connor replied.

"Probably," Sam replied.

"Well, I can't say I wouldn't love to do it, but I'll have to wait a while before I ask my parents if we can do that. My mother's a little touchy about things right now. Long story short, but she saw an alligator in our pond and got all freaked out about it," Connor said.

"I understand," Sam said. "My mom's the same way. Doesn't come near my room because of the snakes. We'll talk about it later."

Mr. Scheuer had the students buddy up and then repeated a lot of what Mr. Talbot already said. He explained about the trails that they would be going on this morning and told them to be on the lookout for the butterflies and birds that Connor had mentioned to his mother. He said that they would be going by a beaver dam too and if they were lucky, they would see one.

As they followed the wooden walkways, Mr. Scheuer would stop and point to a plant or tree that he wanted to talk about and each time they stopped, another insect or animal always came into view. He would get excited and tell everyone to take a picture with their phones. Sam and Connor were doing that before he even mentioned it, but most everyone else in the group was not that interested.

They saw several bald eagles, an osprey, and two blue herons and Connor heard the sora many times. Mr. Scheuer excitedly pointed out a few alligators that popped their heads up as they walked by and when they got to the beaver dam, they stood there for about ten minutes hoping to see a beaver, but none ever appeared. Connor was taking a picture of one of the many butterflies when he saw the first snake. It was a water moccasin, just like the one in their pond. It ignored everyone who was watching it as it swam across the top of the water before disappearing into the murky shadows of the large cypress trees and their many knees that suggested they had stood there for a very long time.

They got back to the welcome center at about 12:30 for their lunch break. Sam and Connor sat down on an old tree stump that had been carved out in the shape of a bench.

"Cool place, huh?" Sam asked.

"Yeah, it is," Connor replied. "My mom will love all the pictures of the butterflies I got. Too bad we didn't see more snakes."

"Yeah, but on this next trail, we'll be going by a real marshy area. It doesn't look like that from the path, but I know it pretty well. This trail is a great place for different plant life and I know our guide will be pointing out a lot of the plants and insects and some of the skinks that are everywhere. Heck, I have those same skinks in my backyard, and the plants, well, I could do without that dissertation. This marshy place I'm talking about is not too far off the trail and it's a great place to find snakes. We could go over there and look around for a few minutes and be back up with the group before they even miss us," Sam said.

"It's not off a wooden pathway, is it?" Connor asked.

"No, but it's in the woods. Why?" Sam asked.

"Just wondering," Connor replied. He didn't need to tell Sam about the promise he made to his mother.

After lunch, Mr. Scheuer and Mr. Talbot gathered the group and told them the trail they were going on this afternoon was a dirt pathway and they both reiterated that it was safe but everyone needed to stay on the trail. Within minutes, they had "buddied up" again and Mr. Talbot took a roll call. With everyone accounted for, they headed down the trail.

After about twenty minutes, Sam elbowed Connor and nudged him off the trail into the woods. They could still hear Mr. Scheuer talking about the plants as they made their way into the marsh. It wasn't long before Sam grabbed Connor's arm and pointed at the ground. To their right was a black racer and it seemed to stare at them for just a second before it disappeared into the brush.

"Damn, those things are fast!" Sam said as they moved further into the marsh almost up to their waist in the boggy area. Connor saw the movement first and snatched Sam back. The two of them stood frozen as they kept an eye on the large tan snake that was moving through the water. Connor guessed it was about nine feet long as he watched the hypnotic movements of the brown blotchy patterns on the large snake.

"That's a Burmese python," Connor whispered to Sam and Sam whispered back a "yeah."

They both knew that snake shouldn't be here in this swamp. It had to have been left there by some irresponsible owner. They just didn't understand how it had managed to survive the weather in Georgia. They weren't supposed to be able to do that. Sam and Connor followed it as it led them down further into the marsh until they were almost next to the water. They were both recording the movement of the large snake on their phones when they heard Mr. Talbot's voice behind them.

"What are you boys doing back in here? I told you to stay on the trail! It can be very dangerous back here." That's when he saw what the boys were pointing at.

"Oh my God!" Mr. Talbot cried as he felt something painful against his leg.

"Hellfire!" he yelled as the large ten-foot alligator rose out of the murky water and clamped onto his shoulder and dragged him down. Mr. Talbot's body was spun around as the alligator went into its death roll. Connor and Sam saw one of Mr. Talbot's arms float to the surface, followed moments later by his head. His mouth and eyes had a frozen hysterical look about them as the head bobbed in the water. It looked like he was still screaming, but Connor and Sam heard nothing except the alligator moving around and continuing to gulp down its food.

Connor pulled Amos's knife from his backpack and Sam's eyes widened when he saw the large blade.

"You hold onto my shirt and lead us out of here," Connor said to Sam. "I'll make sure we don't end up on this son of a bitch's dessert menu."

Sam directed Connor out of the marsh and back onto the trail. When they heard Mr. Scheuer talking about some pitcher plants, Sam yelled out to him and he and the students turned and looked. Sam waved his arms and cried, "Help!" Mr. Scheuer told the students to wait there and not move. He ran toward them while Connor tucked the knife back in his pack. Sam whispered urgently to Mr. Scheur and told him what happened and Connor watched as his face turned white and then saw a worried but determined look take over. He asked Connor and Sam if they were comfortable waiting there until he could return with some help and they both nodded their heads yes.

Mr. Scheuer announced to the other students that the tour was over and they needed to get back to the welcome center as soon as possible. He said Mr. Talbot had been hurt and needed some help. They heard him call 911 on his cell phone as he told the students to follow him as fast as they could. Connor and Sam both knew there was nothing anyone could do for Mr. Talbot but they understood why Mr. Scheuer was saying what he did. As the rest of the students hurried back to the welcome center, Connor and Sam were quiet for a moment, keeping an eye on the woods around them.

Sam broke the silence first. "What do you think, Connor?"

"I think that alligator was chasing down that python."

"Yeah, that's what I was thinking too. But, if we hadn't been there, this wouldn't have happened."

"But we were there Sam and we can't move backward in time. If Mr. Talbot hadn't come after us, one of us might be dead now."

"Yeah, that's what I was thinking," Sam replied.

"It was an accident, Sam. A very bad accident. We didn't want anyone to get hurt but they did. There was nothing we could have done."

"Yeah, that's what I was thinking," Sam replied.

"I don't think the school will be coming back to Phinizy Swamp for a long time and I'm sure we won't be camping out here anytime soon."

"Yeah, that's what I was thinking," Sam replied.

Chapter 30

Therapy

"Hurry! We don't have time to wait!" Mr. Scheuer cried as the EMTs ran up to the welcome center. They followed Mr. Scheuer to where Connor and Sam were waiting on the trail. As they started off the trail, one of the EMTs hesitated.

"Hold on just a minute. We need to find out what's going on before we just run off into these marshes. I've hunted out here, just outside the park and it can be quite intimidating if you don't know what you're doing and watch yourself."

Sam looked at Connor for a reply and Connor provided one. "It won't matter," he replied. "Mr. Talbot is beyond hurt. A ten-foot alligator got hold of him. We only saw body parts on the surface of the water. One of them being his head."

"God all mighty," the other EMT muttered.

"Do any of you have a gun?" Connor asked.

"Yeah, I have one with me," the first EMT said. "I figured we might need one." He pulled out a 9mm Glock. One of the Georgia wildlife experts that Mr. Scheuer had called to help said he had one too. He also pulled a machete out of his backpack.

"Those will be helpful." Connor reached into his pack and pulled out his knife.

"Holy shit!" Mr. Scheuer shrieked.

"We think the alligator was chasing this." Connor held out his phone for all of them to see.

"God damn," Mr. Scheuer said. "That's a python!"

" What's a python doing in this swamp?" the EMT asked.

"I suspect it was put here by an owner that didn't want it anymore. It must have been left out here sometime in the spring. It wouldn't have survived a winter here," Mr. Scheuer replied, still shaken by what was happening.

"Are you ready to go?" Connor asked.

"Yes if you're ready to lead the way," the EMT with the Glock responded.

"Okay, follow me." Connor began to follow his tracks back into the woods. It wasn't hard. The limbs of small trees were broken off and there were footprints in the mud until the water started to cover the land.

Though Connor wouldn't have believed it, the arm and head of Mr. Talbot were still floating on the water like a gruesome buoy when they reached the spot of the attack.

"I don't think we need to look around too much in here, do you?" one of the EMTs asked Mr. Scheuer.

"No, it probably wouldn't be wise. We'll need to come back with more trackers," he said as he looked at the other Georgia wildlife personnel for agreement.

"The alligator is more of an issue than the python," one of the wildlife experts said. "And I'm sure it's still around here somewhere. We need to get out of here as soon as we can and then come back with others that can hunt down that alligator and that python. I think everything else that may have been Mr. Talbot, is long gone."

The EMTs placed the arm and head into a red biohazard bag and together, everyone backed away from where they were with their heads on a swivel. Watching Sam and Mr. Scheuer lead them out, they kept looking back over their shoulder for the large reptile that they did not want to see reappear.

All of the students at the welcome center were waiting and watching the trail for a sign that things were okay. As they saw everyone return, they began trying to identify who was missing from that group. The awareness of who was not there was almost simultaneous among them and it felt as if an exposed electrical cord had been dropped down into a large pool of water in which they were all standing.

Neither Mr. Scheuer nor the Georgia wildlife personnel was prepared to handle the shock or questions that were forming like large word balloons and hovered over many of the students. Unseen but waiting to burst and explode with emotion. One of the EMTs realized what was getting ready to happen though and took charge. He told Mr. Scheuer to contact the school principal about what had happened and to request that grief counselors be available today and for the rest of the week. He then volunteered to speak to the students.

The students were told that Mr. Talbot had been attacked by an alligator and before he could say another word, several of the girls screamed and began crying. Their friends hugged them and they cried together as they continued to listen. He explained that they were safe and that they needed to get back on the bus and call their parents to come to the school and meet them. He said he was sorry and it was a terrible accident and one they should never have had to encounter.

The students were quiet as they got back on the bus and then slowly began making calls to their parents. Connor, though, was thinking of how close he had come to being attacked by an alligator twice in just two weeks. After the first time, he had said he would never put himself in that position again, but he had once again allowed that to happen. *The damn pond. I allowed myself to think pond and swamp were not the same things. How stupid was that*? He knew he was alive today because Mr. Talbot stood between him and the alligator. He had his knife but it was still in his backpack. He didn't even have it out as they trudged through the marsh. *How stupid was that* he thought again. He would not live to be seventeen if he didn't wise up. He knew Mr. Talbot had died a horrible death and he was sorry that had happened, but the alligator was only doing what it was supposed to do. Find things to eat. Survive. He wasn't angry at the alligator. He was angry at himself for not being prepared.

Most of the parents were there when the bus returned to school. Emotions were strong. Anger, relief, sadness, fear - all of those emotions filled the air and the principal and the grief counselors tried their best to address them, but in that particular moment, they were of little help. The best they could do was just listen to the outbursts, nod their heads and tell everyone they would be there to help when they needed them.

Sam looked at Connor and shook his head as he looked around at all the pandemonium. "Man, this is going to be messed up for a while."

"Yeah," Connor replied. "Are you going to be all right?"

"I don't know. Mr. Talbot. I mean, I liked him. He was a good teacher. What happened, it's just…I don't know."

"It could have been one of us. But we need to turn his death into something positive, Sam. He deserves that. The only thing we did wrong was not being prepared for what could have happened. We got lucky."

"It's hard to relate our luck to his death," Sam said.

"Yeah, it is. I think talking to the counselors will help. I know I'll be seeing one."

"Yeah. Well, I'll see you later, Connor," he said as he recognized his dad's truck in the parking lot.

Connor pulled his phone out of his backpack and stood there looking at it for a few minutes. After practicing several times in his head what he was going to say, he called his mother.

"What's up, son?" Maggie asked as she answered the phone. "Is something wrong?"

Already he thought to himself. *Without saying a word, she knew.*

"Yes, there was an accident at the park. Our teacher was killed."

For a moment, Connor heard nothing on the other end of the phone, but he knew his mother was there. He was prepared for the silent response.

"An alligator attacked him. He was with me and Sam. Sam was showing me a place where he knew some cool snakes were. We were off the trail, but not the wooden pathways. I made a promise to not go off the wooden paths and I kept that promise. Sam had been to this place before and was familiar with it. It was in the woods, where a lot of unique plant life grows. We got distracted by a python that shouldn't have even been in the swamp and then the alligator attacked Mr. Talbot," Connor said.

"But I'm okay mom. I am very sorry about what happened to Mr. Talbot, but it was an accident. All I can do is get through this moment right now and I'm going to need you to help me do that and I need you to do that too. Can you do that?"

Connor heard his mother crying. He knew it was best if he let her cry and process what he had told her. Maggie couldn't believe what she was hearing at first but somewhere in her brain, she heard the words "I'm okay," and that's what she focused on. She remembered what Beth and Sable had told her. *Be there in the moment.* That's what her son was asking her to do. Be there in the moment for him and for herself. Realize that he was alive and safe and that this was an accident that was out of their control. But she knew. Mr. Talbot was just like Amos. If they hadn't been there, she doubted if her son would be alive.

"I will be there as soon as I can," Maggie said as she hung up the phone and rushed out of the house. She had to stop several times as the emotions overwhelmed her, but each time, she heard her son asking her to be there for him. And she was going to do that. He had always been there for her and he needed her help now.

Connor was one of the last students remaining in the parking lot when she drove up. He was talking to the principal and one of the grief counselors. She didn't get out of the car to talk to them. She was afraid of what she would say. She was afraid of what they may say.

Maggie hugged him when Connor got in the car, trying to fight back tears. She heard her son say several times that he was okay but they didn't talk on the way home. Maggie wasn't sure what to say and Connor was afraid to say anything else.

She finally broke her silence when they got home. "The alligator wasn't supposed to be there, was it? Not in the place where you were?" she asked.

Alligators could be anywhere in the swamp and considering where they were, Connor knew he would be lying if he said it wasn't supposed to be there. He knew what his mother wanted to hear. But he had made a promise not to lie to her.

He held up his phone and showed her the picture of the python. "It was chasing this." That was his answer to her question and he hoped she didn't pursue it any further.

"What is that?"

"A Burmese python. It was someone's pet that they wanted to get rid of. They can't survive in the swamp here. It gets too cold."

"And you and Sam and Mr. Talbot were there?"

"Yes," he answered.

Maggie nodded her head and told Connor that he should go shower and get in some clean clothes. He went to his room and closed the door. Maggie waited a few minutes before she tiptoed down the hall and stood outside his room. She heard him talking again. He was saying Mr. Talbot had no reason to be there and if he hadn't been there, he would still be alive. She heard him say the knife he took with him would have saved them.

She knocked on the door and Connor opened it with a towel around his waist.

"Were you talking to yourself?" Maggie asked. "Talking about what happened today? I do that sometimes. Talk to myself. It helps me process things. Helps me sort things out."

Connor looked at his mother and started to say he hadn't said a thing but her eyes told him to say something else.

"It was an accident. There was nothing we could do to save him. It was just a horrible accident," Connor said.

"You can only control what you can control. And no one has control over accidents. I'm sorry you had to see that, Connor, but you can't accept blame for what happened."

"I know."

"Good." Maggie placed her hand on his cheek. "Good," she repeated as she closed the door and went back down the hall. She poured herself a glass of wine and waited out on the patio for Sean to come home. She had finished almost an entire bottle by the time he arrived and like Connor, she had rehearsed what she was going to tell him. When he came outside, she smiled at him and got up from her chair.

"Would you like a drink?" she asked. "I'm going to get another glass of wine."

"It looks like you've had several already," Sean grinned.

"Yep. And it was a very good bottle of merlot," Maggie said. "There's not enough left to give you any but I can open another one."

"No. But I will have some Crown over ice," Sean said.

"Yep. Got it."

When she returned with his drink, Sean had removed his tie and was just sitting there wondering what was going on. He didn't have to wait long to learn the answer.

"Connor's teacher was killed at the swamp park tour today," Maggie said as she took a drink of wine.

"What?" Sean shouted. From the look on Maggie's face, he could see that he needed to dial it back a bit. He took a sip of the whiskey and leaned back in his chair.

"An alligator attacked him," Maggie said calmly. "The teacher and Connor and Sam were looking around in the marsh and they saw some python. Which I'm not sure if you know or not, is not supposed to exist there in the swamp. The alligator was chasing it and as it went by them, it decided that the person standing there in the marsh would be just as good."

"And Connor?" Sean asked.

"He's fine. He will be fine. Pretty traumatic though to see the person next to you get eaten by an alligator, I would think." Maggie sounded like she was reading a newspaper account of something that frequently happened to people as if the recurrent nature of the event would diminish the traumatic experience.

"Oh my God," Sean said as he took another drink. "Oh my God," he repeated.

"It was an accident, Sean. An accident that occurred and we can't do anything about it. We can only control what we can control and that is how we react going forward."

Sean looked at Maggie. What he was hearing was some of the wine and some of the therapy she had undergone throughout the years. And perhaps some of the medication and the wine interacting. He didn't care if was one or all three of those things combined. He was just glad to see that she seemed to be in control of her emotions. And what was even more encouraging, was what she was saying was true. Connor didn't kill the teacher. But Connor could have been killed and he paused to think for a moment. The thought of it made his stomach do flips.

"I'll get you another drink," she said. "I can see that you need one."

Before Maggie could get back with the other drink, Connor came outside. Sean jumped up and hugged him. "How are you doing?"

"I'm okay," Connor replied.

"Sit down, talk to me. Tell me what happened."

"Sam and I were looking for some snakes and saw a Burmese python. Look." Connor showed the video to his father. "I have to admit when we saw that snake, we were so focused on it, that we let down our guard a bit and the next thing we knew, Mr. Talbot was asking us what we were doing. Right before he was attacked."

"So, are you saying you were somewhere you weren't supposed to be?" Sean asked as Maggie came back out.

"They had walked off the trail just a bit," Maggie replied before Connor could say anything. "His friend Sam had been there lots of times. They weren't doing anything wrong. It was an accident."

Sean looked up at Maggie and then back over at Connor. He wanted to hear what Connor had to say. "Answer the question," Sean said. "Were you somewhere you shouldn't have been?"

"Yes. You are not supposed to go off the trail, but Sam had been there several times before and wanted to show it to me. We were only going to be gone a few minutes."

"Shit," Sean said as he lifted his drink and drained it.

"Look Sean," Maggie started. "If the park isn't safe, they shouldn't be taking kids out into it. They went off the trail for a moment. That's all. Connor and Sam didn't kill their teacher. A large alligator did. How do you think the park and the school are going to react to this? They can't blame this on our son and his friend. Considering the fact that a teacher was killed, I would think they would be worried about a lawsuit."

Sean looked over at his wife. Again, what she was saying was true. Neither the school nor the park could blame anyone. Both of them could be considered negligent in this situation regardless of what the park or school said about the trip.

"Was there a permission slip sent home that detailed the dangers of the park?" Sean asked.

"There was," Maggie replied. "Even more reason for the teacher to be extra vigilant when you have thirty lives for whom you are responsible."

"Were there fences up along the trail you were on, Connor?" Sean asked.

"No. You stop all along the trail and look at plants and animal life. The trail is just a dirt path through the woods."

Sean finally took a deep breath. There was nothing that anyone could say that would implicate their son was at fault. He didn't think they would need to talk to an attorney but he would ask his boss tomorrow for the name of a good one just in case.

"We're going tomorrow to talk to my therapist," Maggie said. "Me and Connor."

"That will be good. Yes, good idea," he said as he smiled at his son.

Maggie didn't add that the appointment had been set up before this happened and she didn't think she needed to. What was important was that they were going. Connor noticed his mother didn't say the appointment was set up days earlier either. He knew his father was okay with everything for the moment and he didn't think that information added anything of value. What he needed to hear was that they were going to see the therapist.

Maggie and Connor got to Hazel's office just before one o'clock and Janice told Maggie she could go right in to see the doctor. Maggie nodded her head and told Connor she'd see him in a few minutes. Connor smiled and told her that he wasn't going anywhere.

"Oh hello. Maggie," Hazel said as she looked up. "You're one of those 'right on time' people, aren't you?"

"I do try to be," Maggie agreed as she sat down in the chair in front of the desk.

"I like those kinds of people. I happen to be one of them myself. So, how are you doing?"

"I have a lot of concerns about my son," Maggie replied.

"Yes, I understand that, but before we talk about those concerns, tell me about you," Hazel replied. "Are you taking your Zoloft as prescribed?"

"Yes. Every day."

"Good. Still enjoying your waterfall and the pool?"

"Yes, very much so. The waterfall every day. And I get out to the pool as much as I can. It's still warm enough that's for sure. We painted the guardhouse, which looks great. I thought of that and the neighborhood agreed it was a good idea."

"Sounds like you've been quite busy. And are making quite the impression in the neighborhood. Made any new friends?"

"Yes, several more. If not for them and the medicine, I don't think I would have held up as well as I have considering everything that has happened."

"Let's talk about that. Tell me what has happened."

"Connor has been attacked by an alligator twice now. If you recall, the first attack was in the pond in our neighborhood. My neighbor, who killed that first alligator, got his foot cut off by an animal trap in his yard. My son found him and we got him medical help. Then another neighbor cussed me out at the neighborhood cookout and her husband called me a dirty name, so

Connor pushed him into the pool. And oh, yesterday, his teacher was eaten by an alligator."

Hazel had heard a lot in her forty years as a therapist but she had to admit that the list of items she had just heard from Maggie would have been overwhelming for someone even without psychological issues. For someone who was bipolar with severe anxiety, they had to be devastating. But when she looked at Maggie, she didn't appear devastated. She seemed a little anxious but otherwise, very calm. And that concerned her. *Zoloft is good. But is it that good?*

" Your son's teacher was eaten by an alligator?" she repeated.

"Yes, at Phinizy Swamp. I'm surprised it wasn't on the news this morning. I'm sure it will be coming out soon. Connor witnessed it. If not for my neighbor the first time, or the teacher the second time, I'm not sure he would be alive right now." Maggie rubbed her forehead as if she was trying to massage away what lay beneath the skin.

There is a sign of stress that I would expect Hazel thought. "Would you like a glass of water?" she asked.

"Do you have any wine?"

Hazel smiled and got a bottle of water out of a small refrigerator behind her desk and handed it to Maggie. "So, Connor witnessed the alligator eating his teacher?" Hazel asked.

"Yes. And if he hadn't been there, Connor would be dead." Maggie fumbled with the cap of the bottled water with shaking hands but finally got it open. She took several long drinks and then tried to put the top back on the bottle but couldn't manage it.

Hazel pulled her seat closer and took the bottle from Maggie. She laid her notepad down and took her hands in hers. "I am so very, very sorry Maggie."

Maggie broke down upon hearing those kind words. Hazel let her cry and then handed her some tissues as she hugged her. Maggie felt her body's release of bottled-up emotions wash over her.

"I'm sorry," Maggie finally said as she dried her eyes with the tissues.

"You have nothing to be sorry about. I'm pretty amazed you had the ability to drive over here and walk into my office considering what you've told me. Your son is with you, right?"

"Yes, he's out in the waiting room."

"Good. And did you tell your husband about the first alligator attack; that Connor was in the pond?"

"Yes, and Sean took it well. Better than I imagined. In fact, I think it made us all a little bit closer. He didn't get mad. He was impressed with Connor and the way he had thought about how he should handle things in the future.

And he appreciated the fact I didn't keep that information a secret, so to speak. You were right about trusting in each other. I don't remember saying how much my son loves animals. I tell people if it flies, walks, crawls, swims, or slithers, my son wants to know about it. Especially the things that slither."

"Yes, you mentioned it last time."

Hazel wanted to say, "Oh my God!" but she knew as a therapist that wouldn't be appropriate. But silently she said the phrase several times in her head. *She is a stronger woman than I knew. Depression and anxiety be damned. She has made it through all of this; coping with one emotional arm tied behind her back. She is a very strong woman indeed.*

"Maggie, what you have described to me would place an emotional strain on anyone. A strain that would be hard to endure and yet here you are. Frazzled, yes, but broken, no. I'm glad you reached out to me and I'm so glad you brought your Connor with you. He sounds like someone I want to meet."

The empathy and kind words made Maggie feel better They bolstered her spirits and her attitude. She was right the first time. She could share anything with Hazel.

"And you say your son found your neighbor with his foot cut off by an animal snare?"

"Yes, the same neighbor that saved his life. His name is Amos Morgan."
Again. Oh my God, Hazel thought.

"Where did the animal traps come from?"

"I don't know, but I think Amos may have put them out there around his waterfall. Someone killed the koi in his pond earlier. He is a Vietnam war vet. A war hero. He suffers from PTSD at times. Forgets things. But his heart is good. He has the heart of an artist. He is a very talented artist. He paints sunrises and sunsets. Beautiful sunrises and sunsets," Maggie said as she looked off into the distance for a moment.

"And he saved my son's life." Maggie started to cry again.

Hazel made a note of 'Amos Morgan and vet with PTSD, animal traps and forgets things.' She would talk more about that with Maggie in a later session.

"You said you were worried about your son. Not only from the physical trauma he witnessed but from some other things. What do you mean by that?"

"Connor has always had a desire to protect me. My other therapist said it was because he would see me depressed and very sad. Or very anxious. He felt like it was his job to make me better. When he pushed my neighbor in the pool because he called me a derogatory term, he seemed detached. Like he wasn't really there or what he had done was wrong."

"What did your neighbor call you?"

"A nasty little cooch."

"Why?"

"Because they are alcoholic assholes."

"They?"

"His wife threw a drink in my face earlier."

Hazel knew there had to be more to that story but she didn't feel it was important enough to go into now, considering everything else that had happened. She noted the hostile and angry tone Maggie took when she referenced the neighbors but she wasn't so sure that her angry tone wasn't appropriate and reflective of everything else that had occurred. She made another note to explore it at the next session.

"Okay, he appeared detached from the situation. I understand. What else?"

"I heard him talking about it in his room. I went back to check on him after the party and he was talking about how he should have thrown Jim's wife in the pool too. And he was talking to himself about the accident with his teacher. Over and over he said it was an accident and that he needed to be better prepared. And he talked to me about the traps he found over at Amos's house. He went over to his house looking for them. Setting them off and then brought them back to our house. Setting them off! They are big traps. He could have been seriously hurt doing something like that and when he was showing them to me, he mentioned how the body at the lake wouldn't have come to the surface if these traps had been wrapped around her legs. You know the body of the young girl they found at the lake? The one they say committed suicide?"

Yes, a dangerous thing to do and yes that was a strange thing to say, Hazel thought as she nodded her head.

"He did this before. Talk to himself. Right before the fire," Maggie said.

Hazel waited for her to continue. Waited for her to tell her things she still had bottled up.

" I dreamed about him killing Mr. Talbot – Alex's teacher - last night," Maggie started. "In a fire. Like the one that burned down most of our house in Florida. I know Mr. Talbot didn't harm Connor but he should have been watching over my son. Why do people we entrust with our children's safety end up trying to harm them? Why do they do that?"

What are you still not telling me, Maggie?

"My other neighbor down the street isn't well," Maggie said before she realized what she was saying. It was like she was in a trance and the words were a response to a hypnotic suggestion. "She's a whore and is having an affair with her yardman. Our neighbor says she's had multiple affairs. She doesn't like me at all. She showed how petty and mean she was to everyone at the guardhouse painting project and again at the neighborhood cookout. And then when we showed her the picture of her when she was a little girl sitting on a horse with Amos, she tore it up and burned it. She hates Amos for some reason. And she denied that they were related. But we know. We know better."

"Who is this neighbor you say isn't well? And who knows better?"

"Beth Stevens is the adulteress. Barbara Gillespie and Sable Skye know about the picture. Barbara is who recommended you to me. She and Sable have been like rocks for me. I met Jasmine Bartholomew at the cookout and we became friends there. She came to my house the next day to tell me about Beth. She knows about all her affairs. She lives next door to her. She told me she has even tried to seduce her husband several times.

"I dreamed about her too. Beth, that is. That there was a black widow in her car and it fell from the visor as she reached up to look in the mirror. She didn't even notice it fall into her hair because she was talking to herself in the mirror. Is it normal for people to talk to themselves in the mirror?" Maggie suddenly asked as she redirected her focus on Hazel.

"Yes, it's okay to talk to yourself in the mirror in an offhand way. 'How do I look tonight? You look fabulous. Yes, I agree.' That's fine. It's not okay if the person doesn't realize that it's not a real person on the other side of the glass," Hazel told her.

"I dreamed the black widow bit Beth's face and she watched her face dissolve as she looked into the mirror," Maggie said.

Something else is going on between Maggie and Beth. Why did she ask the question about talking to the mirror? It's like her son talking to himself. It could be a manifestation of her depression and anxiety. A way to cope.

"What do you see when you look in the mirror, Maggie?"

Maggie looked at Hazel and paused for a moment. "Someone trying to cope. Someone that wants to be happy. Someone that doesn't want to be sad."

Yes, that's what I thought. The mirror is in her mind reflecting her bipolar conflicts.

"Maggie, I'd like for you to take some lorazepam for the next week until we meet again. Along with your Zoloft. And when you're taking these drugs, you need to minimize your alcohol intake. I'd prefer it if you didn't drink at all. But I know you like wine. So, a glass - and I said a glass - with dinner, should be okay. You have a lot you're working through right now and I can tell it is a struggle for you. It would be a struggle for most anyone, but because of your bipolar condition, it is intensified. I think it would be a good idea too, to stay away from those neighbors you have a low opinion of and create conflict for you."

"You are being kind when you say I have a low opinion of them."

"Yes, perhaps I am. But we'll learn some coping mechanisms for that and how to deal with them in the future. For now, stay away from them. Let's put some order back in your life. Surround yourself with your family. Enjoy the company of your new friends. Help your friend Amos with his recovery. Enjoy the sunrises and sunsets with him. Enjoy your waterfall. Maybe try to learn to do something new. Something that you always wanted to do. Remember how I said in our first meeting how wonderful it is that we can learn something new every day? Take advantage of that. Will you try to do that?"

"Yes, I can do that. But all my new friends like to drink wine."

"That's fine. I like a nice merlot myself. But for now, if you're with them, only have half a glass or have something else, non-alcoholic. Your friends will understand. Tell them you're taking some medication right now that isn't good to mix with a lot of alcohol. Or you don't have to tell them anything. Believe me, friends will understand. And if they don't understand, then they probably aren't very good friends."

"I know what you're saying, Hazel. I get it. Thank you for listening to me and for your help. I feel a lot better from just talking to you about everything."

Hazel smiled and wrote the prescription for her. She escorted Maggie back to the waiting room and they walked over to Connor.

"Hello, Connor. My name is Dr. Nutt. A crazy name for a therapist, isn't it?"

Connor smiled as he stood up and shook Dr. Nutt's hand.

"It's a pleasure to meet you," Dr. Nutt said. "Maggie, we won't be long. There are some nice gardening magazines over there. Might give you some ideas."

Once inside the office, Dr. Nutt offered the chair to Connor and then sat down across from him.

"I know you have spoken with therapists before, isn't that right?"

"Yes. For about a year, I guess. When we were in Florida."

"Good. Then you know that this is a safe environment but it bears repeating. What you share with me, I will not share with anyone. Even your parents, unless you want me to. I just want to talk with you for now. Is that okay with you?"

"Sure."

"First off, let me say I can't imagine seeing someone being mauled by an alligator. It must have been horrifying. How are you feeling about that?"

"It was an accident. A terrible accident. I can't do anything about it. The alligator isn't at fault. It was just doing what alligators do. But seeing the arm and the head of Mr. Talbot floating there in the water. I'm not sure I'll ever forget that."

Good Lord Hazel thought. "No, trauma like that is usually not forgotten. It can be debilitating to some people."

"What do you mean?"

"I mean it, the traumatic event, becomes something that keeps them up at night. Gives them nightmares. Affects the way they go about their life. Sometimes even changes them psychologically to such a strong degree, that it may require some type of treatment before they can carry on with their life."

"I understand."

"Are you having any nightmares?"

"No, but I do have a question."

"Sure. What is it?"

"My friend Sam and I were talking. He was there with me. We realize that Mr. Talbot's death probably prevented us from being attacked. We were wondering how we can turn his death into something positive."

Interesting Hazel thought. *That is such a thoughtful question. He doesn't sound like he's having trouble coping. Was he really talking to himself as Maggie said or were those manifestations of her disease?*

"That's an excellent question, Connor. I'm not sure. But perhaps you can teach others about the beauty and dangers of the swamp. Or maybe you can organize a memorial for Mr. Talbot at the school. Set up a charity for something that he was interested in or a scholarship in his name."

"Those are all good ideas."

"Can we go back to the other alligator attack? The one where you were in the pond and your neighbor killed it before it got to you. Do you have any trouble when you think about that?"

"No. But it made me realize that I need to be better prepared if I'm going into a swamp. I need to make sure there aren't alligators in there. And that I always have something to protect myself with."

"How do you do that?"

"I can throw cherry bombs or firecrackers into the water before I go in it. That noise will bring the alligator up from beneath the water if they are in there. And Amos gave me a knife. A very big knife that will cut through the hide of an alligator, just in case."

He's very intelligent.   He thinks through things as his mother said. Doesn't sound like he takes unusual risks, but I feel like there is something he is hiding. Trying not to reveal. I don't know why I feel that way because he hasn't said anything to indicate that, but I just feel it.

"That's very smart. Your mother said you did something that wasn't so smart though. She said you went over to Amos's property looking for those animal traps that were around his waterfall. Is that true?"

"Yes, but I was prepared. I had metal weight bars strapped to both sides of my leg," Connor said as he indicated to Dr. Nutt with his hands what he was talking about. "And I had on my snake boots which are very strong leather boots. And I had a large metal weight bar that I used to poke around on the ground before I walked. I thought I was pretty safe. Both of the animal traps I found were practically out in the open and the weight bar triggered them without any issue."

Again, a very reasonable plan. He doesn't seem reckless. But what are you not saying?

"It sounds like you gave that plan a lot of thought, but it worried your mother."

"Yeah, I know. She doesn't like what I do sometimes."

"Like what?"

"Well, she doesn't like the fact I'm interested in snakes. She doesn't like being around them. I find them to be fascinating and very beautiful creatures. I like all animals but snakes may be my favorite. That alligator in the swamp was chasing a Burmese python. Here let me show you." He took out his phone and showed Dr. Nutt the video. "They won't survive the winter here. Some stupid person bought it and then just left it out there for whatever reason."

He does seem a bit detached. His teacher was just mauled, eaten by an alligator yesterday. Something he witnessed. Something he said he would never forget. Yet he's treating it like a documentary that he saw on TV.

"Tell me about the cookout. You pushed the host into the pool?"

"I did. He called my mother a nasty word. It was disrespectful. She wasn't doing anything but being nice."

"So, he deserved it?"

"I thought so, yes."

"Do you have any regrets about doing it?"

"No, none."

"Did you want to push his wife into the pool too? Your mother said she heard you talking about that."

Connor didn't remember saying anything like that to his mother or even thinking about that to himself. But if his mother said she heard him, he'd go along.

"I don't remember saying it, but maybe I did."

I don't believe him. He is hiding something. I'm sure of it now.

"Do you know anything about a black widow spider?"

What did his mother say about that Connor wondered? *Why would she bring that up?*

"I found one in our garage. I was going to take it to school to show Mr. Talbot but my mom saw it and it freaked her out. She doesn't like spiders either."

"Aren't they dangerous?"

"They can be. But most spider bites won't kill you unless you're very young or very old. Or have other certain health issues. If you're basically healthy, the bite will just hurt real bad but it will heal over time."

"Let's go back to those traps you found at Amos's house. When you showed them to your mother, do you remember saying something about them and the poor girl who committed suicide at Lake Thurmond?"

Hazel watched as Connor paused and looked away from her for a moment. He doesn't want to answer the question.

"I don't remember saying anything about it, but maybe I did."

The exact words he said about the wife of the man he pushed in the pool. Again, what are you not saying?

"Can you tell me what happened in Florida?"

"A friend of mine was abused by our teacher. She was 14. I was 15. She was actually my best friend. She ended up committing suicide. There was a fire at our house and we had to move."

So much trauma in this young boy's life, but he is a survivor. I understand more now.

"I am so sorry, Connor. What was her name?"

"Allison. Allison Curtis."

"Did you start the fire?"

"Yes."

Hazel reached over and grabbed his hand and smiled at him. "Did your doctor in Florida prescribe anything for you?"

"Yes, but I don't take it anymore. He only prescribed it for a short time and I did what he said. Before I left, he didn't think I needed anything else."

"Okay Connor, thank you. Is there anything that you need from me?"

"Yes. Please continue to help my mom. She likes you. I can tell."

Dr. Nutt promised that she would as she walked him out of her office. She thanked them for coming and told Maggie that she would see her next week and told Connor to stay safe. Maggie and Connor both knew that meant he didn't need to come back. As Maggie tried to process the details of everything, she remembered on the way home that she hadn't told Sean about the traps. She told herself she would do it later. She asked Connor how he liked Dr. Nutt and he said she was nice and he enjoyed talking with her. She asked him what they talked about and he told her about Mr. Talbot and the cookout and the fire in Florida. When she heard him mention the fire, she grabbed his hand and squeezed it. He looked over at her and smiled.

Maggie let go of his hand and asked what he wanted for dinner that evening and he told her pizza. She would have bet on pizza before she even asked and she told him so as they both laughed. Maggie wondered when she would tell Hazel about the fortune-teller or the blue jay or how all of that related to Beth and Jorge. *Soon* she told herself. *Soon.*

After they left, Hazel sat down at her computer and started typing notes about today's visit. She typed:

"Maggie's strong outward appearance today obscured a fragile mental state but she was able to cope by receiving reassurance from her friends and family, especially her son. She also needs reassurance for her thoughts and actions from therapy and benefits from having that professional relationship in her life. She has a very strong relationship with her son and her mental state affects her son's behavior. She says her son is protective of her and he is. They have both experienced a lot of trauma in their lives and are strong-willed individuals that seem to complement each other.

Maggie seems able to find strength when necessary to overcome any of her psychological weaknesses. She can reach down within herself and find a way to act when she needs to but it's possible that leads to a manic state which may trigger anger. Her bipolar conflicts are represented by a mirror within her mind where she works through things. The black widow dream about her neighbor represents her subconscious dislike for the neighbor, which is suppressed for the moment. The medication I gave her should help keep that in balance for the time being, but it will require constant monitoring.

Without question, trying to maintain stability with all of the issues that have confronted her, has been a challenge. But I believe Maggie can manage it with guidance from therapy and with the proper medication. If that does not work, I am afraid she may become lost and disillusioned. A depressive state could overwhelm her and require stronger treatment. Perhaps an inpatient stay for a period of time.

Future meetings should include thoughts about her neighbor Amos and whether her feelings for him are overshadowing some things that should be addressed by social services. Further discussion is needed to assess her relationships and the conflict with those she refers to as her alcoholic neighbors and the person she referred to as a whore. There is a severe dislike for that individual. The 'why' for that needs to be determined. Based on the behavior of those neighbors as supported by what Connor saw, the best way to interact with them may be no interaction at all. We will see how that evolves. I do not believe she is a danger to herself or to anyone else at this time.

Her son Connor is a very resilient and intelligent young man. I believe he is shy around people and may not make friends easily. Probably impacted significantly by the suicide of his best friend, brought on by sexual child abuse from their teacher. He reacted to this trauma by trying to hurt that which he loves. Nature. He set fire to the world around him as a reaction to the suffering he could not understand, but he has overcome that. The medical staff and the police did not believe he was a threat to society since he is not required to see a therapist or take any long-term medication. Though I do not know this to be the case, I suspect his actions were deemed allowable because of what had occurred to his friend and contingent upon the assessment of a psychological professional which he did receive.

He still finds tremendous comfort in nature. Animals don't commit suicide and do not suffer from the plethora of mental ailments seen in man or in his case, woman, i.e. his mother. He has had a front-row seat for witnessing those struggles for some time and retains a strong relationship and love for her, despite them. He may be the most adult sixteen-year-old I have ever encountered. Nature is his coping mechanism and I do not think that is a bad thing for what has been a very confusing world up until now for him. Yes, he can seem like he is removed from the situation but I don't see any harm in that type of behavior considering what has happened to him. I do not think it will worsen or become something that will cause him problems as he matures. Connor still retreats into nature in order to find 'friends' and that serves him well for now. I have no doubt he will eventually live a well-adjusted life and one day do something professionally with animals. Unless he requests it, I do not believe he requires my services any further.

Maggie will require therapy for a long time, if not for the rest of her life."

Chapter 31

At home, At last

"Can we go by and see Amos tonight?" Connor asked as they drove home.

"You and I must be connected mentally somehow," his mom replied.

"Well, that is a scary thought. Does that mean I have to go see Dr. Nutt every week too?"

"Haha, funny. No, you don't need to go see Dr. Nutt every week. I plan to because I find it very helpful. I was under the impression from what you said, you found talking to her was good too."

"I did. I was just giving you a hard time. I'm proud of you Mom. Not everyone recognizes their need to seek counseling when they should. It helped me a lot back in Florida. And it helped me today. I like her and I think she'll be good for you. Another friend to talk to. But one that can certify you are as crazy as bat droppings if need be."

"You do want to eat tonight, don't you?"

"Oh yeah. I meant one that can certify that you are the sanest crazy person she has ever helped."

"Sanest crazy person? I sort of like that description for some reason."

"Hey, I have an idea. Why don't we take the pizza over to Amos at the hospital? I'm sure that's better than the hospital food he's getting."

"Oh, that's a good idea! But I'll need to call the hospital and make sure he doesn't have any diet restrictions."

"Why would he have any diet restrictions for a wound?"

Maggie wasn't sure what to say. She assumed they had found something else wrong with Amos from what Pam was able to tell her, and though Pam didn't say it, she felt like it was something serious. Something in Pam's eyes had suggested that to her.

"Because he was having some more tests," Maggie said. "That's what the nurse told me. They were doing some more tests before they sent him home."

"Okay," Connor replied. "Do you think Dad will want to come with us?"

"Why don't you call him and ask?"

Sean told Connor he would have liked to come but he had a Board of Directors meeting and wouldn't be able to join them. He said it sounded like a great idea and for them to have fun and then asked him to have his mother call him when they got home.

When they ended the call, Sean leaned back in his chair and just shook his head as he thought about his son. *He sounds like everything is back to normal. That's healthy, isn't it? After all, it was an accident. Connor had nothing to do with it. His best friend was sexually abused by their teacher and his teacher here is eaten by an alligator. Yet Connor seemed unaffected by it this time. He's learned how to cope, it seems.*

He did set fire to the house but the psychiatrist said it was a normal reaction for what he had experienced. No one was hurt. Just the house and their yard were burned, but that was because they lived on a twenty-acre lot and no one lived directly next door to them. They were lucky that day. It would have been so much worse if someone was injured. But they weren't. There was something else planned for his son in the grand scheme of things. There had to be. He's been through so much and has come out of everything strong. And Amos. My son found Amos and helped him. No, he's okay. Connor is fine, Sean reassuringly told himself several more times before he began preparing for the board meeting.

Maggie made sure that Amos could have pizza and placed an order with Pizza Joint. They could pick it up on their way. As requested, Maggie called Sean before leaving for the hospital. She told him she had a good talk with Dr. Nutt and she helped her process everything that had been happening. The doctor also prescribed some additional medicine, lorazepam, for her to take until they met next week and told her to be careful about drinking wine while she was taking it. Sean asked about Connor and Maggie told him what she knew, that Connor said they had a good talk and Dr. Nutt didn't say she needed to talk to him anymore.

"That's a good thing, isn't it?" he asked.

"Yes, that's a good thing. I don't know how our son processes things the way he does without getting affected by it all mentally. I think that's the impression Dr. Nutt had too."

"He's a strong kid, Maggie. Probably stronger than both of us."

"I think you are right, Sean."

"I'm glad you guys are taking pizza over to Amos tonight. It will be good for Connor."

"It will be good for me too," Maggie replied. "You know Sean, I see a lot of similarities between our son and Amos."

"How's that?" Sean asked.

"They both like the woods. Nature. They're antisocial. Strong-willed. Determined. Unafraid."

"I would agree with all of that except the antisocial part. Connor isn't antisocial. He's just shy. Reticent to make friends. Well, I wouldn't even say reticent. More like uncomfortable. But he made a friend at the new school right away. With Sam. When people show the same interests as him, he is very comfortable around them. Amos doesn't want to be around people. Although I do think he really likes you and I know he likes Connor a lot."

"Perhaps I should pay you for therapy instead of Hazel."

"You couldn't afford me."

"Maybe we could work out some other arrangement," Maggie replied.

"Maybe. We can talk about that later. I need to get ready for the board meeting. See you when I get home tonight and we can talk about that other arrangement you are referencing."

Just before they left for the hospital, Maggie caught a glimpse of the local news and they were talking about the horrible accident at Phinizy Swamp. They interviewed the director of the park as well as the principal. The swamp was closed until further notice was the last thing the reporter said.

Thank goodness they didn't mention Connor and Sam.

On their way to the hospital, Maggie brought up what she had seen on the news. She told Connor that she would prefer for him not to discuss it with a reporter if they should come by. Just to say it was a horrible accident and that he couldn't talk about it. It was too disturbing to discuss. Connor didn't think it was too disturbing to discuss but he understood what his mother was saying and just said okay.

Amos was smiling when they walked into the room. "Hallelujah!" he cried as he saw the two pizzas in Connor's hands. "I haven't had anything but a little lunch. Something they said was country fried steak but it wasn't very good. The best thing on the tray was jello. And when jello is the best thing you have to eat, then you might as well go outside and put a gun to your head. What kind of pizza did you bring?"

"One with lots of meat, and one pepperoni."

"I'll take some of that one with lots of meat," Amos replied. "I had the nurses leave some plastic plates and even some cokes in here in case you didn't have anything to drink when they told me you were coming with the pizzas.

"I'm impressed." Maggie served up the pizza and watched Amos as he seemed to inhale the first slice and started working on a second. She covered her mouth as she started to laugh.

"What are you laughing at?" Amos asked. "That test I had this morning, well that wasn't so bad. Don't remember that much of it. But last night, they gave me something that made me shit all night. Didn't know I had that much shit in my body. Must've got on and off that toilet they had next to my bed thirty times. You'll be glad it's not in here now, believe me. Thought I'd never get to sleep, but everything settled down around 4 this morning. Had the test sometime this morning. Don't remember much after that until they brought what they considered to be lunch to me. So, I'm hungry," he said as he took a bite of the other slice he had in his hand. "What is today?"

"Thursday," Connor answered.

"They told me I could go home tomorrow or Saturday," Amos said. "Would you be able to pick me up and take me home? They said it would be several months before I can get something for my leg. It needs to heal real good before they can do anything."

"Sure, we'd be glad to come and get you," Maggie said.

"I appreciate that, Maggie," Amos said as he reached for another slice. "This pizza is the best thing I've had to eat in a while. It was really nice of you and Connor to bring it."

"You're welcome," Maggie said as she got up and excused herself. She made it to the hall before the tears fell. *He remembered our names.*

Pam saw her crying and came over to her. "Is there something I can do to help you?" she asked.

"Do you ever get a day or night off?" Maggie asked as she smiled at Pam.

"I work a lot of overtime these days. Are you going to be okay?"

"Yes, I'll be fine. It's just something he said. Or remembered. He said he would be going home tomorrow or Saturday. Is that right?"

"Saturday. He's going to get another couple of units of blood in the morning."

"Why is he getting blood?" Maggie asked.

"Will there be any other caregivers for him other than you?" Pam asked, without answering her question.

"Not that I'm aware of. He does have a family member in town but I doubt she'll do anything for him," Maggie replied.

"Can you give me her number? He says he doesn't have anyone here or elsewhere that is alive family-wise."

"Hold on a minute. It's in my phone. She looked up Beth's information and gave it to Pam. "Her name is Beth Stevens. I'm not sure what their relationship is but I do know they are family."

"Thank you. Here," Pam said as she slipped something into Maggie's hand.

It was a card for a hospice service. Maggie stared at it for a few moments. "What about his prosthetic?" she asked.

"He won't be getting one. Not unless he agrees to further treatment, but from what I've come to know of Amos, I don't think he will. Maybe you can convince him to, but if you can't, you're going to need some help. These folks are very good. They have a lot of experience with veterans. That's all they take care of," Pam said.

Maggie felt the tears welling up again. "Can you tell me what it is?"

"I'm sorry, I can't," Pam said. "Patient confidentiality rules prevent it. But I'll make sure I talk to Amos tonight and ask him that he talk it over with you. I'll make sure he knows that you're very concerned for him and that he will need your friendship more than ever in the next month or so. That's all I can do."

"Thank you, Pam," Maggie said as she hugged her.

"You're welcome," Pam replied. "Amos is lucky to have neighbors like your family."

Maggie gathered her composure before she went back into the room. Amos and Connor were talking about some snakes he found in his waterfall skimmer and she smiled. Maggie let them talk for about another hour before she told Connor that they needed to get back home.

Amos shook Connor's hand and didn't resist when Maggie bent down to hug him. "Where is the sergeant this evening?" Amos asked before they could leave.

"He had to work late."

"Yep, sergeants do all the work. Always have," Amos said. "Tell him I look forward to seeing him when I get home."

"I will Amos, and your neighbors are anxious for you to get home too," Maggie replied.

"Even those lesbian neighbors?" Amos asked.

Maggie didn't bother to say anything. She just shook her head at him and Amos smiled.

On the way home that evening, Maggie considered what she should tell Connor about Amos and hospice care. She decided not to say anything. He didn't need to know. They could just spend time together and Connor wouldn't need to worry about anything. She would tell Sean though. He needed to know.

"Do you want to go to the zoo in Columbia tomorrow?" Maggie asked all of a sudden.

"I have school tomorrow," Connor reminded her.

"You look a little ill to me. I think a trip to the Aquarium Reptile Complex might make you feel better."

Connor coughed in a fake manner. "Oh, I, uh, have been feeling kind of bad tonight," he said as he looked over at his mother and smiled. "Thanks for tonight and thanks for tomorrow."

"You're welcome, son," Maggie said. *And, thank you for being my son.*

That evening Maggie told Sean about Amos's condition and said that she wanted to help him as much as they could. That he wouldn't have anyone else that would. Sean took her in his arms and kissed her.

"We will do everything we can for him," Sean said.

Maggie, Connor, and Sean went to the VA on Saturday afternoon to pick up Amos. He was in his room, in a wheelchair ready to go when they got there. In his lap was a large jar and he held it up proudly.

"This here is my foot. It's in formaldehyde right now, but I have a taxidermist friend who said he would fix it up for me. Bronze it. He lives off Gordon Highway which is on our way home. He said he'd be home if we could bring it by and he'd get started working on it. Will that be okay?"

"Sure Amos, not a problem," Sean replied.

"Thanks, Sergeant," Amos said. "I appreciate that. I'll let you use it later on if you want to."

Sean laughed and said, "I just might take you up on that!"

Connor got behind the wheelchair and pushed Amos out of the room, trying not to laugh as he looked at the expression on his father's face. The nurse handed Maggie some crutches for Amos to take with him. On the way to his friend's house and then back home, Connor sat in the backseat with Amos and showed him pictures of their trip to the zoo, and recited interesting facts about every reptile. As they drove into the neighborhood, they drove past Amos's house and through the covered bridge.

"Hey, Sergeant. You missed my house," Amos said.

"I did, didn't I?" Sean replied as he turned into their driveway. When they got to the top there was a large banner and Amos's neighbors standing there waving at him.

"What the hell is this?" he asked.

"It's a welcome home party."

"You gonna cook out steaks and have beer?"

"We sure are," Sean replied.

"Then get me the hell out of this car!"

Connor lifted Amos into the wheelchair and helped him up to the flat part of the back yard where he saw his cooler waiting for him. He smiled as he leaned over and got out a cold beer. When he popped it everyone cheered and came over to Amos to welcome him back. All of the neighbors were there except the Stevens and the Thompsons and though Amos didn't know most of their names it didn't matter to him. Maggie warned Jennifer and Frances that he would be most excited to see them and they laughed when they heard that and told her she didn't need to worry. They said that Amos had always been a gentleman and Maggie was surprised when she saw how he reacted around them. He was indeed as much a gentleman as he could be. *He just admires good-looking women,* Maggie realized. *Nothing wrong with that.* She even told Sean that if she wasn't committed to the team she was on, she could be tempted to switch sides looking at Jennifer and Frances.

"Is that so?" Sean asked.

"Well, I don't think I really ever could," Maggie replied. "I prefer having the bat in my hand or in the batter's box too much."

Sean looked down at his wife and kissed her as he put her hand on her butt and squeezed it.

"Be careful there," Maggie said. "You're still on deck for a while."

After the party was over, Maggie and Connor took Amos home. Amos kept saying over and over how that was one of the best days of his life. Connor reached over and grabbed his mother's hand and shook his head telling her not to cry. *He knows what I'm going to do before I do* Maggie thought as she looked back over at her son and told herself not to cry.

Maggie and Connor followed Amos as he wheeled himself into the den. He went straight to his Bible and began looking through it. *Oh my God. No. He can't be looking for that* she thought, but she was wrong.

"Damn," Amos said.

"What's wrong?" Maggie asked.

"I can't find the picture of my granddaughter and me on her eighth birthday. We were on a horse."

Holy shit! Beth is Amos's granddaughter! I don't know whether to scream or cry. Connor could see the reaction on his mother's face and though he didn't know what Amos was referring to, he knew that she did.

"That was the last time, I really ever saw her," Amos said. "Everything today made me feel so good about things, I felt like seeing it again. I don't look at it very much, but every once in a while, I get it out and remember the better days."

"Why don't you see your granddaughter anymore?" Maggie asked.

"Never liked her father. Cheated on his wife, my daughter. Got in a big fight that day with him. Punched him in the nose. He said I broke his jaw. My daughter said I broke his jaw and his nose. Regardless, he didn't press charges. He knew I would tell all of his rich asshole buddies about his lowlife ways. Don't know what happened to Elizabeth that day, but she wouldn't have anything to do with me after that. I was too stubborn to do anything about it and you know, time just went by.

"I see her every once in a while. She doesn't go by Elizabeth anymore. She prefers Beth. I think a lot of people that see her prefer another name. Bitch. She's got the same temperament as her father and grandfather. And I don't just mean her father's father. I can be an asshole too sometimes. At least I have been told that. It's too bad," Amos said as he sat there and just stared at the wall.

Connor opened the cooler and handed Amos a beer. Amos smiled at him. "When I die, will you take my foot for me? I'm sure it will look real nice when my buddy is done with it."

"I'd be proud to have your foot," Connor said. "Might help me kick ass one day."

Amos laughed. "It might just do that for you. Sure is good to be home. That party made me feel real good. One of the best days I've had in a very long time." He looked all around and whispered, "Home at last," and smiled as he looked over at Maggie and Connor.

Chapter 32

A difference of opinion

"Okay, show me how you can get around your house before we leave," Maggie said to Amos.

"What do you mean?" Amos asked as he turned his wheelchair around.

"Can you get everywhere in the house that you need to in that wheelchair? Without us being here?"

"Well, let's see," Amos said as he rolled himself into the kitchen and then back down the hallway to his bathroom and bedroom. He was able to open the front door and also the back door to the porch. He opened the door to the garage where his art supplies were. Several steps were leading down to the floor. As he looked at the steps, he started to get out of the wheelchair when Maggie told him that they would get them for him.

"I'll get them," Amos said. "Just give me one of those crutches."

Maggie did as he asked and Amos was able to get out of the wheelchair and down the steps with the crutch under one arm. He picked up a canvas and went back up the steps putting it next to the door and then went back for his art supplies. He placed them next to the canvas and then got back in his wheelchair hanging onto the crutch with one hand.

"I'll be fine," he said as he backed his wheelchair into the kitchen.

"It does appear that way," Maggie had to agree.

"But that doesn't mean you shouldn't check up on me," Amos said. "I might be hungry for a steak or some more of that cake."

"I'll come by every day," Connor spoke up. "I can check on you in the morning before I go to school and then again when I get home."

Amos looked at Connor and then over at Maggie. "You got some of the sergeant in you, boy," Amos said. "But you got a whole lot of your mother in you too. And because of that, I bet you'll be able to do just about anything that you put your mind to."

Maggie kissed Amos on the head and hugged him. "See you later, Amos," she said as she went out onto the porch and started crying again. She heard

Connor tell Amos goodbye and she wiped away her tears as her son came outside.

"You okay?" Connor asked.

"Fine," Maggie replied. "I'm fine."

"I'm not so sure about that. You've lost a lot of water the past several days. Are you re-hydrating?" Connor asked.

Maggie laughed and elbowed her son. *He knows what I need to hear every time. He is a special boy, my son. A very special boy.*

On their way back home, Connor asked his mother about the picture.

"You knew what picture he was looking for," Connor said. "I could tell you knew."

Maggie knew the next question coming.

"Was that little girl in the picture with Amos, Mrs. Stevens? It was, wasn't it?"

"Yes, it was."

"That's a shame she doesn't want to know Amos. He's a good man."

"You are very wise. And you're a good person. Don't you ever forget that. Nothing that you have seen or witnessed should tell you anything else. You are a strong young man and I am very proud of you."

"Thanks, Mom. Don't go getting all sappy on me," Connor teased as they walked into the kitchen.

Sean was in the den watching football when he saw them return. Connor said he was going to his room to play video games and would see them in the morning.

Maggie sat down next to Sean and put her head on his shoulder. "What kind of neighborhood did you bring us into?" she asked.

"Is this a game where I guess the answer?"

"No, it's not a game. But you are not going to believe what I'm getting ready to tell you. Are you ready? Amos is Beth's grandfather."

"Sure he is." Sean laughed sarcastically.

Maggie sat up and looked at Sean.

"No, really. I found a picture of a young Amos while I was cleaning up his house the other day. He was sitting on a horse with a little girl. The little girl was Beth. When I showed her the picture, Beth tore it into pieces and set it on fire. She wouldn't admit it was her, but all four of us knew it was. And now Amos said that picture was of him and his granddaughter on her eighth birthday. That was the last day he saw her. Got into a big fight with Beth's father and the words 'the apple doesn't fall too far from the tree' is most appropriate in her situation. Her father cheated on her mother all the time, according to Amos, and I know Beth has had multiple affairs. I told you after the party that she is having one now with the yardman. And there were others that Jasmine knew about."

"Who are the four people you're referring to?" Sean asked.

"Me, Barbara, Sable, and Beth."

"Shit," Sean replied. "How fucking crazy is all this?"

"I don't think we've seen all the crazy yet." And before Sean could ask, she continued that line of thinking. "And no, it won't be the 'excitable boy' or me. I'll control Connor's anger and my own. I'm much better prepared for this type of thing because of all the therapy I've had and the medication that I'm taking. And Hazel said the best thing I could do right now is to avoid Beth and her drunk neighbors. So that's what I'm going to do and I'll make sure Connor does too."

Sean looked at Maggie in disbelief. Surely this was not one of her exaggerated versions of what occurred. She couldn't make all of this up. In particular what Amos had said or what Jasmine has told her. She appeared to be in control of herself and her emotions and telling the truth.

"Connor knows that Beth is Amos's granddaughter too, but I'll make sure he stays away from her. He'll be so focused on Amos that he won't have time for Beth. And speaking of Amos, the nurse at the VA wouldn't be specific because of privacy rules, but she handed me a hospice card for him before I left the other day. Something is killing Amos and he won't do anything about it. Connor doesn't know that and I'm not going to tell him because I don't know how much longer Amos has to live. That is a worry he doesn't need. I'm hoping I can get Amos to talk to me and perhaps convince him to get some help but that remains to be seen."

"Let's stop and think about that for just a minute, Maggie. Amos is a Vietnam war veteran. Has seen a lot of death in his lifetime," Sean started before Maggie interrupted.

"He has a bronze and silver star," Maggie said. "He is not just a vet. He is a war hero. And I think that party today meant more to him than just coming home from the hospital. I believe in his mind it was a thank you for coming back from the war."

"Even more reason for what I'm about to say. I'm sure the doctors told him what was wrong with him and I'm sure they told him that if he didn't do anything about it, he would die. But that decision is for him to make. And I know you're going to say he doesn't understand, but I think he does. And as such, I think he wants to go out on his own terms. He doesn't want to fight another war. He is through fighting wars, Maggie, and I think we should respect that. And now that I know about him and Beth, it's just another example of what I'm saying. It sounds like he has avoided that war for probably close to thirty years now."

Maggie didn't want to admit that what Sean was saying made sense. It was logical and probably right. But that didn't mean she wasn't going to ask. And try. *At least try,* she told herself.

"And I'm very proud of you, Maggie," Sean said. "For going back to a therapist and listening to her. Trying to make yourself better. Not only for you but for your son."

"What about for you?" Maggie asked.

"And me too. Very much me too," he said as he took her hand and led her back to the bedroom.

"Batting practice?" Maggie asked.

"Yes," Sean replied.

The next morning, Sean and Connor went to church, but Maggie said she wanted to go over and check on Amos. Before she left, she sent out an email to the neighborhood asking for their input on adding some lighting on the covered bridge and around the pond. Within seconds, she got a response from Jennifer stating that was a wonderful idea.

Well, they must be home, Maggie thought and she emailed Jennifer back, thanking her for her quick response. She asked if she would check with Frances and see if she ever met someone named Luna when she was helping Sarah Cayman with her medical needs. Jennifer replied with a "yes." Maggie then asked if she happened to know her last name. "Yes, it's Garcia," Jennifer responded. Maggie sent her a "thank you" and started looking through the computer for an address for a Luna Garcia.

Within minutes, she had the address. It was in downtown Augusta, in Olde Town, on Broad Street.

"I will be coming by to visit with you this afternoon, Luna," Maggie said out loud. "But first, I've got some things to do."

She called Barbara and Sable and told them they needed to meet again. She said she was going by to see Amos first and would meet up with them in thirty minutes at Sable's house.

Maggie could see Amos in his wheelchair on the front porch, an easel and canvas beside him. She waved as soon as she saw him, but he didn't acknowledge her. *Maybe he doesn't see me* she thought as she neared the steps and greeted him.

"Good morning, Amos." Even though he was looking right at her there was still no response.

"Did you paint a sunrise?" Maggie asked. She turned to look at the canvas and saw that it was blank.

"What's wrong, Amos?"

"I've lost my best friend. Hank. He was in the hospital after we crashed. I was over at the hospital just the other day, but I couldn't find him."

"I'm so sorry," Maggie replied. "But do you remember being in the hospital? You know for your leg?"

Amos looked down at his leg. "How did that happen?"

"You stepped into an animal trap," Maggie replied.

"I bet that woman down at the end of the road put those out there."

Yes. I've heard you say that before. But you did it, Amos. You did it to yourself. How can you be so lucid one minute and so confused the next? It's more than PTSD, isn't it? Early-onset dementia maybe?

"Do you remember the doctors talking to you about your foot or anything else?" Maggie asked.

"No, they didn't talk to me about anything. But I remember them telling me Hank had died. Yeah, they told me that he had just lost too much blood. I remember seeing blood when I was there at the hospital. I think they took some from me to give to Hank. I guess they just couldn't get it to him fast enough. I'm going to miss him. He didn't get to have a coming home party. I did. It was wonderful. I wish Hank could have been there. But I'll get to see him again someday. And I'll tell him about it over a beer. Someday soon I think."

He remembers getting the transfusions but he's confusing that with his friend's death. Sean was right. He knows he is going to die and I should respect that. Just be there for him, Maggie. Comfort him when you can. That's what he needs.

"Did you have any breakfast this morning?" she asked.

"No, I don't think so."

"Can I make you some?"

"I ain't got nothing to make breakfast with," he replied.

"What if I run out and get you some biscuits? Would you eat those?"

"Will they have bacon or sausage on them?"

"Yes, if that's what you want."

"Sure, that sounds good. Can one be sausage and one be bacon?"

Maggie smiled as she patted his cheek so tenderly that Amos thought it was just the wind blowing by his face. "I'll be back in a little while with some food, okay?"

Amos sat silently in his chair gazing straight into the woods. She was leaving when she heard him call out, "Hello, Maggie!" and waved. She just shook her head and waved back and then went straight to Sable's house where she and Barbara were sitting out on the back deck.

"What's up?" Barbara asked. "What did you find now?"

"That picture, that picture of the little girl and Amos. It was Beth. Amos told me last night. He is Beth's grandfather," Maggie said.

"Oh my God!" Barbara said. "Are you kidding us?"

Maggie shook her head no.

"Wow! I would've never imagined that! So, what now?" Sable asked.

"Nothing as far as I can see will come of it," Maggie replied. "The nurses were going to call Beth and ask her if she is related to Amos so she could possibly help with his care and I bet she tells them no. And even if she says yes, we all know, Beth isn't going to do anything to help him. And he's going to need our help.

"He is dying. He won't admit it. But they found something while he was in the hospital. I'm guessing some sort of cancer. I was going to try and get him to tell me what it was, but Sean said I should just leave it alone. That if Amos wanted anyone to know, he would tell us. I disagreed, but after seeing Amos this morning, I've changed my mind. He's dying and he knows it. The best thing we can all do now is to go by and see him. Take him food. Keep him supplied with his beer. Visit with him. I'm not sure how long he has but the nurse gave me the name of a hospice group to call when it becomes necessary. And I don't think they give those cards out if they think you're going to be around for a long time."

Barbara got up and took Maggie in her arms. She hugged her tight without saying a word. There were no words needed.

"You have a good spirit, Maggie Brodie," Sable said as she got up and hugged her too.

"You sound like Red now," Maggie said as her voice cracked and she began crying.

"Yeah, I suppose I do," Sable replied.

"Thanks for coming over and telling us," Barbara said as she sat down. Sable sat down too but they watched as Maggie just stood there. Not moving.

"Maggie," Barbara said. "Sit down before you fall down."

Maggie looked at them and shook her head no.

"Now we know why Beth talked about discussing Amos with a therapist. She did that because he was her grandfather. Not because he was some crazy stranger at the end of the street. Seeing how she treated her own grandfather it makes even more sense to me."

"What are you talking about Maggie?" Barbara asked. "The look in your eyes, it's a little scary."

"She'll do anything to anybody to get what she wants and it doesn't matter who she hurts to do so. She and Jorge. They have been sending me warnings. I think she is trying to intimidate me."

"What kind of warnings?" Barbara asked.

"I can't say yet. Not until I'm sure. Hazel told me to stay away from them for the time being."

"Then that's what you should do," Barbara said as Sable looked at her in a puzzled manner, not sure who the person was that Maggie referred to.

"But you aren't going to do that, are you?" Barbara stated.

"I am going to stay away from them," Maggie replied. "I just want to find out some more information. But I have to go get Amos some food first. I'll be okay. Thanks for being my friends," she said as she hurried away.

Sable turned to Barbara. "Should we be worried and who is Hazel?" she asked.

"A therapist friend of mine. Took good care of me when I got sick. I thought I told you about her, but maybe I didn't. And I don't think we need to be worried yet. But we need to keep an eye on things. Maggie is right about Beth. She will do anything to anybody at any time," Barbara said.

Maggie picked up some biscuits from Hardee's, got a few things from the grocery store, and delivered them to Amos. He thanked her many times for the biscuits. On her way out, she told him about the milk and frozen dinners that she had put in his refrigerator. *And if he doesn't remember that, he should see the piece of paper that I taped to the refrigerator door,* she thought. *And Connor will be by later.* She reassured herself that he would be fine as she drove to Luna Garcia's house.

Luna answered the door and Maggie introduced herself as a friend of Sarah Cayman's who lived in the same neighborhood as she had. When she described where she lived, Luna said she knew the house well and that it was a pleasure meeting her.

"What can I do for you?" Luna asked.

"I am looking for your nephew," Maggie replied. "Jorge."

Luna looked at Maggie curiously. "I don't have a nephew named Jorge."

"The young man that was at the funeral service with you. Wasn't that Jorge?" she asked.

Luna knew at once that there was more to this being just a friendly question. "No, it wasn't," Luna replied. "And what do you want with that young man, may I ask?"

Maggie realized she should just cut to the chase and just tell her why she came by today. She should know about the person that she was trying to protect. "He's having an affair with a married woman in my neighborhood and you and I both know that is wrong. It will hurt that family if her husband and children find out," Maggie said. "And I think he may have done some things to me. To threaten me."

"It's Brodie, isn't it?" Luna asked.

"Yes."

"Mrs. Brodie, I do not want to ever see you at my house again. My nephew wouldn't do what you are saying. He is a good man. And if you want to accuse him of something, you best be sure that you have all the evidence that he did it. Because if you are just profiling him because he is a Latino, then I'm afraid, you and I are going to have some issues with how we go about resolving our difference of opinions."

Maggie started to walk away but then stopped and pointed to the driveway. The blue Chevy truck was parked there.

"I recognize his truck," Maggie said as she pointed to it. "He's probably here right now. And if I see it around my house, I will call the police and let them sort it out. If he continues to have an affair with Beth, Beth Stevens, he will end up in jail. Not because of me, but because of her. He doesn't know what kind of person she is and what she will do to him."

Luna closed the door and stood there as she listened as Maggie's voice got louder.

"Tell him. Tell him I know and I'll be watching. Tell him that for me," she said as she stood by her car and pressed down on her horn until she saw the neighbors come out of their houses, looking at her. *That's what I wanted. I want your neighbors to remember me and my car,* she said to herself as she got in and drove away.

Luna watched Maggie drive away and then went back to the kitchen where Emiliano had been eating lunch with his nephew and niece. Luna quietly told her children to go to their rooms and sat down across from Emiliano. She didn't have to say anything as she looked at him. His face confirmed what she had just heard.

"It's true, Luna," Emiliano said. "What she said was true. I'm trying to stop the affair with the woman, but she is like Mrs. Brodie said, very vengeful and full of poison. It is humiliating to be with her but I thought I had to do what she said so I could get my company going. But I will end it. I promise. Now I know I must protect myself or she will indeed send me back to jail. She will lie about everything and send me back to jail."

"Did you harm that woman?" Luna asked.

"I put some bugs in her mailbox and garage but nothing serious came of it. And I won't do anything like that ever again. I know better now. I believe you when you say I have been given a second chance and I don't want to mess that up. I don't ever want to go back to jail. I will fix this. In the right way. I promise you."

"It breaks my heart to hear you say that Sobrino," Luna said. "It breaks su Abuela's heart. And you know why I know that? Because she is here," she said as she pointed to her chest. "For a very long time, you gave her nothing to be proud of. But she believed in you and so I believed in you. I became convinced that you would be a good man one day. That deep down inside, you had a good heart. I believed in you, Emiliano. I still believe in you and I wouldn't have said that if you had lied to me today. The other Emiliano I knew would have lied to me when I asked these questions. But the one I know now stands up. He owns up to his failures and says he will do better. That is the man that I want to be around me and my family. But, if that old Emiliano shows up and the Emiliano I am looking at right now goes away, then I will have a different opinion."

Chapter 33

The Garden Gnome

Emiliano sat and looked at his aunt. *She stood up for me. She protected me.* He realized she had been doing that his whole life. He didn't tell her about the fish that he killed in the pond but he didn't need to do that now. He would tell her after he fixed everything.

"You know you will have to apologize to Mrs. Brodie, do you not?" Luna asked.

"Yes, I understand. I know what I must do to make things right. I promise Luna. Y tu, Abuela," he said as he looked up to the ceiling.

Luna smiled and called for her children to come back down and finish lunch. "What about we go to a movie this afternoon?" Emiliano asked. "To that fancy theater. The one with the reclining chairs."

"Riverwatch Theater?" his nephew asked. "I've been wanting to go there."

"Then we go there," Emiliano said as he looked over at Luna.

Luna looked skeptical as she asked her son what was showing that they could all go see. He told her "Jurassic World 2" was playing. She asked what the rating was and her son borrowed Emiliano's phone to find out.

"PG-13. It's fine. We saw the other one. You said you liked all the dinosaurs."

"Si, si, creo que recuerdo," Luna replied. "And you can afford this, sobrino?"

"Yes," he replied.

"Then I think we go see the dinosaurs," Luna replied and everyone started laughing.

It cost Emiliano almost ninety dollars for the movie and snacks. When Luna realized how much it cost she tried to give him some money but he wouldn't take it. He whispered to her that he had never spent money more wisely. He enjoyed the movie with his family but what he enjoyed the most, was his nephew and niece talking about the movie after it was over. With him. Thanking him for taking them and saying what a wonderful afternoon it had been. He hadn't felt that good in a very long time.

The following day, his thoughts were consumed with Beth. He knew he had to have evidence, a picture or video of them in the act, or she would claim he raped her. Maggie Brodie was right when she said Beth would send him to jail. He meant nothing to her. He needed proof that she was a willing participant. Once he had that, he knew she couldn't hurt him.

The threat of losing business because of his relationship with Beth had already become a reality. Mrs. Bartholomew had canceled his services last week. When he asked her if she was unhappy with his work, she told him it had nothing to do with his work. It had everything to do with her neighbor and him. He knew he would lose more yards by making Beth angry but if she knew he had that picture, perhaps he could use that as leverage. So that she wouldn't say anything to the other neighbors. *No*, he told himself. *That is the old Emiliano talking. I must accept what happens. The picture of us together is just so I don't go to jail. What happens with my business will just have to happen.*

He dreaded Wednesday but the day came anyway. He drove slowly to Beth's house arriving at nine o'clock, just like he had always done. He switched his phone to video mode and slid it into his pocket as he walked around the back of the house. Beth was lounging in a pool chair, wearing a skimpy bikini.

"Feel like going swimming today?" she asked.

"I didn't bring a bathing suit."

"Who needs bathing suits? Get undressed," she directed.

Emiliano heard a chain saw revving up in the yard next door. He looked around and saw the end of a pole saw extend upward over the fence and begin cutting down leafless tree limbs.

"Don't worry about that," Beth said. "That's just my neighbor. I asked him to cut down some dead tree limbs months ago. He probably hasn't been sober enough to get to it until now."

Emiliano got undressed and Beth smiled when she saw him standing in front of her.

"You are quite the specimen," she said. "Get in the pool and swim around for a minute. I want to see if the water can do anything to shrink that thing between your legs."

She pulled out her phone and began recording him as he was walking to the pool. *This is it*, he said to himself. *I don't need my phone. I can steal her phone. And once I have it, it's over. All I need to do is copy that video onto a flash drive. And it's over.* He got into the water and made sure he smiled back at Beth. *It's not a silent movie, Emiliano. Speak.*

"Why don't you come get in the water with me?" Emiliano asked. "I think you will like what you'll find."

"Oh, really?" Beth replied. "What do you have over there in the water that I want?"

"Come and see," Emiliano replied.

"No, come show me."

Emiliano came up the pool steps. "Damn," Beth said as she continued the video. "Water does nothing to that big old thing, does it? Come here and let me make sure the pH of the water is in balance."

Emiliano walked over to her and she bent down and filmed her newly acquired oral skills. Once she had taken as much as she wanted, she held it next to her face as she looked into the cell phone.

"Do you like tacos Jorge?" Beth asked. "You love tacos, don't you? Take my bathing suit off," she commanded as she kept recording. "Show me how much you love eating tacos, Jorge."

Emiliano removed the bottom of her bathing suit. He spread her legs apart as she pushed his head down. After a few minutes, she dropped the phone. *Shit,* he thought as he continued to do what she wanted. He moved his lips up to her stomach as he looked down at the phone. Beth's eyes were closed and he reached up and grabbed her breast with one hand as he turned the phone over with the other so it was pointed toward them.

"You're not through, are you?" she asked.

"No, just getting started."

Beth had never felt anything like what Jorge was doing to her. Darrin couldn't even come close to making her feel like she did now. She was moaning out loud but she didn't care. As long as she didn't scream, she was sure the sounds would be muffled by the noise of the saw. She grabbed his hair as she opened her eyes and she saw her child's playhouse and the guard to the playhouse; the garden gnome, with his wide-open eyes staring at her. *Look all you want, you little orange-hatted freak.*

"Don't stop," she said as she looked down at Jorge and pushed his head into her body. She opened her eyes again and started to scream when she saw a different set of eyes. The eyes of her neighbor standing on a ladder, looking at them over the fence. The saw was not on and he was smiling as he watched them. She wanted to tell him to fuck off but she couldn't find the energy to do so as Emiliano climbed on top of her. *Fuck him and fuck me* she thought and smiled.

Once Emiliano was finished, Beth reached up and ran her hands through his hair just before she pushed him away. "That was worth at least three more homes," she said as she sat up and put on her swimsuit bottom. She could see out of the corner of her eyes that her neighbor was still watching them. *I'll make sure that son of a bitch drunken perv pays for his little peep show. He'll realize he shouldn't have done that,* she told herself as she picked up her phone to go inside.

"I'll watch this video over and over. At least until next Wednesday," Beth smirked. She handed Emiliano a piece of paper from the table with the names and addresses of more potential clients.

"You don't need to trim the hedges today. They're fine. Just do the yard," Beth declared as she walked into the house and closed the door.

Back to work, he told himself, but this time he looked forward to mowing Beth's lawn because he knew he would soon have what he needed to end this humiliating affair. He was nothing but a dick to Beth and that wouldn't have bothered him at all in the past, but it did now that he was beginning to understand what self-esteem meant.

The phone rang as he was getting his tractor from the truck. When he saw his aunt's name pop up, he knew it was something bad. His stomach clinched when he answered and heard her crying. In between the pauses and the moments she tried to gather her composure, Emiliano heard his aunt explain that his sister was dead. She was killed attempting to rob a liquor store with her boyfriend.

Emiliano wasn't sure what to say. At one time in his life, he had looked up to his sister. She didn't take crap off of anyone and she was a strong leader in the gang they were both a part of until she moved out to California. They didn't keep in touch but he knew from Luna that she was still involved in the gang life. He hadn't thought it was that big a deal when he had learned that but now he realized how hard it was for Luna to have to give him that information. *She probably saw the good in her too* he thought. But in her case, if it was there, it was now gone, concealed in a red stain on the concrete.

"I am so sorry, my Emiliano," Luna said. "I don't think Malia ever really had a chance. I prayed for her many times and I only hope she asked for forgiveness before she died. It will be the only thing that gives me any comfort going forward. Hoping that she did that."

"I am sure she asked for forgiveness before she died." He doubted that she did, but he knew what Luna needed to hear.

His aunt was still crying. "That could have been you, Sobrino. That could have been you, but for su Abuela. She would not allow that to happen. Just remember that I love you," Luna said as she ended the call.

Emiliano placed the phone in his pocket and made a cross on his chest. He finished mowing Beth's yard and as he started on the Thompsons's, he saw Jim sitting on his back deck with a bottle of scotch on the table beside him. He waved him over to the table and Emiliano walked over.

"How are you this morning, Jorge? Did you have a good breakfast?"

Jorge thought that was an odd question but he told him yes, he had a good breakfast.

"How are the American-made tacos? Are they as good as your kind?"

Emiliano now understood the question. He knew he had seen him and Beth. And though he was angry at the racial slurs he was glad that he had seen them. *He would be a witness. He could say that Beth was a willing participant.*

He knew what Mr. Thompson wanted to hear and so he told him with as few as words as possible. "Si, muy Bueno," Emiliano said.

"I bet." Jim laughed and offered him a drink. "I know this is scotch, but I have some tequila over there at the bar."

Emiliano wanted to lash out at the racist fat man sitting in front of him but he knew he couldn't. He felt he deserved the humiliation so he just nodded his head no and went back to finishing his lawn. Afterward, he drove his tractor over to Mrs. Cayman's yard and smiled at the sight of the hedge full of roses.

He thought about Malia. Her name meant 'bitter' and he wondered why his parents would name a child something like that. *Perhaps, she was always bitter,* he thought and as he did, he could remember his grandmother chastising her for something she had done. And his sister throwing her a bird as she turned her back. *Yes, she was probably well named.* But he still felt a loss inside and he was sorry that she had never been given a second chance. He lifted his head as the fragrant scent of the roses floated over to him and made him feel better.

It was getting dark when Connor came back from Amos's house and told his mom that he had stopped to check on Amos and that she needed to come with him to see his foot because it was so cool.

"The foot? Are you kidding me? He has it already?" Maggie asked.

"Yes, his buddy John just brought it over to him. I think they had quite a few beers too. Amos seemed to be in a pretty good mood and there were a lot of empty cans in the kitchen. But it looks pretty damn awesome."

"It is a person's foot, you know," Maggie replied. "How would you like it if I got breast cancer and had my breast bronzed and placed on the wall?"

"Nice, Mom. Nice analogy."

Maggie realized what she said was cold and disrespectful not only to Amos but to every person she had known that had struggled with breast cancer. "I'm sorry. That was a poor attempt at humor. And I'm sorry I said it. But I doubt that I'm going to find Amos's foot that cool."

"Well, you won't know until you see it, will you?"

"No, I guess not. So let's get it over with." Connor was running toward the road when Maggie saw Jim Thompson's Cadillac heading their way. She yelled at Connor to stop and just as he did, Jim's car swerved toward him and their mailbox. Connor had to jump back as the car clipped the stone mailbox and then righted itself before weaving its way through the covered bridge. *Someone needs to do something about that* Maggie thought as she raced down to Connor.

"Are you okay?" she asked frantically.

"Yeah, I'm fine. I saw Mr. Thompson talking on his cell phone. He must not have been paying attention," Connor said.

"Yeah," Maggie replied, though she thought the phone was just a small part of the reason he was swerving toward her son. *He'll pay for that.*

Maggie heard Amos yell out their names. *He recognizes us. That's good* she thought. *Probably has something to do with Connor.*

"Hello, Maggie," Amos said as they came up to the house. "Care for a beer?"

"No thanks. I came up here to see the foot. Connor said I had to see it." The beautiful sunset that Amos had painted today was sitting on the easel.

"Do you like it?" Amos asked as he followed her eyes.

"I love it! You are a very talented artist."

"You can have it."

"Well, I already have one of your paintings, Amos," Maggie said.

"You do?"

"Yes, and it's one of my favorite things in my entire house. You know besides this guy over here and the sergeant."

"You think that big tall Indian fella that lives next door to me would like it? He likes doing art stuff."

"He would love it, Amos."

"Good. Then can you give it to him for me?"

"I would be glad to, Amos."

"You reckon the other neighbors would like a painting too?"

"I bet they would all love one."

"Well then. I'll paint 'em all one. Well, maybe not all of them."

Maggie felt like she was going to cry again when she heard him talking about doing a painting for his neighbors, but his remark about "not all of them" made her regain her composure, and then she heard her son.

"Look what Amos gave me." Connor pulled out the alligator billfold. "And look at his belt."

Amos pushed out his stomach so Maggie could see the belt. The craftsmanship of the belt and the wallet was amazing.

"You have been a busy man," Maggie said. She didn't want to remember that day but seeing the dead alligator in the form of a belt and wallet was probably something she could live with. The more she looked at them, the better she felt about that day – seeing that something beautiful had come from that awful incident. And then she remembered Connor's teacher and all of those bad emotions came rushing forward and she turned away for a moment while she took a deep breath. *Pull yourself together, Maggie. Amos doesn't know about that and he doesn't need to* she thought as she turned back around to face him and her son.

"I have. Felt like I needed to be," Amos said as Maggie looked into his eyes.

Maggie knew why he was saying that and this time she did cry but, again, Connor came to her rescue.

"Come on, mom. You haven't seen the best part yet," he said as he nodded his head toward the inside of the house.

Amos wheeled himself into the house and Maggie followed them to the back porch where the bronze foot and a small garden gnome held open the door.

"My friend John found that old thing in the garage as he was poking around in there," Amos said as he pointed toward the garden gnome. "He said I now had a gnome foot," Amos said as he burst out laughing.

Connor was laughing too, but Maggie wasn't sure what they found so funny.

"Get it? A gnome foot," Connor said.

Maggie stared at them, unsure of what they found so funny, and then it hit her. A gnome foot. A numb foot. She groaned and then started laughing at the pun.

Amos smiled. "It gets even funnier when you say it after you have had twelve or so more beers."

"I would imagine it does."

Chapter 34

The burning ground

"Amos, you may be the only person in the world who has a bronze foot. His own foot, bronzed for all to see. I'm sure you are the only person in Augusta with one," Maggie said.

"And I am giving it to your son when I die. Don't you forget that," he reminded her.

"I haven't forgotten, Amos. I'm just trying to figure out where to put it in our house."

"It stays in my room," Connor replied. "He's giving it to me, remember?"

"Ah, yes. I thought it was for all of us to enjoy, but I see now, you want to keep it for yourself. Fine. Fine. I'll just have to be okay with that," Maggie said as she was thinking, *Thank God.*

"There's a couple of other things, if you have a minute, that I'd like to talk to you about," Amos said as he looked over at Maggie. "Can you come inside?"

Once in the den, he pointed at the lamp and began to tell Maggie about it. "That's an old lamp that my wife bought a long time ago. She knew a lot about antiques and, anyway, it's the only thing I think I still have that she bought back in the day. Sold a lot. Gave away a lot. And may still have some other things out in the garage I have forgot about, but that lamp. That lamp, she was mighty proud of it. Said it was worth a lot of money. I want you to have it, Maggie. I ain't got anyone else to give it to, you know."

Maggie felt the tears again. "So I get that old thing by default, huh?" she said jokingly, trying to keep herself from falling to the floor in the fetal position and crying like a baby, as she wiped away the few tears that had escaped the emotional restraints she had placed on her eyes.

"I know, I know. I didn't care too much for it but she sure liked it and it made her happy. And she told me not to sell it, so I am trying to abide by her wishes. If you want to sell it after I'm gone, then you'll just have to deal with my wife's spirit haunting you," Amos said as he winked at her.

Maggie carefully lifted the lamp and showed the bottom to Amos. "This is a Tiffany lamp. A real Tiffany lamp. Made in the early 1900s. It's worth a small fortune. Somewhere between four and five hundred thousand dollars in an auction, I'm guessing. You should sell it. Buy something with…" She stopped in mid-sentence as she realized what she was going to say, would mean nothing to him. He wasn't looking for more things. In fact, in a moment of clear-headedness, he was putting his affairs in order. His response confirmed that for her.

"I don't need anything else. Maggie. Got everything I need right here. My house is paid for. I got a yard full of pretty plants, and trees, and shrubs. Got a nice waterfall. Get to see sunrises and sunsets every day and drink a beer when I want one. Not sure I could ask for more than that. Except, maybe a good grilled steak every now and then and maybe some help getting my beer and groceries. Maybe even have those people who were at that party the other night get together again. Boy, that was something."

"Thank you, Amos," Maggie said as she walked over and hugged him. She felt him return her hug for the first time and all of the checks and balances she had in place unraveled and she began to cry. Amos patted her on the back and told her everything was okay and that made things even worse. She held on to him even tighter and cried even more.

After a few moments, Maggie heard Amos ask if she would like a beer and she managed to say no as she continued to cry. He waited a few more minutes before asking her if it would be okay if he got one for himself. Her tears mixed with laughter as she grabbed one for him.

"There is one more thing," he said.

"Damn, Amos," Maggie said. "I'm not sure I can take any more news today."

"Hasn't this been a good evening so far?"

Maggie had to admit it had been as she looked at the clear but bloodshot eyes of her friend. His mind was lucid and he seemed to be so happy. She understood that everything he had done, everything that he was doing was making him happy. It was just hard to accept that he was doing these things because he knew he was dying. But then she heard Sean's voice telling her how Amos had seen a lot of death. How he had been in a lot of battles and that he was tired of fighting them. He was okay with the knowledge he didn't have to fight very much longer. She needed to be okay with that too. She had told her friends she was, but she wasn't acting like it tonight.

"It has been a good evening, Amos, a very good evening. What else do you want to tell me?"

"I have a Ford F-150 out in the garage. It's an old one. Made in 1986, but it still runs like a champ. I've taken good care of her, and she's taken good care of me. If you will allow your son to take me to the grocery store and places I need to go, and I ain't talking about titty bars or anything like that, but maybe over to John's or to get something to eat. Well, if you will allow him to do that for me, he can have the truck when I don't need it anymore. I'll make everything legal so nobody thinks he stole it. I know he isn't a thug, but some people may get that impression the first time they meet him," Amos said as he looked at Connor and laughed.

Connor was now more surprised than his mother. And even more shocked when instead of protesting or coming up with many reasons as to why she couldn't allow him to do this, Maggie did what she said she would do. She would provide her friend support and try and make him happy.

"Yes, Amos, I think that would be fine - on one condition," Maggie said. "You need to show Connor how to take care of the truck. How to change the oil, check the tires, all the things you did to keep a thirty-two-year-old truck running."

"Deal," Amos said as he tilted his beer to Maggie and smiled.

"Is there anything else before we go, Amos? Perhaps something that we need to dig out from behind the drywall that you have hidden there?"

"Well, I do need some clothes washed," Amos answered sheepishly.

Maggie burst out laughing and asked him where the washer and dryer were. He pointed her in the right direction and she put a load of clothes in the washer and promised that Connor would be back in the morning to move them to the dryer. They would be okay in the washer until then.

"Thanks, Maggie. I appreciate that."

She gave him a quick hug and then told Connor it was time to go. Connor thanked Amos for everything and said he would see him in the morning. Maggie expected Connor to bombard her with questions as they walked home about why he was giving everything away but he didn't and she was thankful for that. Until she began to wonder if Amos had already told Connor something and though she wanted to ask, she didn't. If either of them wanted her to know anything else, they would tell her and she needed to just be okay with that.

When Maggie got up the next morning, Sean and Connor were gone but there were two notes for her next to the hot water kettle. She made her cup of tea and walked outside before she opened them. The first one was from her husband telling her how proud he was of how she was handling everything. The other was from Connor and in it, he wrote that he appreciated everything she was doing for him and Amos.

"Nope, nice try you two, but not going to cry again. I'm just not," she said out loud as she drank her tea and every so often, reread the notes and smiled. Before she went to see Hazel that afternoon, she went by to have Amos's picture for Red framed. Barbara had recommended the place and the owner of the shop helped her picked out the perfect frame.

She arrived at Dr. Nutt's office promptly and Janice told her to go right in. Maggie opened the door and found Hazel typing at her desk.

"Be right with you, Maggie," Hazel said as she finished up her notes and closed her computer. "I'm sorry about that. I'm usually ahead of myself but the last session was somewhat difficult."

"Anything you wish to talk about?"

Hazel laughed. "So how are you, Maggie?"

"I'm doing okay."

"How is Connor?"

"He is amazing. Like a rock. He just seems to move forward every minute. Understanding things that I think few adults would understand or be able to work through."

"What do you mean?

"Well, as you suggested, I've been trying to avoid certain people in my neighborhood. But even though I've tried, things have happened that continue to bring us together and they somehow involve Connor."

"Can you explain?"

"Well, I found out that Amos, the neighbor who had his foot removed, the one who saved Connor's life – well, he is Beth's grandfather. You know, the woman who is having an affair with the man that takes care of her yard?"

Hazel was trying to understand the connection and waited for Maggie to make it.

"Well, her friend, the alcoholic neighbor, almost killed my son the other night as we were going over to see Amos."

"What?" she exclaimed.

"Yes, he was swerving in his car as he was driving down our road. Connor said he was talking on his cell phone but I suspect he was drunk. He hit our mailbox and Connor had to jump back to keep from being hit."

"Interesting. Why do you suspect he was drunk?"

"Because he is drunk all the time according to his neighbor. She won't go out with him and his wife anymore because they drink so much. And from the two interactions I've had with him, I have seen it too. He's a damn drunk. No doubt."

"Perhaps he needs help. Professional help to deal with the problem you say he has."

"He does, and I am not making any of this up."

"I'm not saying you are, Maggie."

"You kind of implied it. You said 'with the problem I say he has.' I'm not the one that called someone he barely knew 'sweet cheeks' and then called her a 'nasty cooch' later that same evening."

"Agreed. That is bad behavior."

"And like I said, he almost ran over my son the over evening. He did hit our mailbox."

"If he was drunk, as you suspect he was, why didn't you call the police?" Hazel asked.

"That's a good question. I think I should have. I will next time."

Hazel made a note regarding Maggie's rational acceptance of how she should have handled things. Her anger was controlled. She would refer back to that going forward as they continued to discuss conflict resolution. "Tell me about your neighbor. The one with PTSD."

"We brought him home from the hospital. Connor has been wonderful with him. They have developed a strong relationship and I have to admit I've gotten pretty attached to him too. He is dying," Maggie said matter of factly. The abruptness of her comment took Hazel by surprise.

"Dying?" she repeated.

"When we picked him up from the hospital, the nurse told me he wouldn't be getting a prosthetic for his leg. When I asked why she said she couldn't say. You know, because of patient confidentiality laws, but she gave me a hospice card before we left. I don't have to tell you what that means. I wanted to find out what was wrong with him, but my husband told me to let it go. That Amos would tell us if he wanted us to know. I had a hard time dealing with that at first, but I realized that Sean was right. Amos has accepted his fate. He has fought as many battles as he wants and I need to accept that. When I talked to him last night, I finally came to terms with that."

"What happened last night?"

"He was talking about making paintings for his neighbors. I can't remember if I told you what a fantastic painter he is, but he is amazing. He told me about some things that were special to him and he wanted to make sure they were taken care of. His amputated and now bronzed foot, for one," Maggie said as she looked off to the side and chuckled.

"And then two other things. A lamp his wife had bought. She bought a lot of antiques. She had, well Amos has, a Tiffany lamp. It's one of the wisteria lamps made around the early 1900s. I think that lamp would sell for a fortune at auction. I told him he needed to use it to buy himself something nice, and he just looked at me and said he had everything he needed." Maggie took a deep breath and tried to control her emotions.

Hazel could see that Maggie wanted to say more so she sat and silently encouraged her to continue through the facial expression she had perfected after forty years of listening to people talk to her about anything and everything.

"And then a car. Well, not a car, but a truck. If Connor would drive him around, to the grocery store, to the beer store, to see his friends when he wanted, then the truck would be his after he's, uh…gone. He wanted to give that to him."

"Have you heard Connor talking to himself anymore?" Dr. Nutt inquired.

"No. No, I haven't."

"Maggie," Hazel started. "It seems to me that Amos has some wonderful neighbors. Actually, neighbors is not the right word. Has some wonderful friends that are willing to be there for him when he is going to need them the most. From what you told me earlier, he had shunned his neighbors in the past and now you're saying he wants to make paintings for them. That didn't happen accidentally. That happened because of the connection you and your son made with him. He wants to be remembered now instead of forgotten by his neighbors and probably by the granddaughter who lives down the road from him. You have given him a gift. One that will provide him support and dignity in the final days that he's now ready to face."

Maggie felt angry when tears welled up in her eyes. "Shit, Hazel, I think I've cried every day for two weeks now. I can't remember when I didn't cry and it's pissing me off."

"It's not pissing you off, Maggie. You think it makes you look weak. But in reality, it shows how strong you are."

Maggie accepted a tissue from Hazel and wiped her eyes. *She is so easy to talk to. Next time I'll tell her about the Renaissance Fair and the bluejay. She'll understand why it has caused me so much angst.*

Hazel reminded Maggie to keep taking her medication and said that they would talk about more conflict resolution techniques in the future. She also told Maggie she appreciated her honesty and her efforts, and that she looked forward to seeing her next week.

Maggie drove home feeling better. She was encouraged and hopeful. When she got home, she changed clothes and smiled at herself in the mirror.

"You look good today," the image said.

"I do look good, don't I?" Maggie replied.

"You need to stay away from your neighbors," the image warned her.

"I know that. I'm supposed to call the police the next time, just like Hazel told me."

"I hope you do," the image answered.

"You talk too much sometimes," Maggie said as she turned around and shut the door. She went outside and thought about all that had been happening with Connor, Sean, and Amos. *I think I should say something to Jim. I won't be hateful or mean. I will just talk to him and tell him in a matter of fact manner that if I see him swerving down the road again, I'm going to call the police. That should be fine. Yes, I think I'll go tell him right now.*

Jim was sitting on his patio nursing a scotch. He was surprised he had to make a run to the liquor store the other night. He never ran out of Scotch. He blamed it on Renee being away for a couple of days. She usually made sure the liquor cabinet was stocked. But it didn't matter now. He had three bottles and she would be home tomorrow so he should be good until she returned.

He had finished over half the bottle as he looked up at the tree and the ladder beneath it. There were still some limbs that needed to be cut down, but he would have to use the pole saw while standing on the ladder. He wasn't sure that was wise considering how much he had drunk, but then he realized, people who have been drinking never seem to get hurt when they fall. He could testify to that. They just roll with the punches it seems. He chuckled as he poured another glass and drank it.

When Maggie reached the cul-de-sac she saw Jim in his yard, standing on the ladder with a pole saw in his hands. She saw someone who looked like Beth walking toward him. She ran to the front of the house so she could listen to their conversation.

When he saw his neighbor approaching, Jim turned off the pole saw and looked down at her. "Well, I have to admit, I didn't expect to see you. How are you doing today, Miss Queen B?"

"Sober, unlike you, you son of a bitch drunken perv," she yelled as she pushed the ladder with both her hands and watched Jim fall. He hit the ground hard and was knocked out. Because of his weight and the height he fell from, his body was unable to withstand the force with which it hit the ground. Bones cracked and limbs were turned in a way that should not have been possible. "I hope when you wake up, you will have learned a very important lesson. And oh, by the way, I wouldn't lay there too long because there are things out here in the weeds and woods that will hurt you."

Maggie saw Jim lying on the ground. She didn't notice any of the malformations on his body, because she didn't want to see them. She only saw him lying there on the ground, unconscious. She walked up closer, leaned down, and could hear him breathing, and decided he would be okay. And so, she left. But as she walked home, she began to feel sorry for him.

She told herself that she would remain calm and truly make an effort the next time she saw him and they spoke.

She was certain that he would have learned a very important lesson today regarding his neighbor and because of that lesson learned, she was sure he would be much more receptive to her concerns. Hazel would be proud of the way she was handling things she told herself and she looked forward to telling her about how she had started the process of conflict resolution with Jim.

Jim was on the ground for about thirty minutes before he opened his eyes. His entire body was screaming at him. Telling him to get up and get help. He attempted to get up but the pain made it impossible to do anything but stay there and hope that it would soon pass. He felt nauseous and when he looked down at his legs, he saw something white and jagged sticking out through a hole in his sweat pants. "My God-damn leg is broken," he said and then he saw the foot on his other leg twisted backward. "Holy shit!"

The porch was only about a hundred feet away but to reach it would be like crawling over broken glass; each move sending shock waves of pain through his body. He then checked his hands as he realized he would have to drag himself to the porch. His right hand looked like it had been stuck in a garbage disposal. Fingers were twisted in all sorts of different directions and several of them looked like they could fall off his hand at any time.

"God damn it!" he yelled and even doing that made his body hurt. It was at that moment that he noticed the reddish-black line moving in his direction and the large mound from which they were coming. It was as if a small volcano had erupted and the lava was moving toward him in a rapid straight line.

He soon felt the stings and burning sensations created by the first wave of fire ants that arrived at his body. He tried pushing onto the ground with his left hand and though his body moved, it only moved an inch and he thought he would pass out from the pain. At first, the stings of the fire ants were just a nuisance, but as more and more of them descended upon him, the pain from their stings began to surpass the pain he felt from his broken bones.

He took a deep breath and pushed down on the ground with his hand and again he moved. More than an inch this time but no more than a foot. He knew he couldn't stop though because the army of ants marching toward him made it look like the ground was moving. They began to bite and sting his neck and his face. He swatted away as many as he could with his one good hand but he knew if he continued to stop to do this, he would soon lose the battle.

He strained and grunted and pressed down with all of his strength and this time he moved several feet. The pain racked his entire body but he did it again and again until he was about halfway to the porch. He was beginning to think that he might make it when he glimpsed down at his chest. It looked like a crimson pond that was flowing back and forth unconstrained by any borders.

The ants were swarming in and out of his ears and all over his head. He closed his eyes as he swiped at them but for each one he killed, ten more took its place. He had to keep his eyelids closed or they would inject their venom into his eyes. The eyelids became shields that endured a constant barrage of bites and stings that seemed to be tearing and burning away the thin layer of protection. He dragged himself another few feet, but the ants were overwhelming his body.

He could feel them going up his nose and when he opened his mouth to take a breath, ants poured into it. They were crawling around the inside of his cheeks and all over his tongue. It felt as if someone had poured lighter fluid and a lit match into his mouth. He tried to scream but no sound came out and he choked on the ants that fell and wriggled down his throat. It was harder and harder to breathe. The ants had replaced the air in his lungs and he was suffocating. He reached up and swiped the ants away from his eyes and opened them one last time as he stared at the dead tree limb that had survived another day.

Chapter 35

Scotch Tape for Sale

On Friday afternoon, Renee returned from visiting her friend in Atlanta. It was the same routine each time she went there. Sleep late. Have a light salad and a bloody mary for lunch. Shop. Find a new restaurant that evening. Drink, eat, and drink a lot more and then repeat. But she was glad to be back home, as she was much more tired than usual.

She saw Jim's Cadillac in the garage when she parked her Mercedes. She walked into the kitchen with her arms full of shopping bags and several new bottles of twenty-year-old scotch that she always picked up for Jim at one of their favorite liquor stores out in Buckhead. She called his name telling him she was home but there was no answer. *He's probably out back at the bar* she thought as she walked out to the patio. She saw her husband lying under the tree he had been working on. A ladder and pole saw were on the ground close to him.

"Goddamn it, Jim. I told you not to get up on that ladder with a pole saw. I told you that you'd end up hurting yourself if you did, and it looks like I was right," she said as she marched over to him. When she got closer to his body she stopped abruptly. Though the swarm of ants had dissipated, there was still a large contingent of them biting his hands and fingers, tearing the skin away into small transportable segments that they could take back to the colony. Several of his fingers were just bones and she gagged as she turned her head and threw up.

She forced herself to look back at his body. A large bone was sticking out of his pants leg and his foot appeared deformed due to its position in relation to his leg. His face was almost unrecognizable, red and swollen and covered with thousands of bite marks. She started backing away from the body when she spotted the ants crawling out of his nose. She pulled out her phone and called 911 and went back up on the porch and poured herself a drink.

Beth heard the ambulance siren as it raced down the street and she rushed outside to see where it was going. It pulled into the Thompson's driveway and drove toward Renee who was waiting for them. She saw Renee talking to paramedics and watched until they disappeared behind their house.

"I wonder what happened to Jim? You've got to be careful when you go out into the woods, Summer. I told you that before, didn't I? Yes, I did," she said as Summer giggled at her mother, hearing something familiar and seeing the smile from her mother's face. Beth then turned around and calmly walked back inside.

Renee told the EMTs that she had just gotten back from Atlanta and found her husband in the backyard. She had warned him before she left about getting up on the ladder and using a pole saw, but it was apparent that he didn't listen to her. Renee watched as they took a large broom and began sweeping the ants away from Jim's body and spraying them with ant spray that they found in the garage. They soon had an area cleared around his body and started to assess the extent of Jim's injuries. They placed their stethoscope on his heart and against his neck but could not detect a heartbeat or pulse. As soon as they touched the body, they didn't expect to. His body temperature told them he had been dead for a while.

They turned to Renee and told her that they were afraid he was dead and reached out to comfort her. She backed away from them, stumbling toward the porch when one of them reached out and stopped her from falling. He helped her to a chair in the shade and got her a glass of ice water and told her to drink it in slow, steady sips. Renee listened to the person talking to her and did what he said, but she didn't feel like she was really there.

She closed her eyes and she could see Jim when she was young and in college. They were at a Georgia football game cheering and drinking rum and cokes from a bottle of rum that they snuck into the stadium. She saw them on a riverboat cruise that they took last year through Europe. She loved that trip even though she remembered Jim getting so drunk that he fell off the boat and had to be rescued.

"God damn you!" she cried. "You didn't listen to me then and you still didn't listen to me, did you?" *God damn you* she said again in her head and then opened her eyes to see the EMT holding her wrist as he checked her pulse.

"Your pulse is pretty weak right now. My name is Chuck, by the way, and that's my partner, Webb. We're very sorry about your husband. Are you a diabetic or do you have any heart conditions?"

Renee shook her head no.

"Any blood pressure issues?" Chuck asked.

Again, Renee indicated no.

"Have you eaten today?"

"Yes. You should be able to see some of it over there next to the body. Though it doesn't look like it now, it was a chicken salad sandwich."

Damn, she's rather feisty, but it's no wonder she lost her lunch Chuck said to himself and nodded his head. "Okay, just keep sipping the water. We believe this death is an accident, but we're required to call the police and have them come out and investigate everything before we can move the body."

"Do whatever you need to," Renee said as she finished the water and picked up the scotch she had started before they got there. She sat back down to drink it while they waited on the police.

Within about twenty minutes, two police officers arrived. "I came as soon as I heard, Mrs. Thompson," one of them said as his partner went over to inspect Jim's body. "Tell me what happened."

"I came home from Atlanta around one today and found him out here. He had been wanting to cut down those dead tree limbs and I told him he couldn't do them all by himself. That he would fall off the ladder if he tried to use that damn saw while standing on it. But you know Jim. He doesn't listen to anyone. He does what he thinks or wants to do and that's just the way it is. Has always been like that. You know that, Tom. You've been to our house enough times to know that."

"Yes ma'am, I do know that," Tom replied. "Let us take a look around and talk to the EMTs and then we will go from there. Hopefully, we should be able to finish this investigation pretty quickly."

Tom examined Jim's body and the ladder and the pole saw. The compound fracture in the leg and the ankle made him wince. He saw the hand and the bones on the fingers that were now exposed. *God damn,* he thought. He then saw the fire ant mound. *Fuck. That's pretty sickening.*

He determined that Jim must have been near the top of the ladder when he fell to have caused so much damage to his body and he could understand why it happened considering how big and out of shape he was. He also knew he should ask a few more questions considering he had been to the house several times for domestic squabbles. Neither one of them had ever pressed charges against the other, but he had seen more than one black eye and busted lip on both of them over the years which caused him to pause for a moment to think. He was certain it wouldn't have mattered if he had tried to take either one of them in for a domestic dispute. One phone call and he would have just been told to walk away. He had learned that the first time he came out here.

The EMTs confirmed his thinking about the height of the fall and that considering his weight, the broken bones would not be unexpected. Tom then asked if they had any idea as to the cause of death.

"Well, we can't say for sure, but we think he suffered a severe allergic reaction and his tongue was swollen so much that it cut off his oxygen supply. He hurt himself very badly too when he fell off that ladder. Those breaks in his body would have been so painful, he must have yelled for help. But not sure how long he could have done that. He may have been in and out of consciousness and when the ants started to attack, well, I don't think he had much of a chance at that point. With those breaks and the condition of his body, it would have been almost near impossible to get away from them. Pretty dangerous to be out here doing what he was trying to do with a ladder and pole saw. You need someone there holding the ladder if you're going to do that, and then it's still risky. We see a lot of falls off ladders because people do some stupid things," Chuck said.

When Renee heard Chuck imply her husband was stupid, the color immediately returned to her face and she stormed to the edge of the porch. "Who the fuck do you think you are, lecturing anyone about my husband's mental capacity because of what you just found on the ground? Do you give people timely tips on gun safety when you find them shot or do you wait and tell the family member later as you zip up whoever was shot in the body bag? That son of a bitch lying there at your feet had three degrees. He had a BBA in finance, an MBA, and a Law degree. So, don't say anything about him being stupid."

Tom had seen this type of behavior before and had been on the receiving end of the tirade several times. He had learned there was not much you can do except just stand there and take it at that point. It appeared Chuck was about to learn the same thing.

"And unless they have started putting doctors on ambulances, I doubt you know for certain what killed him. So, I want you to take him to the University hospital morgue. I'll call the administrator there and tell him I want a god damn autopsy done by someone that might have a little more knowledge about things than an ambulance jockey. Do you think you and Webb over there are capable of doing that? Or do I need to call someone else?"

Chuck wasn't sure what to say as he looked over at the officers. Tom held up his hand indicating for them to not do anything for a moment.

"Renee, I'll have them do as you requested, but we need to ask a few questions before they can move the body. Is that okay?" Tom asked.

"Ask what you need to, Tom," she replied.

"Can you tell me who you were visiting in Atlanta?"

"Kate Simpson. Her number is 678-466-5690. She can tell you everything you need to know," Renee answered. Tom turned to his partner who understood what he wanted and began to make the call to that number.

"And you got home when?"

"About 1:00 and then when Jim didn't reply to me as I was calling out to him in the house, I came out here. I then called 911 and then they called you and here we are. Standing here looking at a stubborn man that refused to ever listen to a woman's advice and fell off the fucking ladder. God damn him," she said as she drank her scotch.

Tom walked over to Beth's house while his partner inquired at the Bartholomew's home. Jasmine told Tom's partner that she didn't hear or notice anything strange but she was gone most of the day. Beth told Tom that she saw Jim up on the ladder the other day, but didn't pay much attention to him. She did wonder if it was safe for him to be up on that ladder, but she figured he knew what he was doing. And echoing Renee, she said Jim was pretty stubborn and she knew it wouldn't have done any good for her to offer her opinion to him regarding whether what he was doing was safe or not.

Tom nodded his head as he recorded Beth's statement. He thanked her for her time and met his partner out by their squad car to compare notes. Renee's story about Atlanta had checked out and they both agreed that the neighbors had no relevant information to add, so there was nothing that raised any unusual concerns in their minds about Jim's death.

They walked back to Renee and reported that they hadn't discovered anything that suggested it was not an accident. Nevertheless, Renee said she wanted an autopsy done. She watched the EMTs prepare Jim's body. They cleaned the ants off his body, and then carefully and respectfully placed him in a black body bag and zipped it up. They lifted him to the stretcher and wheeled him to the back of the ambulance.

"I'm very sorry," Tom said. "The coroner in Newberry is one of the best. We'll have a definite cause of death after she does her assessment."

"Yes, we will," Renee said. "I know her quite well. I should have said that to begin with but I let my anger get the better of me when I heard them call my husband stupid. He was a lot of things, but he wasn't stupid. Though, God damn it, falling off a ladder doesn't do much to suggest otherwise, does it?"

Tom just shook his head. He knew better than to say anything right now. Just let her talk and then leave.

"When I first saw him, there were ants covering his body. Some of them tearing away the skin of his fingers. Sons of bitching little ants. Can you believe it? A big man like Jim killed by a bunch of fucking ants. Would you mind setting fire to that ant mound for me before you leave? Those little fuckers don't deserve to live another minute."

"The best thing to do is get some fire ant pellets and pour them around the mound. I'll be glad to get some and bring them by for you. God knows you and Jim sure did a lot for the police department. It's the least I can do," Tom said.

"Thanks. I appreciate your kindness and respect for my husband and me. I'll make sure to tell the chief how professionally you handled things. I'll be here if you need to talk to me more. I won't be going anywhere," Renee said.

"Again, I'm very sorry about your loss, Renee," Tom said as he and his partner left.

Renee went back inside and opened one of those bottles of scotch she had bought for her husband. She drank the first full glass in three swigs and poured another one before going over to her neighbor's house

"Hey, Renee," Beth said once she opened the door. "Is Jim okay?"

"The police didn't tell you? Jim is dead."

"Oh my God!" Beth said as if she cared.

"Yes. Did you happen to see him - up on the ladder with a pole saw?" she asked.

"Yeah, I did," Beth replied. "As a matter of fact, I thought what he was doing was kind of dangerous. I was worried about him."

"Well, thanks for your concern, Beth," Renee said as she took another drink.

"I told him before I left not to get up on that ladder with a pole saw. I told him he would end up falling off of it and killing himself. I told the son of a bitch that and he doesn't a bit more listen to me any more than that stupid Maggie when I told her she was a know-it-all that didn't know shit at the party the other night. You could tell something bad was going to happen to him, couldn't you?"

"I could," Beth said. *In fact, I was sure of it* she said to herself.

"Oh shit, Beth. What the fuck am I supposed to do now?" Renee asked as she finished her drink.

Beth saw her empty glass and took Renee by the arm and led her into the kitchen. She retrieved the bottle of scotch that she kept put away for whenever the Thompson's came by. She walked outside and refilled Renee's glass.

"Thank you, Beth. I just don't know what I'm going to do."

"You grieve, you mourn, you move on," Beth replied. "You always move on."

"We've been married for forty-five years. I knew more about him than he knew about himself. I knew what food made him fart like a damn patient laying in the recovery room after a colonoscopy. I knew what he was going to say each and every god damn time he watched the news. Every fucking night I heard the same shit as he ranted and raved about what was going on in the country. I told him to just quit watching the shit, but again, he didn't listen. I knew when he wanted sex and what kind of sex before he did and there were many times I just ignored his desires. But on occasion, we did what he wanted to do because I wanted to do it too. I knew what car he would buy, what clothes he would buy. What food he would buy at the grocery store. Every god damn time, he had to stop at the bakery and get a chocolate éclair. But one thing I can say about Jim was that he always supported me. Made sure I had what I wanted. And he never complained one time about the money I spent. Not one time. I think he liked seeing what made me happy. I always appreciated that about him. He wanted me to be happy."

I remember how that was. Beth thought about her father and grandfather. *It was a good feeling. I understand what you are saying word for word.* "I'm sorry, Renee. Very sorry. Can I help you with any arrangements?"

"No, they're doing an autopsy before we bury him."

"An autopsy?" Beth asked. "Was that really necessary? I mean it was an accident, wasn't it?"

"Yeah, he was probably half-lit, when he was up on that ladder. Trying to reach a limb with that pole saw and his body couldn't manage the imbalance. He was so big that when he hit the ground, he was hurt badly and knocked himself out. And those god damn fire ants. The EMT's think he died from suffocation brought on by their bites. Fucking little ants killing someone so big and powerful. Doesn't seem possible, does it? But I'd prefer you just keep that to yourself until I get the official cause of death," Renee said.

"Of course."

"You can tell Darrin but don't send anything out to the neighborhood yet. I'll start making some phone calls. I know what he wanted to be done for his funeral. We had talked about it several times."

"I understand."

"Thank you, Beth. You've always been there for me." Renee said as she hugged her and then left.

On Saturday evening, the coroner called Renee with her report. Jim had multiple fractures that were indicative of a fall that were survivable. What killed him were the numerous bites that triggered a severe allergic reaction which caused his tongue to swell and impaired his ability to breathe. He died from asphyxiation. She also told her that he had an aggressive form of lung cancer that had gone undetected. He would have most likely been dead within six months without any treatment. She didn't tell her about the cirrhotic liver that would have killed him in a year's time if he hadn't stopped drinking because she knew Jim and Renee Thompson very well. She just said she was sorry.

Renee thanked her for the call and went outside to sit, carrying a new bottle of Scotch. She was staring at the pole saw and ladder when Tom drove up with some fire ant pellets. He poured the entire bottle out on the mound and around the yard.

"By tomorrow, they'll all be gone," Tom said. "Want me to move this saw and ladder for you?"

"No, I don't, but thank you for killing the fire ants and for offering. Care for a taste of some really nice scotch?"

"Love some," Tom replied. He thought it was strange that she didn't want to move the ladder or pole saw but he told himself that it must be some way in which she was processing Jim's death and he didn't say anything more about it.

Renee poured him a drink and they toasted Jim. She thanked him again for his professionalism and asked him if he would like Jim's Cadillac. Tom laughed and said sure, thinking she was kidding but she wasn't. She pulled out the keys and gave them to him.

"I'll have my attorney take care of all the paperwork. It shouldn't raise any eyebrows from anyone and if it does, I know how to deal with raised eyebrows," Renee said as she poured herself and Tom another drink.

"I don't know what to say. I'm speechless. Uh, thank you."

"Thank you, Tom. You saw Jim and me in a lot of bad moments and I always thought you were kind and understanding. You knew you didn't need to do anything clsc whcn you came out here except separate us for a moment so that we could get our bearings. It meant a lot to me. And I think it meant a lot to Jim."

Tom held up his glass and said, "To Jim." They had a few more drinks before he got up to leave. She told him to enjoy the Cadillac and he smiled and told her he would every day.

There was a large crowd at the funeral for Jim Thompson on the following Wednesday, but only one family from his neighborhood. The Stevens family.

Maggie could still hear the ambulance going down the street at different times of the day and night and it made her anxious as she remembered Jim lying on the ground. She should have done something for him when she saw him there but she didn't. She could have helped him. She hadn't told anyone that she was there that day or that she had seen Beth. She was going to tell Hazel though and then she was going to tell Sean.

The morning of the funeral, Beth texted Jorge to say that her husband would be home that morning, so they would not be getting together. She said that her drunk neighbor had fallen off a ladder and killed himself. She asked him if he remembered the sound of the pole saw last week and added a smiley face emoji and a picture of a taco. Emiliano replied yes. She then sent a text telling him to just come do the yard and that she would do him next week. Emiliano wasn't sure how to answer but he didn't have to, because Beth continued the message.

She added that she wasn't looking forward to going to the funeral that afternoon, but she needed to be there for her neighbor and wife of the deceased, and it was a good thing her husband would be driving her to the church. Otherwise, she was pretty sure she wouldn't be able to sit up in the pew as she attached a liquor bottle and a crossed eyes emoji to the statement. As soon as he realized they were both going to be out of the house, Emiliano knew what he was going to do but he needed to make sure Beth didn't. He sent her a lips and taco emoji and said he looked forward to next week. Beth texted him that she was too.

That afternoon, during the funeral, Emiliano drove to Beth's house. He started trimming the hedges in the front and worked his way to the back of the house. He left the hedge trimmer on as he set it down on the ground and broke into the house through the sliding glass door. It was very easy to unlock. He looked around the basement but he didn't see what he wanted. He was praying he would be lucky and she would have left her cell phone at home. He spotted it as he walked into the kitchen - sitting out on the granite countertops. "Gracias, Abuela," he said as he looked up and crossed his chest. He grabbed the phone and hurried back outside. He quickly finished cutting the hedges and then got in his truck and left.

Just before sunset, Maggie walked down to the end of the road to take Renee a dish of her manicotti. *That's what Hazel would want me to do, even though Hazel doesn't know how good my manicotti is. It doesn't matter, Maggie. Even if it is the best in the world, it's still just a casserole. It's the thought that counts and Hazel will understand that.* As she got toward the end of the road, she was surprised to see a For Sale sign in front of Jasmine's house. She hadn't mentioned anything to her about selling her house. *What is going on? I'll just check in with her first* she thought as she detoured to their house and rang the bell.

Jasmine answered and told Maggie that she had convinced Caleb it was time to move. Even though they called Jim's death accidental, she was suspicious of everything. She wasn't sure if Renee or Beth had anything to do with it, but she didn't want to be around to find out. She knew it was time to move; the place where they lived had a strange feeling about it now that she didn't like. She knew what her neighbors were really like and she didn't want to be living next to them anymore. There was also too much death around this place, with Jim dying and Sarah passing away not that long ago. Maggie said she understood and told her that she would miss her and they would talk more later. Jasmine told her it was nice of her to take Renee a casserole considering the way she felt about her and Maggie just smiled.

"I'm trying," Maggie said as she left. With each step toward the house, she remembered the night of the cookout, and several times she thought about going back home, but she knew she needed to do this. She needed to do the right thing, even if that meant she got a casserole dish thrown in her face.

No one answered when she rang the doorbell, so she knocked and the door opened. She looked around and then walked cautiously into the house, calling out, "Hello!" She moved through the living room but didn't see anyone, only a lot of food and several empty liquor bottles on the table. She put the casserole dish down and kept calling out Renee's name as she opened closed doors looking for her.

When she opened the door to Jim's study, she found Renee.

Jim had always told Renee that duct tape could fix just about everything so she wanted to try and see if that was true. She twisted the tape several times around a very large pair of antlers, wrapped a lot of it around her own neck, and then slid down the wall. The tape didn't break as it strangled her. The two bottles of scotch she had consumed that day helped her resist her brain's inclination to fight. Renee welcomed the tightness around her neck. It reminded her of Jim. She hung there as she looked around the den at all of the animal heads that Jim had mounted on the wall. She smiled as she looked at the rhinoceros head and its horn. She didn't realize how big that horn really was until now. *I don't even know what some of these animals are* she thought until her ability to think and see became blurred and turned into a darkness that would obscure any semblance of light forever.

Maggie looked around the room at all of the animals and considered how sad they all looked. She thought it looked even sadder now, as she studied their newest club member. She turned to walk out of the house and just before she closed the door, she remembered the manicotti and went back in to retrieve it. She told herself that after calling the police she would need to call Jasmine and tell her if they received a reasonable offer, they needed to take it. Otherwise, that "For Sale" sign might be in their front yard for quite a long time.

Chapter 36

Manicotti

As soon as she stepped into the Thompson's front yard she heard Jasmine calling her name.

Shit, Maggie thought. *What the hell do I do now? I shouldn't lie to her. She'll find out anyway as soon as I call the police.* She turned around and saw Jasmine standing at her front door.

"Was she not home?" Jasmine asked as she saw the casserole dish that was still in Maggie's hands.

"I'm not sure how to say this Jasmine, so I'm just going to say it. I found Renee dead in the house. When I knocked on the door, it just opened and so I went in. I called for her and looked around and found her in Jim's study. She hung herself."

"Oh, dear God!" Jasmine fell back against the door. Maggie watched as she slid down the door and sat there on the floor. For some reason, Maggie saw Renee going through that same motion as she hung herself hours earlier. *Yep, another nightmare to try and deal with,* she thought as she ran toward Jasmine.

Caleb heard the door hit the wall and rushed in from the den and he and Maggie met at the door. Caleb asked his wife what was going on but she didn't answer. Maggie asked Caleb to get some water as she bent down next to Jasmine. When Caleb returned, Maggie took the cup and threw the water in Jasmine's face.

"What the hell are you doing?" he asked.

"She's helping me," Jasmine said as she reached up and wiped the water from her eyes.

"What are you talking about?"

"Maggie found Renee dead in her house just a moment ago. She hung herself. We need to leave this place, Caleb. We can't leave soon enough."

Maggie leaned over and hugged Jasmine before she got up and thought, *I might as well get this over with now.* She pulled out her cell phone and called 911. When she gave them the address, the dispatcher realized they had just been to that house recently and asked the reason for the call.

Maggie said, "I just found Mrs. Thompson dead in the house. She appears to have committed suicide by hanging herself." The dispatcher asked her not to leave and said the police would be there in ten minutes along with the ambulance service.

Maggie walked back to Renee's and waited on the front porch, holding her manicotti, and just like the dispatcher said, they were both there within ten minutes. Tom was one of the police officers and asked Maggie what happened as she led him and the paramedics to Renee's body. They cut the duct tape and tried administering CPR but there was nothing they could do. They looked up at Tom and shook their heads indicating she was gone.

"Shit," Tom said as he looked down at Renee's dead body, though he wasn't really surprised at what he saw. He remembered the ladder and pole saw that still laid out in the backyard and he felt the keys to the new Cadillac on his key ring. *She was telling you, Tom, that she was going to kill herself and you ignored the clues. You should have seen it* he said to himself as he walked away from her dead body.

Maggie watched them take Renee's body away in the ambulance. Jasmine and Caleb were standing at their window and Maggie was glad they had not come outside. She then saw Beth over in her front yard rushing toward her.

Shit, shit, shit, Maggie thought. The police officers were still there and watched as Beth confronted Maggie.

"What the hell did you do, Maggie?" Beth screamed. "What did you do to Renee?"

Tom walked over to them, and before Maggie could say anything, held out his hand and touched her shoulder, so Beth could not move forward.

"Don't put your hand on me," Beth said indignantly.

"Ma'am, you need to lower the tone and get rid of the attitude," Tom replied. "Mrs. Brodie did nothing except try to help Mrs. Thompson. Are you a friend of Mrs. Thompson?" he asked.

"Yeah, right," Beth said. "Mrs. Brodie did not like Mrs. Thompson nor her husband. What did she do to Renee? Did she kill her like she killed Jim?"

Tom looked at Maggie and told her that everything would be okay if she wanted to leave. He had her statement and would call her if he needed anything else. Maggie said thank you and glared at Beth. Though she should have left as Tom suggested, something inside of her wouldn't allow her to go without saying something to Beth. Saying something that she knew she shouldn't. Saying something that she knew she might regret.

"You are one of the reasons Jasmine is moving away, Beth. You are a total and absolute one hundred percent fucking bitch. Why don't we talk about your grandfather who lives right up the street and yet you haven't even bothered to talk to him in almost thirty years? Or maybe talk about you and

Jorge or your dead neighbor, Sarah Cayman, and how all of that is related? Or Jim? Maybe we should just talk about Jim. I came here tonight to give my condolences to Renee and found her. She had hung herself. Probably had enough of you yammering in her ears like a little lap dog. There was only so much alcohol she could consume to drown out your shrill voice."

Beth pushed Tom out of the way and shoved Maggie to the ground. Tom and the other officer pulled them apart. Maggie wanted to smile but she knew it wouldn't be appropriate. But she was almost giddy thinking about how everyone, especially the police, was now witnessing the real Beth.

After he had a moment to study her face, Tom remembered seeing Beth with Renee at the funeral. He recognized she was a close friend of Renee's even though he couldn't remember her name.

"Ma'am, because I know this has been a traumatic day for you, I'm going to let you go home, and suggest to Mrs. Brodie that she doesn't press assault charges against you. Mrs. Brodie, are you okay with that suggestion?"

Maggie didn't say anything as she looked at Beth. *Why not tell them everything? Tell them about Jim, Jorge, Amos, Sarah. Hell, officer, the whole damn neighborhood can tell you about this woman. Then you'll see what a bitch you have on your hands.*

She started to talk but heard another voice telling her that by saying nothing, Beth would suffer more than if she told all that she knew; that the best way to get back at Beth was to let her think and worry about everything.

Let her think about her friends that are now gone; that she might as well have shot with a gun. I don't need to do anything but let her think about what the police just witnessed her do and say. Yes, I called Beth a bitch but the police saw that wasn't just an embellishment. I mentioned enough names for the police to question things in the future if need be. No, this is all I need to do now. Maggie looked up at Tom and nodded her head in agreement as the other officer helped her to her feet.

Beth knew that she needed to walk away. She had let Maggie get to her. *She's a lot like Amos in that way. Fucking bitch has probably sat there with that asshole Amos listening to God knows what regarding me and my family. Stories that I don't want to respond to now. Not now in front of the police. You won this round,* Beth said to herself as she looked at Tom and smiled. *No, there were too many things Maggie could bring up that she didn't want to discuss tonight.*

"You're right, officer, I shouldn't have acted the way I did, but as you said, it has been very emotional for me. I just buried one of my best friends and now I find out his wife has killed herself. I'm distraught and I have to admit that I don't like the woman over there," she said as she pointed toward

Maggie. "But that doesn't give me an excuse to act the way I did. I said things I shouldn't have and I shouldn't have pushed her to the ground. I'm sorry for my actions and I hope you can forgive me, Maggie. I let my emotions get the better of me. I apologize. We can talk later about all of your concerns. I'm sure we can resolve them."

Beth didn't wait for Maggie to respond. She just walked away. She told herself over and over again not to turn around and say anything else. And she did exactly that as she went straight back to her house and closed the door.

Maggie understood the apology from Beth was a load of bullshit but the veiled threat was real. She knew the police hadn't picked up on it but that was okay for now. They had seen the anger that was a part of Beth. It could no longer be hidden.

"Are you guys hungry?" Maggie said as she looked at Tom and his partner.

"Police officers are always hungry," Tom replied.

"Well, I don't mean to brag but I make probably the best manicotti in the United States, and I would hate to see it go to waste. Would you and your partner like some?"

Tom didn't have to look at his partner. He knew what his answer would be. "We'd love some," Tom said.

"Do you think it would it be okay if we went back into the Thompson house and found something I can put this in for you? I'd like to give some of it to my neighbor. He's a Vietnam war vet and doesn't get too many home-cooked meals," Maggie said.

"I think it would be fine," Tom said as he accompanied Maggie back to the front door and opened it for her.

Maggie quickly found a plastic container and divided the manicotti. "Just find a microwave later this evening and heat it up for about five minutes, stirring it around at three. It will be good and hot then. I think you'll love it. But if you don't, don't tell me about it - and remember, it was free," Maggie said as she smiled at the two officers.

They thanked her and offered her a ride home. She turned them down, saying that it was a beautiful night and she would enjoy the walk home. It would give her a chance to think about everything that had just happened.

Tom stopped before getting in his car. "Were the Thompsons close friends of yours?"

He can tell, Maggie said to herself. *Even without Beth's damnation of her, he could tell.* She knew he would be able to tell if she was lying.

"No, we weren't good friends at all," Maggie said. "I didn't particularly like either one of them. I thought they were abusive alcoholics and they were very mean when they got drunk. But that didn't matter. Renee still deserved my sympathy and my condolences."

Tom was very familiar with what Maggie was saying. He had been to the Thompson's house too many times to not recognize the truth in her words. The Thompsons were abusive drunks. Abusive drunks who had a lot of money and influence in the community despite their inability to cope with each other in a positive and loving manner.

"Be safe walking home," Tom nodded to her as he and his partner got in the car.

"I will. Hope you enjoy the manicotti." As she walked toward home, she looked forward to seeing Amos and telling him she brought him some dinner. She smiled as she thought about him asking her if there was meat in the manicotti. She could even hear his response when she said yes. He would laugh and say, "Then heat it up and let's get at it." He might smile even more when she told him about that woman down at the end of the road acting up in front of the police. In fact, he might like that better than the manicotti.

Chapter 37

The Walking Dead

Maggie leisurely walked down the road to Amos's house as she processed what had transpired over the past several days. It was hard to believe that Jim and Renee Thompson were now both dead. Though she didn't like either of them, she did feel sorry for them and the way they died. However, her sympathy didn't extend to Beth. She knew she had made things worse for their relationship by saying what she did, but she didn't care. The police now had a nice image of an angry Beth and of her willingness to act on that anger, which could prove to be useful in the future.

She would make sure Hazel knew about it tomorrow too. She might even tell Hazel that she was worried about what Beth was capable of and ask her what she should do about it. *Yes, that would be a nice touch* she thought. Not only would it put her on record with a professional that Maggie had concerns for her safety, but it could be something she could bring up later if need be.

She walked by Francis and Jennifer's yard and saw that they had put out some annuals around their large hostas. The outdoor lighting acted like magnifying glasses that intensified their colors among the leaves of the green plants. *I need to get inside their house. Their yard is so beautiful, I can only imagine what the inside of their home looks like.* She passed Red and Sable's house and smiled when she saw the "Montana" cabin sitting on top of the hill in Georgia. *I wonder if the painting for Red and Sable has been framed yet? I need to check on that.*

Maggie paused to admire the large industrial lamps that had been installed over the entries to the covered bridge. *Those things look amazing and they give off a lot of light. Another great idea you had, Maggie!* Just before she entered the bridge, she saw the dog standing at the far entrance under the light. She had never seen this dog before. There was a ragged rope around its neck and she thought how pitiful it looked. Its body was emaciated and indicated it had been abused or neglected for a long time. She wanted to run over to it, but something held her back.

The guttural sounds that came from the dog told her it was scared. Scared of the world around him. Scared of the person he saw standing several hundred feet in front of him. Scared of the way his body felt and made him act. There was something wrong with this dog besides hunger and malnourishment. The low-pitched growl invoked fear, not empathy, and Maggie started backing up slowly while keeping her eyes on the dog.

When it saw Maggie move, it started to come toward her but then stumbled and fell several times. It reminded Maggie of something she would see on "The Walking Dead" and then she realized: the dog was the walking dead. It was consumed by a virus that was killing it, making it want to kill whatever got in its way. *Shit,* she said to herself as she remembered the animal traps out in her backyard. *One of those sure would come in handy right now.*

The dog staggered in her direction and Maggie threw the manicotti on the ground and started running back toward her house. She hoped the smell of the meat would slow it down but she saw it emerge from the covered bridge running toward her as fast as it could make its body move. It didn't want food. It wanted to bite something. The virus was controlling all of its actions and she knew the only thing she could do was get back into the house before it got to her. As she ran into the garage, she tripped over a watering can and fell. She turned around and saw the dog getting closer. Close enough now that she could see the foamy saliva dripping from its mouth. At this distance, it looked more like a child blowing bubbles with soapy water but she knew there was no innocence at all in that sickness that came toward her with a maddening whine and growl.

She yelled for Sean and Connor and ran for the kitchen door. Maggie couldn't see the note that was taped to the refrigerator door saying they had gone out to get some ice cream and would bring home some of her favorite, pistachio. She tried the doorknob but it was locked and she didn't have a key.

"Are you fucking kidding me?" she shrieked as she hit the garage door closer but the watering can that had been knocked over was blocking the beam that triggered the system to engage. The dog was now in the garage and coming toward her so she jumped onto the hood of her car. With her back against the windshield, she felt the drool of the animal on her ankles as it tried to climb up after her.

She pulled her legs up into her arms as the animal tried over and over to get up on the hood, but each time it slid back and the nails on its paws made a screeching sound on the metal. The dog would lay on the floor for a minute as it looked up at her, angry and confused that it couldn't reach her, before trying again.

Maggie put her hands over her ears to try and drown out the sounds from the sick animal and closed her eyes as she tried to think of what she could do. For a moment she didn't see or hear anything and when she opened her eyes, she couldn't see or hear the dog. She crawled up on the roof of the car and looked around but still didn't see anything. Then she spotted Sean's tools hanging on the pegboard about four feet from the car. She quickly examined the tools and decided the only one that would help her was the hammer. But, getting it and then using it was going to be risky.

She sat there for a few more minutes as she continued to look around and listen for the animal but she saw and heard nothing. She began to wonder if the disease had killed it but she was sure she would have heard something. She didn't know what she would have heard indicating that it had succumbed to the virus, but she was sure it wouldn't just pass away peacefully as it took its last breath. Then a sound came from somewhere under the car that was like nothing she had ever heard before. It was a cry of anguish and torment that she was certain others in their neighborhood must have heard. It was inhuman and inhumane all at the same time.

Maggie knew now was the time to act. She gathered her strength and leaped off the car and grabbed the hammer just as the dog lunged at her from out of the shadows. She swung the hammer at its head and heard the jaws of the dog snapping into the air around her. The hammer made a squishing sound as the claw embedded itself into the dog's brain. There was a whimper, followed by a thud as the dog fell forward onto her feet. She reached up and grabbed a screwdriver and drove it into the animal's ear as she pulled her feet away.

She huddled in a corner of the garage and waited for the animal to move but it never did. It seemed like she had been waiting there for an hour before the sound of a car made her jump. Sean pulled to the top of the driveway and stopped before entering the garage. Maggie leaped into the back seat and started crying.

"Good Lord, what's wrong?" Sean asked as he and Connor looked back at her.

For a moment, Maggie could only cry as she reached up and hugged her son and then her husband.

"How were we supposed to know you wanted something else besides pistachio?" she heard Connor say and Maggie started to laugh and cry at the same time.

What would I do without you, she asked herself as she looked at her son. She then looked over at her husband and saw that he was ready to defend her against whatever was upsetting her. *And what would I do without you too? My rocks. Always there for me. Regardless of what kind of fucked up mess I am, both of you have always been there for me.*

"Do you have your gun?" Maggie asked Sean.

"Yes," he answered slowly. "Why?"

"There is a rabid dog in the garage. I think I killed it but I'm not positive."

Sean wasn't sure what was going on but he drew the Smith and Wesson .45 out from beneath his seat. He pulled the car up closer so that the headlights were pointed into the garage, which revealed the dog lying on the garage floor. The screwdriver and hammer were still in its head and blood was pooling up on the floor. In the bright lights of the car, it looked more pitiful than monster-like and Maggie shuddered as she looked at it. "Oh God," she groaned.

Connor told his father that if it was rabid, it would be important not to get any of the fluids on him and that they needed to burn the body as soon as they could. Sean nodded his head as he got out of the car. When he stood a foot away from it, he knew he wasn't going to need the gun. The dog was dead. The handle of the screwdriver was the only visible part as it stuck out of the dog's ear and the hammer's claws were buried so deep into the brain that he was surprised they hadn't come through its face.

"It's dead," Sean told them as he put his gun back into its holster and under the seat of his car. Connor got out to inspect the dog and confirmed what his father had said as he came back to the car.

" It's going to be a mess to clean up," Connor said. "We need gloves and Clorox and some large trash bags. And we'll need to throw those tools away. Burn them along with the dog. You'll need to get rid of your clothes, mom. Burn them too. Did the dog bite you or get anything on you?"

"Just saliva."

"You need to clean yourself off with Clorox and then take a long shower. The virus doesn't live long outside the host but you still need to be careful."

Neither Sean nor Maggie questioned what Connor was saying. They didn't know how he knew all this stuff but he knew it.

"I'll get the Clorox for you," Connor said, "and some towels you can wrap yourself in while you undress. Dad, can you go and get a metal trashcan at the store? We won't want to use it for anything else after we burn everything."

Maggie knew everything was okay now, but she still didn't want to get out of the car. Sean opened the back door and looked at his wife and she started crying again.

"It's okay Maggie. It's dead," Sean said as he tried to reassure her.

The image of Renee and the confrontation with Beth had been suppressed because of the encounter with the dog, but now that she realized she was safe, all of those pictures came rushing forward as if she was watching one of those live police shows that permeated the cable network these days.

"You have no idea what I've seen tonight, Sean," Maggie said. "The dog; it was just a nightmarish end to what happened to me after I went to see Renee."

"What do you mean?"

"When I went to her house, I found her dead in Jim's den. With all his fucking dead animals on the wall. She was like some sick animal rights activist making some horrific statement. You know the ones you see on TV that set fire to themselves in front of some foreign consulate no one has ever heard of. She had hung herself with duct tape around some antlers of some kind of animal. Right there as soon as you walked into the den. I didn't like her at all and if she was trying to get back at me, she succeeded. I will never forget what she looked like."

"What?" Sean asked, not sure of what he heard.

"I called the police and they came and the ambulance people came and then Beth came out of her house and accused me of killing Renee. She got so mad, she knocked me to the ground. The police had to intervene. I'm not sure what she would have done to me if they hadn't been there."

"Oh, my God! There's no excuse for that, but she just probably lost it when she heard that Renee was dead, after just having buried Jim too. It was probably just too much. You were a convenient punching bag for her."

Maggie wanted to say, "I don't want to be a convenient punching bag for that bitch." but she didn't. She simply looked up at Sean and said he was probably right. He always took the high road. She loved and hated that about him.

"I don't want to tell Connor about any of this. It would not be good for him to know what Beth did to me and we can tell him about Renee later."

"You're right Maggie. I completely agree. Since you're contaminated, I don't suppose Connor would approve of me hugging you or giving you any ice cream, but you're going to have to get out of the car so I can go to the grocery store."

Maggie nodded her head and though she wanted to jump into his arms she held back and waited on Connor as Sean left for the store. Connor returned with the Clorox and washrags and towels and told his mother what to do. She scrubbed her ankle where she had felt the drool, and then wiped her entire body, not knowing if anything splattered on her when she killed the dog. She left the clothes there in the yard and then went into the house and showered.

After Sean returned, he and Connor put the dog in the trash can, poured gasoline over it, and set it on fire. They cleaned the garage and then went inside to decontaminate themselves. Afterward, they all sat down in the den and Sean asked Maggie to tell them the whole story of what happened with the dog. "I thought I recognized that casserole dish on the road when we drove out of the bridge," Sean said. "I mentioned something to Connor about it."

Maggie told them everything and then Sean's phone rang. It was the hospital. They heard Sean say he would be there in about thirty minutes. He hung up and told them a psych patient was missing at the hospital. They thought his children had come to visit and left the door open for him.

"Is he a danger to the patients?" Maggie asked.

"I don't think so, but you never know. I'm going to meet the police over there and go room to room looking for him."

Maggie looked at Connor and asked, "Would you help me escape from a psych ward if I asked you to?"

He shook his head no.

"Why not?"

"I can't let a maniac loose into the world," Connor replied. "We both saw the movie 'Maniac.' I can't have that on my conscience."

" Connor, I'm not a serial killer who places the scalps on mannequins up in the attic. I'm not ready. I don't think I have enough mannequins yet."

Connor laughed as Sean just shook his head. He didn't always get it, but he didn't care. Connor was making his wife laugh and considering what had happened to her tonight that was quite remarkable.

"Would you help me get out, Sean?" Maggie asked.

"Nope. I would just get a divorce and try and escape the madness."

"Stay away from the hills," Maggie replied. "They have eyes."

Sean looked puzzled but Connor and his wife were laughing again. *Must be a reference to some other horror movie* he told himself.

"Don't wait up for me," he said as he got up. "I don't know how long I'll be."

"Is it okay if I kiss my husband goodbye?" Maggie asked as she looked over at Connor. "I don't need a hazmat suit, do I?"

"I suppose it will be okay," Connor replied.

She kissed him goodbye and he said, "I'll see you two later," and left.

"Weird, isn't it?" Connor asked.

"What?"

"Crazy people loose at the hospital. Crazy dog loose in the neighborhood. Sounds like a movie of some kind."

"Not one I want to watch," Maggie answered as she remembered the forlorn look of Renee's eyes and the angry look on Beth's face. *Shit.* She went into the kitchen and poured herself a glass of wine and took several anti-anxiety pills. She went to the window and looked outside.

She knew it was okay for Connor to think of this evening as weird. He didn't need to know about all the other things that had happened tonight. They might change his opinion to something more disturbing. When Beth pushed her to the ground, she had seen Connor pushing Jim into the pool and it scared her. She took a sip of her wine and felt the tears rolling down her cheek. For some reason, everything that happened tonight seemed interconnected in some way. It was as if the animals on Jim's wall were seeking revenge and Maggie thought how close they came to finding it.

Chapter 38

Conflict Resolution

Maggie didn't hear Sean come home that night. He didn't get in until three in the morning and she never even moved when he got in bed. The two glasses of wine and medication made her unaware of his presence and she only wished they had helped keep her from dreaming.

She saw herself opening the door to the den and Renee hanging there from the antlers. She heard an animal on the wall informing her that those were two red deer stag horns the angry woman was hanging from. She then heard the rhinoceros, in what she thought was a very high voice for an animal of that size, say she didn't like the woman hanging there and asked if Maggie would be kind enough to move her to a tree outside.

"She is certain to start smelling soon," the tiger's head said. "Humans have a very unique smell and start decaying soon after they are dead, but I think she may not rot as quickly. All the alcohol in her body will delay the process for a day or two. But after that, it will be very bad. Not that I mind rotting human flesh, mind you, but it has to be a certain kind of rotten if you know what I mean. If it's been lying there for several weeks, I just refuse to eat it. I'll let those hyper and annoying hyenas have it then."

"Are you friend or family?" the wolf said as it looked down at Maggie.

"Neither," she replied.

"Oh, a thief huh?" the wolf said as it smiled at her. "He has a coin collection in a false drawer over there in his desk. The gold coins in there are worth a fortune. Take them all. I hated the son of a bitch."

"Yeah," all the animals called out in agreement.

"And after you get the coins, would you mind just setting fire to this place? We don't want to be hanging on the wall for the rest of our lives. It's so undignified. We were majestic animals at one time. Some of us were leaders within our pack or pride or dance troupe," the wolf said as it winked at the antelope.

"That's hate speak," the antelope said. "And sexual harassment. Did you see how he winked at me?"

"Artie, Artie, Artie. Just relax," the wolf said. "I am just messing with you. I could care less what you did out there in the woods. I'm sure you would taste good regardless of your sexual orientation."

"Oh honey, I know I tasted good," the antelope replied.

Maggie yelled out for them to stop talking and they all looked down at her in a surprised manner.

She then felt someone grab her hand and she looked over and saw that it was Renee. She was smiling at her.

"You know, Jim was right," Renee said. "Duct tape can do just about anything."

Maggie tried to pull away but Renee wouldn't let go. "Would you mind getting me a glass of water?" Renee asked. "My throat is parched."

Maggie reached over and tried to pry Renee's hand from her wrist and as she pulled back Renee's fingers, they began to fall off one by one. "I knew this would happen if I laid out in the sun too much," she commented and sighed.

Maggie ran from the room and then remembered what the wolf had asked. Set the room on fire. She found some matches in the kitchen and then went back to the den with a trashcan full of paper. She ran by Renee, placed the trashcan in the middle of the room, and set it on fire.

"Thank you!" the animals cried in unison as Maggie looked up at them. They all seemed so happy now. Renee tried to grab her again as she left the room.

"They'll know it was you," Renee said.

"No, they won't," Maggie replied. She picked up two of Renee's fingers and jammed them into the electrical socket next to the antler coat rack. Sparks flew out of the wall followed by smoke.

"Electrical wiring short," Maggie explained as she walked out and found Tom standing in the hallway with an empty plate.

"That manicotti was really good. Do you have any more?" he asked.

"Yes, at the house," Maggie said as she took him by the arm.

"Do you smell smoke?" he asked.

"No, I don't smell anything," Maggie concluded.

The alarm clock buzzed at 6:00, but Maggie turned it off and went back to sleep with her arm around Sean. At 7:30, she heard Connor knocking on their door asking if anyone was going to take him to school or was this another unofficial holiday.

Maggie threw on some jeans and a football jersey, combed her hair, and gargled some mouthwash before she came out of the bedroom. "That will be me," she said as she hurried down the hallway. "I think your father came home late and is still asleep. I'm assuming he plans to go in later. Did you eat breakfast?"

"Yeah. Had some cereal. Took Amos some pop tarts. He loves those things by the way. I poured him a glass of milk and he doesn't have much left. The sunrise he painted this morning was extra nice. He said it was for the lesbians."

"Jennifer and Frances," Maggie said. "We don't call them the lesbians."

"I was just saying what Amos said," Connor replied.

And before Maggie could give him a speech, Connor added. "It's funny when Amos says it. It doesn't matter what they are. I know that. I would only say that with you or Amos or Dad."

Maggie smiled as she looked over at Connor. *What did I do to deserve you* she asked herself. *You are so grown up and yet you have a shyness about you around people. But as Hazel said, you'll find the right person or persons sometime. Sometime soon. I know you will.*

Maggie arrived about thirty minutes before her appointment time with Dr. Nutt but she didn't care. She sat and read some of the gardening magazines until Janice told her the doctor was ready to see her.

"Hello, Maggie. How have you been since we last talked?"

"My neighbor Jim died. You know, the one that my son pushed into the pool after he called me a dirty name. Well, he fell off a ladder and died. I took his wife, Renee, a casserole the evening of his funeral and when I went to her house, I found her dead too. She had hanged herself in her husband's study. When I called the police, Beth, who I don't need to repeat to you what I think of her, came running out and accused me of killing Renee and shoved me to the ground. And then after the police intervened and told her to calm down, she walked off, saying she would deal with me later. Which I found rather threatening. And then on the way home after all of that, I saw a dog. Thank goodness we put those lights up on the covered bridge as I told you we were going to do, or I might not have seen it. Anyway, the dog was rabid and chased me into the garage and onto the top of my car. I killed it by putting a hammer through its brain."

Hazel looked at Maggie and felt a sense of déjà vu. *Oh my God,* she thought. *How is this possible?*

"I'm going to have to stop asking that question with you," Hazel said as she smiled. "Let's go about this another way. How is Connor doing?"

"He's fine. He was like someone from the CDC as he told Sean and me how to clean up the garage after I had killed the rabid dog. Explained how we needed to burn everything. The dog, our clothes, the tools that I used to kill the animal. Went about doing it as if nothing happened. He is going over and checking on Amos every morning and evening. He has even convinced the Phinizy Swamp people to set up a $1000 scholarship in Mr. Talbot's name for a student who plans to work in the life sciences. Vet, botanist, etc."

He did just as I suggested Hazel thought. *It's quite amazing how he just pushes through all of this trauma. And after that meltdown with his friend. Quite amazing.*

"You should be very proud of your son, Maggie."

"I am. Very much so. He and Sean are like rocks for me. They always hold me up."

"And how are you holding up in the midst of all these traumatic events?"

"I'm trying to do what you told me to. I avoided the Thompsons and Beth as much as I could. Even stayed away from Jim's funeral because I didn't want to upset Renee or Beth with my presence. But I thought it would be a nice gesture on my part to take Renee something to eat on the night after her husband's funeral. I didn't expect to find her dead and I didn't start the fight with Beth. She attacked me."

"That was very smart on your part to stay away from the funeral. And it was nice of you to go to Renee's house. It's shocking that you found her dead though. In that manner too. It must have been awful."

"It was."

"And you said Beth came over and just pushed you to the ground while accusing you of killing Renee?"

"Yes."

"You didn't say anything to her? Nothing that would be construed by her as antagonistic?"

Maggie paused before she answered. But she knew pauses in front of a therapist only meant one thing. The patient was trying to find a way to answer the question.

"I may have said some things she didn't like," Beth said. "But I could have pressed charges of assault against her. The police asked me if I wanted to do that and I told them no. That she had suffered enough that day." *And will continue to suffer* Maggie added to herself.

"Why do you think she threatened you?"

"She said we would resolve all the things I brought up at a later date. She didn't want the police to hear her have to explain the way she has ignored her grandfather, who lives just down the street from her, for thirty years, or how she has been having an affair with the gardener for some time now. Or now Jasmine."

"Jasmine Bartholomew? You mentioned her once before."

"Yes, she lives down there in the cul-de-sac next to the Thompsons and Beth. They're moving. Jasmine said she couldn't stand to live in that environment any longer with all the death around her and because of what she knew about Beth. Sarah Cayman, one of her elder neighbors died of COPD. Now Jim and Renee Thompson have died. I understand her reason for leaving, don't you?"

"Yes. And you said you were chased by a rabid dog?"

"Yes. Sean and Connor had gone to get ice cream and they locked the door thinking I had a key. I didn't and had to jump on my car to stay away from the dog. It was trying to claw its way onto the car. I got lucky. I had one chance to stop that dog and I did. After that, I have to admit, I had more than one glass of wine that night."

Hazel smiled. "The same night you found Renee, were confronted by Beth, and then chased by a rabid dog? I think more than one glass of wine that night would be understandable."

"I have nightmares, Hazel. I can hear the ambulance all the time going down the street. Going to find Jim. I saw Renee hanging in that den and all the animals on the wall were talking to me. Telling me how awful Jim and Renee were. Telling me to burn the house down because the way they were hanging on the wall was undignified. When I did what they asked me to, Renee reached out and tried to stop me. While she was hanging there. Talking to me. Telling me I couldn't do what the animals were telling me to do. Her fingers fell off of her hand when I tried to get her to let go of me. It was horrifying. But I did what the animals told me to. I set the room on fire."

"I think the reason the ambulance bothers you, Maggie, is because you had unresolved issues with Jim. The ambulance reminds you of that and makes you feel like you failed. The same with Renee. Dead people reaching out to you making you feel bad because you do feel bad. Perhaps even worse now that they're gone and you cannot do anything to make peace with either one of them. The fact that they were mean to you or alcoholics doesn't matter once they are dead. You feel remorse regardless."

Maggie nodded her head.

"You say Jim's study was full of animal heads?"

"Yes. I'm guessing he was a big hunter. There were very exotic animals mounted on the wall. Even a rhinoceros and tiger."

"Sickening in my opinion that they allow that, but nevertheless. The animals asking you to set them on fire, I think reflects your burning of the rabid dog, and in all likelihood, your house that burned down in Florida. Horrifying event. You were very lucky Maggie. If that animal had bitten you, the treatment, well, let's just say, you wouldn't have liked it."

Again, Maggie nodded her head. She wanted to tell Hazel about the Renaissance Fair and the blue jay but she didn't know how to start that conversation. And she hadn't told her about confronting Jorge's aunt.

"Before we talk about some additional conflict resolution tools that you can use with Beth, it looks like you're trying to tell me something else. Is there something else?"

You could tell her about the encounter with Jorge, but you didn't actually confront him. You just saw his aunt. So, you don't need to tell her about that. Tell her about the bluejay. Now is the time to tell her about the bluejay.

"My friend and I were talking one evening. His name is Red. Red Skye. He is a very talented artist of Indian heritage. While we were talking, a bluejay flew right into the window I was standing in front of and he told me that meant something in his culture. That I needed to overcome obstacles in my life before I could be happy. It resonated with me that evening and has ever since. Is it wrong to put such belief into that type of old saying? Just some Native American myth?"

"Depends on what you would do as a result of seeing that. From what you've told me, you have overcome a lot of obstacles. You told your husband about the alligator and your son. And got through the trauma of your son witnessing his teacher being killed. You have never doubted your son and been there for him when he needed you in the past, as well as right now. You helped him with Amos and worked through the fact that Amos was dying. And learned to accept that death in a noble way, helping your friend live out his last days, happy and content. You even found the strength to go to someone you don't like, someone who threw a drink in your face, and say you were sorry. I don't know Maggie, if all of that came from you working to fulfill a Native American myth, then I think it was probably a good idea to believe in it."

Maggie smiled. Hazel always knew what to say to make her feel better.

"There is one last obstacle though and that's Beth. You're going to have to learn how to deal with her. She will not let it go, it appears. And you cannot make things worse when you interact with her."

"Yes, I know."

"The first thing you need to do with her, Maggie, is to eliminate any misconceptions you have about her. Our minds are very good at filling in blanks when we don't have all the real information. It creates anxiety and anger within us. Those two things can be overwhelming and very destructive.

"So what do I do?"

"It won't be easy but you need to clear up anything that is still not one hundred percent factual in your mind about her. There are still things you don't know for sure about Beth. Perhaps you can start with Amos. Maybe you can convince him to paint a picture for Beth. I bet you can. And tell her that you want to have a nice neighborhood just like she does. That is something you both have in common. I hate to say it, but it might be easier now that her alcoholic friends are no longer there. Those types of relationships can be so destructive. Tell Beth you are sorry about her losses. Invite her over for a gathering with all the other neighbors, including Amos. That might be a very good way of bringing them together."

"What do I say about the affair?"

"Nothing. That's none of your business. You can't fix that, so don't try to."

"Hmmm. Say I get Amos to do a painting for her and have a party and I give it to Beth and tell her I'm sorry and she takes the painting and burns it like she did the photo and tells me to fuck off?"

"Then you tell her that you expect her and all of her flying monkeys to stay on their end of the street and you'll stay on yours and if she doesn't, you'll throw a bucket of water on her and watch her melt."

Maggie started laughing and Hazel smiled. "You are a very strong woman, Maggie. Much stronger than you realize. If things don't go well with Beth, it won't be the end of the world and you will know that you tried. That's all you can do because you have so many other things in your life that are much more important than that one person down at the end of your neighborhood. Make one more sincere effort and if it doesn't work, then move on with your life."

"Thank you, Hazel," Maggie said as she let out a big sigh. "I'm not sure what I would do without you."

"Get into a big fight with Beth for one thing," Hazel said as she smiled.

Maggie laughed again. "See you next week, Dr. Nutt."

On her way home, Maggie considered all they had talked about and decided she liked the idea of the party. She picked up a few grocery items that she and Amos needed and stopped at his house to drop them off.

"Is there beer in those bags?" he asked as Maggie approached.

"Yes."

"Outstanding," Amos replied. "Outstanding. What is your name again?"

Oh shit, Maggie thought as she walked up onto the porch. *He's in one of those funks. I won't be able to discuss anything with him.*

"It's Maggie."

"No, it isn't. It's Maggie Brodie. Mother of Connor and wife of the sergeant," Amos said as the grin on his face told Maggie, "Gotcha."

Maggie laughed as she went by him and unloaded the groceries in his kitchen. She came back out on the porch with a six-pack and saw the sunrise painting Connor had mentioned.

"Amos, the picture, it's…"

"It's pretty good, isn't it?" he asked.

"Yes, it's better than pretty good."

"I'm getting better. I made this one for the lesbians."

"Jennifer and Frances," Maggie corrected. "Amos, what would you say if I told you I would take you over to their house so you could give them the picture in person. Would you be interested in doing that?"

"I would love that!"

"Okay. I have another question and I don't want you to say no without thinking about it first. Deal?

"Deal."

"Would you paint a picture for Beth? If you do, I'll have a party and you can give it to her at that party. You never know, but it might start something good."

"Thought about it. Nothing good will come of it," Amos said as he took one of the beers and put the rest in the cooler.

"Well, would you think about it a little bit more?"

Amos popped open the beer and looked at Maggie. "You and Connor and the sergeant would be there?"

"And the rest of your neighbors. The ones that were at your welcome home party. They would all be there."

He sipped on the beer a few minutes before answering. "Yeah, I'll do it, but there has to be beer there, and steak, and banana crème pie."

"Banana crème pie?"

"Homemade banana crème pie. Not store-bought. And I will be able to tell the difference."

"Deal," Maggie said, without allowing her euphoria to spill out onto the porch or Amos.

Amos smiled as he gazed out into the woods. "Sure has been good since I got home. Never felt better. Can we go to the lesbian's, I mean Frances and Jennifer's house now?'

"Yes, we can, Amos." *Conflict resolution 101, Chapter 1. Excellent job, Maggie Brodie* she said to herself as she helped Amos and the painting into the car.

Chapter 39

Animus

When Beth returned home from the funeral on Wednesday, she realized that her phone was gone. And she didn't even bother looking for it. She knew where it was. On Friday morning, she sent a text to it.

Emiliano had called Miguel to see if he could break into an iPhone. Miguel said sure, but couldn't meet him until Friday. They were together that morning trying to figure out how to unlock the phone when the message popped up on it. They both saw it at the same time. It read: "Jorgeeattacos."

Miguel looked up at Emiliano. "What the fuck man?" he asked as the same message was repeated.

Emiliano sighed. "Shit. That's the password for the phone. Just do what it says. That will open it for you."

Miguel typed in those letters and just as Emiliano said, the phone opened. "What next?" Miguel asked.

Before Emiliano could reply, Beth sent another text.

"I don't think you'll find what you're looking for on the phone that you took from my house, Jorge. I have two phones. One that I keep with me at all times. That's the one you want. The one I use for special video recording. The phone you have is just a phone with pictures of my children and my husband on trips to Disney World, the Cayman Islands, the Virgin Islands, Europe. You should take a look at them. I doubt you'll ever get to visit those places."

"Who is this puta?" Miguel asked. "And who the hell is Jorge?"

"Fuck," was all Emiliano said before Beth texted another message.

"Just bring the other phone back when you come next week. Now that I know how much you like the video we made, I'll make sure we watch it again on Wednesday. Maybe make a new one. See you next week."

Emiliano slammed his fist down on the table. "Puta perra!"

"Tell me. Who is she?" Miguel asked. "What was on the phone that you needed to get?"

"A woman. She is married. She filmed me having sex with her. I need to get that video to make sure she can't do anything to me. Otherwise, she'll have me por mis bolas," Emiliano said as he gripped his crotch. "She is rich. White. Nice neighborhood. All-American home. You know, all that shit. I am fucked without that video because if I don't do what she wants then she'll say I raped her and then I'm gone for the next forty years. And I haven't raped the bitch. She's the one that came onto me. But no one will see it that way. She knows it. I know it. And now you know it."

"So why don't you go get the other phone? And if she gets in the way, make her wish she hadn't. There are ways you can do that. I know a couple of guys that can help you."

A month ago, Emiliano would have jumped at the chance and told Miguel to call his friends so that they could plan the break-in, knowing that the friends that Miguel was talking about would want to rape Beth.

"Fucking puta," Emiliano yelled again as he threw the phone against the wall.

"Here, use this." Miguel handed Emiliano a hammer.

Within a few minutes, there was nothing left of the phone except tiny bits of plastic, glass, and minute particles of gold, silver, and copper.

"So you want me to make the call?" Miguel asked.

"No," Emiliano replied. He promised his aunt and his Abuela that he would never take that path again. The path that was just around the corner of his building. Through an alley and down a few blocks to a bar. And even though he had never been to that bar, Emiliano knew what it looked like inside and out.

Emiliano told Miguel he would see him later and left the pawnshop. He got in his truck and drove onto Broad Street and parked his truck. He walked by the James Brown statue and over to the Augusta Commons and sat down. It was a beautiful day and he knew he had some work to do but it would just have to wait. He needed to think about what he was going to do. He closed his eyes and asked his Abuela for her help one more time and he heard her voice.

"You know what to do," was all she said. And he knew she was right. He was going to end the affair with Beth and whatever happened with his business would just have to happen. He hoped that he could keep some of his customers, but even if he lost all of them, he would just start over. His equipment was paid for and he was a hard worker. He could make it. He told himself he didn't need Beth and for the first time, he believed in himself.

The words from Luna swirled around him as he sat there.

"I believed in you, Emiliano. I still believe in you and I wouldn't have said that if you had lied to me today. The other Emiliano I knew would have lied to me when I asked these questions. But the one I know now stands up. He owns up to his failures and says he will do better. That is the man that I want to be around me and my family."

That is the Emiliano he was now, even though that Emiliano took great pleasure in destroying Beth's phone. Considering everything else he could have done, he told himself that was okay. Next Wednesday he would end everything with Beth. And then he would apologize to Mrs. Brodie. And accept the consequences. Even if he had to go back to jail for what he did to Mrs. Brodie, he would still be a free man. Capable and willing to do the right thing even when no one but himself told him to.

Beth laughed as she sent Jorge that last text. She could imagine him opening the picture and videos and seeing her and her family in all of the resorts that they had visited. He would be looking at them and swearing something derogatory about her in Spanish. That made her laugh even more. She knew he might destroy that phone once he got the message but it didn't bother her. If she lost those pictures of her family, she would just make more. To other mothers, the loss of their young children's images would be devastating, but to Beth it was inconsequential.

Beth loved her children because they helped define her. April, May, and Summer were just little girls that she happened to give birth to. Beautiful girls like their mother. She would take care of them. Provide them everything that money could buy because that's how she wanted to live. She would revel in their accomplishments even though she wasn't all that concerned with what they did. But it was important that whatever they did made them look good and more importantly, made Beth look good.

It was the same type of love she had for Darrin. He was handsome and a good provider. And did what she told him to. He made her look good. He had given her a great home and she loved living in their gated community. She shouldn't be expected to live anywhere else but in a gated community. She still felt privileged and would always feel like she was better than the people around her. That's why she did volunteer work. Not because she was sincere in helping those less fortunate than her, but because it made her look good with those in her social circle. She came away from those events feeling even more superior considering everything she had in her life.

For Beth, the material things in her life still mattered very much. The ability to exercise her superiority in everything she was involved with, was part of her DNA. Everything she did was to elicit a certain image. She wanted to maintain that portrait because of what she knew existed just below the surface on the blank canvas. She was still a cruel and petty woman who did not like being told what to do or to be embarrassed in front of anyone. To be put in her place in front of the police was not acceptable and she could not allow that to go without some level of retaliation.

She saw Connor riding his bike up and down the road on Friday evening after school. *He's probably out looking for something in the woods,* she told herself. *He's kind of geeky like that.* She knew there was something in the woods behind her house that would surprise him. As he came into the cul-de-sac, she hollered out to him. "Hey, Connor!"

He stopped his bike and looked over at Mrs. Stevens.

"I've seen a snake in my backyard but I'm not sure what kind it is. I think it might be another copperhead or something poisonous. I don't think it's a rattlesnake but I guess it could be. I didn't get close enough to make it rattle. Would you mind taking a look at it and if it's poisonous remove it so my children don't get hurt?"

"Be glad to. I just need to go back home and get some things but I'll be right back," he said as he took off on his bicycle.

He picked up his snake grabber and an Igloo cooler. That would be much easier to carry than the aquarium he had used for the water moccasin. And now that he thought of it, he wondered if its male counterpart had come back to the pond looking to mate yet. He told himself that he would have to check tomorrow. It was getting too late in the evening to do it today.

He attached Amos's knife to his belt before leaving the house. He wasn't going to tell his mother about this until it was over. She would try to stop him and he really wanted to see what kind of snake this was. He pulled his bike into Beth's driveway and parked it in front of the garage.

"Thanks for coming to do this," Beth said. "I hear you're quite the wizard when it comes to snakes and that sort of thing."

"I try and know as much as I can, but there's still a lot I don't know," Connor replied.

Beth saw the big knife on Connor's belt. "Wow, that's an impressive knife! Where did you get something like that?"

"My friend Amos gave it to me," Connor replied. He wasn't going to avoid the subject around Beth. He felt no need to and he thought it was her problem, not his.

He watched as Beth tried to ignore what he said about Amos and he wanted to laugh as he identified the fake smile that she manufactured. It looked more like she was constipated and trying to dislodge a large turd than smiling and though Beth couldn't see it in his face, he was laughing his ass off at that image.

"Can you show me where you saw the snake?" Connor asked. "You don't have to take me all the way out into the woods. Just take me to the area where you saw it and get me as close as you can."

"Follow me," Beth said as she walked into their backyard. "Once you get past the fence," Beth said, "we have about another seven acres of woods that go all the way down to a pond. I think snakes come from that pond quite a bit. It's real swampy down there. I would have had it dredged up some time ago but I was told it was wetlands and I need a permit to get rid of it. I haven't been able to get that permit yet but I'm still trying."

The mention of the pond certainly caught his attention, He would have to be smart about everything though and he didn't have his cherry bombs with him, so he couldn't go in that pond. *Have to stay one step ahead, Connor. Remember that.*

Beth took him to the tree line and pointed north into the woods. Connor told her to go back to the house and he would look around until it started getting too dark and then let her know what he found. "Once I get this snake out of the woods for you, would it be okay if I explored your pond back there someday?" he asked.

"Sure, anytime." Beth went to her patio and sat down as she watched Connor search for the snake. She had not seen a snake that day or any other day.

She hadn't seen any snakes, but Beth had seen more than the shadows of the trees earlier. As she watched Connor look around in the woods, she saw the shadows of her past that still hung around and taunted her on occasion. To say they haunted her would be like saying one of those feeble attempts at a haunted house that sprung up every Halloween, haunted her. She wasn't haunted or terrified by them. It just made her aware of them on occasion and when she saw those shadows, she always said the same two words: Fuck off.

No, the only shadow that interested her today was Connor's and another one she had seen very recently. Running through the woods and tearing up the ground. One that people walking around in the woods would be smart to avoid.

Connor ventured deep into the woods and looked down at his watch. He only had about thirty to forty more minutes of sunlight. The tree's canopy was already darkening the ground around him when he saw something red. "That's a snake," Connor whispered as he moved closer to it. He saw it moving as he approached, slithering underneath the pine needles and fallen leaves where it preferred to stay.

As it moved, more of its body became visible and he couldn't believe what he was seeing. There were bands of red, yellow, and black. "It can't be," he said as he gently brushed aside some of the pine straw covering its body. They weren't supposed to be this far north but there it was. He repeated the rhyme, "red on yella, kill a fella. red on black, friend of Jack."

A damn coral snake. Yep, this would have hurt your kids all right. I can't wait to show this to Sam, he thought as he followed its movement and then tripped.

Some old barbed wire had been strung up between the trees long ago when all this property was farmland. The wire was rusted but it got tangled around his legs pretty good. It looked like there were two or three strings of it altogether and he could feel it scraping against his skin. As he worked on getting his leg free, he kept his eye on the coral snake. For some reason, it had stopped moving. It had stopped moving because of the vibrations it felt on the ground, which Connor couldn't feel but he definitely heard.

He reached over and snagged the coral snake with his grabber just as he removed the knife from his belt. The wild boar charged out of the woods toward him. His pants were still caught on the barbed wire and he was unable to get away. He screamed in anguish as the boar attacked his stomach and tried to rip away the middle part of his body. It didn't have time to go for his face because Connor drove the knife into its skull causing it to jerk back. Connor quickly pulled the coral snake forward and threw it on the boar's back, where it bit into its neck before the boar tossed it off and killed it.

The boar didn't seem to know what to do next as it felt the venom coursing through its body and the blood leaving its body even faster. It stumbled toward him and when it got close enough, Connor sliced open its throat. It backed up and staggered a few steps before it dropped dead.

Connor clutched his stomach and saw that he had been hurt very badly. But even though he had lost a lot of blood, he knew he still had a chance. He pulled out his cell phone and called 911 and gave them Beth's address telling the dispatcher that he had been gored by a boar in his gut and he was losing a lot of blood. He knew that the best thing he could do was to just be still, so he laid back and looked up at the trees and thought about the coral snake he had just seen out in the wild. *That was a first. Maybe the first one in Augusta* he thought before he closed his eyes.

At the sound of the ambulance siren, Maggie knew Connor was hurt. She didn't know how she knew but she knew. She ran down the street and saw the ambulance in front of Beth's house and Connor's bike down in the driveway. Jasmine came out to her as Maggie stood next to the ambulance yelling Connor's name. When she saw the stretcher being pushed toward the ambulance, it was not covered with a black body bag. But her son was on it with several IVs hanging above him.

"That's my son! How is he? Tell me how he is!" she cried. One of the paramedics stopped for just a moment and said, "He's got a chance," but they needed to get him to the University Hospital trauma unit right away. She fell to the ground as her knees buckled and watched them drive away.

She heard Jasmine trying to comfort her but all she focused on were the words, "He's got a chance." That was until she heard Beth coming up from behind her. Telling her she was sorry that she had asked Connor to search her backyard for a snake.

Maggie stood up and turned toward Beth. "Don't stand there and tell me you didn't know what was out there because you might choke on that lie. I might even choke you myself if I hear you say another word. I won't need to tell you what I will do if my son dies. You stay the fuck away from me and my family, you god damn whore."

Beth didn't say anything else or try and tell Maggie that Jasmine was a witness to her threats. She wasn't even sure what Jasmine would say but she knew she should once again just turn around and leave. Only this time as she walked away, it wasn't because she lost. No, she had accomplished what she had set out to do today and she smiled as she opened her door and walked back inside.

Jasmine drove Maggie to the hospital and on the way, Maggie managed to call Sean at work and tell him that Connor had been hurt. She didn't know what had happened yet but he was hurt badly and he needed to meet her at University hospital right now. When they arrived they were told that Connor was in the OR and were shown where to wait.

Five hours later, the surgeon came out and asked to speak to them. He told them that they had done as much as they could for him and that the next forty-eight to seventy-two hours would be critical. As he started to explain things to them, he could tell they didn't have any idea what happened to Connor and began to tell them what he knew.

"Your son was attacked by a wild boar, according to the paramedics that arrived on the scene. Connor is a very tough young man. Most people wouldn't have survived an attack like that, much less kill the animal that attacked him, but he did. That knife he had saved his life. The boar tore up his insides pretty bad but your son stopped him from getting to his renal artery. If that had been cut, he would have bled out in minutes. His small intestine was cut up pretty bad as well as his large intestine, but amazingly, his kidneys were untouched. His stomach, liver, and spleen were lacerated and that's what caused him to lose so much blood."

Maggie felt like she was going to faint but she knew she had to hear everything the surgeon was saying. She needed to be strong for Connor now like he had been for her but she was struggling. Sean felt her starting to fall and held her up as he moved her back to a chair so that they could sit down. Once seated, the surgeon continued.

"We removed the spleen, cauterized the wounds of the stomach and liver, and stitched up his intestines to the best of our ability. He has a colostomy bag now, but we're hopeful that will just be temporary. He used a lot of blood during surgery. Sixteen units, but he's stable now and has a good hemoglobin value. It's 9.5, which is very good considering everything. He also has a few fractured ribs, but those don't worry me. The biggest concern over the next two to three days will be infection and blood loss."

The doctor paused for a moment as he saw them trying to absorb all he was telling them and then continued. "I have a son about his age and I know if I had a doctor telling me about him I would want to know everything so that's what I am trying to do, even though I understand some of it is pretty difficult to hear."

"Yes, we want to hear everything," Maggie said as strongly as she could which was only a whisper.

"Well, having your bowel contents spread around in your abdominal cavity will make him prone to infection, but we're pumping him with multiple antibiotics and I have consulted with the infection control guy to check on him and make sure we stay ahead of things. I think we have the blood loss controlled. His blood pressure is good, very good. Like I said earlier, he's a strong young man, which is a very good thing.

"He will be in ICU on a ventilator for now because we need his heart and lungs to get some help and not have to work so hard. Not that there is anything wrong with either of them, but they have been stressed quite a bit just getting him to this point. If everything goes as we hope, we can get him off that ventilator in a short time. He won't feel it. He won't feel anything for a while as we have him in a drug-induced coma to let his body heal, and let the drugs do their thing. I know I've said a lot, but do either of you have any questions for me?"

"Your name?" Maggie asked.

The surgeon shook his head. "I'm sorry. I was so focused on what I was doing and telling you I just…"

"Don't apologize," Sean replied. "I'm glad you are that focused on our son."

"I'm Dr. Buchanon. Dr. Joseph Buchanon, but I'm just one of several surgeons that operated on your son. Dr. Ray and Dr. Tomeo are trauma gastrointestinal specialists and they helped me in the OR because the surgery was so complicated. Here's the number to my cell phone. You can call me any time of the day or night and I'll answer it."

"Can we see him?" Maggie asked.

"Yes, you can, but I want to caution you. He will not look like your son. There will be three or four IV's going. He is still getting blood and he's on the ventilator. It's hard to look at when it's your child lying there. But I promise you, we're doing everything we can for him."

Maggie and Sean followed the doctor to the ICU where he introduced them to the nurse who was caring for Connor that evening. Maggie heard Sean tell her their names as she went over to the bed and took her son's hand.

"I'm here, Connor. I'm here and your Dad is here too. We love you so much. You fight, son. I know how strong you are and you fight, you hear me? My Connor, my boy, whose spirit doesn't know how to quit." Maggie's voice cracked and she fell into Sean's arms.

Chapter 40

A clogged skimmer

Dr. Buchanon reminded them to call him at any time if they had concerns or questions. He told them to make sure they gave the nursing staff a contact number. Sean nodded his head that he understood and thanked Dr. Buchanon for everything he had done and watched as he walked out of the ICU room and over to the nurse's station. Connor's room was directly across from the nurse's station and Sean knew that was good.

"It's Aya, right?" Sean asked the nurse.

"Yes, Aya Robinette. I've been working in this ICU a little over a year now."

"Do you maintain a one-to-one nurse to patient ratio in here?" Connor asked.

As soon as he asked that question, Aya understood Sean worked in healthcare. "Most times we do. That's the goal," she said knowing that's not what he wanted to hear, but she knew she shouldn't lie. "I can assure you, with your son's condition and the extent of his injuries he will get one-to-one care."

"Thank you. That's reassuring to know."

Aya looked at Maggie who hadn't taken her eyes off her son as she conversed with Sean. She walked over to Maggie. "We will take very good care of him," she said and upon hearing that, Maggie looked into Aya's face for the first time.

"Can I stay here with him?" Maggie asked.

"No, but let me show you where you can stay," Aya said. "First let's go by the nurse's station and write down some phone numbers and then I'll show you where you can wait. We open up the ICU for visitors every two hours for ten minutes."

Sean and Maggie gave the ward clerk their contact information and she recorded it on the front of Connor's chart. Then Aya took them into the ICU waiting area where there were chairs that functioned as beds.

"You can stay here as long as you want. There is a green light on the wall next to the clock. When it goes on, it means visitation time. If you happen to be asleep, I can come and get you if you want. You two must be exhausted and I would encourage you to get as much rest as you can when you can."

"I want you to come get us," Maggie said. "I don't want to miss anytime with him."

"I understand."

The ICU waiting room was filled with family members who were sleeping, watching TV, or checking a device of some kind. There was only one vacant chair left that converted to a bed but there was another regular chair right beside it.

"Go ahead and lay down," Sean said. "I'll sit up and let you know when it's time."

"I'm not going to sleep for a while," Maggie replied. "Oh my God! Jasmine. I need to go check on her. I forgot all about her."

Maggie found Jasmine still sitting in the OR waiting room. She took a deep breath as she told Jasmine everything that the doctor had said. She also thanked her for bringing her to the hospital and asked her to let everyone in the neighborhood know about Connor. Jasmine told her she would do that and would be praying for all of them.

Maggie and Sean didn't sleep at all. Each time the green light flashed on; they were the first through the door. At 6 a.m. Aya told them she would be getting off in an hour and a nurse named Shirley would be taking over. Shirley had been an ICU nurse for twenty years and would take excellent care of Connor.

Maggie hugged Aya and thanked her for watching over Connor through the night and asked how he was doing.

"His vital signs are very strong," Aya said. "I just checked his hemoglobin and it was good too, so his bleeding seems stabilized. He's not running a temperature, which is good, and they'll be doing some more bloodwork this morning to see how everything else is doing. But all in all, it was a positive night."

"Will you be back tonight?" Maggie asked.

"Yes, tonight and tomorrow night. I work Fridays, Saturdays, and Sundays."

"Your name. What does it mean?"

"In Japanese, it means an angel who knows magic," Aya said as she smiled.

Maggie returned the smile. "You are a real person, aren't you? I haven't been imagining things even though your name suggests I may have been."

Aya laughed. "You're sleep-deprived. You need to rest. We'll take good care of Connor, I promise you."

Maggie nodded and she and Sean went back to the waiting room. "I know neither one of us has slept, but let's do this. I'm going to go home and run. I feel like that will help me. Then I'm going to eat some breakfast and take a short nap. I should be back by eleven at the latest. Why don't you go downstairs and get some breakfast and then shut your eyes for a minute? You may not sleep, but then again you might. You heard what Aya said. I'll bring you a change of clothes and some toothpaste and things. Does that sound ok?" Sean asked.

Maggie said that was fine and followed him to the elevator. Just before they left the ICU waiting room area, one of the older women sitting there introduced herself as Esther and told them she would watch their chairs for them. Maggie thanked her and asked if she could bring her anything from the cafeteria. She said she would love some biscuits and gravy, adding that, "they make real good biscuits and gravy down there."

"Ok I'll back with them soon," she replied. Esther tried to hand her some money, but Maggie shook her head no. "We're in this together now, Esther."

The elevator carried Maggie and Sean to the first floor and opened its doors. They stepped out into a maze of halls and corridors made worse by their lack of sleep. Though Sean was used to this type of confusing infrastructure, even he felt somewhat overwhelmed looking for a familiar symbol or letters on a sign that would indicate they were headed in the right direction.

Maggie held onto Sean's hand, unaware of where they were or where they were going. When she heard Sean say, "There it is," she looked up and saw the Cafeteria sign, and then she remembered. She was going to get some biscuits and gravy. Sean kissed Maggie, handed her some money, and told her that he would see her in a few hours.

Maggie got a cup of tea and some biscuits and gravy and then walked outside into a garden next to the cafeteria. There were tables and a large fountain and she thought how nice the water sounded. For a few minutes she stopped thinking about her son and she felt normal. Like she was at home on her patio, but that image faded as soon as someone sat down across from her at the table.

She smiled at the person who sat down even though it disrupted her sense of normalcy. She stayed until she finished her tea and then remembered the woman in the ICU and her request. She left the cafeteria after getting another cup of tea and Esther's food but then realized she had no idea how to get back to the ICU and came back to ask the cashier for directions.

The cashier began explaining to Maggie how to get to the elevator that would lead her back to the ICU but she soon realized that she was speaking a foreign language to the woman in front of her. She told Maggie to wait just a minute and got someone from the kitchen to take her place at the cash register. She then led Maggie back toward the elevator.

Along the way, the cashier talked to her, telling her about her family and how long she had worked at the hospital. She didn't ask any questions. She knew better. This wasn't the first time she had seen someone in her cafeteria that didn't appear to understand English. Most of them were family members of someone in the ICU, so she had made this walk to the elevator many times. She accompanied Maggie back to the waiting room and said she would be praying for her and her family member, but she wasn't sure the woman heard her. She was okay with that. It happened sometimes.

Esther recognized the cashier and thanked Doris for bringing Maggie back. Doris asked Esther how things were going and she said they appeared to be getting better. Doris smiled and said she was hoping to hear that. She said goodbye to Esther and Maggie and walked away, not knowing if she would ever see either one of them again. But that was okay because she had learned that happened and could only hope that a kind word had helped. Her kindness was seldom forgotten.

Maggie sat down next to Esther, who told her she had put some blankets in the chairs they were sitting in earlier. "They will let people know those seats are taken. Most everyone in here goes along with that, but on occasion, there is someone who doesn't seem to care what it means. And then I have to step in and explain things to them. Thanks for the biscuits and gravy," Esther said.

"Step in and explain things to them." Maggie found that comment amusing considering it was uttered by a tiny little woman not more than five feet tall with hair as white as cotton. From what she was saying, it seemed to Maggie that she had spent quite a lot of time out in this waiting room, so she asked about her situation. Esther explained that her husband of fifty years had fallen off a ladder and knocked himself out. When they brought him to the ER, they found a brain tumor.

"Didn't expect that at all," Esther said between bites of the biscuits and gravy and sips of her coffee. "He's been active all his life. Never once slowed down even though he's been retired for about ten years now. He's seventy-five, be seventy-six next month. He married a much younger woman. I'm only seventy-three," Esther said as she winked at Maggie.

Maggie returned her smile as she looked at the pixie grin on Esther's face. "What's your husband's name and how long has he been here in ICU?" she asked.

"Well, today is Saturday, so I'm thinking it will have been three weeks tomorrow. Yep, that's right. We came in on a Sunday after church. He was cleaning out the gutters. Never believed any day was a day of rest even though the Bible says Sunday is. I never stopped trying to convince him of it though. His name is Francis but he hated that name. Everyone calls him Frank."

Three weeks. How does she do it? She seems so positive and she's been in this place for three weeks. "How is he doing?"

"Better. A little better each day. The doctor says if he keeps improving, we'll get moved to the rehab unit in a couple of days. He's had a series of small strokes since he's been in here. His left side is real weak and he's going to need some help adjusting to that, but if God's willing, he will. Why are you here Maggie?"

"My son, Connor, was mauled by a boar," Maggie replied. She started to say more, but she couldn't right now. Not without falling apart, so she stopped.

"Land's sake, child! How did that happen?"

"He was out in the woods doing what he loves to do," Maggie replied, again stopping before she said anything else. She didn't want to say it was an accident because she knew it wasn't.

"So far, so good."

"Well, I'll pray for Connor," Esther said.

"Thank you, Esther. I'll do the same for Frank and for you," Maggie said as she looked at her watch. It was almost 8:00 and she knew the green light would be coming on any minute. She watched the clock up on the wall and as soon as it turned green, she got up and hurried into the ICU.

"Morning," the black woman said as Maggie entered Connor's room. "Are you Mrs. Brodie?"

Maggie nodded her head as she went to Connor's bedside and grabbed his hand.

"My name is Shirley and I'll be taking care of Connor this morning and afternoon."

"Call me Maggie," she said as she turned around and smiled at the nurse.

"I'll do that, Maggie. Have you got any questions?"

"Is he still doing okay?"

"His hemoglobin dropped just a little bit so we're going to give him another unit of blood and some of his blood chemistries are a little off. In particular, his kidneys seemed a little bit more stressed than they need to be right now. So we're giving him some medicine for that and will continue to monitor it. His blood pressure and heart rate are both good. And no temperature. Every time you hear us say 'no temperature' that's a good thing."

Maggie kissed Connor's cheek. "You don't get a temperature, Connor. Did you hear the nurse? No temperature! And keep fighting. Your mom and dad are here for you. We'll be here night and day until you are better."

Shirley smiled as she listened to Maggie talk to her son. "Keep talking to him. I believe he can hear you. Some nurses and some doctors think they don't and just as many of us think they do. So you keep talking to him."

"I'll do that Shirley. I will certainly do that," Maggie said as she felt a tear on her cheek.

Stop it, Maggie. Stop it. You need to be strong for your son now. No crying. Talk to him.

"When you get better, we'll go to that Cape Fear Serpentarium, that you've been wanting to go to. And the one in Edisto Beach too. But you have to get better. Do you hear me, Connor? You have to get better."

"Serpentarium? Is that one of those snake places?" Shirley asked.

"Yes, he loves snakes. Don't ask me why. I hate them, but he loves them. He knows a lot about them. He knows a lot about all kinds of animals."

"He doesn't have a pet snake, does he?"

"No, not yet."

"Good. I don't like those things at all. I didn't want you bringing it in here for him to look at when he wakes up. Lord have mercy! I couldn't stand that at all."

When he wakes up, Maggie thought to herself. *I heard her say, "When he wakes up."*

"Don't worry Shirley," Maggie said as she turned around and hugged her. "We won't bring any snakes in here but you've got to get my son better. Deal?"

"Deal. Have you had any sleep in the past twenty-four hours?"

"No, I don't guess I have."

"Well, you need to get some or you won't be able to think straight. I know. Been doing this a long time. Connor is doing pretty good right now. I want you to go out there and get some sleep now, you hear me?"

Maggie didn't have the strength to argue with Shirley. She laid down when she got back to the waiting room and shut her eyes. She heard Shirley saying "when he wakes up" over and over in her head until she fell asleep. Shirley came out at the 10 a.m. visitation time but saw Maggie sleeping and didn't bother her since there had been no change in Connor. Maggie slept until she felt someone holding her hand. She opened her eyes and saw Sean beside her.

"How long have you been asleep?" he asked.

"Since a little after eight," Maggie said as she looked up at the clock on the wall. It was almost noon and visitation time.

"That's good. I packed a little suitcase for you. Hope I got what you needed."

"Did you put some wine in there?"

Sean smiled. That question was a good sign.

When the green light flashed, they went in to see Connor and Maggie introduced Sean to Shirley. He asked her if there was somewhere that Maggie could get cleaned up and change clothes. Shirley shook her head and held up her finger. "Give me a minute," she said as she walked away and then came back.

"Come with me, Maggie. The doctor's sleep room has a shower. I'll stand outside the door while you take a shower. You okay with that?"

Maggie said yes and followed Shirley to the doctor's overnight area. It felt so good to get a quick shower and brush her teeth. Shirley even let her get another quick look at Connor before going back to the waiting room. Maggie re-introduced Sean to Esther and told her about her husband Frank. "And by the way, Esther is in charge of the waiting room so don't cross her," she added.

Esther laughed and pointed two fingers at her eyes and then at his telling him she was watching him. Sean and Maggie laughed too as they sat down to wait. Throughout the day, friends from the neighborhood came by to spend time with them. It seemed like just as one couple left another one came. So much so, that Maggie eventually asked Jasmine if their visits were planned.

"Yes - Barbara assigned everyone a time to be here. You've got coverage through the day, every day," Jasmine said. "Until you and Connor come home."

Maggie hugged her and then sent a text to Barbara thanking her for organizing the visits but added that it really wasn't necessary. She would be glad to keep her in the loop about Connor's progress and that everybody didn't need to keep coming by.

Barbara replied saying she was sorry, but she had already made out the schedule and that schedules could not be broken. She should know that and then added for her to not bring it up again with a heart and smiley face emoji. Maggie knew better than to argue with Barbara as she smiled and showed Sean the texts.

Saturday night became Sunday night and Connor's condition had not changed; he was no better, but also no worse. As Sunday night was becoming Monday morning, a "Code Blue to ICU" came on the paging system. Maggie jumped up and asked Esther what that meant even though her husband could have told her. Esther explained it meant that someone in the ICU had gone into cardiac arrest and that the code team was coming to the unit to help resuscitate the patient.

Maggie looked back at Sean. She couldn't feel her arms or legs. Everything was numb and she couldn't move. She saw Sean come and get her but she couldn't hear anything he was saying. He led her over to the chair and sat her down as he held her hand. Everyone in the ICU watched the door waiting for someone to come through and ask to speak to a family member, knowing that as soon as their name was called, whatever they were about to hear, would either bring them relief or words that would take all their breath away.

Twenty minutes went by before a nurse came through that door and walked over to Esther. Maggie heard a loud "No!" and buried her head into Sean's shoulder, knowing what that "No" meant. Esther didn't come back to the waiting room. A nurse came into the room about an hour later and gathered up Esther's belongings. A wave of loss and loneliness washed over Maggie as she watched.

Maggie didn't sleep at all that day and didn't speak much to any of the friends who continued to come by. With each visit, their friends would speak to Sean privately and ask him if Maggie was okay. He would explain to them each time what had happened that morning. Then all of them, including Sean, would shake their heads and say they understood. But they would all be wrong.

They didn't understand what was going on in Maggie's mind since Esther's husband had died. The death of her husband made Connor's death seem inevitable and imminent. She tried to tell herself that wasn't true, but her arguments were unconvincing. She was becoming more and more depressed and that depression was being masked by what people believed to be a normal concern for her son's well-being. But with each hour of the day, she was sinking into a dark cavern that had no end.

On Tuesday afternoon Barbara came by and found Maggie sitting alone. She inquired how Connor was doing and Maggie gazed up at her as if she didn't know her. She asked her again how Connor was doing and this time she heard her sigh and then saw the recognition on her face.

"Hey, Barbara. How are you doing?"

"I'm fine Maggie. How is Connor?" she asked again.

"He's holding on. He has a low fever but they said they weren't too worried about it right now. His other vital signs are good and he hasn't needed any blood so far today."

"That's good. Where is Sean?"

"He went home for a little while to get some sleep. He'll be back later this afternoon. He's exhausted."

He's exhausted? You haven't left this place in five days she thought and wanted to tell her she needed to rest but she knew it wouldn't matter what she said. All she could do was be there and talk to her and take her mind off of things, if just for a moment.

"I told Agathe not to wear her penis necklace when she came to see you. She hasn't, has she?"

Maggie smiled. "No, she hasn't. Have you seen Amos? I haven't even asked anyone about him. Connor went by there every morning and every evening. I need to tell someone to check on him."

"It's okay, Maggie. We've got it covered. Jasmine and Sable and I have been checking on Amos. He's fine."

"Does he know about Connor?"

"He does."

"I wonder why he hasn't come by to see him?"

"He can't, Maggie. He kind of slips in and out of reality when we talk about Connor. He starts talking about his friend Hank."

"Yeah, I remember him doing that when he was in the hospital. I can understand now why he can't come by. Oh, the green light is on. Would you like to come in and see Connor with me?" Maggie asked.

"Yes, of course," Barbara said as she put her arm around her friend and walked into the ICU.

Barbara felt like crying when she saw Connor but she pinched herself so that she felt pain instead of the overwhelming sorrow that looked up at her from the bed.

"He looks okay, don't you think?" Maggie asked.

"He does, Maggie. He sure does. Connor is a very strong boy. He'll be okay. You just have to have faith in that."

"Yeah." Maggie took Connor's hand and stroked his arm until it was time to leave.

Barbara stayed until Sean arrived and told Maggie that she would see her tomorrow and Maggie answered, "Sure."

Sean and Maggie talked all through the evening and he got them some pizza for dinner. He told her that she and Connor would be eating pizza together soon and Maggie nodded her head. Every two hours they went in to see Connor and each time found that nothing had changed. Maggie heard the same report from the nurse each time, regardless of which nurse it was.

Sometime after the 2 a.m. visit, Sean nodded off and at 4:00 Maggie walked into see Connor alone.

There were several nurses in the room working with Connor. Maggie saw things happening in slow motion as one of the nurses pressed the button on the wall and she heard "Code Blue" over the pager. She felt herself floating out of the room as people were rushing past her to get to Connor. She turned and walked out the door and kept going all the way to the front lobby and asked someone to call a cab for her.

Maggie had the cab driver take her home. She used a hidden key to get into the house and get some money to pay the driver. She checked her watch and saw that it was about 5 a.m. and went into Connor's room and sat down as she looked around. She picked up some of his favorite things and took them with her as she wandered outside.

At 6:00, she walked over to Amos's house. He was sitting on the front porch with his easel looking at the sunrise.

"Good morning, Amos."

"Well, good morning, Maggie. Are you and Connor home now?"

"No, just me. I wanted to come by and watch you paint a sunrise. I always wanted to do that."

"Not sure how interesting that will be. Sitting here watching an old man paint."

"It will mean a lot to me," Maggie replied. "Would you make this one for Connor?"

"I sure would. That's a good idea. This one will be for Connor. How is he doing?"

Maggie wanted to tell Amos the truth but she couldn't. "He's doing fine. I think he'll be out of the ICU soon."

"Like hearing that," Amos said as he started to paint. Maggie sat and talked with Amos while he painted; about his wife, painting, the koi, anything she could think to distract her from thinking about Connor.

It's beautiful," Maggie said as he finished it and she held it up against the sky. "It will mean a lot to him and to me. Thank you for this morning, Amos." She kissed his cheek before she turned to walk away.

"Don't you want to have some breakfast with me? I've got some blueberry pop tarts. Connor got those for me the other day."

"No, not today," Maggie said. "Maybe later." She remembered Connor saying how much Amos liked pop tarts. She smiled as she thought about them sitting there on the porch eating them. Connor drinking milk and Amos probably drinking a beer. *I'm so glad that Amos came into our life.*

After she got home, Maggie laid down on Connor's bed and went to sleep.

When he couldn't find his wife, Sean thought about the one place she would be, and he was right. As soon as the doctor permitted him to leave, he drove home as fast as he could and ran down the hall to Connor's room. She was there, just as he thought.

He debated with himself as to whether he should wake her or let her get some rest. He decided she needed rest more than information now, as none of the information he could give her would provide any real comfort. Not yet at least. *Best let her sleep a little longer*, he said to himself as he thought about what the doctor said.

An infection came on very quickly, causing some organ failure, and sent Connor into cardiac arrest. The resuscitation was successful but this bug that they had identified as the culprit was a bad one. The doctor said it was called Serratia marcescens and because of the stress to his body and the endotoxins being released into his bloodstream, Connor was in a very critical state.

Maggie might not know the reason why Connor was so sick now, but Sean was aware that she knew her son's condition had worsened. The nurses told him she was there when he coded and when he realized that Maggie was gone, he knew why.

The doctor told him that they were using three antibiotics in heavy doses to combat the infection, but the next few hours would be touch and go. They were going to start Connor on dialysis and hope that the antibiotics would stop further damage to his body. His vital signs were good considering everything, but that could change in a minute. Dr. Buchanon said he would be there in the ICU until Sean came back and that he needed to go find his wife.

Sean put all of that information into a note, framing it in the most positive manner he could, and then taped it to her mirror and left. He prayed for Connor as he drove back to the hospital and prayed that he had done the right thing with Maggie.

Maggie only slept for an hour and woke up thinking she heard someone in the house. She called out for Connor and Sean but didn't get a response. She got up and made herself a cup of tea and went to sit on the patio. "Forgot something," she said suddenly. She went inside and took Amos's painting off the dining room wall. She laid it on the big oak table, poured gasoline on it, and then set it on fire. *Amos was right* she said to herself. "The picture wasn't perfect," she said out loud as she walked back outside to finish her tea.

About thirty minutes before Jorge arrived, Beth was floating on a raft in her pool and watching the video that she had made several weeks ago. *Maybe we'll do that in the hot tub this time* she thought. Her raft bumped against the skimmer several times and the third time it happened, Beth turned around and pushed back against the skimmer lid. Her raft drifted out into the middle of the pool.

She didn't realize that when she pushed on the lid, she dislodged something that was inside the skimmer clogging it up. It was the larger snake that Connor had told Maggie would probably come to the pond looking for the female he had relocated some time ago. *He was much bigger than the female* Maggie thought as she retrieved it from the pond that morning. She was proud of the way she used Connor's snake grabber as she was able to get the snake with one deft lunge. Actions she had seen Connor make many times. It was waiting in the reeds as if it knew she was coming for it and only snapped its head toward her once as she placed it into the Igloo cooler.

The water moccasin that now glided toward the raft was almost six feet long. It attacked Beth's arm first and as she jerked her arm back to see what bit her, the large serpent crawled over her chest as it reared back and injected its venom into her neck. Beth dropped the phone and watched it float to the bottom of the pool as the snake swam away from the thing that was disturbing it.

She could have survived the bite on the arm but the additional punctures to her neck were right over her jugular vein and carried the venom straight to her heart. She tried to paddle to the steps but found it hard to breathe with the venom circulating in her body so rapidly. She was able to move off the raft but she fell into the pool, gasping for breath. She was taking in large amounts of water which only exacerbated her inability to breathe. She was dead after the fourth large gulp of water.

Emiliano was anxious about seeing Beth this Wednesday. As he pulled up to the gate, he spotted a large plume of smoke billowing from the front of the neighborhood. He entered the code and as he drove down the road, he saw the house up on the hill and the woods around it on fire. He thought he heard Sarah Cayman's voice telling him she couldn't breathe and that he needed to help her as he drove up the driveway into the smoke that looked like gray clouds had come down from the sky and now floated close to the ground. He covered his mouth to try to filter the smoke, as he shouted the name "Brodie" over and over. It was very difficult to see and he could feel the heat from the fire as it consumed the house and trees that surrounded it.

He then heard someone yell out, "Connor!" and he made his way toward the voice and found Maggie laying on the ground, just below the layer of smoke.

As he carried her out of the smoke, the gasoline in the back of his truck exploded and he and Maggie were propelled to the ground. He shook his head to clear his thoughts and realized there was only one thing they could do to survive. He picked Maggie up and ran to their pool and jumped in.

The cold water shocked Maggie into a gasping breath of responsiveness as she looked at the fire all around her. She thought she might be in one of Amos's paintings because of all the orange and red she saw but then she realized Jorge was standing next to her. Holding her up. *He wouldn't be in Amos's painting* she said to herself. She looked back at the flames that surrounded her and remembered setting fire to the painting.

Connor couldn't say he set the house on fire this time. He won't have to make up a story like he did last time. It made her feel good knowing her son wouldn't have to lie this time, which was a burden that he had carried around for so many years. She knew she would see him again soon as she closed her eyes and felt the cold water all around her body. *It is really cold the further you go down into the dark cavern.* She knew that from experience.

Chapter 41

Reflections

When Connor went into cardiac arrest, Maggie immediately thought of Esther's husband Frank and Connor's friend Allison. She knew what was coming next and she couldn't stay there to witness it. She had been there the day when Frank had died and she had been there the day that Allison had died. She was there when the doctors came out to the waiting room and took Allison's mother and father off to the side and told them that she had no brain activity and that they should consider taking her off the ventilator.

Maggie could still hear Allison's mother sobbing and her husband's attempts to comfort her. The cries were deafening and kept her awake at night for a very long time. Allison was Connor's best friend and she watched him try to stay strong when he was told that she was dead, even though Maggie knew his heart was breaking. She had been certain Allison was the young girl that Connor would know for the rest of his life. They would be high school sweethearts and eventually marry. She wasn't supposed to be the girl in the newspaper who had been sexually abused by their teacher and then shot herself. She wasn't supposed to be the girl whose parents said she was such a sweet young girl whose innocence had been taken away too soon. She wasn't supposed to be the girl whose parents were described as being so brave because they donated her organs so that others could live.

Her son, who was awkward when it came to making friends, had hit it off with Allison the first day they met. She was supposed to be THE girl for Connor. She was supposed to live. Maggie could not comprehend how any of that could have happened and she retreated into a dark world that welcomed her. One that didn't judge her or ask her to talk about trivial things. It was a world that allowed her to just be. Asking nothing in return, only her presence. She set her house on fire later that week when the darkness around her became so black that she couldn't see anymore. She was hoping the fire would help her see. Connor understood that. He told everyone he started the fire so his mother could heal.

Maggie didn't look right. She wasn't acting right either Amos thought and he struggled to remember something he had seen before. Something that reminded him of Maggie. And then he saw it. His face. He had seen the look in Maggie's eyes, in his own eyes before and he knew what that look meant.

He smelled the smoke before he saw it and called 911. When he looked across the street, he could see the smoke and the tentacles of fire that were now jumping out into the yard and onto the top of the roof. He got out of his wheelchair and dragged it behind him as he crawled down his steps. Once he was on the sidewalk, he pulled himself up into the wheelchair and headed toward Maggie's home. Before he could get to the end of his driveway, he saw the blue Chevy truck driving up toward the fire. He watched as it disappeared into the smoke and heard an explosion a few moments later.

"God damn it, Maggie!" he yelled as he heard the fire truck crash through the front gate and stop in front of the Brodie's house to hook up the hoses to the fire hydrant. The water slowed down the fire in the woods but it was too late to save the house. Amos watched as the roof tumbled in and the sides of the home fell apart until all that was left were a few pieces of blackened, water-soaked framing.

The firefighters fought for at least thirty minutes before they could get into the backyard to tackle the fire that was consuming the woods behind the house. The Brodie house and over twenty acres of woods were destroyed that day and never once did the firemen expect to find anyone alive within that natural furnace. But they did.

Maggie and Emiliano were in the pool. The concrete walls of the pool were charred but remained intact and they were able to stay alive by slipping under the water when it got too hot and finding little pockets of air within all the smoke. They were too exhausted to even try to call out for help.

Many of the neighbors came up and joined Amos as they watched the ambulances arrive.

"What happened, Amos?" Barbara asked. "Do you know what happened? Is anyone home?"

Amos knew what happened but he wasn't going to say. "Must've been some sort of short or something. It went up real quick-like," Amos said. "That fella in the blue truck went up the driveway when he saw the fire. He was trying to help when I heard his truck explode. So, I know he's there. Not sure about anyone else."

The women exchanged glances when they heard Amos mention the blue truck. They knew that was Jorge's truck. They could see the same question in each other's faces. *Why would Jorge try and save Maggie? Maggie thought he was trying to hurt her.*

Within a few minutes, the EMTs wheeled two people into the ambulance and drove off. The fire was still burning in the woods but was pretty much controlled when Phil walked up the driveway to talk to one of the firemen.

"They found a young man and a woman in the pool alive," Phil told the ladies when he came back. "The man, his name was Emiliano, drove his truck into the fire to try and see if he could help anyone and found Maggie on the ground. She had almost suffocated due to smoke inhalation and he picked her up and jumped into the pool. The fireman said it was the damndest thing he had ever seen, but what he did saved him and Maggie."

"Oh my God," Barbara said as she hugged Phil.

Amos smiled when he heard that Maggie was alive. Knowing what he did, he wasn't sure if she was okay, but at least she was alive.

"Do you know where they're taking them?" Amos asked Phil.

"Doctors Hospital, the burn unit," Phil replied.

"We need to call Sean, no, wait, we can't call. We need to go see him," Barbara said. "And tell him what's happened."

"I want to go with you," Sable and Jasmine both said.

"I appreciate that, but why don't you two go to Doctors and check on Maggie and that guy they called Emiliano? Maybe you can find out if he's related to Jorge. They have to be, don't you think? They can't both have a blue Chevy truck, can they?" Barbara asked.

Barbara and Phil found Sean in the ICU waiting room and could tell by the look on his face that he was very worried. "How is Connor?" Barbara asked.

"Hanging in there. He coded," Sean said as he tried to control himself and his voice. He cleared his throat and was explaining what happened when the nurse came out and asked to see him.

Barbara started to cry as she held on to Phil's arm.

When Sean returned there were tears in his eyes, but he was also smiling.

"They think he's turning the corner. The fever, they have it under control. His vital signs are good. They think the combination of drugs and dialysis has helped him. May have saved his life. My son - he's a fighter." Sean's voice broke and he could no longer hold back the emotions he had been trying to keep in check.

Barbara and Phil surrounded him and held him in their arms as he let go of everything that had been bottled up inside. For several minutes he just stood there and cried and without Phil and Barbara both holding him up, he would have fallen to the floor. Sean gathered his composure and thanked them for being there. He said he needed to call Maggie and give her the good news.

Barbara couldn't find the words to tell him what had happened and the look on her face told Phil that he needed to talk. "We need to tell you something Sean," Phil started. "About Maggie."

The color drained from Sean's face. "Let's go over here and sit down," Phil said.

Phil calmly explained everything he knew about the fire. Sean just put his head in his hands and wept. He knew what Phil was telling him had been a possibility and if he had been thinking clearly when he found her at the house this morning, he would have called one of the neighbors to come over and stay with her. But he didn't. What happened to Maggie was his fault. He would not be able to live with himself if she died.

"Do you know if she's okay?" Sean finally asked as he looked up into Phil and Barbara's face.

"We don't know anything," Barbara replied, "but Sable and Jasmine are over there checking on her. Let me call them." Barbara went into the hall to make the call. She returned in a few minutes and took Sean's hand.

"She's going to be okay," Barbara said. "She suffered some smoke inhalation but no burns. And that's all the doctors will tell them. You should go over there and check on her. We can stay here and keep watch over Connor."

"Thank you." Sean took a deep breath as he got up to leave. "But call me if there's any change at all."

Maggie was asleep when Sean arrived. She was getting oxygen through a nasal cannula and had an IV in her arm. The nurse told Sean she was in shock and they had given her a heavy sedative which should make her sleep through the night. Maggie had been unresponsive when she came into the ER but not from her injuries; it was more like the reaction from a PTSD victim. Sean told the nurse that she suffered from depression and they should consult with Dr. Nutt about her condition. She was caring for her and would need to see her. He kissed Maggie's cheek and whispered, "I'm so sorry, baby."

After a few minutes, he told the nurse about his son who was still in ICU at University, and that he needed to get back to him and asked her to call him as soon as Maggie woke up. The nurse said she would and that she would be praying for him and his family. Sean thanked her and then went down to the ER before leaving the hospital to ask about the man that had come in with his wife.

They asked Sean if he was a family member and he said no, but that he had saved his wife's life and he just wanted to meet him. The nurse nodded her head and told him to follow her. Emiliano was also getting oxygen through a nasal cannula but was sitting up drinking a ginger ale. His heart began racing when he saw Mr. Brodie. He wasn't sure what was going to happen. But Sean just walked over to him and took his hand and squeezed it with both of his, thanking him for saving his wife. He asked him his name and he answered with his real name this time. Emiliano Martin.

Sean asked him if he had a brother named Jorge and Emiliano smiled and shook his head no. He said Jorge was his father's name and he had used it as he started his business. He was afraid people wouldn't hire him if they knew his real name and found out about his past. He told Sean everything about why he went to jail and that he was trying to atone for his previous actions. Sean assured him that his actions today went a long way toward doing that and if he needed help getting back on his feet, he would be happy to help him. Emiliano said thank you and asked if Mrs. Brodie would be okay. Sean said, "Eventually," and smiled.

Sean returned to the ICU just as Phil and Barbara were coming out from the last visitation. Connor was doing fine and they asked about Maggie. He told them she was sedated but doing well.

When Darrin got home that evening, he found Beth in the pool and called the ambulance. Phil and Barbara had to pull over just before they got to the entrance to their neighborhood as they watched the ambulance speed past them and turn down Lavender Lane.

"What the hell now?" Barbara asked. "Do you think it could be Amos?"

"It could be," Phil said but as they followed the ambulance into the neighborhood, they watched it speed by Amos's house. They drove further down the road and saw it parked in front of the Stevens' home.

"God only knows what that can be," Barbara said. "Either Beth killed Darrin or maybe Darrin found about everything and just snapped. I wouldn't blame him at all for that."

They saw Jasmine standing outside in her yard and Phil parked in front of their house. They got out and stood with her as they waited to see what was going on. Jasmine told them she didn't hear anything and had no idea what was happening. She had just gotten back from the hospital too and came outside when she heard the ambulance. Jasmine asked how Connor and Sean were doing and they told her Connor had turned the corner and Sean was walking a tight rope. They would all need a lot of support over the next several days.

After about ten minutes, they saw the stretcher and the black body bag on top of it.

"Dear God," Jasmine whispered as they watched them load the bag into the back of the ambulance and drive away.

"Who's going over there to find out what happened and who was in that body bag?" Barbara asked but before anyone could volunteer Darrin came to the door with his children. As he was strapping the youngest into his car Jasmine walked over as Barbara and Phil watched them talk. They saw her put her arm around his neck and then come back to them.

"This place is fucking haunted," Jasmine said. "Fucking haunted, Beth was killed by a water moccasin. The snake bit her in the neck. In her jugular vein, the EMTs said. She didn't have a chance. Beth, Renee, Jim, Sarah. And then Connor getting hurt so bad. It's not safe around here. We're moving just as soon as we can. We'll miss you guys but we're getting the hell out of here."

Connor continued to make progress, but Maggie's condition only got worse. She was in a catatonic state and had been placed on the psychiatric ward. As Sean and Dr. Nutt talked, she asked if he had ever heard her say anything about seeing things that weren't really there. Sean said she had a tendency to exaggerate things at times but he couldn't remember her "seeing" things except in her dreams.

"Strange," Hazel said. "I've put her on some different meds, but she'll need to remain in the psychiatric ward until things improve. This severe trauma has just overwhelmed her. What she needs, I think, is to see her son. Is he well enough to visit her?"

"No, not yet. He's off the ventilator and is healing, but the doctors don't want to take any chances yet with an infection. Maybe another week or so before he can get out. He still has a colostomy bag."

"Well, the best we can do then is to keep visiting and talking with her. She probably won't respond but you never know with these types of disorders. She can come out of it any day."

Sean wanted to ask what she meant by "these types of disorders" but he couldn't bring himself to do it. All he could do was listen and try to look positive.

Hazel saw the hopeful look on his face and knew she needed to make sure she wasn't giving him false expectations.

"Sean. You need to also understand that it may be days, or weeks, or even months before she comes out of it. Or it may never happen. I don't want you to think that it may be tomorrow even though I did allude to that. There is something else going on here with Maggie that is much more serious than I realized. This catatonia is reflective of a more severe form of mental disorder. Has your wife ever tried to harm herself before?"

Sean shook his head no, as the images of the past swirled around his head like smoke and confused him. Hazel could see she had asked enough questions for now and patted him on the arm, saying she would stay in touch and that he could call her anytime if he needed to talk.

Over the next few weeks, Connor continued to improve so much that he was moved out of the ICU and into a regular hospital room. Dr. Buchanon was able to successfully reverse the colostomy and told Connor that if everything went as planned he could go home soon. But first, he had to have a successful shit, and Connor and Sean laughed. They hadn't laughed in a long time and the laughter made them both think about Maggie.

One week later, Sean came into Maggie's room and told her that she had some other visitors. She was staring out the window as she always did and Sean turned her around as Amos wheeled himself in. Behind him was Connor who walked over and took his mother's hand and started talking to her. Though she didn't appear to be responding, she was. She was hearing her son's voice and she could see Amos and Sean now. She even saw the two paintings that Amos brought and put beside her bed, one was a sunrise and one a sunset. Just before they left, Connor felt his mother squeeze his hand and he motioned for his Dad to look down and he saw it too.

Sean called Hazel and reported what happened and she agreed that was a good sign. She would alter some of the medicine and hopefully, with continued visits from them she would come out of it soon.

Just before the sun went down that evening and everyone had left, Maggie looked into the window and saw her reflection for the first time in a long time.

"I look like shit, don't I?" Maggie asked.

"Well, you've been in this damn place for over a month. What do you expect?" the image asked.

"True. But, I'll be going home soon. And I will get better. Look better and feel better."

"Don't you think people will start asking about things?" the image asked. Maggie thought about what the reflection in the glass was referring to. She knew she had nothing to be worried about or sorry for. She had promised herself after Allison died that she would never let anyone hurt her son again. No one. And as soon as she remembered that promise, the memory of the day that Jim died came back to her. She saw him fall off the ladder and heard him ask for help, but she just turned and walked away. He had almost hit her son while driving drunk and he needed to pay for that.

She saw the broken bone sticking out of his pants and the twisted foot and the mangled hand and the fire ant mound that was only several feet away. She heard his pleas for help for many nights within her nightmares.

"He deserved what happened to him," Maggie said. "He could have killed Connor. And if Renee hadn't done herself in, I'm pretty sure she and I would have had a serious discussion, somewhere down the road. Get it, somewhere down the road. Like her husband. It's a pun. Humor. Laugh."

"It wasn't that funny. And people will start talking. They always do, you know," the image replied.

"Yes, they always do, but everything was an accident. Everything except Renee. She killed herself, but you know that. I wish I could have seen Beth when she saw that snake. I bet it scared the shit out of her but at least she knows now. She knows she shouldn't threaten my family, especially Connor. I don't even think Renee will haunt me anymore. I'm feeling much better about a lot of things. My son is well. Did you see him today?"

"I did," the image responded.

"And did you see these paintings?"

"I see them."

"They are beautiful. As close to perfect as they can be, I think," Maggie said.

"What about Jorge or should I say Emiliano?" the image asked.

"He saved my life. Everyone deserves a second chance. No one knows that any better than me."

"That's for sure."

"You know I will be leaving you here in this place where they have put me temporarily," Maggie told the reflection.

"You'll be in here a long time though," the image reminded her.

"I will be, but I'll go home eventually and you'll have to stay here. Locked up. But that's where you belong. You know that, don't you?"

"Yes."

"When I get out of here, Sean and Connor and I will build a new house. I think I'd like one like Red and Sable have. And I'll get Red to frame those pictures that Amos made for me. Damn, I wonder if that picture for Red is still at 'Frame it Now'. Oh well, it doesn't matter. I can get it later. I also need to ask about that stained glass transom he was making for Beth. I wonder if he ever finished it."

A bluejay landed on the window sill and Maggie smiled as she saw it twist its head several times to look at her and then flew off. She remembered when Red had told her what the dead bluejay had meant. Removing an obstacle. She knew neither he nor Hazel would ever know how good she was at removing obstacles, especially in her son's life. It took her a while to figure that out but she finally got it.

"I will miss you," Maggie said to her reflection.

"I'll be around," the image answered.

Sean helped Emiliano get a bank loan and an official business license and Emiliano promised him free lawn care once they rebuilt their house. Emiliano went out to Essie May Washington Branch Park one last time to see if the water moccasin was still there. He had been waiting for about an hour when he saw the snake swimming across the water and into the weeds. It ignored Emiliano just like it had before but he knew el Serpiente de algodon was aware of his presence. It had shown him what Beth was and had made him a free man.

On the way home that evening, Sean asked Amos and Connor if they wanted to stop and get something to eat. Amos said Steak n Shake was his favorite so they stopped there. Connor took Amos's order and he and his father walked into the restaurant. On the way in, Sean saw some trash littering the doorway and picked it up.

Among the empty candy wrappers, receipts and napkins was a pay stub. After they had ordered, Sean asked to speak to the manager and showed him the trash. The manager thanked him for bringing it to his attention and after noticing the pay stub, he looked over at the young man at the cash register in frustration. The manager told him that he would like to see him in his office after his shift and the young man just nodded his head as he watched Sean and Connor leave.

Connor looked back at the young man at the register as they walked away remembering his name and what he looked like. He knew he was going to be reprimanded or maybe even terminated by the manager for littering the ground. He had heard his father talk about that happening at his hospital. But Connor wasn't worried or scared about the young man getting even with him or his father. His mother had taught him how to handle people that threatened the family.